# DANCING WITH SHADOWS

Lynne Pemberton was born in Newcastle-upon-Tyne. She had a highly successful career as a model before becoming a founding director of Pemberton Hotels, a Barbados-based group which encompasses some of the most luxurious hotels in the world. Her novels include the bestselling *Platinum Coast, Eclipse, Sleeping with Ghosts* and *Marilyn's Child*.

**Acclaim for Lynne Pemberton:**

'One for the holiday suitcase'                    *Tatler*

'This fast pacey book is ideal for the summer'
                              *Girl About Town*

'A tale of glamorous lives and ruthless ambition – impeccable'                    *Manchester Evening News*

'Romantic suspense, mystery and intrigue in a tropical setting – a terrific read'                    *Annabel*

'A bittersweet love story to keep you on tenterhooks'
                              *Woman's Realm*

LYNNE PEMBERTON

# Dancing with Shadows

HarperCollins*Publishers*

HarperCollins*Publishers*
77–85 Fulham Palace Road,
Hammersmith, London W6 8JB

The HarperCollins website address is:
www.**fire**and**water**.com

This paperback edition 2000
1 3 5 7 9 8 6 4 2

First published in Great Britain by
HarperCollins*Publishers* 1998

Copyright © Lynne Pemberton 1998

Lynne Pemberton asserts the moral right to
be identified as the author of this work

ISBN 0 00 649942 2

Set in Aldus

Printed and bound in Great Britain by
Omnia Books Limited, Glasgow

# Acknowledgements

I would like to thank Lucy Ferguson, my editor, for her valuable contribution. My agent Jonathan Lloyd, for his pragmatic advice. Merill and Gerald Powell, for their generosity, and constant support, during a particularly tough patch. Ralph Kreitzman in New York, for spending precious billing time on my legal research. Edna and Peter Goldstein for their friendship, and the use of their house in Spain. And finally Angie Creme for her wise and valued counsel. Thank you Ange, very much.

*For Michael Pemberton Jnr,*
*my only son, whom I love with all my heart.*

# Chapter One

It was the last day of February, white and crisp, and very cold. *Cold enough to freeze the balls off a brass monkey*, Jay remembered the saying, and how strange he'd found it the first time he'd heard it. But he'd always found Hal Jefferson's English mannerisms inexplicable. The man had talked in riddles; Cockney rhyming slang had constantly embroidered his conversation and he'd have to translate. 'Apples and pears – *stairs*; Jack and Jill – *bill*, geddit?' Sure he'd got it, but he'd never understood why Hal had bothered using three words where he could have used one. Nobody had.

Jay's face creased a little, it wasn't a smile, more the effort of trying to put a date on the time he'd first met the dapper Englishman nicknamed 'Hal' because of his halitosis. Once, Jay had asked him what his real name was, suggesting that he use it instead of the derogatory reference to his breath. Hal had stuck his face in Jay's, breathing heavily, emitting a smell like rotting meat. 'So I've got bad breath; who cares?'

Shaking his head Jay wondered why it mattered, then told himself it didn't; not any more. The nightmare was over, past, done; *finito*. But was it? Or would he carry the faces and voices of the inmates in his head for the rest of

1

his life? Would they always be with him, muttering the banalities that at the time had seemed of the utmost importance? In those days it somehow brought colour and character to the grey walls, the grey days, when all he had to worry about was staying alive, staying sane and getting out before he got too old.

He saw her before she saw him. Her back was turned towards him. She was stooped and clothed from head to foot in crow black. He wished she'd worn something bright; red would have been heart-warming, or meadow green. A narrow shaft of late winter sun, stark in its brilliance, glanced across the top of her head where the pale pinkness of her scalp could be seen shining through a sparse covering of granite-coloured hair.

Then she looked up. Her eyes were upon him, the same colour, or so they seemed in this light, as her hair. Yet as she came closer he could see they were blue; not the blue of the cornflowers he'd likened them to as a child, but a cold, milky shade, the brightness dulled by age. Jay stood very still, watching her approach. He couldn't remember how old she was, seventy-one, seventy-two maybe? He tried to recall how old she'd been when she'd had him, almost forty-six years ago.

When she was a couple of feet away she stopped and, pulling herself up ramrod straight, looked directly into his eyes. There was no tenderness there, only searching, and in that instant he knew what he'd always known yet had never allowed himself to accept. She had never believed in him; but, worse, she'd never forgiven him. He hoped she wouldn't want to hug him, to take him in her arms, to hold him close; not yet, he wasn't ready. Jay needn't have worried, her hands were pushed deep into her coat pockets, and she made no further move. Neither of them spoke.

Her face, he noticed, was a strange yellow colour, darker around her mouth and under her eyes. She looks sick he thought, picturing her weariness clinging to her stick limbs like moss to an ancient stone. But then he was older too, his once coal-black hair was threaded with silver, and lately he'd found white streaks in his pubic thatch. Deep lines etched from his nose to the corners of his mouth, and the crisscross tracery of fine lines around his eyes had nothing to do with laughter. He wished it had.

It was Jay who broke the silence. 'Thanks for coming, Mom.' The words came out flat like meat forced through a mincer.

A mist of breath rose, like smoke, out of her open mouth. 'It was the least I could do, son, you ain't got nobody else.'

He wanted to say that he had a few friends, decent men he'd met inside, who were either innocent, misguided, or just plain desperate when they'd offended. But he said nothing.

'It sure is cold,' she said, shuffling from side to side and pushing her hands even deeper into her pockets. She was wearing rubber-soled brown boots, the mass-produced type sold cheaply in supermarkets and discount stores across the country. They were down at heel. Jay knew she could afford new boots, but she was frugal, mean

3

with herself, deriving immense pleasure from penny pinching. A sudden and unexpected image ju___ his mind: his mother was bent over the kitche_ her lips muttering figures as she calculated the wee household accounts. A lifetime of hards___ _f scrimp___ and saving, of making do. *Old habits d__ h___ if at all.*

Her eyes had now darted to the building behind Jay. She stared long and hard, as if looking at something or someone in particular. 'You want a last look?'

*A last look?* What a fucking stupid question. The pile of bricks and mortar he'd just left would remain with him for the rest of his life. As would the noise, the smell, the loneliness and the fear. Every square inch of Cedar State Penitentiary was indelibly printed on his subconscious as surely as if it had been branded there with white-hot iron. Jay felt like crying. He'd dreamt of this day, this special day, planned every moment in minute detail all those countless times when loneliness had visited, and revisited, inviting him to despair. He'd longed to taste the air on the outside, certain it would smell and feel different from the stuff he gulped every morning in the exercise yard. What would he have become by now without his dreams? Whenever he'd doubted his sanity, his carefully maintained diet of hope had sustained, comforted and enriched his miserable existence. And always in his imaginings this day had been in springtime; a blossom-bursting, sun-filled morning, with deafening birdsong and an intoxicating sense of euphoria. So why did he feel like shit? Why had a black cloud slipped

4

common
ell, none
other and
hat lasted
when she
Hotel. Jay
e discreet
vation for
t hotel on
rt out an
ven got a
play the
his bag
other out
her hand
ng, it felt
it looked

round his shoulders? Where was
-anticipated for so long, the sense
aved? Had he been too optimistic;
been incarcerated for twenty-five
thdays, twenty-five Christmasses
nagged at his eyes; yet something
*on, Jay; don't feel sorry for your-*
*years ago. This is the day you've*
*'s an anticlimax, what the hell . . .*
*f the rest of your life.*
er question. 'You want a parting

ight ahead at nothing in particular.

look at her son, Rebecca lowered
't begin to articulate how she felt.
od with words, she'd left that to
her fast-talking, no good husband. And now when she
desperately needed to tell her son how sorry she was,
she couldn't find a way. She took a step closer to Jay,
her face was impassive. 'I think we should get the hell
outta here.'

The drive to New York was a nightmare, the amount
of traffic scary, and even more terrifying was Rebecca's
habit of looking directly at him when he spoke. Jay was
convinced they were destined for a head-on collision.
Having survived twenty-five years of imprisonment, he
mused, how ironic if he were killed on his first day of
freedom by his mother.

There wasn't much to say to each other: n[...]
bond; no shared interests; no memories. [...]
that Jay wanted to recall, and eventually m[...]
son settled into an uncomfortable silence t[...]
for most of the journey. Both were relieved [...]
finally stopped the car in front of the Lowell [...]
glanced at the uniformed doorman, then at t[...]
lobby, recalling his agent's voice: *Made a reser[...]
*you at the Lowell, 28 East 63rd Street. Smar[...]*
*the Eastside. You can stay there until you s[...]*
*apartment. Your suite's on the seventh, it's [...]*
*baby grand in the living room, so if you car[...]*
*keys* ... He got out of the car first, hande[...]
to the hovering doorman, then helped his m[...]
of the driving seat. They stood side by side, [...]
resting on the open car door. Jay was smili[...]
awkward but he kept right on doing it, hoping it look[...]
sincere.

Then Rebecca smiled, too, for the first time. 'You
remind me of your pa, except the way you speak. You
don't talk the same as you did, Jay; you've got a fancy
accent.'

Jay made no comment, he couldn't be bothered to
explain that he'd been nicknamed 'the Gent' in prison,
having acquired the new intonation from Hal, the ex-
butler from England who'd poisoned his employer – some
rich old dame who'd left him a couple of million bucks in
her will.

As Rebecca's smile faded, her mouth slackened and
in that moment she looked profoundly sad. Jay thought

about his father, then cursed himself and hated his mother for mentioning that he looked like Ellis Kaminsky. It was the first time he'd thought about his father since ten years ago when he'd come across an inmate who had met an Ellis Kaminsky while doing a prison stretch in Illinois. Jay had denied any connection. Ellis Kaminsky had sired him, but that was his only claim to fatherhood. For the first twelve years of Jay's life, his father had been conspicuous by his absence. A long-suffering Rebecca had always quietly defended her husband. *Your father works hard to get nice things for you and your sister. He has to spend time away from home to earn more money so we can have a better house.* The move to a bigger house never came, nor did the much promised gifts, like the fishing pole Jay had asked for. After frequent similar disappointments, Jay had begged, then prayed, and eventually given up. Until the day when Kaminsky had left home to work on a construction site in Kansas, promising to bring the pole back for Jay and a bicycle for his sister Fran. They never received the presents, because Ellis Kaminsky never returned. Jay had been fourteen; Fran, twelve. After that their mother had slowly deteriorated, losing sense of who or what she was, given to fits of prolonged depression and introspection. The 'head of the house' role had automatically fallen on Jay's shoulders. He'd tried to console his needy mother and be a father to young Fran. But although he'd tried to make everyone happy, he'd tried too hard and failed miserably. The effort had fuelled both his hatred for his father and his own will to succeed. *Perhaps now I can finally make amends*, Jay

7

thought. But even as the thought was born, he doubted it was possible. Ellis Kaminsky had taken a large piece of Rebecca's heart when he'd left, and Jay knew his mother had never completely recovered. And Fran was lost to him; lost to herself, if the stories his mother told were true. Sometimes he doubted this, because on each occasion when he'd enquired about his sister, his mother had been evasive to the point of downright secrecy. Fran was living in Florida, so Rebecca said. Alone, and working as a waitress. Five years after his imprisonment, Fran had moved away from Sand Springs in Montana to California. She'd only visited Jay three times after that and her weekly letters had become monthly – quickly scribbled paragraphs – gradually dwindling to annual events before stopping completely. Where was she now, he wondered, as he was gripped by a vivid recollection of his freckle-faced, plump-cheeked sister – her single pigtail, the same colour as the corn, flying out behind her. It was an age-old image, yet the only one he had. He felt a sharp pang of sadness at the realization that he doubted whether he would be able to pick her out in a crowded room now. The cliché said it all for him . . . *Too much water under the bridge.*

Jay inclined his head towards the entrance to the hotel. 'You want to come in, Mom?' He wasn't sure he wanted her to join him, but he was afraid to walk into the lobby alone. He felt his heart hammering. *Get a grip, it's only a hotel for Christ's sake.*

When Rebecca shook her head, he felt immensely relieved. The prospect of trying to make small talk with this stranger, his mother, was too daunting. He wanted her to go, and go quickly, but inwardly berated himself for his churlishness.

'Naw, I've got a long drive back. Anyway, Jay, I think you've got some adjusting to do. Pick up some of the pieces. You got your release, your freedom. I never thought I'd see the day. It's going to take some time to feel right on you, and you don't want yer old ma getting in the way.'

Jay nodded. 'Perhaps you're right, but some time I'd like to talk; just you and I.' He held out his hand.

She took it, tentatively at first, then grasped it, and held on very tight as if she was drowning. 'I know, son, I want to talk, too; there's a lot to say, twenty-five years of catching up to be done. But not right now. You know me, I never was much good at talking.' She no longer met his eyes and with a faraway expression on her face, she looked into the middle distance. 'I'm sick, Jay, been sick for a good while now. I didn't write you, no need, you got troubles of yer own.' Still gripping him tight, she blinked rapidly.

He looked at the back of her hand, a patchwork of white skin, knotted veins, and dark brown liver spots. 'Sick with what?'

'Colon trouble, last year they gave me a handy little purse to shit into. But lately it's not been working so well, and they want to operate again. So who knows, I might get a classy designer version this time round.'

Her stab at humour failed to mask the dread resignation he detected in her small voice. She was dying; of that he was certain. He didn't want her to die, but he knew he wouldn't miss her. But then who would he miss? He thought about the few friends he'd made inside, and that was it. Concerned, but not devastated, Jay reproached himself and said, 'I'll make some enquiries, Mom, find the best surgeon, and we'll get you fixed up with an appointment.'

'You'll do no such thing. I don't want any fancy docs. I'm OK with the one I've got. Charles Cornwell is a good man, he's doing fine by me. Listen, son, I ain't getting any younger and we've all got to go some time, it's only a matter of how.' Jay opened his mouth to speak, but she beat him to it. 'I'll tell you all about it when you come home.'

Jay thought about home; where was home? The ram-shackle wooden house in Sand Springs, Montana that poverty had hijacked long before he'd left? It was where he was born, where he'd started his journey, and he had no intention of ending it there. His mother had refused to leave, even after he'd had his first royalty cheque, and had offered to buy her a new apartment near her sister in a better neighbourhood.

'I've got a few things to sort out here,' he said, return-ing to the present. 'As soon as I've done that, in a couple of weeks, I'll come home, I promise.'

They both knew he was lying.

'Well I ain't goin' nowhere so when you're good and ready, son . . .' She paused. 'Then we'll talk.'

For a few minutes neither moved. They held hands, like lovers reluctant to part, saying nothing, lost in thought.

Had they compared those thoughts, they would have been surprised at how similar they were. Both were of deep regret.

'This is great stuff, Jay!'

Ed Hooper was tapping a deep pile of foolscap on top of his battered desk. It was the manuscript of Jay's latest novel. With the flat of his other hand the agent stroked the mahogany surface, thinking about the day he'd bought the desk. Spring 1968. His buddy, Abe Lesser, had been selling second-hand furniture at the time and Ed recalled how he'd haggled with Abe, who'd insisted the desk was early nineteenth century. Ed had beat him down to a hundred and twenty dollars; more than he could afford at the time. The antique was intended for a big space, and it had incongruously filled his shoebox office in SoHo. He'd named it 'Samson', after Bill Samson his first client, and in 1976 Samson had moved uptown with him to his new office on 76th and York. The grander premises suited Big Samson admirably; solid and important, the desk dominated the twenty-foot-square room. Samson had hosted six secretaries' butts; been party to ten mega deals, hundreds of major deals, and thousands of minor ones. One crazy night after a party, Ed had even had a blow job under the desk; and he'd fucked his first wife over it. Samson could tell a tale or two. It was part of him, the one piece of furniture he'd ever felt really attached to, the one constant in his life. Samson looked good when cluttered; two cigar boxes, one for the legal cheroots the other for black market Cubans, helped the effect. As did a monogrammed ashtray from Ed's mother, and the eclectic mix of junk he'd collected or been given over the years, including an engraved golf ball on a silver plinth from his teenage son, Josh. And a framed photograph of himself, and Josh at fifteen, on a fishing trip in Key West. Ed liked to put his feet on Samson, happy in the knowledge that he wouldn't receive a scathing comment from his ex-wife Carole, who had repeatedly asked why he insisted on keeping such a beat-up old relic. Thank God he'd resisted her influence; he liked his office exactly as it was. The floor was carpeted in moss green; the walls were painted white and left unadorned; there was a free-standing rosewood veneered bookcase full of titles he'd handled, and of twentieth-century classics. The room also boasted a couple of leather chairs picked up wholesale twelve years before, and a Tudor oak chest acquired by Carole in a furniture sale. She'd kicked up a stink when he'd used it as a coffee table. But then Carole, after six months of marriage, had kicked up about mostly everything he did. Ed narrowed his eyes, registering the ironic fact that next week he'd be signing divorce papers on the very same spot where he'd first had Carole six years ago almost to the day. *Bitch. Double-crossing, money-grabbing, beautiful, devious bitch.*

Turning his attention back to the manuscript, he stroked the paper lovingly, a smile creasing his battered face. A 'lived-in' face, he liked to think, as he tried to convince himself every morning that what he saw in the bathroom mirror was *not* a short, pig-ugly, fat Yid, who'd inherited his maternal grandmother's leathery pockmarked skin and deep-set eyes. His father, God rest his soul, had given him very little except a long hooked nose and a rubbery bottom lip. The pair of them had a lot to answer for. Ed hated being ugly. All his life he'd surrounded himself with beauty; had idolized beautiful women. This was a weakness for which he'd duly suffered, yet he kept repeating the pattern. His father always said that everybody makes mistakes; it's only fools who don't learn by them. If that was true then Ed had to accept that he was a prize turkey. He was addicted to beauty, basking in its reflection, hoping some of it would rub off. Just like those dumb idiots who married intellectuals on the same principle. Only it never quite worked out that way. His best friend Joe, when they were teenage kids, hanging out and trying to get laid, had said that with a face like his the only way to get beautiful women was to become successful. *Make money, Ed, lots of it. Women love rich, powerful, ugly men. Look at Henry Kissinger, he's had more pussy than he's known what to do with.*

Ed smiled. It softened his features and for a split second he looked like an old teddy bear; the kind kids cherish for life. Then he was talking again, doing what he did best: negotiating; bullshitting; doing the deal; making a buck, making a million bucks.

'When I say *great*, I mean fucking brilliant, Jay! Like, the best. You're a great writer, man; you know that? You're a fucking born-again Hemingway. You listening to me, Jay?'

There was no reply. Ed shrugged, lit a cigar, and mentally digressed back to the time he'd read Jay's first

13

manuscript, *Killing Time*. A man calling himself Ivanov had delivered the three hundred and sixty pages in a brown paper parcel tied with tatty string. He'd refused to be questioned, saying that there was a letter from the author inside which would explain everything. He was referring to Jay's simple note explaining that he'd read about Ed Hooper in the *New York Times*, and wanted an honest appraisal of his first novel. He could be contacted at the Cedar State Penitentiary. The story, a harrowing account of a hitman's revenge on the Mafia godfather who had destroyed his family, had captured Ed from page one. He would never forget the churning in his gut after the first chapter, or his mounting excitement when he'd thought the narrative couldn't get any better, and it had. He'd put all his other work on hold, finishing the book in one sitting. The knowledge that in Jay Kaminsky, alias Will Hope, he'd discovered a great talent, and the fact that he had a hot property to sell, had kept him awake for several nights.

'Come on, Jay, say something. I just called you another Hemingway! What more do you want?'

He was talking to Jay's back, clothed this morning in new jacket and slacks, and a button-down cotton polo shirt that hung loosely on its wearer's narrow frame. Jay felt uncomfortable in the designer clothes. Yesterday he'd allowed Ed to lead him into the strange and terrifying world of Madison Avenue. They had started in Ralph Lauren. To begin with, the sight of so much merchandise had been daunting; later Jay had felt like a kid again, let loose in a toy shop, unable to make up his mind what to have first. Oh, the joy of touching the huge array of suits and shirts – wool so fine it caressed the fingertips; crisp cotton, cool to the touch; the smell of polished wood, mingled with a spicy fragrance which Ed informed him was Polo aftershave. The young sales assistants, both male and female, dressed in *de rigueur* designer gear, impressed Jay even more than the customers who graced the sensual emporium. Heads held high; flawless skin; perfect teeth and supremely confident smiles. Short skirts; panty-hosed legs so shiny they looked gloss-painted, breasts and pecs straining against well-cut fabric. All selling sex, selling the Lauren lifestyle, the dream. Wear a Polo shirt, or a Ralph suit, and you'll be considered upwardly mobile, recognized as tasteful, sexy, desirable. Jay had been reluctant to try on the clothes Ed picked out for him, and had agreed only after much encouragement from a very attractive girl called Jodie. He'd fumbled with zips and buttons, overcome with embarrassment when Jodie had pinned his trouser hem, and he'd felt his cock get hard.

Meanwhile Ed had been surveying the back of Jay's head. His hair, cropped to an inch long all over, revealed the end of a narrow scar that ran from the side of his left earlobe to the back of his neck. When Ed asked how he'd got it, Jay had dismissed the question curtly, muttering something about a fall in the prison yard. Ed had seen knife wounds before and knew Jay was lying, but also knew better than to pursue the subject. No point in arguing with convicted killers. He didn't want to take any chances, even though Jay had professed his innocence, and Ed believed him. There was something profoundly honest about Jay Kaminsky; he exuded a quiet sort of dignity that Ed had encountered only rarely in his life. Photographs of Jay at twenty-one, during his trial, had shown a fresh-faced type, ripe for handsome manhood. A regular sort of guy, the one every mom wanted for her daughter's prom date and every pop wanted for a son-in-law. Jay had looked exactly how Ed Hooper himself had always longed to look if only his gene pool had been a little more discriminating.

Now, though, Jay was no longer handsome in the conventional way of his youth. Bitterness had eaten into the angular face dominated by high cheekbones, giving it a taut and slightly menacing edge that could have been described as mean but for his generous mouth and wide eyes. Those eyes had lost their sparkle, yet none of their warm amber glow. And prison regime had kept Jay in good shape; he was lean and supple with the body of a man half his age.

'This is the best work you've ever done, Jay.'

Jay could hear Ed's voice, but he wasn't listening. *Hemingway*, for Christ's sake! A few months before it had been Capote. He'd heard it all before; it was literary agent bullshit-speak. Tell the boy he's great; make him feel good. Feed his ego; take a bigger slice of the pie. Sighing, Jay stared into an office across the street, the room clearly visible through one large sheet of plate glass. There was only one occupant, a woman in a red dress, blood red. It was short and had gold buttons running from the scooped neck to the knee.

She was wearing black hose and black shoes as she moved slowly towards a computer screen, leaning forward so he couldn't see her face. Jay willed her to look up, wanted her to be beautiful, and longed for her to smile in his direction. She had very long hair, it was black, shiny and scraped back from her face. Her head dropped slightly to one side, a long glossy tail of hair falling over one shoulder. As her fingers began to move rapidly across the keys, she chewed the end of a pencil. Computers, information age, techno babble, digital TV, communication satellites, fax: a whole new language, a confusing technological world beyond anything he could have imagined. Yes, sure he'd read everything he could lay his hands on in prison, but seeing it, being part of it, was awesome. *Shit, I've missed so much,* Jay thought as he continued to watch the woman, feeling himself get hard as he imagined undoing the buttons of that dress, exposing her breasts. He envisaged them as milk-white, and big, like melons, plump and soft, spilling out of his grasp as he pushed her face down on the desk – taking her there and then, with the screen displaying its information as he spread her smooth thighs, rounded and soft in his imagination. First he would probe into her fleshly warmth and moistness, and then the moment of exquisite bliss, when he thrust himself deep, then deeper inside. In that instant, as if on cue, the woman looked up; not at Jay, but towards a man who had entered the room.

'Schnieder and Smith are going to –' Ed paused. 'Jay, could I have your attention for one minute? I'm trying to tell you something important here, we're talking big money.'

Jay spun round. 'Ed, I need to get laid; like soon, like right now . . .'

This sort of distraction Ed could understand. He puffed on his cigar a couple of times, coughed to clear his throat, then pointing the cigar in Jay's direction he fixed him with a new-moon grin. 'I know just the gal for you.'

'How long has it been, honey?'

Jay couldn't bring himself to tell the truth. 'A long time,' he muttered. 'A very long time.'

It had been over twenty-six years since he'd made love to a woman. How could he tell this to a stranger when he had no voice for such an admission, no words to describe his loss. Yes he'd had sex, if you could call it that. However hard he tried, he'd been unable to erase from his memory the face of the man who'd raped him on his second week in prison. He knew with absolute certainty he would carry that face with him to his grave. 'Taurus' was the prisoner's nickname, *the bull*. Jay never found out his real name; he never spoke to him at all except to beg him to stop. But the more Jay had screamed, the more Taurus had enjoyed it. And it wasn't until Luther Ross gave him something to relax his anal muscles that the excruciating pain ceased. Luther had even cleaned him up, gently stuffing him with cotton wool to staunch the flow of blood.

After four months Taurus was transferred to another prison, and Jay healed on the outside anyway. Even now the thought sickened him, not of the act itself – that was disgusting enough – but of how he'd got used to it, become immune.

Jay raised his eyes to the ceiling, then back to Cheri who was staring at him in an odd way.

There was something in his expression she'd seen in her own face many times. *This guy's had a tough time, but it hasn't hardened him, not totally, and he certainly doesn't sound or act like a criminal.* She felt a sudden and unexpected empathy for the man lying between her thighs. The emotion surprised her; it was a long time since she'd felt anything but distaste, at best, for a client. *No time for sympathy*, she reminded herself. You turned tricks, got paid, got out; no mileage in feeling sorry.

Yet even as she listened to the reasoning in her own head, she found herself saying, 'Listen, honey, Ed's told me where you've been since nineteen seventy-three. He says you're a good boy and to look after you, so you wanna go again – a blow job on the house?'

Jay buried his head in the soft folds of her cleavage; he inhaled her scent. She smelt of lavender, spiced with sweat and a strange woody odour, but above all she smelt of woman.

'I want to go on for ever; it's like I never want to stop.'

'You're cute, but I've got a living to make. All night's gonna cost you . . .' The prostitute began calculating the rate.

Jay moved his head to one side. 'What did you just say?'

'I said it's gonna be . . .'

'No, before that.'

She looked blank. 'I think I said you were cute.'

Jay looked incredulous. 'I *am*?'

'Sure, honey. If you could see some of the mothers I've got to go down on. Jesus! Yeah, you're very cute, great ass.' She patted his butt. 'Very tight, like a young boy. And what a big boy.' She pointed to his flaccid penis. 'Take a word of advice from a gal who knows. Don't let any fancy lady friends tell you that big ain't important. For me in this line of business, well it don't make no difference . . . but I'm telling you, boy, big *is* beautiful.'

Her lips were dark with lipstick, and there were black smudgy lines around the bright hazel beads spattered with brown flecks which were her eyes. Jay liked her. He liked her small pot belly, and plump buttocks – dimpled and spongy to the touch. Her pubic hair was cut very short and shaved into a neat mound exactly like the adolescent sprouting he'd seen when Jenny Crawford had pulled her knickers down for him in Bakers Creek when they were both twelve. Jay's lips moved to Cheri's right nipple. It was very pale and very pink, like that of a pubescent girl, not a thirty-four-year-old woman. He didn't care how old she was, she was warm and soft and pliant. She was feminine, she was bliss. He began sucking the nipple, rolling it around his tongue, feeling it harden against his upper gum.

'An allnighter is – '

Without looking up, Jay placed a finger on her open mouth. 'I've got the money, baby.'

# Chapter Two

After Cheri left, Jay slept like a baby. He slept like he hadn't slept for more than twenty-five years, and when he eventually awoke he felt different. He wasn't sure in what way, but he felt a definite change. As he lay in bed very still, chain-smoking and deep in thought, his eyes roamed the luxurious room. He felt cosseted, cocooned, safe; yet strangely detached.

Eventually he rose and, naked, he padded to the window. Yesterday the world outside had seemed scary; today it looked a little less daunting. It was raining hard, slanting off the black umbrellas that moved like a swarm of insects seven floors below. A stretch limo, dark and sleek, pulled into the kerb – a fountain of water spraying the sidewalk. Transfixed, Jay watched the scene which was all in black and white like a silent movie playing in slow motion. He considered the years ahead. If he was lucky he had twenty good years left. He was almost forty-six, looked younger; at a pinch he could pass for forty. At least prison life had kept him fit: regular exercise; balanced diet; no alcohol and only the occasional foray into drugs. His intellect had been his salvation; his writing cathartic, as well as lucrative. As he thought about his future, his dreams surfaced –

and he'd had plenty: fodder for the imagination; dreams of such glorious extravagance. Los Angeles, producing movies in the Californian sun. Beaches, beautiful babes, great sex. And love. Love with a wonderful woman; an intelligent, sensitive soul mate – his wife. He'd even invented his ideal mate, an enduring fantasy that had for many years inhabited his imagination; as real to him as a living person. Her name was Colette, she was petite with a cute, slightly retroussé nose and full mouth. Her hair was the colour of old gold and it fell in soft waves to an inch below her ears. And they had a daughter who looked like him, dark haired with her mother's cobalt blue eyes. They laughed a lot, the three of them, and loved. Oh how they loved; hugs, kisses, stroking, bathing together, picnics, walking hand in hand, always tactile, very touchy feely. And every morning he awoke covered in white cotton, in their duplex apartment overlooking the sea, with Colette's toasty body slotted neatly beside his, the faint scent of her musky perfume awakening his senses. The scenario always ended the same way with Colette telling him he was going to be a daddy again, and the three of them celebrating the good news. The prison shrink, Doc Kramer, had confirmed what Jay already knew. His fertile imagination, aspirational dreams and erotic fantasies were normal and important. They would keep him psychologically balanced. *You mean keep me from going stir crazy in this fucking zoo*, Jay commented. Simon Kramer had laughed, a deep mellow sound that had warmed Jay's heart. From that moment, the two men had struck up a rapport and they had talked about anything and everything except psychology, literature, commerce, politics and chess. It was unusual for Simon Kramer to enjoy the company of his patients, but then he recognized that Jay Kaminsky was an unusual inmate. The day before Dr Kramer had retired he'd shaken Jay's hand and patted him on the shoulder. It was the first time Jay had been touched with affection for six years, and he'd felt tight-chested and close to tears. Kramer went on to say it was a pleasure to have met him, and that unlike most convicted felons Jay had the strength of character and the will to survive a long-term sentence.

The sound of the telephone interrupted his introspection, and made him jump. For the last few months he'd been nervous, strung out. Jay knew he was paranoid about life on the outside, unknown territory changed beyond recognition since he'd been imprisoned. Would he lose his marbles like so many ex-cons did, and end up drinking himself into oblivion? The day before yesterday when the prison doors had slammed shut behind him, he'd panicked. Learning to live independently again after twenty-five years was going to be no picnic; it was a mind-blowing prospect, and he was more scared than he'd thought. As he picked up the phone, Jay realized it was going to take much longer than he'd anticipated to re-enter the human race. Even the simple task of learning how to use a digital telephone made him grimace.

It was Hooper. 'How did you get on with Cheri?'

'She was great, Ed, just what I needed.'

'What did I tell you! Cheri's a good girl, she really

goes, gives great head. I've known her since she started out at seventeen. Wow, then she had an ass . . .'

Jay interrupted, 'Like I said she was great.' He sighed. 'I'd forgotten how good it feels to be inside a woman.'

Ed guffawed. 'You and me both, buddy.' Then without waiting for a reply, he continued, 'Lunch is on for tomorrow, the vice president of Maxmark Productions wants to meet you. They're pitching for the movie rights on *Killing Time*. This is big-time Hollywood, pal.'

'That's great news, Ed! I'm on; where and when?'

'Indochine, Lafayette Street, take a cab, be there for twelve-thirty. Your publisher, Bob Horvitz, is coming too. Says he's dying to meet you in person at last. Bob is one of those dudes who likes to eat the same way he talks, fast. I'm warning you he doesn't even draw breath, let him have his head and leave me to do the negotiations.'

Jay said, 'So who needs me?'

'Bob's keen to hang on to you for Schnieder and Smith and to get the next book in the bag. I've told him what a great guy you are. The personal touch always helps.'

'Spare me the bullshit, Ed. I'm a convicted felon who's spent the last twenty-five years in the pen on a second degree murder charge. What's with the nice guy routine? He likes the way I write, period. Schnieder and Smith have made big bucks outta Will Hope, but I sure as hell know that Bob Horvitz couldn't give a damn about what sort of guy I am.'

'You're way too touchy, Jay, still over-sensitive. It's gonna take time; you're on a learning curve, man, you've gotta lighten up.'

24

'Yeah yeah; I hear you. Don't worry I'll do what I'm told. I'll wear the nice new Brooks Brothers shirt and tie. Eat food I can't pronounce, listen to the suit and make the right noises in the right places.'

'That's my boy; see you at twelve-thirty sharp.'

Jay replaced the telephone, walked to the mini bar and, marvelling at the selection of drinks and confectionery in the small fridge, he took out a beer. He returned to the bed, and using the remote control spent twenty enjoyable minutes surfing the channels. He was about to switch off when he saw her. Like a bolt of lightning her face shot on to the screen. He jumped up, running towards the TV to get a closer look and dropping to his knees. It was Kelly, he was certain, he would recognize her anywhere. In fact she hadn't changed much in all the intervening years. A little fuller around the middle, but the same twinkling-eyed wide smile – a tantalizing mixture of warmth and mischief. The kind of smile that turns heads, melts knees and knots guts. He felt his own insides respond now, bunched in a hard ball.

Kelly was standing next to Senator Todd Prescott, the man tipped to be the next Republican president. Jay knelt rigid, mesmerized. He couldn't hear what they were saying for the loud buzzing in his ears. Then Kelly was gone, replaced by the newscaster's face. *Kelly Tyler, Kelly Tyler,* he repeated her name in his head. She'd been the girl of his dreams, the one who'd broken his heart, his first love. His thoughts sped back down the years, back to the fall of 1972. It was after a summer of the Eagles and Santana. He'd been invited to spend the day at Susie Faber's house. He remembered that day as if it were yesterday. It had started out warm, had got more so, and by midday was perfect. He'd picked Kelly up in his beat-up Wrangler jeep. And on the way home, later, much later that evening, they'd made love on the back seat. He would never forget the way she'd looked that day. Her long dress, flowing to her ankles, the curve of her body clearly silhouetted by the sunlight through the diaphanous fabric. When he'd commented on it, she'd told him it was only cheesecloth. Fooling around, someone had put flowers in her hair, and he remembered carefully picking them out by the petals and saying something gauche about her smelling sweeter than any flower. He'd been nervous, fumbling, inept; she'd been the opposite – calm and self-assured, and guiding. He'd taken her for an accomplished lover. He was wrong; it was her first time. Yet making love, she explained afterwards, felt as natural to her as walking, eating or sleeping. She'd helped him unhook her bra and giggled when he'd been all fingers and thumbs with the buttons of his jeans. He'd never forgotten how ashamed he'd felt about his performance; even now he recalled his stumbling apologies and repeated reassurances that it had nothing to do with her.

Kelly had merely smiled in an enigmatic way and reminded him that everyone said the first time was often a disappointment, so it could only get better. She was right; their love-making had improved to the point of glory. Torrid romps in his jeep; outside in some remote spot; or in her room on campus; whenever they could steal a little time together ... It always felt, for him at least, totally complete, and something he wanted to repeat again and again.

In the space of four months his love had blossomed to a point where he cherished her, desired her, wanted to possess her, to make her his wife.

That was how Jay had felt about Kelly Tyler, and how he'd believed she felt about him. Until Matthew's death. It was then that Kelly changed. For as long as he lived he would never forget the indifferent voice of the judge passing sentence. The noise in the courtroom had faded to a dull drone, then pin-drop silence. A crushing pain in his head had followed, as if his skull was in a vice, the cool steel getting colder and colder as it clamped tighter and tighter against his temples. Kelly had stood in the aisle staring at him, her face framed by a waterfall of golden hair. Slightly parted lips, tears falling from big luminous eyes the colour of burnt almonds. To him she had never looked so beautiful as she had in that moment, the last time he'd seen her. Then her features, except for those eyes, had become fuzzy, and textured, like those in an old photograph.

In the first few years of captivity, it had been impossible to put Kelly out of his mind however hard he tried. A deep sense of betrayal had nagged his senses like a persistent dog with a bone. She never came to see him, nor did she write, not a single word. Every week for months he'd flicked through his mail, searching, longing, for a glimpse of her handwriting. Eventually, just staying alive, staying sane, came to demand all his wits and helped crowd out the memory of her. But the hunger to see her face, touch her soft skin just one more time, had never abated. And now, seeing her on screen had brought her back to life, renewing that hunger deep in his belly. It was like the ache that used to keep him awake as a young boy whenever he'd dared to answer his father back. In those days he would receive a beating and be sent to bed without food until forced to apologize.

'I'm going to find out who killed Matthew and why, and then I'm going to write about it.' Jay wasn't shouting, yet his voice sounded too loud in his own ears. A title sprang instantly to mind.

*Remission*. He liked the sound of it, it had a good ring. He repeated it again and again. '*Remission, Remission, Remission*.'

He began to pace the void between the bed and the wall, a habit he'd developed in prison. It had helped him to shut out the noise of the zoo all around, and enabled him to concentrate. With a sense of dread, he acknowledged that to find out what had really happened on that awful night, he would have to go back to when it had all started.

For years he'd vowed he wouldn't take that path, sworn he would go forward, opening only the doors that led ahead. But stronger still was his primeval urge for vengeance. Revenge was normally another luxury that prison squeezed out of you. Yet here he was, only hours on the outside and ready to hatch plots, schemes of retribution and pay-back. But it wasn't just about revenge, Jay knew that. It was about knowing, finding out, making all the pieces fit.

During his imprisonment, his vengeful schemes had been the one thing that fed his fervent intellect – until the early eighties when Al Colacello had come into his life and his writing had begun. A vision of Al, the first time Jay had seen him, crossed his mind. That face would always live with him. A big cat face, sleek and malevolent. With eyes so dark, they were almost black; so shiny, they were almost inhuman. Al had eyes that stripped you naked in seconds, read your mind. And they had looked into the faces of more than twenty-eight men before he'd killed them. All hits, good clean eliminations. 'The best cleaner in the business.' That was how Al had referred to himself.

Al had boasted to Jay that he was so good he'd earned himself the nickname 'Teach 'n' Reach', or just 'Teach'; there was nobody whom he couldn't teach a lesson, nobody he couldn't reach. Al Colacello had been Mario Petroni's lieutenant for twelve years, and his best friend. Mario was known as the 'Dapper Don' after he'd been indicted on three charges of corruption and grand larceny and had appeared every day at his hearing immaculate in hand-stitched Savile Row suits, Hermès ties and cashmere overcoats. Al had been a key witness in his defence, his testimony crucial to Mario's subsequent acquittal. Al and Mario: both born on the same day, within hours of each other, in the mean backstreets. Al in Naples; Mario in Sicily. Both emigrated to America in the late fifties; Al with his family, and Mario to stay with his uncle.

Somehow innocence managed to bypass them both, they had no time to be kids – too busy finding food to put in their empty bellies, and organizing some new scam to finance the next few days of existence. Bosom buddies, kindred spirits, until Al had made a mistake, almost a fatal mistake. He'd screwed up big time.

Jay recalled Al's voice the night he'd told him about Mario's daughter Anna. 'What would you have done?' he'd asked Jay. 'If this beautiful girl, like she's sixteen, with huge tits, and an ass like a ripe peach, slips into bed next to you and begins going down on you. Only coming up for air and to beg you to fuck her. Like I've got the biggest fucking hard-on, and suddenly she's pushing her tight little pussy down on my cock. She's no virgin, and as I go inside she's screaming to fuck her hard, cause that's the way she likes it. Man, believe me I tried to stop! I tell you, I really tried. All the time, I'm telling myself she's my best friend's daughter. But Christ, she's gagging for it and pumping me like crazy.

'I stayed away from Anna after that, tried to avoid her, but she kept coming on to me. Until one night she warns me if I don't fuck her she's going to tell her father I raped her, took her virginity. I call her bluff. I knew it was a risk, but I'd no choice.'

At that point Jay had glimpsed a chink in Al's armour of arrogance as he said, 'One fuck, one simple fuck loused up everything. Mario didn't believe me. I was lucky to hang on to my cock, and to this day he still thinks his fucking daughter is Mother Theresa.'

After this confession Al and Jay had struck up a rapport, and a friendship began to grow. Jay knew it was an incongruous pairing and one that would never have existed on the outside. Theirs was a meeting of opposites, but nevertheless he felt at ease in Al's company as he knew Al did in his. Day after day, week after week, Al had poured his dark and innermost secrets into Jay's greedy ears. He had kept diaries of his time with Mario, detailed and comprehensive memoirs of their twelve-year partnership. And night after night, while his cell-mate slept, Jay had stayed awake scribbling in his notebook, recording Al's life – a life of organized crime, littered with dead bodies. It had fascinated Jay, gripped him from the first telling, and he'd listened avidly to how Al had met Mario Petroni when they were twenty-year-olds, young hell raisers with the smell of fresh blood on their hands. From the tenement basements of Hell's Kitchen on Manhattan's Westside they hatched ambitious schemes of how they were to become big Mafia dons, bigger and better than any before.

And during the three years he'd shared a cell with Al, Jay had also quietly observed his gradual decline into insanity. The end came when Teach was found dead in a pool of his own vomit, his face the same colour as the concrete floor of the prison cell. Al Colacello the invincible, the teacher, had done something really stupid – shot up on smack from a supplier who was known to cut his drugs with baking powder when he could get it, rat poison when he couldn't.

In a strange way Jay had missed Teach; missed his crude

street humour, his outrageous arrogance. Above all he'd missed the protection Al's friendship had afforded him. The gangster's life and death had inspired *Killing Time*, and he would always be grateful to him – killing machine or not – for that at least.

Jay finally stopped pacing. He stood perfectly still for several minutes as he bottled his memories, then moved back to the bed. He lit a cigarette and filled his lungs with smoke. *Why go back?* he asked himself. *Let it be, leave it alone, let go.*

But then the nagging sense of injustice returned, and with it the need for revenge, as it had countless times before. An eye for an eye. Get the motherfuckers who framed you and tell the world about it. Anyway, he concluded, it wasn't about going back, it was about going forward. Because then and only then could he begin to live again. Exhaling, he watched the smoke rise into the air and evaporate. He was feeling better already.

It was Todd Prescott's persistent erection pressing between her buttocks that finally woke his wife Kelly. With her head buried deep in linen-covered duck down she stifled a groan. Then lifting a blonde tousled head, she whispered, 'I've got to pee.'

Gently Todd grabbed her hips, his fingers pressing into hard flesh. 'You're not getting away with that old line . . . Come on, honey, be nice to your baby. You know how horny I get before congress.'

Kelly pushed her ass into her husband's groin, biting the corner of her lip as she felt his hot hands ease her buttocks open. If there was one thing she detested about Todd, it was his hands. It wasn't the only thing, but they were high on the hate list. Hairless soft hands, the small fingers capped with tiny white nails. 'Your husband's got a politician's hands like pumping wet fish,' her brother had commented on more than one occasion. She was forced to agree.

Kelly loathed watching Todd's limp fingers stroke her body; clamped her eyes shut when they slid into her pubic hair; and usually thought about a new Donna Karan dress, or the big beefy hands of her yoga teacher and occasional lover, when the baby fingers probed inside her.

But this morning she was thinking about something she'd read late last night in the *Boston Globe*. The headline had been running through her brain like tickertape ever since. 'Kaminsky Released from Cedar State Pen.' A grainy photograph of Jay as a nineteen-year-old Harvard freshman had accompanied the article. Lantern-jawed, with heavy-lidded chestnut eyes that could look dark brown depending on his mood. Thick hair, shining like ebony, slicked back above a high tanned brow. Her prom date, her first 'let him go all the way' date; her sweet, considerate, innocent teenage love.

As Todd pumped, she thought about Jay. She wondered if prison had destroyed his good looks. Would all that bitterness and anger have warped not only the inside, but also the outside?

Todd's shouting intruded just then. 'Baby! My sweet baby.'

Wiggling her bottom, Kelly contracted her internal

muscles at the same time to hurry her husband along on his final lap. Two more thrusts and it would all be over. Kelly was counting. It took four. Until the next time, she thought, and there always was a next time.

It was the story of her life. Ever since her father's death when she was nineteen, then losing Jay, she had been filling in the gaps in a desperate quest for the one thing that constantly eluded her. *Love*. The word rang in her head, bouncing back and forth like a tennis ball.

She felt Todd's hands on her shoulders, and suppressed the urge to recoil. His voice was whispering in her ear, but it was her father's words she could hear. *Kelly, you are a beautiful princess, and there will always be men who want you. But you were one of the lucky ones. God was generous; he gave you a brain as well. And so there's nothing you can't have, no place you can't go. Don't waste a minute.*

Paul Tyler had been right. At forty-three, there were few places she hadn't been and there had always been a man. Her first husband, Maynard Fraser Jnr, a wealthy Wasp businessman, had showered her with gifts. Jewels were his thing, and Kelly wore his success. The purchase of a new tower block would be followed by Kelly's glittering appearance in an antique diamond choker. But three years into the marriage, when Maynard was fifty-two and Kelly a few days off her twenty-ninth birthday, he was killed in a light aircraft somewhere in British Honduras. His body was never found. Kelly had never loved Maynard; she'd been fond of him which was a totally different thing. Yet she was genuinely sorry to lose him, and in the first few months of bereavement she missed his ebullient presence in their vast apartment on Manhattan's Eastside, and their sprawling beach house in East Hampton. To ease the loss, Kelly threw herself into Maynard's electronics business, doubling the profits in the next two years as the technological age began to grip the entire world. A merger with the giant multi-national Cirax diluted her stake, and the much-publicized battles between its megalomaniacal head and Kelly Fraser made 'Beauty and the Beast' headlines more than once in the *Wall Street Journal*.

In 1986 Kelly had sold out and bought a house in the Caribbean, where six months later she met the man who was to become her second husband. Tim Reynolds, two years younger than herself, was a budding film producer, overflowing with creative angst and poetic romanticism. They met on the beach: she was searching for shells, and he was pretending to read whilst watching her over the top of his book, catching her off guard. This time, with Tim, she had told herself, it's for real, like in all the schmaltzy movies and love songs. And for two years Kelly believed in the myth, convinced herself that she was loved and in love. Whenever yet another bizarre film scheme floundered, she backed her husband both emotionally and financially – until the final straw, the one that breaks even the most ardent camel's back. She found Tim in their bed with one of her so-called best friends, a guy called Jack Silvers.

In the next few years Kelly had managed as much as humanly possible to forget. Yet occasionally something would remind her of what she privately referred to as her 'twilight time'. She couldn't remember half of the men she'd slept with; they'd all merged into one huge grey mass. It was her friend Weston Kane who had rescued her, rebuilt her self-esteem and persuaded her to go back into business, and in 1990 Tyler Publications was born. The media had proved a natural arena for the gregarious and charmingly devious Kelly. At last she had found her forte, and she could honestly say that the last few years as head of Tyler had been the happiest of her life.

Kelly slid out of bed, ignoring Todd's glancing peck on her right shoulder, and his muttered, 'That was great, baby.'

She crossed the large room, her bare feet making no sound on the deep pile carpet. As she stepped into the bathroom, she felt Todd's hot sperm dribbling down her inner thighs and shuddered with distaste. The door closed behind her with a quiet click and she walked towards the shower at the far end, passing white walls, white handbasins and stacks of white towels. Even the travertine marble that cooled the soles of her feet was white. Everything was white and, according to the interior designer, the absolute last word in minimalist chic. It looked like a luxurious hospital theatre on first impression, and Kelly's comment to Todd that it was ridiculously large for one person had produced a dismissive shrug. She'd gone on to say that an entire family could live in her bedroom and dressing room; combined, they were bigger than the average apartment. Then she'd quickly reminded herself that this was where she'd always wanted to be. The ultimate

'Chez nous', the biggie, the colonial spread on Capitol Hill: M Street, Georgetown, Washington DC. Complete with European antiques, impressionist paintings, fully equipped gym and a state-of-the-art kitchen that she rarely went into.

Suddenly a voice sprang into her mind, interrupting Kelly's musings. It was saying something she had buried deep, so deep that it sometimes felt as if it had happened to someone else. Kelly wanted to scream like she had as a child when she'd turned over a stone to find a teeming mass of worms underneath. She turned on the shower, but made no attempt to step into the cubicle.

Placing both hands against her ears she pressed hard, humming a tune, but the words would not go away. *'Jay Kaminsky, you have been found guilty of the manslaughter of Matthew Fierstein. I have no option but to . . .'* Kelly blinked, and at the same time a shutter clicked in her brain: she saw Jay on the day he'd been sentenced, his face a study of total incomprehension. He looked like a frightened little boy who'd misunderstood the sentence and was certain the judge and jury would tell him they'd made an awful mistake and he could go home soon. Jay's shocked expression had plagued her for months afterwards; so much so, she'd thought at one point she would go mad. When the image had finally disappeared, she'd prayed it would never return. And it hadn't until today.

Kelly stepped into the steaming cabinet and turned the temperature up high. She pushed her right hand into an exfoliating glove, and with slow deliberate movements she began to scrub her body. Round and round she rubbed, until her skin smarted. Yet she continued to rub, harder and harder, and with each circular motion she repeated in her head the maxim, the one the Pact always used in times of stress. *Stay calm, stay cool, but above all stay in control.*

# Chapter Three

Weston Kane arrived at the restaurant ten minutes early. Carlos, the owner, waved, adopted his most ingratiating smile and extracted himself from a tight knot of chattering people. Swiftly he negotiated the closely packed tables, greeting Weston with what she knew was genuine warmth. She had known him since her father, Sinclair Kane, had first taken her to Umberto's on her eighth birthday. Then Carlos had been a young maître d' with the looks of a matinée idol and the kind of quick wit and instant charm that made whoever he was talking to feel special; as if he'd known the person all his life. Carlos had approached Sinclair Kane to finance a new restaurant; there had been no hesitation, and ten months later Carlos had opened the doors of Umberto's.

Now, thirty-four years and five restaurants later, Carlos was no longer handsome. His love of food and late nights had added an extra thirty pounds of all too solid flesh. And age, though he swore it was worry, had taken most of his once thick hair. But time had not dulled his enthusiasm, nor had it robbed him of his sense of humour and unquenchable zest for life.

'Miss Kane, you look younger every time I see you. How do you do it?'

Weston found herself smiling in response to his trademark flattery. 'It's in the genes.' She pinched his arm. 'The same as your charm.'

It was his turn to smile. 'You're the first, Miss Kane; you want to wait in the bar?'

'I'll go straight to the table, Carlos, thanks, and I'll have my usual.'

Carlos gestured to a passing waiter. 'A vodka martini, shaken, with a twist for Miss Kane. Her usual table.'

Several heads turned as Weston Kane crossed the crowded room to a corner spot where she always sat. After leaving college she'd often lunched with her father in the several top restaurants he used in Manhattan. In each establishment Sinclair always had the same table. If it wasn't available for him, which was rare, he didn't eat there. And on one occasion when he was promised his table and didn't get it, he left and never set foot inside again. He called it the power table, the best one in the house – far from the noise and activity of the kitchen, far enough from the door to avoid the hustle and bustle, yet close enough to see exactly who was coming and going, as well as being able to scrutinize the entire restaurant in one sweeping glance. Part of the game, the social hierarchy game.

Weston slid her long legs under the table. She was tall, over six foot in high heels, with a square handsome face. The azure blue eyes she'd inherited from her mother scanned the room as always. They were spaced wide under a high brow and complemented the collar-length

Titian hair which was her legacy from her father's Scottish forebears. The tight auburn curls she'd hated as a child had been hacked off several times, once with a kitchen knife when she was eight, and on many occasions since. As a teenager, she had ached for long straight blonde hair, the silken type, without a vestige of curl, and had tried every straightening method known to mankind – from reverse perming to a hot iron and greaseproof paper. She shifted on her seat, picked a fleck of cotton off the taupe skirt of a suit she'd had for ten years. It still fitted perfectly. Weston cared little for clothes; in fact she was happiest in jeans and T's in summer, and jeans with good cashmere sweaters in winter. When she did buy clothes, she bought good ones. It was the only lasting influence her mother Annette had achieved over her. On their rare shopping trips she was constantly accompanied by Annette's high-pitched sing-song sighs of approval or disdain.

Such forays had filled her wardrobe with practical, simple well-cut outfits. Pants, invariably St Laurent; Armani jackets; and Valentino or Dior for evening. She knew she was a disappointment to her impeccably dressed mother, but then Weston had no desire to follow Annette on to the 'Ten Best Dressed Women in America' list; she didn't need to. Her height, presence and minimalist style turned heads without fanciful flourishes. The two were completely different in every respect, so much so Weston often doubted her parentage; how could the capricious, totally vacuous Annette Elizabeth Sinclair be her mother? A woman whose main interests ranged from shopping

41

and lunch to more shopping, followed by hair and beauty treatments. And when the shops were shut, Annette's time seemed to be dedicated to modelling her purchases. How the bored young Weston used to hate the preening and pouting in front of the dressing-room mirror as her mother fished for compliments, interrogating her daughter in search of approval and adoration. She grew to abhor her mother's lifestyle, her loathing only increased by her father's worship of the empty-headed beauty he'd loved passionately for forty-six years. Weston had often longed instead for a fun mom, and later in her teens she'd longed for a friend.

From as young as six Weston had lain awake long after she was supposed to be asleep, planning how she could create mischief and mayhem to gain attention. But by the time she was sixteen, she had simply decided that the lifestyle of her mother and her contemporaries was a ridiculous charade. Massaging precious egos, and playing sex games with philandering power brokers was not to be her fate. She set out to become highly successful, extremely rich and very powerful in her own right, and in that order. By twenty-eight she had produced her first television series; it was nominated for three Emmys and won two. A year later she'd joined forces with Imogen Irving, a fifty-two-year-old Hollywood legend and movie producer, who taught her all she knew about motion pictures and also initiated Weston into the joys of sapphism. Weston had never looked back.

She had gone on to head up her own production company Summit, and had recently negotiated a billion-dollar merger with Avesta Inc, a multi-national media giant spanning digital TV, cable, satellite and the Internet.

Now she was hungry for more power, more control. It was like a potent drug, addictive, the ultimate high. *But be careful, Weston, power also corrupts*, she could hear her father's voice whispering in her ear.

The waiter had arrived with her drink; she swirled the olive around the glass before taking a sip, her thoughts digressing to her two closest friends, Beth Morgan and Kelly Prescott, who were both joining her for lunch. They were the two most important people in her life, the result of a friendship that had survived untarnished through three decades, since they'd all met at Wellesley College. This year was the twenty-sixth annual celebration of the special bond the three women had forged in their sopho-more year. They had been hedonistic young feminists with far-reaching ambitions and ruthless energy, and had formed an immediate rapport. While other girls discussed vacations, boys or clothes, they had spent long hours working out how they would help each other achieve positions of real power. They agreed it would take time, it was a man's world and they had to find a way to crack it, each giving the others a leg up the ladder whenever they could. The end of the century was their deadline – the millennium. And that was the pact they secretly swore: the Millennium Pact.

Way back in 1972 when they had called themselves sisters, the world was still waking up to female equality and as the balance of power between the sexes began to shift, they had been ideally placed to take advantage of the changing times. At that time the year 2000 had seemed so distant, yet here they all were nearly at the dawn of a new century, having achieved even more than they had aspired to in those early heady days. They still met six times a year, but their lunches never involved small talk or gossip. They spoke only about themselves, their careers, the next rung, and how each could help the other. Their get-togethers were more like board meetings, brainstorming sessions in which each new move was planned with the sharp precision of a military campaign. And now on the birthday of the Pact they could at last congratulate themselves, give each other a resounding pat on the back.

They had made it.

They had beaten men at their own game, and come out on top. Weston glanced at her watch. Beth, she knew, would be on time; she was punctual to a fault. Kelly, on the other hand, would be late for her own funeral. But she was so beautiful, so adorable, Weston would have forgiven her anything – especially after that night, that perfect night in the Hamptons. A vision of Kelly lying by the pool last summer entered her mind. Weston had been swimming and had surfaced where Kelly lay gloriously naked, milky white triangles of soft flesh emphasizing the secret places the sun hadn't seen. Weston had warned her to wear sun screen, and then had moistened her lips with naked lust as she'd watched Kelly smooth the cream into her delicate skin, massaging it into her full and home-grown thirty-six DD breasts. She was a natural blonde, the all-American dream girl. The one all the guys talked about in the showers after the game, the one they thought about when jerking off, the girl every smart-assed jock had wanted to take to the prom. Weston moaned inwardly as the vision remained before her eyes. She blinked but Kelly was still there, opening her legs wide to apply the cream to her inner thighs. She felt the heat rise between her own, and her belly begin to ache thanks to that never-to-be-forgotten memory.

It was six years ago, spring 1992; Weston had hosted an intimate dinner party at her house in South Hampton. A select gathering, spelling power and influence. It was a celebration: Kelly's publishing company had just won two prestigious awards; one for a cutting-edge, investigative magazine that she had purchased three years previously for next to nothing, increasing the circulation to over half a million; and another for Editor of the Year. Weston had closely observed Kelly chatting to Todd Prescott, an extremely wealthy senator. The naturally gregarious Kelly had been in a strange mood all evening, and Weston had thought her distracted and withdrawn. After dinner Todd left, and Kelly had asked to stay the night. She and Weston had sniffed a few lines of cocaine, and listened to music. It was Marvin Gaye singing 'I Heard It Through the Grapevine' that prompted Kelly to dance. With her long hair whipped across her face, she had laughed, urging Weston to join her. Weston had refused, happy to watch her friend gyrate; happy to bask in the warm flush that spread from her nipples to her groin when Kelly began to take off her clothes.

Stripped to her panties, hips swaying, she'd danced

till the end of the tape, then she stood very still in the middle of the room, panting, breasts rising and falling, her hands running up and down the entire length of her body leaving glistening trails in the sheen that clothed her. Kelly, not taking her eyes off Weston, had slowly slipped her panties down her legs and, sinking to her knees, she crawled to the sofa where Weston sat.

'You want to eat me, don't you?' Kelly had said.

Weston, her mouth suddenly very dry, had merely nodded and watched, lost in desire and anticipation. When Kelly turned round, for a moment she'd thought she was going to crawl away. But instead she bent over gracefully, provocatively, and arched her back, thrusting her tight ass in the air. Weston had gasped when Kelly spread her legs, hands reaching back to ease her buttocks apart and tracing a line that ran down to the bud of her clitoris, which was being rubbed by one finger.

Weston could recall muttering, 'You're so beautiful,' as she opened her mouth to taste Kelly. A fresh and faintly peachy sensation.

The following morning, over breakfast, Kelly had dismissed the encounter. She'd wanted to have a woman, been curious; the cocaine had made her feel horny, she'd needed to come, nothing more. They never mentioned it again.

Weston now took another sip of her drink to drown the memory before it engulfed her. Looking up afterwards, she spotted Beth coming into the restaurant – true to form on the dot of one o'clock. Weston saw her friend before a waiter directed her to the table, and had the opportunity to observe her unawares. Beth was wearing what she always wore, a badly fitting suit. She had appalling dress sense, and no idea what was right for her big-boned, pear-shaped frame. In summer she favoured either a cotton or linen suit, always with a sleeveless tank. The winter version was invariably in wool and usually worn with an assortment of bright polo-neck sweaters, or high-necked starched white shirts. Today she had opted for a black pinstripe, with a long jacket and knee-length skirt. Underneath she had chosen a canary yellow cable sweater, with a brightly patterned scarf tied at the neck. Her freshly cropped dark hair was gelled flat to her head, she wore no make-up save a slash of scarlet lipstick that made her white face look like a death mask. As Beth neared the table, Weston rose.

'How long have you been here?' Beth asked between kisses.

'Not long, I got out of my meeting early so I thought . . .' Weston pointed to the half-empty glass, 'why not have myself a quick shot before you guys arrive.'

Beth dropped to a chair, black eyes darting round the restaurant. The pupils always reminded Weston of shiny jet beads.

'I need a drink, too. Douglas is the prize prick of the month. I'm telling you the man is a shit, and if I wasn't such a lady I'd punch him in the mouth.'

Weston laughed, teasing Beth as she summoned a waiter. 'Being a lady's never stopped you in the past.'

Beth grinned. 'He's bigger than me.' Then to the waiter who was hovering, 'Get me a Scotch on the rocks.'

'Since when did you start drinking Scotch?'

'Just. That Douglas creep has driven me to drink.'

'So tell me about it. On second thoughts, I think you already have. The last time he dumped on you, and the time before that. I did warn you not to marry him. Come on, Beth, the man is gorgeous; women come on to him, he can't resist. Why don't you take my advice, and lose him? Like once and for all.'

'Would you believe me if I told you we still have a great sex life? And that I love the louse?'

Weston raised her eyes. 'Now that I can accept. It's as good a reason as any for staying with the sonofabitch.'

The Scotch arrived and Beth took a sip, wrinkling up her tiny nose as it hit the back of her throat.

'No, you're right of course, I should dump him. But a gal's got to do what a gal's got to do, and I need a little pleasure in life. Running the numbers, playing the financial markets, acquisitions and mergers . . . moving billions of dollars around the world; believe me, it gets mighty tedious. And after fourteen hours of that every day, getting smashed and getting laid becomes top priority. Doug is convenient and he does it good, better than anyone I've ever known; he knows exactly how to ring my bells.' Beth winked. 'Know what I mean?'

Weston was about to retort that it had cost Beth dearly, both financially and emotionally, when Kelly swept into the restaurant – causing heads to swivel and subdued appreciative whispers.

Weston felt her heart leap. Kelly had that effect on most people, men and women alike. She was, to say the least, beautiful. But more than just on the surface; she had a radiance, a charismatic aura that was tangible. It was a rare man who was not immediately intoxicated by her; a rare woman who didn't immediately want to be her. Today she was wearing her long hair piled high on her head in a fashionably messy topknot, several strands fell on to her oval face and down the nape of her long neck. When she reached the table she was smiling, but it wasn't with her usual all-consuming warmth. This smile was taut, forced, polite, the type normally reserved for an unwelcome or distant acquaintance. Weston knew instinctively there was something awry. Reaching across, she covered Kelly's hand with her own.

'What is it, Kelly, is there something wrong?'

Kelly nodded, meeting Weston's enquiring eyes and acknowledging Beth with a sigh. 'I need a drink.' She sat silently until a large glass of white wine was placed in front of her. Then she raised it. 'First and foremost I want to drink to the Pact.'

The three women raised their glasses and drank. Weston was impatient but she knew not to press Kelly, she would tell all in her own time.

'To the Pact.' They said it in unison.

Kelly took three deep gulps of wine, placed her glass down carefully and looked first at Weston, then Beth.

'Three guesses who I've just seen on the corner of Fifth and Fifty-second?'

'Kevin Costner?' Beth piped up, giggling.

'This is serious, Beth.'

With a shrug of her shoulders, Beth retorted, 'So don't play games; who did you see?'

'Jay Kaminsky.'

Weston and Beth both stiffened. Nobody spoke.

Eventually Weston broke the silence. 'I knew he was out. You got my fax? I read the piece in the *Globe*.'

Kelly nodded. 'He's here, in Manhattan, and –' She stopped speaking, squeezing Weston's hand tight.

'It was a shock seeing him like that, just hanging out at a news-stand buying a paper, looking for all the world like he was on his way to an office on Madison or Park. He was dressed like an uptown lawyer or advertising exec. He's only a few blocks from here right now. In fact he could walk into this restaurant at any moment. I knew he'd got out, because all the papers announced it. And we all knew his sentence was up. But to see him like that, so close, after so long; wow, it freaked me out.'

Beth had paled. 'And today of all days.'

'Yes, today of all days,' Kelly repeated.

'So what if Jay Kaminsky is out, what difference does it make?' Weston tried to calm the other two. 'How can he harm us? What can he do? He's a convicted felon, an ex-con; who's going to take any notice of him? Come on, Kelly, relax.'

When Kelly did not respond she turned her attention

to Beth. 'This year is the twenty-sixth anniversary of our Pact; this is celebration time. We can't let Kaminsky get in the way. We didn't back then, so we're certainly not going to now.' Weston looked from one apprehensive face to the other. 'Come on, what's done is done, no turning back. We're going forward into the twenty-first century on top, in power, in control.' Keeping hold of Kelly's hand, she took Beth's from her lap and holding it reassuringly tight said, 'We've got each other, nothing and no one is going to change that. Let's drink to our continuing friendship, and our journey into the next century. Together we can surmount anything: we're strong, empowered, united.'

Weston raised her glass and drained the last dregs. Kelly took a sip of iced water, and Beth finished her whisky. Their hands were still joined as Carlos came to the table.

'Message for Mrs Prescott.'

Kelly was handed a slip of paper. On it was one line, neatly handwritten in black ink: *The past always has a future.*

The flight to Washington landed on time. As she walked through the arrivals terminal, Kelly searched the sea of faces for her driver, Jim. A moment later she spotted him rushing through the revolving entrance doors. He waved and stood still watching her approach.

Kelly felt tired; thoughts of Jay and too much white wine had combined to keep her awake for most of the previous night. Todd was out of town, and wouldn't be back until later that evening. She moved towards the chauffeur, determinedly pushing all thoughts of Jay to the darkest recesses of her mind.

> When she walks
> She's like a samba
> That sways so sweet,
> And moves so gentle,
> And when she passes
> He smiles but she doesn't see . . .

Jay hummed the tune but the words that rumba'd through his head were not about 'The Girl from Ipanema'. They were about the girl from Temple Texas who went on to become the girl from Capitol Hill.

Long-limbed, with an ease of movement more usual in a Polynesian princess than an apple-pie, homespun American girl, Kelly looked graceful, sleek and majestic to Jay as he watched her cross the arrivals hall. He had a clear view from his vantage position in a telephone booth facing the busy concourse.

She was carrying a fur coat and a small tan leather bag. Clad in a midnight blue suit, jacket nipped into the waist, straight skirt skimming her knees, Kelly held her neat head high – flaxen hair like a slick of gold paint across her shoulders. Several male heads turned, eyes bewitched, blatantly undressing her, and for a brief possessive moment Jay wanted to hit one particularly lecherous pot-bellied executive. Yet the object of all the attention was totally oblivious. Jay supposed it was the nature of the beast: such a combination of beauty, charisma and raw sex appeal was bound to be so acquainted with admiring glances and goggle eyes that it becomes immune to them.

He fell into a quick trot behind her, only holding back as she strode out into the sunlight and dipped into a waiting limousine. Moments later, Jay was in the back of a taxi. The black stretch, three cars ahead, inched forward, indicating left. The taxi followed, fitting in behind on the Beltway leading to the I-75 that went into Washington. As the limo picked up speed, Jay imagined Kelly in the back sitting with legs crossed. Idly he wondered if she was wearing pantyhose or stockings, and, if the latter, whether her garter belt was white, black or the flesh colour of her skin.

In prison every time he'd seen a film clip of a couple in the back seat of a limo, he'd had erotic fantasies of hitching up a full skirt to find stocking tops and milky white thighs belonging to a beautiful, scented woman who wanted him. Always, he would go down on her, while the driver politely readjusted his rear view mirror and turned up the radio.

The cab had followed the limo across the Potomac river, passing the Marriott Hotel where he was staying as of late last night. When they entered Georgetown they got snarled up in traffic, losing the limo for a few nervous moments. Then Jay caught sight of it again and directed the cab driver into M Street, where the limo was gliding to a halt outside an imposing colonial-style house.

Jay looked with a pang of envy at the red brick façade, white portico and gleaming sash windows. The house was seriously elegant, it reeked of money and understated grandeur. He watched Kelly get out of the car and go inside before he asked his cabbie to take him back to the Marriott.

An hour later he was in his room, freshly showered, wearing a towelling bathrobe and sitting in front of a club sandwich and French fries. He'd just taken the first bite when the phone rang. Jay picked it up after four rings. It was the call he'd been waiting for.

'Good to hear you, Luther. When did you get in? Hotel OK?'

Luther's voice sounded jaunty. 'It sure beats the dump I've been living in for the last eight months.'

'Good, I suggest we meet for breakfast here in the coffee shop – eight-thirty in the morning.'

'Have you located the – '

'Yes,' Jay interrupted abruptly; he didn't trust telephones. 'We'll talk tomorrow.'

'I'll be there.'

Jay replaced the telephone and sat down on the bed, closing his eyes. But he had too much going on inside his head to contemplate sleep. In prison the nights had been his time for solitary contemplation. How he'd longed for the zookeepers to lock the cages, to shut out the incessant and repetitive male babble. The close of another monotonous day in hell had always been, for him, a relief. Time to dream.

But tonight, on the outside at last, there was no time

for dreams or introspection, tonight was for plans. Jay believed in careful and strategic planning. Every move had to be thought out, like chess of which he was a master, with precision and patience. He had both and he relished the long hours ahead; while others slept he would plot. And by dawn he knew he would be more alert than if he'd had eight hours' undisturbed sleep.

Jay hadn't seen Luther Ross for six years, but he would have recognized his big head anywhere. It was still shaven and gleaming like a bowling ball. When Jay approached the corner table, Luther looked up and his button black eyes were the same, if a little duller, and the gap-toothed grin hadn't changed – it was as broad and as warm as Jay remembered. He'd used bits of Luther for a character in his first book; not the best bits either, yet Luther had been delighted, thrilled to taste a meagre morsel of fame.

When the other man stood up he seemed smaller than Jay recalled, but maybe that was the outside – on the outside the world seemed to dwarf everyone in it. As if to compensate Luther had gained a lot of weight and his stomach protruded over the top of his trousers. He extended his hand.

'Jay, man! Good to see you.'

Jay felt Luther's firm grip. Genuinely pleased to see the ex-boxer, he returned the greeting. 'It's good to see you too, Luther.'

Luther was smiling as Jay slid into a chair. He began the ritual of ex-cons everywhere. 'You been out long?'

'Just a few days, but it seems like years. Hell, it feels strange after all that hoping, waiting, longing for a normal life on the outside. Living through movies and books doesn't exactly prepare you for the real thing, does it? I wake up in the middle of the night convinced I'm still in the pen, waiting for the familiar sounds, and it takes me hours to get back to sleep – if ever. Some days I feel like I'm acting, like this is not real life and I'm going back inside when it's over. Weird. I suppose it's going to take a long, long time. I've been locked away for a quarter of a fucking century.'

Silently Luther nodded, he'd heard the same story too many times, from too many friends encountered on the outside. He let Jay continue.

'Thank God I started to write; when I think back I don't know what I'd have done without that as an escape. My sales are doing well, so my agent tells me. According to him, I'm the Hemingway of the nineties, and – check this – Hollywood is interested in *Killing Time.*'

'Geez, man, you're doing good! Fucking great, Jay. Waddya say I look after security on the set. Uh?' Luther laughed.

A waiter approached and Jay ordered coffee, eggs sunny-side up, bacon and toast.

'So how have things been for you, Luther?'

'Not so good, buddy; but then . . .' He pointed to his temple, 'You've got a great brain, man. I got no muscle up there. I think when Randy Lewis knocked me out in sixty-eight, I left a whole heap of brain cells on the canvas and forgot to pick 'em up.'

Grinning, Jay said, 'You working?'

'Kind of.' Luther paused, sipped his coffee, then said, 'I was straight for three years.' He stuck three fingers in the air. 'Worked as a kitchen porter, room service waiter, and a cab driver. I was real straight, man; no shit. I met a woman, a good woman. A great-looking broad with a good job, a duty manageress in the St Regis Hotel.' He whistled. 'Legs, like you've never seen legs! Long enough to be continued. And an amazing butt, big and beautiful. Oh yeah, and the face of an angel. Believe it or not, Jay, this incredible chick fell for Luther Ross. Can you imagine? She's crazy about me. It's enough to send anyone straight. So we get ourselves an apartment together. Not a bad place on the lower Eastside. Shirley, she does it up real smart – white sofas and white cotton sheets. I ain't never slept on cotton like that . . . yunno? White folk cotton. Anyway I have the best time of my life – I mean the best, man. And just when I'm telling myself it can't get any better, Shirley goes and quits on me.'

He clicked his fingers with a loud snap, lowering his head at the same time. 'Big C, man. First it's in her right breast, they take that away. Then they find some more of the shit. But this time they don't operate cause it's gone into her lymph glands, and spreading fast; like fucking weed, man. She was dead within six months.'

Luther took a deep breath and there was a long pause until Jay said that he was sorry.

Luther looked into the bottom of his empty cup. 'I knew it couldn't last.'

The eggs and bacon arrived. Jay took one look at it, and pushed the plate to one side.

'I lost it after that. Did some drugs, went a little crazy, got in touch with a couple of old contacts. I've done a few odd jobs. Nothing big, I'm getting too old for the really heavy stuff. Just small heists. Clean. Easy. In, out. It pays the rent.'

Jay bit into a slice of toast as Luther looked at the discarded plate

'You not eating?'

'I just lost my appetite.'

'I ain't lost mine, you mind?'

Jay pushed the plate in front of him. 'Be my guest.'

Luther sawed into a strip of bacon before speaking again. 'So whaddya need, buddy?'

'I need a wire job on Senator Todd Prescott's house. I don't want to hear what the senator has to say, I'm more interested in what his wife is up to.'

As Jay slid a photograph of Kelly across the table, Luther let out a low whistle. 'Ouch! I sure know what I'd like to say to this babe.'

Jay nodded but made no comment. He was afraid his voice would betray him. 'I need a neat job, and I need it done now. I know from the press that the senator's away campaigning from next week.'

Egg yolk trickled from the corner of Luther's mouth as he looked at the photograph again, then pointed at Jay with his fork. 'It's a hot gig, heavy security; high risk, I'm not sure.'

Jay's eyes narrowed. 'That's why I want you. You're the best.'

Luther's grin confirmed to Jay that the big man's ego had kicked in.

'How much?'

'I'll pay you three grand,' Jay said, knowing Luther would ask for five at least.

'Come on, man, this is a senator's pad; they can be mean bastards, as mean as the mob when they get upset.'

'OK, five,' said Jay, knowing Luther would have asked for ten if he'd offered five thousand bucks in the first place.

'Five, plus expenses,' urged Luther.

Jay nodded and held out his hand, aware as he did so that Luther was wondering if he'd asked too little. 'OK, five plus expenses it is. We got a deal?'

Luther wiped his right hand on the table top, before holding up a meaty paw in front of Jay. 'Am I allowed to ask why?'

Jay trusted him. 'I was in love with this woman.' He pointed to the photograph. 'So was the man I'm supposed to have murdered. She was very close friends with two other women; she still is. At the time of my trial I had a hunch they were hiding something. It's only a hunch, but I've got to start somewhere. Kelly seems as good a place as any.'

Jay's eyes had not left the picture of Kelly and Luther had noticed. 'You sure that's all it is, man?'

Jay seemed dazed. 'It'll do for starters. You on or not, Luther?'

'What do you think? Gimme five for five, man.'

Jay slapped palms as he was told, 'We should be on line this time next week.'

Both men smiled.

# Chapter Four

Weston woke up at six-thirty a.m. with a hangover. She rarely had headaches, in fact she'd been ill on only half a dozen occasions in her entire life. 'Weston's as strong as an ox,' her father had been fond of saying. 'Kane genes! Gets it from me.' Sinclair Kane was still bragging about his own consistent good health when he dropped dead of a coronary thrombosis at sixty-five. Weston missed him more than she would have believed possible. She had lost count of the times she'd longed to speak to him again. Her father was the only man she'd ever loved and long before realizing she was a lesbian, she'd known with a certainty that scared her that he would remain so.

The phone rang and she staggered to the bathroom, allowing the answer machine to intercept the call. As she threw up she vowed never to drink champagne again; well, at least not two bottles on an empty stomach. She spoke to her reflection, 'Oh God, you look about a hundred.'

*Not a pretty sight,* she thought as red-rimmed, blood-shot eyes stared back at her out of a face the same colour as the white marble of her vanity basin. Her stomach made an odd gurgling sound, and she braced herself as a wave of nausea swept through her body. *I wouldn't care if the bitch had been worth it,* she thought, her mind returning to last night – spent with a girl she'd met the previous weekend. A very young girl, nineteen, twenty at most, she'd forgotten to ask; far more interested in her full lips and soft body – so smooth it was childlike. A beautiful yet unresponsive body.

Weston breathed deeply, uttering through clenched teeth, 'Shit, why am I such a sucker for the young ones? And why do I always want heterosexual women; what am I trying to prove?'

Scraping her hair back, she moved closer to the mirror. *Time for a face lift,* she thought, then instantly rejected the idea. Her mother had recently had her third: a seventy-one going on fifty-something *femme fatale,* who reminded Weston of a lamp she'd had in her hall – tall and wooden with a parchment shade that looked best at night when lit. The last time she'd visited Annette Sinclair, Weston had been shocked to discover a pack of tampons in the bathroom. When questioned, Annette had given one of her prim, 'Nothing to do with you, dear,' looks and giggled girlishly without making any comment. The thought had made Weston feel physically sick; her seventy-one-year-old mother still menstruating, presumably with the aid of hormones. Grabbing a couple of extra-strength painkillers, and a 1000 gram Vitamin C tablet, she washed them down with a slug of Evian, then went back to bed.

Three hours later Weston woke feeling infinitely better, and ready to face lunch with Rob Steiner who ran the LA office of Avesta. She had met him only a couple of times since the recent merger of her own Summit television with Avesta, but each time she'd renewed her first impression of Rob. Extremely bright, enthusiastic and intuitive, with the sort of incisive brain that could cut through the crap and stay on track. She liked him, and intended to offer him a fat pay rise to head up her proposed Pacific Rim operation. She showered and dressed in a long-sleeved simple brown wool dress, draping a camel cashmere sweater over her shoulders in preparation for lunch at Le Cirque, where the super-efficient air conditioning almost required fur coats in summer and sleeveless shifts in winter. Armed with her bulging briefcase, she left her bedroom and walked briskly down a wide hallway, heels clicking on the polished ash floor. The first thing she saw as she entered her vast living room was her maid Carmita who was coming out of the kitchen, her head obscured by a large floral arrangement covered in crisp cellophane wrapping.

'Morning, Miss Weston, these just arrived.'

'Morning, Carmita. Or afternoon, almost . . .'

'I careful not to vacuum, I think that you 'ave a late night.'

'I had an early morning, Carmita. I feel a little worse for wear, could you make me a strong coffee? Use that Colombian blend you got last week.'

'All gone, your friend Taylor drank most of it at the weekend.'

Mildly irritated, Weston snapped, 'Use any kind of coffee, Carmita, just make it.'

Muttering under her breath, Carmita left the room.

Weston poked her nose into the cellophane wrapping, jumping back with a sharp intake of breath when she saw all the flowers were dead and shrivelled, brown-stained lilies. She hated lilies. They reminded her of death, and of her father's funeral when her mother had filled the house with them. Nonchalantly she tore the accompanying card off, thinking that Martin the commissionaire had probably forgotten to deliver the flowers to her apartment. It wouldn't be the first time, and she made a mental note to question him about it on her way out. Slowly she moved towards a large white sofa situated in the centre of the room. As she did so, her eyes wandered over the pristine elegance of her apartment, checking for dust. Moving a vase a millimetre as she passed a table, she registered the absence of the Aubusson rug that was supposed to have been delivered from the specialist cleaners two days ago. Weston loved order, was fastidiously tidy and obsessed with her own inimitable sense of style: understated and expensive. Whenever her friend Beth came to the apartment, she always said that she was afraid to sit down in case she looked too messy, or not colour-coordinated with the beige on white, and shades of eau de nil and pewter. Weston was just as unaffected by these playful jibes as she was by her mother's resentful taunts. It had long been her dream to live on Central Park West, an aspirational thing, something she'd promised herself at eighteen when she'd stayed in a similar apartment owned by the family of a friend from college. It would have been very easy, too easy, to have let her father help her climb the property ladder. Sinclair Kane could well afford it. But Weston had wanted to get there on her own. Setting herself goals and meeting challenges were meat and drink to Weston. And the day she'd moved into the nine thousand square feet of lofty space high above Central Park, she had felt very good indeed. Her only regret? Her father hadn't lived long enough to witness her achievement.

When Carmita returned with the coffee, Weston was standing next to the vast floor-to-ceiling plate-glass window, the top of her head glowing like a ball of fire in a sudden burst of brilliant sunlight. The maid busied herself moving a pile of glossy magazines to make room for the tray on the coffee table. 'Will that be all, Miss Weston?'

When Weston twisted around, Carmita was shocked to see her employer's face. 'You all right, Miss Weston? You look like you saw a ghost.'

'Ironic you should say that,' Weston whispered almost to herself, then without another word she walked past her maid and out of the apartment.

Carmita shrugged, poured herself a cup of coffee and was about to drink it when she spotted a white card on the floor, close to where Weston had been standing. Dropping to her knees, she picked it up and read the message: *Freedom is a precious gift.*

Carmita propped the card up against the dead flowers before leaving the room.

An hour before Weston received her flowers, Beth also had a gift. She was in her office on Wall Street, a fortieth-floor eyrie with far-reaching views out to Staten Island; on a good day she could see the tourists peering out of the viewing platform high up on Liberty's crown. On a bad day she tried not to look out of the window.

Five years previously she had commissioned an English interior designer to transform the large floor space. The brief was simple: lived-in, old English money, but not stuffy. And the result was a pseudo turn-of-the-century style, more suited to a crusty old barrister in London than a high-flying female banker in Manhattan. But Beth loved it. She loved the mellow oak-panelled walls, specially distressed to look old; the painted faux book-shelves and the original Chesterfield she'd found by accident in a funky little shop selling Indian artefacts in the Village. It was her inner sanctum, giving her a feeling of such calm it was almost spiritual. It was the only room she'd ever inhabited that'd had that effect. Most of her English childhood had been spent to-ing and fro-ing between a rambling, elegantly shabby country house near Cirencester, St Mary's Wantage boarding school, and her father's smart Cheyne Row townhouse in the fashionable end of Chelsea. Until 1968, when her mother had met and married an American TV producer and had dragged Beth, at fourteen, kicking and screaming from her English school to the East Coast American equivalent. The transition had been much easier than Beth could have hoped for. Her American counterparts had welcomed her like a long-lost sister, and she was forced to admit it would not have been as easy if it had been the other way round.

Beth was drinking her fourth double espresso of the day, and thinking that she should give up all toxic substances, when her secretary Julia buzzed.

'Special delivery for you, Ms Morgan; shall I bring it in?'

'What is it?' Beth asked.

'No idea, it was delivered by Fed Ex, it looks like a gift.'

'Sounds intriguing, wheel it in.'

A few seconds later Julia entered the office, carrying a box the size of a wine case. It was expensively wrapped in dark brown paper, tied with black ribbon and raffia. Beth exhaled smoke, as her methodical mind started to eliminate the reasons why she should be receiving a gift.

'It's not my birthday, thank God, and I can't think of any good turns I've done recently. My husband is pissed with me, so I doubt he's bought me a present. And I don't have a lover.'

She began to undo the wrapping, a smile of mild anticipation directed at Julia who looked on eagerly awaiting the revelation. With some ferocity, Beth tore at the paper, standing back with a pant when she pulled it off to reveal the top of a small birdcage. With its yellow handle and red seed tray, it resembled a cage her mother's sister had kept a budgerigar in when Beth was a little girl. The recollection of opening that cage and letting the bird out filled her mind. She had forgotten all about it until now, but she shuddered as she recalled how all hell had been let loose when the bird had escaped.

Julia took a step closer, her nose wrinkled as she pointed at the cage. 'There's something in there.'

Beth stepped forward; she looked down to the bottom of the cage where a baby dove lay in the corner. Its neck was broken; one blood-encrusted eye stared upward. There was a message tagged to the bird's foot; it said simply: *I died inside.*

The box was on the hall table, on top of the *Washington Post* and the unopened mail. It was wrapped in white paper, tied with red velvet ribbon, scarlet red. Kelly didn't see it until she was about to leave the house at ten after twelve. She was screaming orders at her cook from the hall, and checking she had everything she needed for the charity luncheon she was due to attend in less than fifteen minutes. This was the first meeting of the fund-raising committee; what would it be this time, she wondered. A black-tie ball for three thousand of Washington's élite? A musical soirée? A masked carnival? A fashion show? All the same repetitive stuff, and as usual Kelly was dreading the tedious debate and the well-meaning, sanctimonious chatter of the other members. She would much rather be having lunch with her friend Sally Oritz, who made her laugh with her crude bar-room humour.

Kelly grabbed the box on her way out and was comfortably settled in the back seat of the car when she examined the package. It was about a foot long, and a couple of inches wide. There was no message tag, and she suspected by the weight and shape it was an orchid or a rose.

The ribbon came off easily, as did the fine tissue gift

wrap. Inside was a wooden box, it was midnight blue and resembled a long jewellery case. She lifted the lid; the interior was a lighter shade of blue. At first glance Kelly thought it was empty. On closer inspection she realized it contained a string, a musical instrument string, probably part of a violin or cello. It was broken, one end coiled around a card lying underneath. When she picked up the card, her hand was trembling as she read it: *You broke my heart.*

# Chapter Five

He was lucky to get the apartment. It had come back on the market two days ago, after being let for two years. 'A snip,' the agent had said, several times. 'A two-bed, fully furnished duplex on M Street for six thousand bucks a month is a steal.'

Jay had merely nodded silently and handed over three months' rent in advance. The apartment was comfortable in a white-on-white, young designer hot-out-of-school and eager-to-impress sort of way. 'Chic' was the agent's description. Jay didn't know chic from crass, good taste from bad. But it was enough that he was within spitting distance of Kelly and, as of today, on line.

With a self-satisfied grin in Jay's direction, Luther pointed to the equipment he'd set up on a marble-topped console table in the corner of the large living room. Jay was sitting on the arm of the chair, a cigarette dangling from his lips.

'You wanna hear?'

Jay exhaled, and nodded at the same time.

Luther flicked a switch, and Jay heard a man speak.

*'Hi, Kelly.'*

*'You OK, Todd? You sound out of breath.'* Kelly's voice, throaty and deep, caused Jay to have a physical pain in his gut.

'I'm fine, and you, what did the doc say?' There was a long silence then, 'Kelly, you still there?'

In a very small voice she replied, 'Yes I'm still here. And no, you're not going to be a daddy.'

There was another long silence, longer than the last, followed by a deep sigh. Jay wasn't sure whether it was Kelly or Todd sighing. A second later Todd spoke, the enforced joviality in his tone failing to mask acute disappointment. 'That's OK, honey, we can try again.'

'Todd I –' Kelly paused. 'Todd, I'm sorry.'

'It's not your fault. Like I just said, we'll try again. It's fun practising.'

'Tell me the truth. Are you very disappointed?'

Another long sigh then, 'I would love to have a baby with you, Kelly, but if it's not possible it won't stop me loving you, nor will it change our relationship. We've got each other.'

'I'm so pleased you said that, Todd. Because it's exactly how I feel.' Jay detected something in her tone that didn't quite ring true, but then he rejected it as overreacting. It was, after all, the first time he'd heard her voice for over twenty-five years.

'You get some rest now, Kel, I'll call you in the morning.'

'Night, Todd.'

'And by the way, Kelly. I love you.'

Jay did not hear Kelly's reply as the line went dead. Luther flicked a switch and, finger poised, said, 'You want to hear some more?'

'What else is there?'

'A call to her hairdresser, the rest is business. A real cute operator, Mrs Prescott. Did you know that the little lady is about to launch a tabloid called the *Georgetown Gazette*?'

Jay grinned. 'No, as a matter of fact I didn't. But now that this little baby is in place,' he pointed with his cigarette to the electronic playback, 'there isn't much about Mrs Prescott that I won't know.'

'I saw her leave the house this morning.' Luther whistled. 'Sure is one beautiful dame. He added quickly, 'Too much for a dumb ass nigger boy like me.'

'For a dumb ass nigger boy,' Jay grinned and touched Luther's arm, 'you're one hell of an electronics genius.'

But by now Jay was really thinking about Kelly. The sound of her voice had plucked another chord in his memory.

It was the fall of 72; they had been invited to a friend's house at the beach for the weekend. Late in the evening Kelly had suggested a walk on the beach. He'd agreed and hand in hand they had crossed a wide sweeping terrace, bordered on three sides by terracotta pots overflowing with white and occasional pink geraniums. He recalled saying to Kelly that it was how the other half lived. She'd grinned and replied, 'This is how we're going to live, Jay.'

The sound of surf crashing on to the shore at the foot of the garden had mingled with the giggling of two naked couples in the pool, and that of several entwined bodies on the pool side. They never did get to walk on the beach, because Kelly discovered the privacy of the poolroom. And if anything else had been said that night, he'd forgotten it.

Luther noticed Jay's distraction, instinctively aware that he was still in love with Kelly Prescott. He, too, knew how it felt to love a woman and lose her, and at that moment he longed to have Shirley's knack of saying the right thing at the right time. Jay had befriended him on his first week in prison, talking to him like an equal, like he was a fellow college graduate, someone of substance – instead of a punch-drunk ex-boxer, a terminal loser and thrice-convicted felon. He would never forget Jay's painstaking patience when he'd taught him chess.

He watched Jay stand up, stretch and walk across the sitting room of the small apartment, located on the opposite side of M Street, two hundred metres from the Prescott house.

Luther spoke to his back. 'You happy with the reproduction?'

Without turning around, Jay said, 'It's great, you did a good job.'

'It was easier than I first thought.'

'Does that mean I get a discount?'

A guffaw filled the room. 'Come on, man, gimme a break; you're already getting a discount, genius don't come this cheap normally. Anyway it wasn't *that* goddamn easy. The senator was away, and the maid was one of those dumb underpaid greaseback broads who don't give a damn if the rich folks get ripped off, but the security boys took a bit of Luther boy charm to get past. And the telephone company uniform was difficult to get a hold of; you try nicking anything in my size. I had to follow a big black brother around for three days; thank God his security and I.D. card were in the pocket. Discount my ass, I should *double* the fee!'

Jay turned to face Luther. 'A deal's a deal, my friend. You should've held out for more; I was willing to pay you three times as much.'

He watched Luther frown, he knew he was trying to work out if he was joking or not. Then Jay took a fat brown envelope from his inside pocket and handed it over. 'Count it if you like, but it's all there.'

Luther took the package. 'I don't need to count it.'

A look of mutual trust passed between the two men. Jay smiled; he knew Luther would count it later and wished he could be there to see his face when he realized he'd been paid three times what they'd agreed.

'I hope it all works out for you, brother.'

'Thanks, Lu, you take care and never forget what I told you in the pen. If you don't love yourself, why should anyone else.'

In that moment Luther was reminded of Shirley, she'd said something very similar on their second date. Not trusting his own voice, he stumbled out of the apartment, promising to keep in touch.

Afterwards Jay sat next to the window, watching Luther's back until he rounded the corner of M Street and was out of sight. He then switched his view to Kelly's house. He counted the lights in the windows, five in total. Sitting in silence, watchful and predatory, gave him a perverse sense of anticipation. What was he expecting? he asked himself. Why the stake-out, what did he hope to achieve? After twenty-five years would Kelly, Weston or Beth give him even a second thought? And if they did know something about Matthew Fierstein's murder, would they risk talking about it on the telephone? He doubted it, yet maybe if he could rattle their cages, one of them might let something slip in an unguarded moment. By now they would have received his gifts; step one in the flushing out process. He tried to imagine their reactions: Weston would be dismissive; Beth, intimidated; and Kelly . . . ah Kelly, try as he might, he couldn't imagine how she would feel when she opened the box to find the broken cello string and his message. He felt sure she would know the sender though, and he hoped she would experience a twinge of remorse at the very least.

The cat was now among the pigeons. Jay could not resist a wry smile, and with it came the realization that he was actually enjoying himself. His rôle was not unlike that of Mike Flint, the fictitious FBI agent he'd created in *Killing Time*. And where was Mike Flint's alter ego now? he mused. Ron Longman, the FBI operative who'd worked with Al Colacello to indict Mario Petroni, had taken the godfather's money and run. Jay experienced a surge of anger whenever he thought about Petroni who, against all odds, had won. Why is it that good things happen to bad people, and bad to good? He'd asked himself the question many times before, and was always unable to come up with an answer. It reinforced his belief that there was no God.

As he stood up and stretched his torso, the digital clock on the desk was blinking six-fifteen. He moved into the hall and through a door leading to the long narrow, galley-type kitchen – all polished elm units and gleaming stainless steel. Jay made himself a pot of strong espresso, and carrying the coffee in one hand and a large mug in the other, he made his way back into the living room. Once there he sat down in front of the small desk that housed his laptop. He then stared at the blank screen for a few minutes before starting to write.

*REMISSION. Notes: September 1972 onwards. [Me, Matthew and Kelly.]*

There was an electric storm the night before I went up to Harvard. I'll never forget it as long as I live. I watched in fascination from my bedroom window; forked lightning branding the big Montana night sky, and thunder so loud I was reminded of my grandmother's words: 'It's the devil clapping sinners, boy.'

Then the rain came, hard and slanting, ricocheting off my window like a constant barrage of machine-gun fire. I stayed awake all that night, long after the storm had subsided, and at the first glimmer of dawn, while the rest of the house slept, I crept outside. It had been a long hot summer; relentlessly the sun had sucked at the earth, day after scorching day, and now the parched crust was sodden, a great thirst sated; the air moist and still, so still you could hear a leaf fall.

As I stood there completely alone, a rainbow appeared, the colours so vivid they looked like freshly mixed oilpaint. I was spellbound; that colourful ladder to heaven was beautiful beyond belief. I remember feeling very small, a nondescript character in the big scheme of things, and in that moment I believed in God. I don't any longer. I'd kept my promise to my mother: I'd brought in the harvest, breaking my back and eating dust for weeks, and now I had my very own crop; the beginning of what I hoped would be a great and fulfilling adventure.

My feet felt as light as air. In fact my whole body felt light, weightless, elevated. I was ready for anything. My dream, my longed for, hard-fought dream was realized. Jay Kaminsky, second-generation Polish immigrant from Hicksville, USA, had been given his chance. No, not given it; achieved it.

Harvard and I were made for each other, never before or since have I felt so at one with myself and my surroundings. That first day and for many subsequent days I was full of an indescribable sense of wellbeing, a belonging to that hallowed place of learning. I was so full of ideas, ambition and arrogance. Ah, to be back there! In that place and time, not knowing what was in store, what was to be my fate. To taste once more, if only for a moment, that euphoric optimism. I didn't hope I would be successful; I knew I would be.

Matthew Fierstein was the same, a scientific genius destined for great things. Or so we thought. Ingenious Matthew, the brilliant boffin constantly bubbling with enthusiasm for some bizarre new invention. We were campus room-mates; I was in my second year, he was a freshman. I wouldn't have chosen Matt, and I doubt he would have chosen me. We were chalk and cheese: me all sportive and Matthew bespectacled and puny, a Born Again Woody Allen type. He would often joke that we made a great team. I could attract the women, and he could make them laugh.

It was during his first semester that I began to notice glimpses of Matthew's dark side. It was after his mother's visit to Harvard. Matthew was strung out for two days before her arrival and a visible nervous wreck on the morning before she was due. My first impression of Isabel Fierstein was that she was very un-Jewish, if there is such a thing. What I mean is she was Jewish, but not the usual stereotype. Tall, blonde and stunning in an icy Slavic way, and a bit dippy. She reminded me of a second-rate Hollywood starlet from the thirties. Something that Samuel Goldwyn might have auditioned on his casting couch and then cast in B movies. I noticed Matthew recoil when she kissed him, and he seemed withdrawn when she spoke to him. Her every sentence was banal, every word delivered in a jaded, 'I'm very bored with life' kind of way. I thought she was extremely cold, and felt sorry for Matthew who obviously felt ill at ease in her company. After she left he said that he thought his mother was the most beautiful creature in the world, and the most despicable. I was shocked and then Matthew began to bang his head against the wall. Before I could stop him he stopped himself, but when he turned around to face me he was crying. There was a narrow rivulet of blood winding from a graze on his temple to the corner of his eye. He touched it, looked at his red fingertip, then at me. 'I hate my mother,' was all he said before leaving the room without another word.

Matthew didn't come back that day, or the next, and by the third day I was about to report his disappearance when he bounced into a lecture looking and acting as if nothing untoward had happened. I never mentioned his mother, but I did ask him where he'd been. He was evasive and, when I pushed, downright aggressive. With a strange mad look in his eyes, he tweaked the end of my nose saying, 'Ask no questions, get no lies. It's my business, OK?' Then he laughed at my concern, saying, 'Come on, Jay; lighten up. I met a hot girl, we did it for three days, never got out of bed. So I should have called to let you know? I'm sorry; so hit me if you can.' It was the old Matthew again, and he stayed like that for the remainder of the week.

He was in such high spirits that he regaled me with colourful stories of the time he'd spent vacationing in Jamaica that summer. I asked him if he'd been there with his family. He said no, but didn't elaborate. I didn't pry, and we continued to get along just fine on that basis. That was until he fell for my girlfriend, Kelly Tyler.

I'd found her in my first year. We bumped into each other on campus. She was with Weston Kane who I thought was extremely beautiful in a dramatic, handsome sort of way. Not my type, too masculine. Later I saw Kelly on her own and invited her out to dinner. I was over the moon when she accepted.

That's how we began and we were gloriously happy together for our first year. But for some reason, that now seems strange, I ended up asking Matthew to join us for our anniversary of that first dinner. He got drunk and made a play for Kelly in front of me. I got upset and like a dumb jerk walked out, expecting Kelly to follow I suppose. She didn't.

I knew he would be contrite in the morning. I was wrong. Matthew wasn't sorry. Nor was he, as I had anticipated, hung over. When I awoke in our room, he was making coffee. Dressed in shorts and a T-shirt, he was humming a tune I didn't recognize. Before I had time to gather my thoughts he informed me that he'd jogged around the campus twice and felt better than he'd done for years, so much so that he intended to drink himself into oblivion more often. But as he passed me a mug of coffee, his face suddenly changed. His voice sounded different, too, when he said the four words that have been indelibly imprinted in my memory ever since: 'I want Kelly Tyler.'

Shocked into silence, my first thought was that he was joking. I changed my mind a moment later when he repeated, 'And I'm gonna have her.'

Kelly and I were a hot item and I managed to mumble something complacent like perhaps she might not want him. He dismissed this, saying simply, 'I'll make certain of it.'

The sound of screeching car tyres caused Jay to stop writing. He crossed the small room to the window. Tweaking the curtain, he looked across the street. Kelly was walking out of her house, clearly illuminated in the porchlight. She was wearing an open ankle-length coat in beige, and as she moved he caught a glimpse of ivory silk underneath. A pearl choker decorated her throat.

She was waving to someone seated in the back of a parked car, but Jay could not see the occupant. He watched her step onto the sidewalk, her bra-less breasts moving under the fine fabric. An image of Kelly naked except for the pearl choker filled his mind, and for a few blissful moments he allowed himself to indulge in the fantasy.

God, how he'd loved her. Did he still? He left the question unanswered, and watched the car that had come to collect her glide away. He let the curtain slip from his fingers; they were trembling and his heart was banging hard.

It was then that he began to cry.

# Chapter Six

Weston uncrossed her legs and looked directly at Beth, who was sitting opposite dwarfed by the huge white sofa that dominated Weston's spacious living room.

'I think we've got the same admirer.'

Nodding, Beth said, 'I wonder if Kelly got a gift.'

'I don't know. I've tried to call her this morning; she was in a meeting; I left a message on her voice mail.'

Weston leaned forward; she flicked open a box on the glass-topped coffee table, plucked out a cigarette, and lit it with a heavy pewter lighter.

'It's him, I know it's Jay Kaminsky. He's out of the pen, and still harbouring his hatred for me.'

'And me!' Beth added. 'You only got dead flowers; I got a dead bird in a cage.'

Weston was angry. She was controlling it well, but Beth knew. All the signs were evident: high colour at the base of her neck, where a nerve jerked incessantly for a few minutes, stopped for a while then started twitching again. She was chain-smoking. Her voice had become slightly higher pitched, and her speech was faster.

'Sorry, Beth, I'm a little edgy. I must admit I'm worried about Jay.'

'That's exactly what he wants. He wants to shake us

up a bit. If he had any substantial evidence, do you really think he'd be wasting his time sending us sinister gifts; playing mind games? He'd have used it long ago to get released.'

Weston stubbed out her cigarette, and lit another. 'You're right. He knows nothing, but suspects everything. Now I've got the Avesta merger under my belt, I'm all set to negotiate the digital rights for the Pacific Rim. I don't need this in my life right now. Getting those flowers brought it all flooding back. I even had a dream last night about Jay. I was the one in a prison cell, and he was on the other side of the bars looking in at me. His face was in front of a whole bunch of other faces I recognized: there was a girl I knew in high school; my mother; and Dan, my lawyer. They were all pointing at me and laughing. Like a bunch of fucking hyenas. Then all the faces disappeared except Jay's.

'His head was enlarged like a gargoyle's, too big for his body, and when he bent it then lifted it again, it was my father's head.' Leaning back, Weston inhaled deeply. 'It was horrible.'

In all the years Beth had known Weston, she'd never seen her quite like this: vulnerable; scared even. It was unnerving. In their junior years at college she had been nicknamed 'Citizen Kane'. She was always the one who could be relied upon to be focused.

Standing up, Beth crossed the space that separated them. She sat down next to Weston and taking her hand said, 'We did what we had to do; we made a joint decision. It was a long time ago. So long, I've forgotten it ever happened. Listen, Jay Kaminsky is bound to be pissed; so would you be if you'd spent most of your adult life in the pen for something you didn't do. But he's got nothing on us, nor can he get anything. We're watertight.'

'I think *pissed* is a slight understatement. If I was him I'd be bitter and mean. Determined to get the sonofabitch who'd framed me.' Weston waited for her words to sink in before continuing. 'If his suspicions are strong enough, he might be plotting some bizarre form of revenge.'

Beth sighed, shaking her head. 'And risk another stretch in prison?'

Weston wasn't sure. For the first time in years she felt out of control. Enemies she could deal with; she did so almost every day of her life and enjoyed the fight. The game of power-brokering gave her a buzz, spurred her on to fight tooth and nail. But this was different, this was an unseen avenger.

'The guy has spent twenty-odd years inside a maximum security prison. What would that do to *your* psyche, Beth? For all we know he could be insane, completely fucked up, hellbent on just getting even – with anyone. He knows where we live and work; that means he's followed us or had us followed. We're sitting ducks; he can see us but we can't see him.'

An involuntary shudder passed through Beth. 'We need to be very careful.'

'We've got to be more than that; we've got to be one step ahead. First we need to locate Kaminsky. Then at least if he contacts one of us, or sends any more gifts, we'll have the opportunity to confront him – find out what he wants, or what we have to do to make him go away. I thought about using the same guy you used when you had that corruption case a couple of years back.'

The ringing of the telephone interrupted them, but Weston ignored it, allowing the answering machine to take the call.

'You mean Ted Blakeman,' Beth supplied. 'He's the best. I recommended him to a girlfriend when she was collating evidence against her husband in a divorce battle. He came up with the goods in a few days. I'll call him tomorrow; if anybody can trace Kaminsky, Ted can.'

Weston rose to find her diary. 'Good, I'll leave that to you. Tomorrow morning I'm off to the West Coast, so when I get back I suggest we have a Pact meeting. In the meantime contact Kelly if you can, and arrange to meet here as soon as possible, make it a priority.'

Beth had her organizer open on her knee. 'Monday is best for me, on the next day I've got all of Doug's family over for supper. The matriarch from hell, his brothers grim, and their grimmer wives.'

'OK, Monday it is. Just need to contact Kelly and we're on.' Weston replaced her diary next to a photograph of her father. She stared at the image, and for the first time noticed that Sinclair looked profoundly sad. Impulsively she took the photo out of the frame; placing it face down, she made a mental note to replace it with a favourite of herself and her father taken on her graduation day.

The red numerals on her answer machine blinked indicating three messages. She pressed 'play' and listened. The first message was from Kelly: 'Hi, Wes, got your message, I'll be home all evening, call me back.'

Weston began punching out Kelly's telephone number while Beth watched. A moment later she had a connection.

'Hi, Kelly, how are you?'

'Wes! I'm busy as hell . . . so what's new, the first issue of the *Georgetown Gazette* is due out in less than three weeks. It's like I'm on a real high, the adrenaline is popping.'

Weston was deadly serious when she asked, 'Did you receive an unusual gift in the last couple of days?'

'Yeah, I did actually. How did you know?'

'What was it?'

'A string.'

'Don't know what you mean.'

'A violin string, I think; anyway it was broken and placed in a beautiful blue box.'

'Any card, message?'

'Yes.' Kelly paused before saying, '"You broke my heart".'

'Beth and I got presents as well; not quite as romantic as yours, I might add.'

'What did you guys get?'

'I got a bouquet of dead lilies, and Beth got a dead dove in a birdcage.'

'Shit!' Kelly said.

'I've got a hunch the gifts are from an old college friend.' Then before Kelly could reply, Weston continued, 'We shouldn't talk about this over the phone, Kel. I've called an emergency Pact meeting for next week, Monday, here at my place. Can you make it?'

Kelly tried to visualize her diary. 'It couldn't be a worse time for me, with the launch of the paper so imminent. Can it wait?'

'No it can't, it's imperative we talk. You could fly into town for the day.'

'Hang on, I just remembered I've got to be in Manhattan next week for a meeting with my bankers. So I can fly in on Monday afternoon.'

'OK, we're all set. My place at seven?'

'Great, I'll be there. I'll look forward to seeing you guys. It seems a long time since we chilled out properly and dished the dirt.'

Weston could not contain her irritation. 'This is not a girly evening. It's what we started the Pact for; it's about – '

'No, you don't need to remind me, Weston. I need reminding least of all.' Kelly's voice had gone small. 'I'll be there.'

With that the phone went dead. Weston felt contrite for being so brusque and thought about calling back, then decided against it. But as she faced Beth, she was still thinking about Kelly. The child-woman, needy in a way Weston understood but found hard to swallow. The craving to be desired had dominated Kelly's life. And that life was packed with people who told her she was beautiful. Yet Weston knew that Kelly rarely, if ever, believed them; never felt like the goddess she was. And her obsessive need for reassurance was her weakness. Standing in front of Beth, Weston confirmed the Pact meeting.

But Beth was still looking quizzical. 'And?'

'Hers was a violin string, broken. With the message, "You broke my heart."'

Beth felt a tug of remorse. 'I'm sure she did.'

Weston detected the sadness in Beth's voice and, dropping her head to one side, said, 'Excuse me while I throw up.'

'No heart, Wes?'

'Yes, Beth, but no regrets.'

Not wanting to address the issue further, Beth glanced at her wristwatch. 'I'm meeting someone for drinks; I'm due there like now.' She started to walk towards the door. 'Have a good trip to LA, Wes; by the way, are you still seeing Alison?'

Weston pulled a long face. 'Alison got heavy; she's history.'

Beth stopped at the door. 'I wish we could say the same for Jay Kaminsky.'

Jay listened to the tape several times; turning up the volume at the end of the conversation when Kelly said, 'I need reminding least of all.' Why would she say that? he asked himself. Was it simply remorse because he'd been in love with her? Or was it something deeper, darker; a secret the women shared? And was that shared knowledge the basis for this 'Pact' that Weston had mentioned? Jay lit a cigarette, reminding himself that he was chain-smoking and vowing to give up when all this was over.

He walked across the small room, stopping at the window overlooking M Street and Kelly's house. A black cat was running across the drive, its three white paws looked like little gloves and gleamed in the glare of the security lights. There were four sets of double windows on the ground floor, two were lit. Which room was she in now, he wondered, and what was she doing; what she was thinking? Over the last twenty-five years; while she'd been dating, marrying, loving, aspiring, achieving, vacationing . . . doing everything denied to him, had her thoughts ever strayed to poor old Jay doing time, getting old, getting grey, dying inside?

But it was rare for him to feel sorry for himself, and inwardly he chided himself. When this is over, when I find out who killed Matt, it's movies and writing on a terrace overlooking the sea.

The lights in the downstairs windows went out, and he imagined Kelly climbing the stairs to her white bedroom. She had always loved white. He knew there would be a vast bed; white cotton sheets crisp and cool on hot skin.

Moving away from the window, he walked out of the room and went through the ritual of making strong black coffee, before returning to sit down in front of his laptop.

Mug in hand, he watched steam curl into the air as he lit a cigarette. Now he was ready to write.

*October 1973 – continued*

It was at this point that Matthew changed. He was never the same again. He became unresponsive and repressed, given to bursts of uncharacteristic anger. At first I put it down to jealousy. I was dating the girl he wanted. *Tough shit*, I'd joke, all's fair in love and war. But to Matthew it wasn't fair, and he made sure I knew how he felt. For my own part I was hurt and sad; sad that dating Kelly had blighted our friendship. Several times I tried to talk to him about it, expressing how pissed I was with him. If he was a good friend as he professed, how could he resent my happiness? In response he would simply take on a 'holier than thou' attitude, adopting a ghost of a smile. And it was at such moments that I first sensed there was something creepy about him. Forthright and decent on the surface he might be, but underneath there was something devious and Machiavellian. It was almost as if some emotional injury in childhood had healed on the outside, but left the inside remote and dangerous.

Then one night he got very drunk, smashed senseless on a lethal cocktail of vodka Collins and beer. It was then he showed me the letter he'd received from his mother. I didn't want to read it; there was something in Matthew's insistent slurred entreaties that warned me it was not good news. I was right.

Mrs Fierstein had begun divorce proceedings. She'd met an Italian furniture designer, and was leaving America to live with him in Italy. It wasn't so much this that bothered Matthew, he said, it was the fact that she hadn't even discussed her decision with him.

'Not even a telephone call, just that,' he pointed to the letter in my right hand. 'Only eight fucking lines. With four spelling errors. Imagine *your* mother upping and leaving to live with some fucking Italian stallion. No forwarding address, no apology, no *Come see me some time*. No fucking nothing. I feel like killing her, in fact if I could find her I might.'

He drained the vodka bottle then hurled it at the window. It missed and landed on the floor, rolling for a couple of seconds before stopping next to one of Matthew's shoes. I didn't know what to say. I thought 'Sorry' sounded too lame, and kind of dismissive. I considered defending his mother and saying something encouraging like, *I'm sure she's going through a rough time at the moment; she obviously didn't want to worry you, and will be in touch very soon*. But before I'd decided what was appropriate Matthew stood up, his balance perfect, and planted himself too close to me.

'Why are you staring at me with one of your patronizing "I know it all" kind of looks?' He prodded me in the centre of my chest.

'I don't like it, Kaminsky; I don't like it one fucking bit.'

At this I grabbed his hand. 'Come on, Matt, I'm

real sorry about your mom, but it's got nothing to do with me. Go to bed and we'll talk about it in the morning.'

'I don't want to go to bed and anyway I haven't had enough to drink yet. I'm going out to get thoroughly smashed.'

As he started to struggle into his jacket, I barred the door. 'Please, Matthew, listen to me. You're already drunk, very drunk. I don't think you should go out right now.'

'I'll decide if I'm drunk or not. Out of my way, Jay.' He was swaying a little now and there were two bright red blotches on each side of his neck. He snarled again, 'Outta my way!'

I stood my ground and was about to speak when he punched me hard in the side of the face. I recoiled more in shock than pain; then he was upon me, in my face, spitting, seething. An animal.

He yelled again, 'Get out of the fucking way! I'm warning you I'll – '

Angry now, I grabbed him by the throat and pushed him against the wall, pinning him there. 'You'll what?' I squeezed, not hard but hard enough to remind him I was bigger and stronger and I wasn't going to let him hit me again.

A second later I let out an ear-piercing yelp as Matt sunk his teeth into the back of my right hand. I dropped my grip and flew at him, but he was too quick for me – sidestepping and opening the door before I could stop him. I ran after him then stopped. What could I hope to achieve? He'd be back, sorrowful, apologetic, begging my forgiveness tomorrow.

As I sucked the back of my wounded hand, I heard the outside door slam . . . and that was the last time I saw Matthew Fierstein alive.

# Chapter Seven

Kelly was in her dressing room, slowly undressing in front of a full-length mirror. Leaving her clothes where they fell, she ran her hands up the entire length of her body. Her skin was warm and moist. She spotted a purplish-green bruise forming on her left hip, where she had bumped into her desk earlier that day. It was the same size and shape as a dime.

With the flat of her hand she rubbed her stomach. It had been aching all day due to a heavy period. Kelly had known for weeks that she wasn't expecting a baby; yet in spite of her explanations that her late periods were due to a hormonal imbalance, Todd had refused to accept that she wasn't pregnant and she had been unable to dampen his excitement. Todd desperately wanted a baby. He was a good man, he would make a wonderful father, and she was very sorry – no, more than that, profoundly sad – that she wouldn't be able to bear him his longed-for child. Yet her sadness was reserved for Todd alone. Kelly felt no personal regrets; having a baby in her forties was a daunting prospect and the thought of carrying and bearing the child of a man she didn't love was worse. She had only ever wanted to make a baby once. They had talked about it, herself and Jay, on vacation at her uncle's beach house in South Carolina. Jay had said, 'I want my first child to be a girl, and to look exactly like –' He'd paused and Kelly, thinking that he was going to say her, had giggled when he'd said 'Natalie Wood'. Then he'd hugged her tight. 'I don't care who our babies look like, just so long as they're healthy and we have lots, at least four.' She turned away from her reflection; the sight of her own nakedness suddenly seemed repulsive and only served to emphasize her loss.

When she entered the bedroom she heard the sound of a door banging and a moment later Todd walked into the room, beaming at her nakedness.

'Hi, honey.' He opened his arms, frowning as she shrank from him.

'I wasn't expecting you home until Friday.'

'I missed my baby. Hey, you don't look pleased to see me.'

Recovering her composure, Kelly covered the space between them in one stride, giving him her best smile. 'Just surprised that's all. You usually call.'

Holding her by the shoulders, he was kissing her neck. 'Has my baby missed me?'

Allowing herself to be embraced, she willed her body to respond as Todd began to fondle her left breast, his mouth finding the nipple. He sucked hard as he fumbled with his fly. Then he began backing her against the wall and pushing her head down.

'I've got to have you, Kelly. I've wanted you so much.'

In one frantic pull his trousers and boxer shorts were around his ankles. In that instant Kelly wanted to throw up. With a force that surprised them both, she pushed Todd away. He lost his balance, staggering for a couple of feet before falling backwards, his clothing tangled around his feet.

Regaining his balance, Todd kneeled beside his trembling wife. Confused, he scrutinized her face. 'Are you drunk?'

Kelly shook her head vigorously. 'Actually I'm dog-tired and feeling sick.'

'I thought you'd be pleased to have me back home.' He paused and added, 'I kind of hoped you'd want me to make love to you.'

'You call getting yourself a blow job making love to me?' Kelly began to laugh. 'Is that supposed to make me feel desired?' She continued to laugh as Todd stood up with deliberate ease. He pulled up his shorts and trousers, and slowly fastened them. Then he spoke in a tone of voice she'd never heard before.

'Don't *ever* laugh at me again, Kelly. Not if you want to remain married to me.'

Before she could reply he'd left the room. She heard him moving around downstairs, and for a brief moment considered going to him. She hated hurting Todd, but this time he was the one who'd acted clumsily and made her feel like something on a stud farm. Had she driven him to it by not fully reciprocating his love? She had tried, in the beginning, but had never become as emotionally bound up with him as he was with her. *Am I a good wife?* The question jumped in front of her eyes. I'm socially adept, she reminded herself, ever ready to entertain and charm. But is it enough? No. Latterly they had been spending more and more time apart, and the times they were together had become fraught.

Kelly slept fitfully, and alone. When she awoke the following morning she checked the guestrooms to find them undisturbed, and came to the conclusion that Todd must have slept in a hotel.

She had breakfast alone, too, and the next hour was spent skimming through the morning paper. At ten after nine she rang in to her office sick, and by mid-afternoon she was totally smashed. Kelly continued to drink for the remainder of the afternoon, and when Todd returned she was curled up on the sitting-room sofa wearing cut-off blue jeans and a white vest top. Her hair was caught in an untidy pigtail, wayward strands framing her face.

She was in a deep sleep. There was half a bottle of wine on the floor near her. Todd stood very still at the foot of the sofa, observing his wife. She looked to him like a little girl in untroubled slumber. He wanted to touch her face, tell her he was sorry about last night, to talk away the humiliation he'd felt, to be reassured she still desired him. After being away for ten days he'd wanted her so much his groin had ached, and thoughts of making love to Kelly had consumed him in the car driving home. Was that so bad? But then he'd always felt that way about Kelly – ever since they'd first met at Weston Kane's house in South Hampton in the spring of 92. It had been instant attraction for him, and he still remembered how he'd felt like a king because he'd made her laugh.

Kelly stirred, her eyelids fluttered open, and suddenly she was looking directly at him, blank eyes widening.

Inexplicably he felt like a stranger, an intruder in his own home. He even began to stutter slightly, 'K-K-Kelly, it's after six; we're due at the reception at seven.'

Letting her eyelids droop, she said, 'I'm not feeling good, do you mind if I don't go?'

'Of course I m . . . m-mind, this is important.' It was the first time he'd stuttered in years. Todd had been convinced he'd conquered his childhood affliction. As a young politician he'd been plagued with terrible nightmares about his speech impediment returning in the middle of a crucial congressional speech. On such nights he would wake up sweating, overwhelmed by the sense of relief that he'd been dreaming.

'I'm sure they won't miss me.'

Her flip dismissal angered him, and he stuttered again. 'K-K . . . Kelly, I really don't think that's the point. It's an official dinner; you should be there. *I* want you to be there.'

Lifting herself up on her elbows, she swung her legs on to the floor, wondering why he hadn't asked what was wrong with her. Then noticing the half-empty bottle of wine, she assumed he knew and had chosen to ignore it. Todd was a good man, better than she deserved, but just now she resented him for making her feel guilty. Her head ached, and the inside of her mouth felt furry. Dropping her head into her hands, she mumbled through her fingers. 'I feel like shit, Todd; I'm sorry you'll have to go without me.'

He sighed. 'How much have you had to drink?'

'Enough; too much, like I said I feel like a heap of shit. My head hurts like hell. And my brain is frazzled. I'll be lucky to string a sentence together.'

Todd sat on the arm of the sofa, his hand stretched out to touch her hair, then something held him back and he placed it on his thigh.

She heard him sigh and without lifting her head said, 'Where did you go last night?'

'Harvey Kline's place.'

'You slept there?'

'Yeah, Harvey and I did a few beers and I crashed out. It was obvious that you didn't want me here. And sleeping in a guestroom in your own home for some reason feels stranger than sleeping in someone else's house.'

Kelly was irritated by his hurt. 'I was upset about the baby thing, and I thought you could have been a little more sensitive to that instead of storming into the bedroom and expecting me to perform like some circus animal.'

'I'm sorry if that's the way I make you feel, Kelly. I was very upset about you not being pregnant, and I'm sorry if I acted a bit boorish. I was impatient, I admit. I've been away for almost two weeks. I'm a man; what can I say?'

At this Kelly stuck out her bottom lip petulantly. And in that instant she reminded him of his kid sister whom he adored, and who as a child had irritated and amused him in equal measure. His bad mood momentarily abated, he held out his hand. 'Have a sandwich, a couple of large espressos and a hot shower, and you'll feel great. I want you to meet Gary and Diana Rhodes, they're dying to see you.'

Kelly took his hand and allowed herself to be pulled to her feet. She teetered a little, losing her balance for a split second. Todd caught her in his arms, and before she could say another word he planted a kiss on her slightly parted mouth. It was a peck, a gesture, a kiss that said 'truce'.

'OK, Todd, you win; but don't expect me to be the life and soul of the party.'

He was smiling when he said, 'Being there with me is enough.'

Outside it was a clear night, crisp and still. The maple tree below Jay's window stood naked but for a sparkling coat of frost. The tips of the branches glowed like fingers in shimmering icy gloves pointing to the plump moon. Nights such as this always brought back memories of home in Montana. Of camping, cookouts, pine and woodsmoke and those pan-burnt offerings that tasted like a feast after a day's trek under a scorching sun.

Moonstruck ambitions hatched around dying embers under a big blanket of stars. And always with Red Conway. Jay wondered where Red was today; it had been fifteen years or more since he'd heard from him, since he'd had any traveller's tales sent on postcards to the prison. He could picture him now, striding ahead, a giant of a man with a shock of carrot-coloured hair. They had first met when they were thirteen, both chosen for the school basketball team. Red at six feet three inches was the tallest boy in school, Jay was only slightly shorter at six feet. But while Jay grew another two inches, Red went on to become the tallest man in the county.

The beam of light from Kelly's front door drew Jay's attention back to his present surroundings. Todd Prescott had appeared dressed in black tie; it was Jay's first good look at Kelly's husband. He decided he looked like all the other upwardly mobile politicians: groomed, fastidious and ever so slightly oily. Jay pictured an imaginary scenario where parents visited an exclusive store for ambitious Wasp families, where they picked out their off-spring in the form of ideal clones customized for variety's sake. Hair? One with a slight wave please, not too curly, and cropped neat to his head. Brown eyes; not the dark sensuality of bitter chocolate or the warm romantic hue of chestnut, just dull old brown – nothing too striking, lest it frighten the voters. A straight nose, prim mouth and perfect teeth, thank you very much. Average height evenly distributed on a medium frame. Jay reckoned Todd fitted the bill. This evening he certainly looked like the archetypal politician – good posture, ease of movement and flashing white smile directed at Kelly, who in direct contrast looked elegantly sinister.

She was draped in a long black velvet coat with a deep hood covering most of her face in a way that promised mystery and allure. The chauffeur opened the door for her, while Todd let himself in the other side. Jay noted it was the same driver who had picked Kelly up from the airport. As the limo slid out of the drive, gliding slowly past the very window where he stood, Jay indulged in the game that had helped keep him sane inside: rôle-playing. Mentally he too was dressed in black tie and groomed to perfection. But he was a James Bond type who had by devious means, been invited to the same function that the Prescotts were on their way to now. He pictured some smart event held in the Four Seasons Hotel or the home of a fabulously wealthy Republican supporter. When the Prescotts arrived he would be positioned close to the hostess, so as to get an uninterrupted view of Kelly.

Jay savoured her imagined shock when he reintroduced himself, smiling broadly with the consummate ease of the practised small talker, emphasizing empty words to make them sound sincere: it's been *such* a long time no see; it *is* a small world, isn't it? You look *so* wonderful.

Todd would be hovering anxiously behind, wondering who this fabulous man from his wife's past could be. Kelly would mumble nervously, something about being old college friends. Jay would promise to catch up with them later and glide back into the glittering milieu – the life and soul of the party, ringed by eager socialites hanging on his every word and gesture.

He played and replayed the fantasy, like a director going over and over a take. Each time it got more out-rageous, more far-fetched. That was the fun of it, that was what had kept him sane.

His last conscious thought before he drifted into a fitful sleep later on that night, was of how he could wangle a real invitation or ticket to the next event Kelly and Todd attended.

It proved easier than imagined when two days later in

the *Washington Post* there was a paparazzi shot of Todd Prescott leaving a charity function with Kelly on his arm. The caption mentioned his charitable works, and that he was to be the guest speaker at a dinner the following week to be held at the Willard Hotel.

Jay called Ed Hooper. 'Do you know anyone of influence in DC?'

'Don't think so, man, the Big C don't figure in my address book. Hang on, yeah I know a woman I can call at the *Post*. Judy Zedde. She's the health editor; I sold a book for her some years back, it got lousy reviews.'

'Can you call her, Ed. I want to go to a big charity benefit at the Willard. D'you think you could get me an invite?'

'Doesn't sound like your sort of party.'

'It's research. You think your Judy friend might be able to get me a ticket?'

'I dunno. I'll call her, but I can't guarantee she'll be overjoyed to hear from me, she fell off my client list when the book bombed. But we dated a little; had a good time while we were working on things – know what I mean?'

Jay heard Ed's lewd chuckle, and had a good idea of what was coming next.

'Great mouth . . .' Ed sighed. 'She's a pretty important player now, so she might not be so easy to reach.' As he spoke he was flicking through his Roladex; it was battered and nearly as old as him, but he refused to use any other system. He located the *Post*'s number then said, 'I'll call her now, where can I reach you?'

Jay gave him his number.

'Hey, man, I didn't know you were in DC. Whatcha doing there?'

'You don't know everything about me, Ed,' came Jay's evasive reply.

'That's for sure,' Ed said before ringing off. Keeping the phone to his ear he called Judy Zedde. She was in a meeting, so he left a message and jotted a note to call her back if she hadn't returned to him by midday tomorrow.

He didn't have long to wait: an hour later Judy called. 'Ed Hooper, you son-of-a-gun, where you been hiding out?'

'Same place, baby, Eastside Manhattan. Don't wanna go no place else. Suits me here; fine and dandy.'

'Always did, Ed, always did. Remember when I tried to persuade you to go to the Virgin Islands, even went as far as buying the tickets? But you wouldn't go. Preferred to stay in New York and freeze your balls off. You wanted me to come to you to warm them up. Are you still a mule-headed stubborn bastard?'

Ed was grinning, it was good to talk to Judy again. It was six years or more since he'd seen her, and he tried to imagine how she'd look. Older. Who wasn't? But she'd had a great smile, the sort that doesn't age. And laughing eyes that would still be smiling beyond the grave.

'Now to business, the reason I called. Well, not the only reason but – '

'Come on, Ed. Cut the bullshit; this is Judy Zedde, remember. What d'you need?'

'I've got a client, a hot writer. Published under the name of Will Hope, heard of him?'

'You kidding? My husband loves his stuff. Mike just read *Killing Time*, he was raving about it. Will Hope just got outta the state pen, right? Served his time?'

'The same. Got out a couple of weeks ago after twenty-five years. Went down for the murder of his Harvard room-mate – a kid called Matthew Fierstein – you might remember the case.'

Judy didn't.

'Still claims he didn't do for Matthew, and I believe him. The guy's just not the killing type. Anyway Will's in Washington right now. He's doing research for his next book and wants to get into some benefit. It's next week, big Cancer Research gig. Todd Prescott is guest speaker.'

Judy knew exactly what Ed was talking about, her husband was on the fund-raising committee and she'd be going herself. 'Stop right there, Ed. No problem. Where do you want him? Top table or the cheap seats? Ten thousand bucks buys the knee of the senator's wife; a thousand gets the table near the kitchens.'

'Ten grand, are you crazy? That's not fund raising, it's robbery,' protested Ed.

'Look, Mike and I have a top table . . . your man can come as our guest. I'll pay for the ticket and it'll be a treat for my husband. This guy's got to be more interesting than half the stuffed shirts there. And you never know, perhaps he'll agree to do an interview for the *Post* – great story. By the way is William Hope his real name?'

'No it's a pen name. I can't tell you his real one;

he's a very private guy. He doesn't do interviews, but if anyone can persuade him you can. His number in DC is 6285100. He was there a few hours ago so you might catch him now. And, Judy, thanks. Just in case I forgot to tell you last time we spoke, you've got the best ass in the Western world.'

'In the West? Is that all? That's your problem, you promised me the world and only gave me a piece of it,' Judy joked.

'I know, I know, I should have gone to the Bahamas with you in eighty-four, instead of shrivelling my balls in New York.'

'It was the Virgin Islands, Ed.'

'Oh yeah! I knew there was a reason I didn't go.'

Judy started to laugh. 'See ya, Ed.'

'Take care, honey.'

Judy was smiling as she put the phone down, and she was still smiling to herself as she pressed an intercom button to connect her to her secretary. 'I need another seat at my table for the Moore Benefit next week. Send an invitation to Will Hope, you'll find his address if you call this number – '

Judy whiled away the next five minutes doodling pictures of Ed Hooper and reminiscing about the times they'd shared. He was the ugliest man she'd ever been out with, and the funniest. Her secretary interrupted a particularly amusing recollection involving Ed and herself on a boat in Key West. He'd landed a fish big enough to kill them both, and lost it, capsizing the boat at the same time.

'Christine Solange has cried off so there's a place left at your table, Ms Zedde. Do you want to change the seating plan?'

'Just put Mr Hope between Mike and me.'

She tried the number Ed had given her; Jay answered after the third ring.

'Am I talking to Will Hope?'

Only Ed and Luther had his number; Jay felt the small hairs on the back of his neck stand on end. 'Who wants him?'

'*Is* that Will Hope?' Detecting his caution, she chose her words carefully. 'I'm Judy Zedde, a friend of Ed Hooper. He gave me this number. He said that Will Hope has expressed an interest in going to a charity benefit next week. I can make it happen.'

Feeling slightly more relaxed, Jay replied, 'This is Will. I'm doing research for my next book and I want to hear Todd Prescott speak. Ed suggested you might be able to help.'

'I can. In fact I'm ringing to invite you as my guest. You'll get a ringside seat.'

This was better than he could possibly have hoped for. 'Thank you, I'm very grateful indeed. I believe it's black tie, yeah?'

His voice was a surprise; Judy wasn't sure what she had expected but certainly not this 'old money' Wasp accent. Will Hope sounded as if he'd spent the last twenty-odd years working in an established Boston banking house, spending his vacations at Cape Cod or Rhode Island in the family pile, not in a maximum security prison.

'That's right. If you'd like to come to my apartment for cocktails, you'll get a chance to meet the other guests. The event begins at seven, I'll be receiving at six. My address is the Watergate, Virginia Avenue. Apartment 269, tenth floor.'

'I'll be there and thanks again, Miss – '

'Call me Judy. See you then, Will. By the way, my husband's a fan so get ready for some hero worship.'

'I'll look forward to it, Judy.'

# Chapter Eight

Weston strode to the Lear jet ahead of Dan Goldman and Ronald Simpson – Summit financial controllers – and her PA, Jennet Stuart. It was a warm California morning, threatening to become unbearably hot by mid-afternoon, with a storm forecast for late evening. Weston was pleased to be heading back East, relieved to be leaving Los Angeles. She'd recently read an all too apt remark by a journalist writing in *Traveller Magazine*: 'LA is a sprawling nightclub with the lights permanently on.'

To Weston it was a nightmare, like living in a tasteless, tawdry, never-ending soap opera. She hated the weather, if only for its predictable repetition. And the city's lack of a real soul. But what really bugged her, what scared her more than she cared to admit, was that Los Angeles illustrated the American psyche in all its lurid insecurity. The soured American Dream now afflicted the large majority of the population.

Weston loved her country with the fierce pride she assumed some people felt about their offspring. She wanted other countries to look to the US for example and inspiration. She was a version of the great American Dream herself. How could she forget? Sinclair Kane always told everyone that his father had emigrated to

America from Scotland in 1928 with exactly twelve dollars and six Scottish pounds in his pocket. By 1932 he owned a chain of foodstores across the States. Yet she had always known she belonged to the privileged few, not the land of free for all.

After take-off she had a glass of Evian water, talked briefly to Dan, then feigning tiredness, kicked off her shoes, put on her eye shades and pretended to sleep. Sleep was time wasted as far as Weston was concerned; so she snatched a short snooze whenever she could rather than lose a precious eight hours a day. Eight hours, she pondered, that's fifty-six hours a week, 2912 hours a year. How many years in a lifetime? What a waste; how much could be achieved in down-time? How much life was missed?

Five hours, she'd calculated in her Wellesley days, would be enough to energize her for the remaining nineteen. And she stuck to that regime, resenting even that loss. When she was working on a big deal she functioned on less. Even as a child she'd rarely gone to bed before her parents.

Weston knew the recent negotiations had gone well with Avesta. The executive body had liked her expansion plans and were agreed they had to compete directly for their share of the digital and cable market. But it was to the forthcoming evening that she found her thoughts digressing. Serena Harman, society hostess and wealthy patron of the arts, had invited her to the ballet at the Met and later to a private supper at her sumptuous Sutton Place home. She'd promised a special treat for dessert.

Weston knew what that meant, and felt the beat of her pulse begin to race.

Serena, an ex-prima ballerina, was at sixty-two still extremely beautiful. Of Eastern European origin, she had perfect bone structure and huge doe eyes the colour of highly polished sapphire. Four years previously, after a gala night at the ballet, Weston had been introduced to her through a mutual friend. Later that same evening, Serena had tried to seduce her. At the time, Weston was involved with a girl called Catriona and had tactfully used that affair to demur. She was never unfaithful, she'd lied. How could she have told the elegant Serena that she was at least thirty years too old, and that she found her emaciated body completely repellent? However they had become great friends and Serena never failed in her warm generosity towards Weston, especially on occasions like tonight when the services of several beautiful girls would be provided for after-dinner amusement.

This led to thoughts of Kelly. Weston was worried about her and she prayed that Jay Kaminsky would not try anything. She had disliked him from the start; arrogant, self-obsessed and in love with the sound of his own voice. A redneck Montana farm boy who'd believed that being handsome was enough.

He was not welcome on Weston's turf, she had made that obvious from the very beginning of his affair with Kelly. In her mind's eye she saw Kelly getting ready to go on a date with Jay. All excited chatter and frenzied indecision about what to wear, how to do her hair. It had made Weston feel physically sick and she'd warned her to be careful, to take precautions. From the first day she'd met Jay, Weston had known he had a hidden agenda. She'd seen him as intent on breaking her own bond with Kelly, so he could have an exclusive on her.

The plane hit a patch of turbulence and Weston had fastened her seat belt even before the pilot's voice instructed the other three passengers to do so. Taking a deep breath, she returned her thoughts to Jay. She had to give him credit for survival, and the strength of character it must have taken to survive a life sentence and emerge intact. But was he still sane?

The question swirled around her head. How could he not be unbalanced? Bitter and pumped up with revenge? Somewhere the beast in him waiting to attack? But it was impossible to envision Jay, the apple-pie farm boy, as an avenging angel and she couldn't resist a wry smile. He didn't scare her. She'd always been a match for men with ten times his homeboy intellect. But he would have to be nipped in the bud because Kelly was fragile, at risk.

By the time the plane landed at La Guardia, Weston had restructured her strategy for a takeover bid for a cable network in Singapore, and had put Jay Kaminsky firmly out of her mind. Rain spattered the windows as the plane taxied to a standstill. She didn't mind the wet weather; in fact it was kind of welcoming, it felt good to be back. Her regular driver was sick, and the temporary man introduced himself as Lou. Once settled into the back of the car, she told him to take the bridge rather than the midtown tunnel, and not to speak until spoken to and then they would get along just fine.

When she alighted in front of her apartment building, it had stopped raining. Weston squinted, and smiled at the doorman in response to his, 'Good evening, Miss Kane.'

She headed towards the lift, travelling up to the twenty fifth floor alone. She let herself into her apartment, calling Carmita's name as she shut the door. There was no reply. Weston spied a note on the console table in the corner of the large square hall. From the scrawled handwriting Weston learnt that Carmita's husband was ill, and she would not be working today or tomorrow. As she moved into the living room, Weston angrily threw the note at a wastebin, selfishly peeved by the inconvenience of Carmita's problems. Black clouds hung like dirty washing outside the huge glass windows.

Weston flicked two switches and the room was brightly lit, too bright; she adjusted the dimmers and considered sacking Carmita unless she returned tomorrow. When she heard the front doorbell ringing, she picked up the entry phone and snapped, 'Yes?'

It was Beth. Weston opened the door, and her friend breezed into the apartment carrying a manilla envelope in one hand and her briefcase in the other. She was wearing a black suede hat, the brim was battered and the fake leopard trim had moulted in one corner. Weston helped her out of the long fur-lined camel coat that she knew Beth had bought twelve years ago in Vale, on her first and only skiing vacation. Leading the way into the living room, she asked her friend if she wanted a brandy.

'OK, it's past the yard arm.'

Weston poured three fingers of Remy into a brandy

goblet, and then did the same again for herself. 'Have you had any luck with gathering info on our ex-convict friend?'

'Right here.' Beth tapped the envelope on her lap, then took out the contents with a dramatic flourish. 'This,' she held several pages aloft, '. . . makes very interesting reading indeed.'

Weston snatched the foolscap sheets. On them were Ted Blakeman's timed notes of Jay's movements.

'As you can see Jay Kaminsky was released on the last day of February. That afternoon he checked into the Lowell Hotel, and three days later, he flew down to DC on United flight number 4660.'

'That's the day Kelly went home,' Weston commented.

'Yep, he's obviously been following Kelly. He registered at the Marriott Hotel, where he stayed for four days. Ted's working on where he went after that. But my bet is that he's still in DC spying on Kelly. Probably still got the hots for her – all those lonely nights inside, fantasizing.'

Weston nodded. 'Kaminsky could be crazed out of his mind. I think Kelly should get some extra security.'

Beth disagreed. 'Todd Prescott has got more security in that house in DC than the president has in the White House. Kelly can handle herself, she's done all right so far. Seen off two husbands and two lovers that I know of, come through alcohol dependency, made several millions one way or another, survived a car crash and a ski accident. So she was in love with Jay when she was a kid. So what? He's the one that went down. Poor bastard, can you imagine how he must feel, shut away for the best part of his life for a crime he didn't commit?'

'Jay Kaminsky was in the wrong place at the wrong time.'

Beth nodded a silent confirmation. Then, impulsively, Weston jumped to her feet and hugged her tight, kissing her on both cheeks. She said, 'I'm just worried about Kelly that's all. Don't forget what we all promised. We stick together and we take the Pact to the grave.'

The last time Jay had worn black tie was at a Harvard end-of-semester dinner. He'd taken Kelly Tyler of course. The Brooks Brothers suit he'd worn then had cost him two hundred dollars. The Armani he was wearing now had cost two thousand. The salesman had assured him the shirt, by a French designer called Comme des something, was of the finest lawn cotton. And the patent shoes looked like black ice. He'd had problems with the bow tie, and had cursed the salesman for insisting that the DIY version was more chic. He'd even invested in a cashmere overcoat costing roughly what he imagined a two-week vacation in Florida might run to. The limo arrived at five-thirty prompt. One last glance in the mirror, one more tug at the tie, then he was bounding downstairs feeling like a kid on his first date.

'Limo for Mr William Hope.'

Jay nodded, feeling uncomfortable when addressed by his pen name. But it was better to be safe. Mario Petroni was alive and well, and living in Manhattan. Jay Kaminsky knew far too much about the Dapper Don for his own good. Better Jay Kaminsky didn't even exist. Jay climbed into the back of the midnight-blue Lincoln town car. The driver introduced himself as Sammy, then thankfully shut up. Jay was in a state of nervous agitation. This was his first real foray into society.

Sammy spoke for the second time when the car pulled to a smooth stop outside the Watergate apartment building in Virginia Avenue. 'Traffic not bad this evening, we made good time.'

It was ten minutes to six as Jay climbed out. He looked up to the tenth floor, squinting his eyes against the glare of neon light. The lobby was manned by one old guy, small and rotund, who hovered near the entrance, and by another character behind a desk, the back of his head stuck in front of a screen. He was the one who spoke: 'Can I help?'

Jay smiled; it wasn't returned. 'Judy Zedde, tenth floor.'

The doorman called up and after a brief hushed conversation, he indicated to the left. 'Second elevator over there.'

Light-headed with apprehension, Jay strode towards the elevator doors with more purpose than he felt. He got out on the tenth and still walking with a deliberately confident step, he approached apartment 269.

The door clicked open as he rang the bell and a woman's voice hailed him. 'Walk right in, Will.'

A minute later he found himself inside a large hall. It was perfectly square and painted a very dark green. Judy emerged from he knew not where to greet him.

She wasn't how he'd imagined. He'd seen photographs of Ed's women, past and present, and they all slotted into a type. Blonde, beautiful but cold as frost. Not remotely like this raven-haired, animated and voluptuous woman who was smiling with more than a hint of mischief, and whose flashing eyes were the same shade as an alpine meadow. Her ankle-length gown had a very full skirt, and her forthcoming baby was deftly hidden under reams of blue taffeta. She extended a long slim hand; it was attached to a long slim arm with a fine gold band at the wrist.

'Hi, I'm Judy, good to meet you.'

'Likewise, I'm J –' he stopped himself, 'William Hope, Ed's friend.'

'Well, I won't say that any friend of Ed's . . .' she winked. 'Come on, meet my husband.'

Jay followed her into a large open-plan room. Green damask drapes filled one wall, and a small flight of stairs in one corner led up to a gallery with a tall arched window. There was very little furniture, and the walls were decorated in the same sombre shade as the hall.

'Mike, this is Will Hope.'

A tall thin man stepped forward. He was wearing owl-shaped glasses with bright red frames. They perched precariously on his abnormally big face, and looked ready to topple off at any moment. He had a high mop of frizzy brown hair that looked like the bearskins Jay had seen London palace guards wearing in English films.

'Damn pleased to meet you, damn pleased.' He shook Jay's hand vigorously. 'I've just finished reading *Killing*

*Time*, couldn't put it down. They say some of it's true, that so?'

At this Judy prodded her husband teasingly in the ribs. 'Mike, give Will a chance; let the man have a drink and relax a little before you start grilling him. My husband has been a surgeon most of his life. He doesn't know when to stop dissecting people.' Then she asked, 'Now, Will, what will you have? Mike makes a mean vodka martini.'

Jay accepted the suggestion with a smile as Mike began to mix the drink, and Judy excused herself to greet some new arrivals. A few moments later she re-entered followed by three more people, saying, 'William, I'd like you to meet three of my closest friends.'

The first, Tessa, was an enormous woman in a cerise satin tent with a halo of white hair. She had a loud jocular laugh and bad breath. Jay didn't catch the name of her husband – a dapper little man, half Tessa's size, sporting a plaid bow tie and matching cummerbund. Finally a woman called Didi sidled up to him, introducing herself as Judy's best friend, saying they'd gone to school together. She looked at least ten years older than the effervescent Judy, and Jay wondered if they had been in the same year. She was very tall with the emaciated frame of an anorexic, and a porcelain complexion that had undergone several chemical peels. Dressed immaculately in a black tuxedo and white lace camisole, she wore the bored expression of the terminally jaded. Jay disliked her on sight.

Delicately sipping his martini, he exchanged small-talk pleasantries, ducking and diving through the cross-examination. *Where are you from? How long are you in town? What do you do?* Jay was grateful when Judy clapped her hands and said, 'Come along you guys or we're going to be late.' She then marshalled everybody out towards the elevator and on reaching the downstairs lobby, she turned to Jay. 'Have you got a car, Will?'

'Yes.'

'Good. Can you take Didi? We'll take Tessa and Mark and meet you there. You know where it is. The Willard, on Pennsylvania Ave. They have valet parking.'

Jay nodded meekly, following in the wake of all the crinkling fabric and wafting perfume out to the waiting limo. Comfortably settled in the back of the car, Didi offered him a cigarette. He refused, extracting a pack of Ducados from his pocket. 'I only use these,' he explained.

'Hispanic shit. I suppose you acquired that habit in the pen?'

Surprised, but determined not to show it, Jay said, 'That's right.'

'How long were you inside? Judy didn't say.'

'Long enough.'

Smoke drifted out of her mouth. 'Long enough for what?'

Jay could feel his hackles rise. He didn't want to talk to this total stranger about life in prison. 'Long enough to want to forget it, OK?'

'No sweat, just making pleasant conversation.' She flicked a spot of ash off her trouser leg.

Jay decided to change the subject. 'So you've known Judy since you were kids?'

'Yeah, we met at high school. It feels like I've known her all my life. She's a wonderful human being, the best.'

There was a long pause that developed into an uncomfortable silence. Eventually they both started to speak simultaneously, but the car was pulling up outside the Willard Hotel and they each gave up. Side by side they entered the lobby. Didi disappeared to the bathroom, while Jay tried to locate Judy or Mike. After five fruitless minutes hanging around, he began to feel conspicuous. His common sense spoke: *you haven't got a distinguishing mark that sets you apart as an ex-con. You're the same as the rest of the penguins milling about in here. Just relax, act like you do this sort of thing all the time.* Back in the security of the apartment, going to the charity benefit had seemed like a good idea. Faced with the reality, he felt lost. His initial intention had been to confront Kelly on her own turf. To appear suave and sophisticated. To be wearing the 'I'm doing fine' badge. 'I'm a successful novelist; I can afford an apartment on the West side; I can fly first class and eat in fancy restaurants.' He wanted to tell her that his life hadn't been a total waste, and then to ask her if she would talk to him about the past; beg her to go back to the days, weeks before Matthew's death; make her understand that he had to know what really happened.

He turned as he heard someone say 'Jay'. And in the split second that it took him to spin round, he realized it couldn't be Judy – she didn't know his real name.

Suddenly he felt stripped of his battle armour, deserted by all the clever things he'd planned to say. And all he could do was gawk at Kelly Prescott. She was wearing a simple black sheath of silk, a halter neck which exposed her shoulders; they were very square, much more so than he remembered. Kelly was smiling; but it was forced and it showed. He immediately noticed she'd had cosmetic dentistry to fill in the gap between her two front teeth, and he wanted to say he preferred the gap. Instead he used a hackneyed line, feeling like a bad actor reading a cue card in a second-rate movie.

'Kelly. It's been a long time.'

Kelly's smile faded. 'Are you following me, Jay?'

'I'm sorry? I came here as a guest of Judy Zedde. Speak of the devil . . .' he said as Judy appeared at his side.

'Will, there you are, we've been looking everywhere for you.' With a cursory 'naughty boy' glance at Jay, Judy beamed at Kelly. 'Kelly, how are you? I don't know if you remember me, but we met at Sarah Lowen's house last fall. Judy Zedde, health editor on the *Post*.'

Rattled by Kelly's blank expression, Judy turned her attention back to Jay, looping her arm through his. 'Mike and the others have gone in, so if you would do the honours, Will?' Judy steered him away, throwing a goodbye over her shoulder.

'Nice meeting you again, Kelly,' Jay added as he was dragged off to dinner. Kelly said nothing, and when Jay turned to look back she was gone.

During dinner Judy, seated on his right, quizzed him about Kelly Prescott. Deftly he parried all her questions with questions, and succeeded in telling her absolutely nothing. He was even beginning to enjoy himself, and proved to be a willing and able adversary for Mike on his other side when he started to delve into his past.

Whenever there was a break in the conversation, Jay's eyes searched the room for Kelly. And later when coffee was being served he weaved in and out of the perimeter tables, looking for her. When Todd Prescott rose to take the podium to resounding applause, Jay spied the empty chair next to the senator's and assumed with a sinking heart that Kelly had gone home. During Todd's speech, he slipped out and found a phone booth in the lobby. At first Kelly's number was engaged, then it rang out for a long time. He waited, then tried again. This time she picked it up. Before she could utter he said, 'Kelly, please don't put the phone down. I have to speak to you.'

The voice on the other end replied, 'I'm sorry, Jay. I don't want to talk to you.'

'Why not? For Chrissake, Kelly, can't you spare me a few minutes. I deserve that much, don't I?'

His pleading bore no aggression or malice, and instinctively Kelly made a snap decision. 'Meet me tomorrow at Fort Marcy Park; it's a little out of town, off the George Washington Parkway.'

'I'll find it, what time?'

'Ten?'

'Don't let me down, Kelly.'

'I'll be there,' she promised, then the phone went dead.

A trough of high pressure had swept into the Eastern states overnight and at dawn Jay was woken by a thick finger of warm sunlight touching his face. A good start.

As he waited out of town for Kelly to show up, he inhaled the early scent of spring – dewy and fresh and promising. She was twenty minutes late and he thought that she had decided not to come. Then he saw her getting out of a silver Mercedes. Heart hammering, he watched her progress across the parking lot.

Clad this morning in jeans, sneakers and a zip-up skiing anorak, she looked at first as if she'd had her hair cut. It wasn't until she got close that Jay could see it was tied in an unruly topknot, like a docked dog's tail. Apart from that, all he knew was that Kelly was walking towards him, her bent head a golden crown shimmering in the sunlight. He felt a tug of tightness in his chest, a tensing of his muscles. He needed a cigarette and fished in the pocket of his leather jacket for the pack and lighter. When she was about a hundred yards from him, he called her name and waved. She raised her head, a taut smile tugging at the corners of her mouth. A plume of smoke rose out of his own mouth, then she was next to him. He wondered if she felt as nervous as he did.

'Hi, Kelly, how are you?'

Kelly, for the first time in as long as she could remember, had no idea what to say or how to react. *Do what comes naturally*, she heard a tiny voice say in her head. But she had forgotten what that felt like and considered saying something totally incongruous like, *well, I bought a Prada suit yesterday for three thousand dollars.* Eventually she said, 'Great day, uh?'

He nodded. 'We need it; winter seems to get longer every year.'

'You're right, when I was young I can't remember ever having snow in March like we do now, most years.'

'Well you were raised in Texas, that's probably why.'

She grinned. 'You dropped some weight, Jay, it suits you. In fact I've been trying to think since last night who you remind me of. I know now, it's Clint Eastwood.'

'Gee thanks, he's an old guy.'

'I meant when he was younger, your age, forty-five.'

'Forty-six in May.' He felt himself staring. She was as beautiful as he remembered. No, he corrected himself, she's more beautiful, much more. Time had eaten the roundness from her cheeks, leaving a leaner, angular structure with the contour of her jaw a little more pointed, heart-shaped. The fine lines around her eyes could not detract from their perfect oval and his memory had not betrayed him, their burnt almond shade was exactly as he recalled. As familiar as if he'd seen her yesterday.

Thrusting her bare hands deep in her pockets, she said, 'Shall we walk?'

They fell into step side by side, following a tree-lined path. The park was busy, the good weather had brought out dog walkers, lunchtime snackers and an eclectic assortment of roller-bladers. Kelly glanced down-ward, noticing Jay's tan leather boots, good ones. They looked exactly the same as the English-made Churches she'd bought for Todd on a trip to London two years ago.

They walked in silence at first, both looking straight

ahead. Jay wondered if she was travelling back, as he was. Back down a lifetime. To when they were kids, hanging out in parks similar to this one, holding hands, having fun, making love.

'Do you like being married?'

She felt small beads of perspiration break out on the back of her neck. *Calm down*, she told herself sternly, *he's not going to hurt you. What can he do here in a public park full of people?*

'Ought to do. I've been married three times; Todd Prescott is my third husband.' She shot him a sidelong glance. 'But then you know that, don't you, Jay?'

Jay showed no sign of surprise. 'Do I?'

'Let's stop playing games. You've been following me. You probably know *everything* about me. You certainly know where I live; you sent me that broken violin string. Why?'

'Cello actually – too long for a violin – and I sent it to monitor your reaction. I suppose I was playing secret agent games, only not very well.'

'Did you send gifts to Weston and Beth?'

Jay nodded.

'Did you do it for the same reason – to see how they would react?'

He nodded again. 'You three girls were so close at college, joined at the hip. And during my trial I had a hunch that one of you was hiding something. If not all of you. I thought it was Weston, and I still have my suspicions.'

'If you wanted to see me, us, why didn't you do what normal people do and call?'

'Would you have seen me, Kelly? Tell the truth.'

She lied. 'Of course, why not, I've got nothing to hide.'

'You're lying and we both know it, so cut the crap. You're married to a high-flying, powerful senator; you live in a twenty-thousand-square-foot mansion, and – '

'Twelve actually.' She grinned.

'*Touché* . . . but . . . you travel first class or by private jet, and you live the sort of life most people only get to read about or see in the movies. And you're trying to tell me that you'd welcome a friendly tête-à-tête with a convicted felon, fresh out of the pen. I'd be lucky to get past your maid.'

'OK, Jay, OK, but we were just college friends.'

Her casual dismissal angered him, he stopped walking and turned to face her. '*Friends?* Is that what we were?' Jay began to laugh; cynical hollow laughter, it unnerved Kelly. 'We were lovers. I was in love with you: completely, blindly, obsessively. You obviously didn't feel the same way about me. Shame I wasted so much time, and realized much too late. After the trial you never even came to see me, not once. Never answered my letters; not one note, not even a fucking postcard with "Hi Jay, bye Jay." Just nothing, *zilch*. I want to know why, Kelly. I've spent the best part of my life trying to figure it out.'

Without replying, she continued to walk.

'I've served time, a long time, for something I didn't do. Most of my adult life has been spent caged up with animals. Monsters who kill and maim for a living, for pleasure. Have you any idea what that's been like?'

Kelly wasn't ready for this confrontation, and she couldn't look at him. Her mind began to race. 'Look, I'm really sorry for what happened to you, Jay. I don't really know how to put it into words to make you understand *how* sorry. Matthew was fucked up.' She pointed to her temple. 'Screwy, psycho. I'm not sure whether you know, but he used to get off on really hard porno stuff – kids and animals, all of that. On the night of his murder he called me. He was in a rage, babbling about how you and he had fought over me, and that I had to choose between the two of you. I laughed at him, said there was no contest, that I loved you.'

Jay felt a sharp pain in his chest.

'. . . And that we were going to be married.'

Fixated on her mouth, he watched her lips move, pink in the centre and darker towards the edge, the bottom lip fuller than the top.

'I think it was at that point Matthew lost it, he went mad – threatening to kill both of us, you and me. I tried to call, to warn you, but got no answer from your block.'

'Why didn't you disclose any of this under cross-examination at my trial?' Jay somehow managed to suppress his emotions and speak calmly.

'Because I thought it would be damning evidence against you, and . . . in the beginning I didn't for one moment think you'd be indicted, let alone convicted. None of us did. We all believed you'd be acquitted. You have to believe me, Jay, it's the truth.' She dropped her voice to a low whisper, so quiet he could barely hear. 'I have to admit after the trial I made myself believe that

Matt had tried to do what he'd threatened, and that you'd retaliated, killing him in self-defence. It wasn't difficult to imagine Matt in a jealous state – attacking you. I knew how violent he could be and I figured that he'd gone back to your room . . . that you guys fought, and that it got out of hand.'

'No, Kelly, it was exactly the way I said it was. We did argue and he was drunk. When I tried to stop him leaving, he bit my hand. I then went out and got drunk myself and when I got back to the room, Matthew was dead. I've no idea who killed him.'

Suddenly Jay was back there, at Harvard, locking the door of his jeep, a cloying mist like something from a sauna curling around the entrance to the campus. It was exactly ten minutes after midnight; he could hear the guitar strains of Jimi Hendrix coming out of Dan Bryson's room. Strange, he'd completely forgotten that until this moment. He saw himself climbing the stairs to the second floor, bouncing off the walls, feeling no pain – fumbling for the key, dropping it, the door swinging open with a feeble creak. Stumbling into the apartment. Whenever he reached this point, his mind usually went blank, then pitch black. But now everything in his head was lucid and startlingly clear. The room appeared lit like a stage set, and for the first time since his conviction he could see Matthew. His head lopsided, warm and sticky to his touch. He could even smell the blood and see the vermilion patch seeping towards the outer edge of the rug. Squeezing his eyes shut, Jay passed a hand across his brow. It was wet and very cold.

'I've no idea who killed Matt. All I know is . . . it certainly wasn't me.'

Kelly had stopped listening, she was twisting her wedding ring round and round her finger, staring directly ahead at a child in a pram. A long lead dangled from the handle with a spaniel attached. The dog sat quietly while the owner rearranged the baby, thrusting a comforter into a wailing mouth. She looked without really seeing; she felt unwell and wanted a drink. Seeing Jay again had reawakened emotions she'd forgotten she had. It was scary and she tried to think of something else. She couldn't think about Matthew, he was dead, he'd got what he deserved.

She caught a swift shot of Jay's brown gaze. His eyes no longer held the merriment of youth, or the intensity. Something had died. Transporting herself back to 1972, she saw Jay as he was then: strong; young; vibrant; making her laugh. She saw him dropping Hershey Kisses into her navel, and fishing them out with his tongue.

It seemed like aeons ago, even more distant than childhood. So much so, sometimes she believed that she had dreamt that entire chapter of her life. As if waking from the dream, she heard Jay's voice only faintly.

'Why didn't you visit me in prison? Why did you never reply to my letters? What happened to make you ignore me?'

Kelly thought long and hard before she replied honestly, 'I loved you Jay, I wanted to forget, get on with my life. Selfish I know, but I was young. I had everything ahead of me. What did you expect?'

'I think it's a lame excuse, and I didn't expect to be abandoned by the girl I had intended to marry. I was young too, and besotted. I hoped you would believe in me, you who knew me better than anyone else should have known that I wasn't capable of killing anyone, let alone my best friend.'

Kelly wasn't sure if she wanted to cry or scream, both impulses were equally strong. 'I never thought that you could have premeditated Matthew's murder, or even killed him in cold blood. But the evidence was overwhelming. Everyone, even your own mother – '

As she said it, the colour drained from his already pale face, and she wished she could snatch back her words.

'I'm sorry, Jay, I shouldn't have . . .'

'Oh, don't be sorry about that. I know all about my mother. I saw it in her face when I was convicted, and I saw it again when I was released. I know she still believes I killed Matthew. That's one of the main reasons I need to uncover the truth. She's not well, she's been having treatment for a colon problem and it's worse than she admits. I doubt she's got much longer. I'd like her to know her son is not a murderer before she dies. It might help to make up for all those years without me.'

Kelly stopped walking. 'I'm sorry, I'm going to have to rest. I don't feel so good. I've had a virus and I keep throwing up. Do you mind if we sit down for a couple of minutes?'

They found a bench and he sat down first. She followed, deliberately leaving space between them. Taking her hands out of her pockets, she plaited her fingers and placed them in her lap.

'I agreed to see you, Jay, for one reason and one reason only. I want you to stop following me. I live a very high profile life, I'm married to a man tipped to be the next Republican president. I don't need any more complications. We were lovers once, but it was all a long time ago. I'm really sorry the way your life's turned out; if things had been different we might have had a future together. Who knows? Now it's history and I want you to stay away from me. If you don't, I'll have no choice but to involve the police.'

'Are you threatening me?'

With one swift movement she was on her feet, facing him, eyes flashing a warning. 'Yes, if you want to call it that. I can bring harassment charges against you. I'm sure you don't want that so soon after being released?'

This wasn't going the way he'd planned. He'd simply wanted to talk. God, how he needed to talk, to communicate, to relate. Nor had he expected to be so attracted to her, not like this, not after so long. He wanted her, most men would. But it was more than that, he wanted to make love, to lie in her arms, cuddle, kiss long lingering kisses and be touched with affection. Instead he had to listen to her repeated threat.

'If you continue to stalk me you'll find yourself back inside.'

At this Jay jumped up, and before she could move away he grabbed her arm, his fingers sliding on the slippery fabric of her jacket.

Concentrating her gaze on his hand, she told him, 'Take your hands off me, or I'll scream.'

'Scream away, Kelly, scream that you're being molested by a dangerous ex-con, a killer. Go on, then run home to your elegant house, your dinner parties, your glittering friends, your powerful senator man. And while you lie tucked up, cosy and warm in your white cotton sheets, spare a thought for me. Think about going to bed every night in a prison cell where I did things to you in my head.'

He loosened his grip, and was surprised when she didn't bolt. A bird sailed past, a black blot on an other-wise vast expanse of blue. Kelly stood very still, sunlight on her hair, so still she looked like a statue. Suddenly a memory surfaced. It was a day similar to this one, only much warmer, mid-summer. The incessant hum of insects, Kelly's squeals when one flew in her hair, flapping gossamer wings in the tangled strands, and then laughter when the creature took flight again. And later in the fading day, Kelly lying on her back, wiggling her toes in the long grass, her hair a golden fan, yellow on green.

Very slowly she reached up to touch his face, he didn't move as her fingertips traced the line of his jaw. His head was swimming with memories and he didn't hear her when she spoke.

'I'm sorry, Jay.'

His mouth was dry. 'What did you say?'

'I said I was sorry.'

Jay held out his hand, it was shaking and so was Kelly's

when she took it. 'Sorry isn't enough, Kelly. I have to find out who killed Matthew. I can't move on until I know the truth. Will you help me?'

Kelly didn't reply.

He asked again, his voice appealing. 'Please. For the love we once shared will you help me find Matt's killer?'

'I can't, Jay, I can't go back.' Then again, 'I'm sorry.'

With that Kelly pulled her hand from his grasp and began to run. She ran faster and faster, blinded by tears, consumed with one thought and one thought only, to put as much distance as she could between herself and Jay Kaminsky.

# Chapter Nine

'Hi, Wes, it's me.'

'Hi, Kelly, what's up?' Weston Kane could tell by Kelly's voice that there was an urgency involved in this unexpected call.

'Wes . . .' She hesitated, hoping Weston wouldn't be angry. '. . . I met Jay today.' She heard Weston's short intake of breath.

'And?'

'Last night he turned up at a charity benefit in Washington. I left early, and a little later he called me at home. God only knows how he got the number, but he begged me to see him. I agreed and met him today at Fort Marcy Park. It was so weird seeing him again after all this time. He looks great, handsome; he's lost a lot of weight but it suits him. A bit like a young Clint Eastwood . . .'

'Spare me the physical attraction, Kelly. What happened? What did he say?'

'He wanted to know why I hadn't got in touch after his conviction. I told him that I wanted to get on with my own life, and that seeing him would have been too painful. It was OK, Wes; much easier than I thought. I kept cool.'

'Did he mention Matthew or the trial?' When Kelly hesitated again, Weston recognized it as a sure sign that she didn't intend to tell her the whole truth.

'Not much, except to say that he didn't kill him, and that the main reason for wanting to clear his name is because his mother's terminally ill, and he wants her to know the truth before she dies.'

'Do you believe him?'

'Yeah, I think I do. He said he'd thought about me a lot in prison and just wanted to see me again.'

'It doesn't gel, Kelly. Why send us all enigmatic messages if it's just you he wants to see. He must have said more. Did he talk about me or Beth?'

'A little, said he'd had a hunch at his trial that we were covering something up. He admitted sending the gifts, saying he was playing detective, hoping to get some kind of reaction out of us – all based on his theory that we know more about Matt's murder than we disclosed at his trial. I got the impression he wanted to see me again and now that he has, he'll get on with his life, what's left of it.'

'Well let's hope so. But there might be more to this than his hard-on for you.'

'I felt so sorry for him, he looked cut off from reality somehow. That was the sad bit. I wanted to comfort him, make it all right.'

'Sympathy and nurturing is for losers and mothers. You're neither, Kelly. Forget it.'

'OK, I hear you. I only said I was sorry for the guy. He's just spent the majority of his adult life in prison for something he didn't do.'

'Jay will survive, honey; his type always does. The man's acting like a lovesick puppy around you, so what's new?'

'I didn't say that.'

'But that's the effect you have on most men. We still need to tread cautiously, there's a lot at stake.'

'Take it from me, Weston, Jay's cool.'

'We'll talk about it in more detail at the next Pact meeting. You'd better be there, Kelly. And whatever happens, don't see Jay again.'

Beth spent the weekend at her second home in Greenwich, Connecticut. It was close to the water and she liked nothing better than to walk the beach alone. The sea gave her a sense of calm and wellbeing that lately she'd been feeling less and less. She wished she could live and work here in this tranquil backwater, a cosy, colonial haven a million miles from the noise and stress of Manhattan. Often of late she'd dreamt of retirement in the 1920s house she'd acquired fifteen years ago – a year before she'd met Douglas Morgan. But their daughter, Clara was still finishing her school years in New York.

A sea breeze whipped through her hair, chilling her ears and the tip of her nose. She smiled to herself as she remembered a dirty weekend spent with Douglas when he was still living with his first wife Anne. She should have spotted the signs then – what kind of man takes his mistress to his marriage bed? Lust, that was what she'd felt for Doug; unbridled lust from the first moment she'd been introduced to him at a drinks party thrown by an old schoolfriend. Sure he was handsome, but it was more than that. He had a natural talent for focusing his concentration, making whomever he was talking to feel like the only person in the world. And he was funny, quick-witted, with a mischievous 'little boy' charm. He was a devious shit, Beth knew that. But he was also an irresistible shit and despite all his lies and cheating, she still loved her husband. Through her contacts, and her support, his career had enjoyed a heady and meteoric rise from that of an average criminal lawyer in a second-rate practice to that of rising star in a top law firm.

Unknown to Doug, his appointment six years ago as District Attorney was a direct result of one of Beth's clever manipulative schemes. Several times since then she'd considered leaving him. What wife hadn't thought about leaving her husband at least once? And during his latest romantic encounter with Alex Pitman, a woman she'd considered a friend, she'd been tempted to hammer the final nail into his coffin. But he'd pleaded, as only Douglas knew how. And she'd wished, oh how she'd wished, that his ardour had been about saving their marriage, and not saving his face for the forthcoming run-up to the governorship of New Jersey. Douglas would win, she was certain of it. He was a natural politician, with a brilliant future.

The sun was dipping, bursts of tangerine spattering the gathering dusk. Beth started back. The wind was against her now, her black woollen trousers flapping like the wings of a crow as she climbed the grassy bank leading to her house. When she emerged on to the lawn she was surprised to glimpse a light in her bedroom window. Positive it hadn't been on when she left the house, she made her way cautiously towards the back door. It was ajar and the seconds passed silently as she listened with mounting tension for any sound or movement inside. After about five minutes when she'd heard nothing and her heartbeat had slowed, she strode with purpose into the hall. Struggling out of her Barbour, she heard a stair creak. Not moving a muscle, she heard another creak, only louder. There *was* someone in the house.

'Thought I'd surprise you!'

Spinning round, she came face to face with Doug halfway down the stairs, an imbecilic grin plastered across his face.

'Shit, Doug, you terrified me! I thought I had an intruder.'

Like a two-year-old gelding he bounded down the stairs. When he took her in his arms he could feel she was shaking like a leaf. 'Honey, I'm sorry, I didn't mean to scare you. I thought it would be nice to have dinner together. I'll go and get clam chowder from Rick's place – we'll chill out by the fire, like we used to do, remember?'

Gently she pushed him away. 'I wish you'd called. Anyway I thought you had to see Arnold Kimball tonight.'

'He cancelled at the last minute, so on impulse I decided to drive up here and spend the night with my chicken.'

'Come on, Doug, tell the truth. It's me, Beth, you're talking to . . . and I'm no chicken. There never was any meeting with Arnie, I checked. Unless of course you guys were going to meet up in New Orleans where he is at the moment. I called Laurie Kimball yesterday.'

Douglas slapped the palm of his hand to his brow. 'Jeez, Beth, you're so suspicious. What gives you the right to check up on me all the time, like I'm some fucking schoolkid!'

Beth refused to be dragged into an argument. She'd come upstate to get away from the very scenario that looked likely to happen right now: arguing followed by great sex that papered over the cracks of suspicion for a few months more.

'I treat you the way you deserve. Trust has to be earned.' Beth watched the colour drain from her husband's face into his neck before she left him at the foot of the stairs. She was about to enter the living room at the end of the hall when he grabbed her from behind, pulling her round to face him.

'Don't you talk to me about trust, Beth, you're no Mother Theresa. I know all about Jay Kaminsky.'

She felt the blood rush to her ears with a distinct whoosh, and was surprised her voice sounded so casual when she replied, 'What on earth are you talking about?'

'You know exactly what I'm talking about: Jay Kaminsky, your long-lost lover.'

Stunned into silence, she held her breath, her mind swimming.

'Don't try to deny it, Beth. He called the house and left a message on the machine.'

Recovering her composure Beth said, 'So what? I do have male friends.'

'Methinks a little more than a friend in this case.'

'Whatever gives you that impression?'

'I'm asking the questions, Beth; I started the game. First tell me exactly who this Kaminsky is, and how you guys met.'

With a long sigh, Beth said, 'You are as usual behaving like a child. I've no intention of discussing this further.' She was about to move away, when she was pushed against the wall. Doug was so close she could feel his hot breath on her face, and knew he'd been drinking. With that knowledge came the awareness to be on her guard. Douglas could be mean when he'd had too much.

'This Jay asks to meet up with you, says how important it is, how you guys have a lot to discuss about the past, and how you go back a long way. Who is he, Beth, and why have you never mentioned him before?'

'Jay Kaminsky is a convicted felon, recently released from the Massachusetts State Pen. Back in the seventies he was convicted of the killing of his room-mate Matthew Fierstein.'

The name 'Fierstein' rang a bell in Doug's memory. 'I seem to recall the case, college kids both of them. Harvard I think.'

'Yes, Jay was an English scholar; he had a brilliant future. We all hung out together, you know college campus stuff.'

'So what does he want with you, Beth?'

She shrugged. 'Search me, we were never close. He was dating Kelly, they were an item for a while. The guy's just got out of prison, he went down for over twenty years. I suppose he's trying to build a new life, getting in touch with old friends. He might think I can help him find a job or something, who knows?' She hoped her lies were acceptable. She was married to a lawyer after all, he might be trying to catch her out. She had to be careful.

'By the tone of his voice he seemed pretty desperate for you guys to meet.'

'I do believe, Douglas Morgan, that you're jealous.'

He grinned. 'Maybe I was, maybe I am.'

Beth ran her tongue across her top lip, deciding not to counterattack with questions of her own. She knew what would make Doug drop the Kaminsky interrogation. She gave him one of her self-satisfied smiles in preparation.

'You wicked boy. You made Mommy angry so she's going to have to spank you.' The look of eagerness on Doug's face spurred her on. 'In the corner,' she demanded. Meekly he obeyed and with one hard tug she pulled his trousers down to his knees, feeling a quick thrill as she saw the erect outline clearly visible in the fine cotton fabric of his boxer shorts. She longed to touch it, but knew that to do so too soon would spoil the game. Her voice was deliberately shrill. 'Turn round!'

With widening eyes, Doug did as he was told, listening to the snap of her belt buckle as it slid out of the waist-band. The first contact of leather on flesh was always the best for both of them. Doug would yelp, and she would be encouraged to lash until his buttocks were an angry mesh of welts. She always stopped when he began to bleed, but tonight Beth continued. And with every lacerating crack of the belt she heard Jay Kaminsky begging her to stop.

\*　　\*　　\*

An icy wind stung Jay as he left his service apartment on 68th and First. He hailed a taxi and got out on the corner of 78th and York. Feeling the cold bite into his bones, he used his thumbs to pull the collar of his coat up higher, cursing himself for not wearing a hat. He felt the welcome blast of heat from the hot air curtain above the door chase the chill from his face as he entered a drugstore and bought a carton of Ducados. Jay still hadn't got into synch with the nineties. When he'd gone inside everybody smoked everywhere; when he came out nobody smoked nowhere. As he left the store he lit up and, fighting against the wind, battled up two blocks to 1298 on York.

He was propelled into the building on a gust of wind, the double set of plate-glass doors rattling in his wake. A security guard, his apple cheeks flushed from the heating vent, was just visible above his desk.

'Cold enough for you?'

Jay responded, 'Naw, I like it a few degrees colder, brings out the best in me.'

'Well, you might git lucky 'cause they say it's going to git colder, and we can expect some spring snow.'

As Jay pressed the elevator button he wondered afresh why all security guys and taxi drivers were prophets of doom. He came to the conclusion they had such chronically boring jobs that it made them feel marginally better if they made other people feel marginally worse.

Jay could hear Ed on the telephone as he breezed into the twelfth-floor reception of Hooper Brown Literary Agents Inc. The gold embossed plaque reminded him anew to ask where the 'Brown' came from. Knowing Ed, he probably made it up. He was about to greet Ed's assistant when the agent's big head appeared in person at the interconnecting door, with his mouth bellowing, 'Janet, where the hell's my – '

He stopped dead in mid-sentence. 'Jay! You didn't tell me you were coming in today. How are you, buddy?' Beaming, Ed held out his hand.

Jay shook it, pleased to see his agent – who was ushering him into his office.

It was warm in the office, too warm – stifling and stuffy – and Jay draped his coat over a battered leather chair.

Ed whistled, touching the sleeve. 'Nice threads; we chose good, huh?'

'Except for the price.' Jay warmed to the sound of Ed's amused chuckle. 'I wore this as part of the ensemble for the charity benefit. Didn't want to let you down.'

'So how was it? And how was Judy? I'm all ears.'

'Like you said Judy's a doll, she was great. Treated me like a long lost friend. Got me through the whole thing.'

'You said it was all in the name of research, right? So how's the next manuscript working out? You got a synopsis for me yet? Spoke to the publishers yesterday, told them I had a hot new property for them. They're talking about a deal for a three-book contract.' Ed whistled. 'That means big bucks.'

Jay was impressed but nervous. 'What would I do with it all?'

Ed made a few suggestions. 'Get seriously laid, buy

a jet, a yacht, a big spread in Long Island, give it to charity?'

Jay grinned. 'I think the first suggestion is priority. The new novel is called *Remission* and it's about finding out who killed Matthew Fierstein and why.'

Ed raised his eyes. 'You know?'

Jay lied, 'I've got a few leads. But that's all I want to say at the moment.'

Ed knew not to push him; he'd tried before without success. 'Great title,' he said instead.

'Give me a couple of weeks, and you'll have your synopsis and three chapters.'

'That's my boy. And just as icing on the cake, I've got contracts being drawn up at the moment for the movie. Pacino may be on board, he wants Ford Coppola to direct. With those names it's big budget, man.'

'How much?'

'Forty, maybe fifty million smackaroos.'

'What about the screenplay?'

'They want you, Jay. I said I'd speak to you, but it'll mean living out in La La Land for a few months. I suppose you could write it here, but those movie boys work by asking for constant changes and rewrites. It makes more sense for you to be out West. Anyway you look like you could use a little sun. A tan would suit you.'

Ed glanced across to the window. 'LA is a crazy place, does your brains if you stay too long, but at least the sun shines for about forty-six weeks of the year. And the broads are easy. Laid-back LA life.'

'I've got a couple of things to sort out here, then I'd

love to go. In the pen I used to dream about living in California.'

'Well, now's your chance. And if you ever dreamt about big tits, you'll find that the real Silicone Valley's got nothing to do with chips. By the way, how does the charity gig tie in as research for *Remission*? I don't get it.'

'Senator Todd Prescott was the guest speaker and his wife is my ex-fiancée. Kelly was at Wellesley when I was at Harvard; she was a freshman, when I was a junior. I was in love with her, and so was Matthew Fierstein. I've always maintained that Kelly knew more about the murder than she said, but I've never been able to prove it. At the time her two closest friends were Beth Morgan and Weston Kane.'

Ed looked thoughtful. 'I know that last name. Is she Sinclair Kane's daughter?'

'Yes, old heavy-duty money. Lots of it. How much do you know about her?'

'I know that she's a powerhouse lady. Runs a big media corporation. Billion-dollar global stuff.'

'Has she ever been married?'

'No, but I seem to remember some scandal about her a few years ago. It involved a ring of lesbians and underage girls. She hired some hot-shot fancy lawyers and they killed the story, but it leaked out in the *Inquirer*, caused quite a stink around the dinner party circuit on both coasts.'

Jay was all ears. 'Weston Kane's a lesbian?'

'Yeah, the Dutch Dyke they called her at the time,

145

because some of the kids were from Amsterdam, I think.'

'You heard of Beth Morgan?'

'Nope, but there's a Douglas Morgan running for governor of New Jersey. Any relation?'

Jay wasn't sure. 'Maybe, it won't take me long to find out.'

The telephone rang and Ed waited for his assistant to take it. When after six rings she hadn't picked up the call, he yelled, 'Janet, get the phone . . .' There was no reply and he was forced to take the call. It was Clive Norris from Maxmark Productions. Jay heard Ed saying, 'Yeah, I'm fine trying to make an honest buck.' Then in the next breath, 'I'm with him right now, yeah I'll ask him and get straight back to you.'

Ed replaced the receiver. 'It's on, they want us both in LA the week after next. For big powwow.'

'Can't go, I've still got things to sort out here.'

'They aren't asking you to go for ever, a few days that's all. You can sort your business out when you get back.'

Jay made a snap decision. 'You're right, this is too big; the other business can wait. Tell them I'm on.'

Jay wandered to the far side of the office, he looked at the row of spines in Ed's bookcase without registering one title. He could hear Ed confirming they would be in LA the week after next, and he knew he should be bubbling with enthusiasm. This was his big break, what he'd dreamt about: California sunshine, writing next to the ocean. Yet here he was on the eve of his dream thinking of nothing but Kelly Prescott. After the day in the park, he'd been unable to think of anything else.

Ed replaced the phone again and he spoke to Jay's back, voice rising as he punched the air. 'OK, boy, this is it! No shit.'

Jay turned round. 'I couldn't have done this without you, Ed. Not only have you been a great agent, you've been a friend. They're pretty thin on the ground for ex-cons.'

'Nothing to do with me; you're a great writer, man. Anyone could have got you a publishing deal on *Killing Time*. Oh and that reminds me, a guy called yesterday asking about you.'

Instantly alert, Jay said, 'Asking what?'

'Just stuff like when had Will Hope been released; where could he contact you; when was the next book coming out.'

'Who was the guy?'

'Mentioned he was an old friend of yours, said he'd helped you research *Killing Time* in the pen.'

Jay leaned forward, his eyes boring into Ed's. 'Did he leave a name?'

Ed moved a jacket proof off the top of his notepad and without looking up read, 'Al Colacello.'

'You sure he used that name?'

'Yeah, spelt it out for me, said that you would remember, and that he wanted to catch up, talk about old times – thought it would be a good idea to meet.'

Jay could feel his heart banging against his ribs. 'I think that would be very difficult. Al Colacello is dead.'

Ed waved a hand dismissively. 'Look, maybe I misunderstood somehow.'

'Maybe,' Jay said, knowing with absolute certainty that the call had come from Mario Petroni. He grabbed his coat, he wasn't sure where he was going, only that he needed to be alone. 'I've gotta go, Ed, catch you later.'

There was something wrong, Ed could sense it. Jay's body language had changed perceptibly and his face, though always prison pale, was now chalk white. Concerned, he asked, 'You OK, no problems involving this Colacello stiff?'

Jay, his head bent, concentrated on buttoning up his overcoat. 'Everything is cool, just strange someone calls leaving the name of a dead man.'

Ed grinned. 'This town is full of cranks. Probably some guy you met in the pen playing a practical joke.'

Jay was about to reply as the phone rang again. Ed picked it up while Jay started to walk towards the door.

Holding a hand over the phone, Ed said, 'Forgot to tell you. I'm going on vacation tonight, down to the islands, Bahamas. I met a little cutie last week at the track; she's young, busty, lots of chutzpah, just the way I like 'em. Said she needed a few rays and I didn't need to be asked twice, so I made the reservations while she was hot to trot.' A vision of the girl, Jenni, bending over a sun-filled terrace in a skimpy bikini caused a wicked smile to fill his face. Then he finished more seriously, 'A word of advice, if you're considering messing with Weston Kane or Doug Morgan, be careful. They're big shots. Don't get sidetracked into some shoot-out you can't possibly win.'

'Thanks for the advice, Ed; don't worry, I'm cool and focused. There's no way I'm going down again.'

The air felt slightly warmer when Jay emerged from Ed's building on to York Avenue. He decided to walk the eight blocks to his apartment. Cupping a cigarette in his hands he lit up, and with his head bent he set off. He needed to think. The message Ed had received yesterday was very clear. Petroni was on to him, and it was only a matter of time before he found out that Will Hope was Jay Kaminsky. The mob had very long tentacles and very persuasive methods of extracting information. Jay shuddered as he remembered a story Al had told him only hours after they'd met. It had been prompted by the death of an inmate who had snitched to the screws for a measly twenty cigarettes. The unforgivable crime in prison, the unwritten law, *you never ever snitched.*

The offender had been accused, tried and convicted by a kangaroo jury, and subsequently beaten to a pulp by the same men. Jay could hear Al hissing in his ear again, accompanied by the high-pitched hyena laughter that had seemed at times to reverberate off the cell walls. 'He got off lightly! If he'd snitched on Petroni he'd have had a much slower death. Petroni should have lived in medieval Europe, he could have run that, whaddyacallit, the Spanish thing where they put victims on the rack . . .'

Jay had supplied, *The Inquisition.*

# Chapter Ten

Mario Petroni was feeling good. He was lolling on the side of his bed, contemplating getting into it. He'd just enjoyed a long lunch with his only daughter Anna. She always made him feel wonderful, just to look at her was enough: dark flashing eyes and quick smile, so like his own mother. Mario constantly thanked God, and anyone else who would listen, to have been blessed with an angel like Anna. And the chef, Paulo Santorini, had excelled himself; the Tuscan bean soup and pasta with clams had tasted better than usual, and that was difficult. Every week for the last six years, father and daughter had met in Santorinis. It was Mario's cherished time with his beloved princess. A soon-to-be-married princess, his baby no more. The thought of Anna making love to a man, any man, made his guts ache. A sensation akin to when he'd been a seventeen-year-old in Sicily and had seen Carlo, his best friend, making love to Claudia Lorca. *His* Claudia, the one he'd waited two years for, the one he'd wanted to marry.

With controlled anger Mario had watched Carlo's bare ass pumping. It was over very quickly. Perhaps if Carlo had known, while he was thrusting his dick into Mario's property, that it would be for the last time, he might have made it last longer.

We all get exactly what we deserve in life, he mused. The only person who hadn't got his just deserts was Al Colacello. If there was one thing that made Mario seethe it was the thought of Al. He should have chopped his balls off when he'd had the chance.

Mario had already drawn the curtains, leaving only a chink open where spidery fingers of pale sunlight were stealing in to warm the foot of the bed and cast a golden glow over the high-ceilinged, airy room. It was on the thirty-sixth floor, overlooking the East River. A far cry from where he'd been born and raised in the Sicilian backstreets, and an enduring reminder of what he'd achieved. He slipped between the Egyptian cotton sheets, his eyelids felt heavy and were just beginning to droop when the telephone rang. Everyone knew not to disturb him between the hours of three and five. It was Petroni siesta, a daily ritual. He picked up the phone, then growled, 'Yes.'

It was his elder brother, Gianni. 'Mario, you asleep?'

'No, you just woke me, it better be good.'

'I think I traced the writer.'

Alert now, Mario sat bolt upright. 'You sure it's him?'

'I spoke with Ricky Matox a couple of days ago, and this guy fits the description he gave me. Ricky says his name's Jay Kaminsky. He was in the pen the same time as Al, and he writes under the pen name of Will Hope. I've had the agent staked out for months, and then this morning this writer guy shows up.'

'So where is he now?' There was a silent pause,

Mario repeated his question. 'So where is the mother-fucker?'

Gianni didn't want to answer that. 'I don't know what happened exactly, but we lost him. After he left the agency, I – '

Mario sighed. 'You fucked up, that's what happened.'

There was no reply.

'The agent will know how to get to him, so go that route and bring Kaminsky to me. We've got a lot to talk about. Don't call me again, Gianni, just do it.'

The sky had dropped a few feet when Kelly emerged from Bergdorf Goodman on to Fifth Avenue. The clouds, like dirty curtains, draped the upper floors of Trump Tower. She began to walk south past the cathedral and the Rockefeller Center, stopping to fumble in her purse for a couple of dollars. She found a five, and kneeling down she laid it on top of a thin blanket wrapped around the legs of a Vietnam vet. His closely cropped hair revealed a mass of open sores. He thanked her with his eyes, and she gave him a short nod. Laden with designer bags, her conscience pricking, she'd just spent six thousand dollars on frivolity, enough to keep a man like him well fed for a year. Having a conscience wasn't enough, you had to do something about it. She could hear her mother's scalding reprimand. *You have to give back, Kelly, all you do is take take take.*

As she came level with her limousine she pushed the voice to the back of her mind. Concentrate on something superficial she told herself, it always worked. So as she handed her packages to the driver, she thought about her new Gucci shoes and Chanel jacket and slid into the back seat of the limo, saying, Sixtieth and Central Park West.'

The Pact meeting at Weston's was scheduled for seven, which only gave her fifteen minutes to get there. She breathed deeply as she felt panic rise, and the familiar palpitations begin to attack her chest. She told herself there was nothing to worry about. Everything in her life was fine. The meeting with her bankers had gone very well. The credit committee had approved in principle the increased funding she'd requested. They just needed a few more figures from her financial controller, and the working capital on the Georgetown *Gazette* would be in place. The forecasts were looking good and even if the newspaper only managed to break even in the first year, the *Gazette* would still be home and dry. She had a subsequent meeting in the morning to tie up a few loose ends, then back to DC with the finance assured. Kelly looked forward to telling Wes, to feeling the warmth of her approval.

As the limo bumped down Fifth, she spotted a large colour poster advertising jeans. The male model who was undoing his flies was a replica of a young Jay. She felt a sharp pain hit her in the centre of her belly, and her mind began its journey back, back down an avenue of lies. Back to 1973, and the night Matthew Fierstein was murdered. Since she'd seen Jay in the park she had been unable to sleep without dreams of him, vivid repetitive dreams of Jay and herself making love . . . on the beach, in his room, in the car. And always ending with Matthew looming above them, his face painted black, stabbing himself in the heart with a long knife.

By the time the car pulled to a halt in front of the San Remo building, she was rooted to the back seat. She couldn't move, like when being chased in a nightmare, and not being able to run. *I'm not well*, she told herself, *not in shape. But if I keep calm, take deep breaths, I can make it up to Weston's apartment and I can have a drink. I'll be OK then. I can stay with Weston, I'll be safe.*

The driver was holding open the door with a perplexed look. 'Sixtieth and Central Park – this is where you want to be, isn't it, Mrs Prescott?'

Kelly tried to speak, and the words got stuck in her throat. With all the force she could muster, she willed her legs to move. They did, but they felt weightless and separate from the rest of her body. So intent was she on getting to the apartment without passing out, she stumbled past the driver without leaving instructions on how long she'd be. Once in the elevator, she felt a little better and by the time she reached Weston's door she was beginning to feel normal again.

Weston took one look at Kelly, and knew immediately something was wrong. 'Kelly, you OK? What's happened?'

'I'm just so pleased to see you.'

At this Weston opened her arms, and Kelly fell into them. She allowed Weston to stroke her head like a mother would a child. Weston thrilled to the touch and smell of her, and felt a great surge of love. And lust. She berated herself for the latter, yet could barely control the desire to make love to Kelly there and then, against the hall wall. She somehow put all such thoughts out of her head as she led the way into the living room, where she walked to a drinks trolley as Kelly flopped on to the sofa.

Holding up a bottle of Puligny Montrachet, Weston said, 'Drink?'

'That's exactly what I need.' Wine always helped, and after half a glass Kelly began to feel a lot better. She looked around the room. 'Where's Beth?'

'Believe it or not she's held up in a meeting; she should be here soon.'

As if on cue the doorbell rang. It was Beth, who breezed in, making a fuss of Weston and kissing Kelly on both cheeks. 'Sorry I'm late, girls, but someone's plane was delayed, and we had to have a conference before the meeting tomorrow.' She exchanged her coat for a glass of wine, and as Weston was hanging up the former she turned her attention to Kelly.

'You look pale, darling, you OK?'

'I've had a virus, just getting over it, otherwise I'm fine.' Then changing the subject, she asked, 'How's Doug?'

'Douglas Morgan is top of the shop as my old granny used to say. We had a great weekend out at Greenwich, very cosy, like it used to be years ago. And Todd?'

'Pass.'

A look of understanding passed between the two women as Weston rejoined them.

'OK, girls, to business. The objective of the meeting is to discuss Jay Kaminsky, so let's get to work.'

At the mention of Jay's name, Kelly felt a sharp pang of pain like boiling water injected deep into her belly. An image of how he'd looked last week in the park entered her mind, and on impulse she said, 'I think we should stop worrying about him. I don't think he's a threat.'

'You're wrong.' It was Beth speaking. 'He called me earlier and left a message on my machine saying he was searching for the truth, and wanted to talk to me about the past.'

'That would probably be just after you guys saw each other in the park,' Weston said, unsurprised.

Beth looked agog at Kelly on hearing of this, but Kelly made no comment, and Weston was giving 'Leave it' signals with her eyes.

'Has he called you, Weston?' Kelly asked.

'No, not yet, but he will. He's like a dog with a bone, and I reckon he's not going to let go till he's got the last drop of marrow. So how can we be certain he won't find some clue as to how Matthew really died?'

'How could he?' Beth countered.

'Look at the facts. Jay Kaminsky was released from prison at the end of February. In the short time since he's been out he's already managed to follow and meet Kelly. He knows where we all live to send us sinister gifts. He's called you, Beth; and will no doubt be calling me in due course. That's quite good going so far. I don't think we can afford to be complacent.

'Kelly's feeling sorry, poor old Jay, done time for a crime he didn't commit. That's history as far as I'm concerned, and I think we should be worrying about *now*. I'm negotiating a major deal for the digital rights to part of the Pacific Rim; you, Kelly, have got the *Gazette* to launch; and Beth, we all know what a lot you've got on your plate at the moment – what with Doug running for governor, not to mention the Singapore bank takeover bid. Can't you just imagine Kaminsky going to the press with some harebrained story about us, how we were all friends at the time of Matthew's murder and how he thinks we were involved in some sort of cover-up. The tabloids would love it; not to mention our many rivals.'

Beth and Kelly were both silent, letting the implications of Weston's sound reasoning sink in.

Weston knew she had them in the palm of her hand, and continued, 'We must be united in this. If Jay Kaminsky continues to be a minor nuisance, fine; we can tolerate that. But if he becomes a real danger, we have to act.'

'What exactly do you mean, Wes?' It was Kelly.

'Let's cross that bridge if and when we come to it. For now, I just want your agreement that we act if forced to. What do you say?' Weston grabbed Kelly's hand and squeezed it tight. 'It's the only way.'

With a nod, Kelly muttered in a tiny voice, 'I know Weston, I know.'

Then turning to Beth, 'How do you feel?'

'The same as Kelly.'

Feeling triumphant, but careful not to show it, Weston

rose. Pulling Kelly to her feet with one hand, at the same time she grabbed Beth with her other. 'We are sisters; we've come this far together; we can continue if we stay united. Let's repeat the mantra in our heads for a few moments, then we chant.'

The ringing of the telephone interrupted. Weston tried to ignore it then, glancing at the clock, noticed it was seven forty-five and knew it was her vice president calling from Los Angeles. He was spot on time and it was a call she had to take.

'Sorry, girls, if that's who I think it is you'll have to excuse me for a few minutes.' Weston ran to take the call on an extension. When she returned ten minutes later Beth had left.

'Where did Beth go?'

'She had to run – some business dinner she couldn't get out of. Said to give you her apologies and promised to call you in the morning.'

Kelly finished the wine; she held out the empty glass. Weston replenished it, saying, 'You want to talk?'

'Yes. If I don't, I think I'll go quietly insane.'

'So talk, I'm all ears.'

Kelly shifted a cushion at the small of her back, and sighed, 'Seeing Jay again was the most profoundly traumatic thing I've ever experienced since Matthew's death. Neither Maynard dying, nor my father, have hit me quite as hard.' She took a sip of wine before continuing, 'I'm not well, Weston. I keep having panic attacks, I had one in the car coming here. They're really scary, palpitations . . . can't move, and it's happening more and more. Every time I get one, I drink. I know it's not the answer, but it's the only thing that helps.'

'You tried Prozac?'

'Are you kidding? It was invented for me, but it just makes me worse – out of control. And the other thing, I don't want to hack it any longer with Todd. I care for him deeply, but just as a friend. I'm not in love with him, and I don't want to make love with him. It might have been different if a baby had turned up, but that hasn't worked out for us. I can't keep doing it, Weston, the pretence. I'm going to go crazy, or become a soak like my mother.'

She paused to take a gulp of wine. 'I know I've got a wonderful lifestyle and Todd adores me. I keep telling myself all of that. He's got a brilliant future, and so have I as a potential first lady. But what I've got isn't what I want.'

Kelly stood up. She couldn't meet Weston's eyes, which she was sure would be full of the hope that this disillusion might open a window of opportunity for herself. She crossed the room, stopping next to the window and gazed out across Central Park. There was a strong wind, and with their dark branches entwined the trees looked to Kelly like hundreds of withered old arms waving at the sky. Lights blazed in a thousand rooms, a million windows. She wondered what all the people inside the glowing rooms were doing. Were they happy? What *was* happy? A few seconds later Weston was by her side.

Without moving her eyes, Kelly said, 'This view never fails to impress.'

Weston agreed. 'I see it most days, but it still has the same effect on me. It puts me in touch with why I do what I do; why I strive every day; why I live the way I do.'

Kelly clinked the side of Weston's glass. 'I think you do it because you love every minute.'

The narrowing of Weston's eyes made her look feline, and the half smile held a hint of the Machiavelli she was. 'I like the game I admit, and I like to win.'

'And you like the manipulation,' Kelly added.

Weston replied, 'What have we all been doing for the past twenty-odd years? Manipulating men, circumstances, money, chance? You can't accuse me of something you do as well as me. If not better than me.'

'No accusation intended, Weston. I'm just trying to tell you that I'm tired of the game, sick of playing. The glittering prizes seem less intoxicating, the goals less rewarding.'

'What else is there? You give me a better alternative and I'll try it. But remember that I'm a lesbian, a control freak . . . and obsessed with power. Some smartass shrink once suggested I was trying to be my father. I replied that if that means I like building empires, controlling fortunes and fucking beautiful women, then I had to agree.'

Kelly laughed. 'Have you ever thought about kids? You could adopt.'

Weston looked aghast. '*Me!* Come on, Kel, you're looking at the original single-track, single-minded, self-indulgent female. Kids require time, commitment, selfless devotion. You have to get home, or be home, to read them bedtime stories, take them into your bed when they have nightmares. All that stuff is definitely not for me. And in that cosy scenario a father comes in handy. Even I have to admit men are useful sometimes.'

Weston winked, she was giving a wry smile that never lacked warmth when directed towards Kelly. 'I love you, Kelly. Always have, always will.'

It was direct, sudden and unexpected. Kelly made no attempt to hide her surprise. She opened her mouth to speak; Weston closed it with her fingertips.

'Let me finish. I think I fell in love with you in our junior year, only I didn't realize it then. I know you love me too, but your love is based on friendship. I accept that. And I hope that you in turn can accept something from me. *Advice.* You are poised to occupy one of the most important positions in the world: don't jeopardize it; don't throw it away. You and I were destined for great things. It's what we talked about at Wellesley, what we planned. The Pact, the litany, the mantra. We have each other, and together we have a future. That's what's kept me going when I thought I might stumble and fall.'

'Citizen Kane fall?' Kelly shook her head. 'Never.'

# Chapter Eleven

'The orchid, please.' Jay pointed to an early purple orchid. 'Yes, that one.'

'Sure is pretty,' the florist commented, lifting the potted plant out of the window and placing it on the counter in front of Jay. The petals didn't look real, and Jay touched the tip of one to make certain it wasn't fake. 'You want it gift wrapped?'

Jay nodded. 'Red ribbon, please.'

The woman set to work with reams of raffia and oyster-coloured paper, finishing off with a red silken bow. A self-satisfied smile at her handiwork, then, 'That'll be fifty-five dollars.'

Jay gave the exact money and the shopkeeper was smiling when she handed over the orchid. 'Hope she enjoys it.'

With a terse smile and a nod, Jay said, 'I'm sure she will.'

When he emerged from the florist shop, located in the Plaza Hotel, and asked the doorman to call a cab, Jay held the plant close to his body, afraid it might wilt in the wind. A few minutes later he was seated in the back of a yellow cab with the orchid on the floor by his feet. He knew exactly where he was going: the wire tap in Kelly's

Washington home had given him a precise time and the location of Weston Kane's apartment building. He asked the driver to park across the street and wait.

Forty minutes later he spied Beth Morgan coming out of the building; she took a cab from the corner of the block. After another hour and a half, Kelly emerged on to the sidewalk and a waiting limo pulled up in front of her. Jay could see only the top half of her body as she slipped into the car.

The yellow taxi followed Kelly's car across town to Madison and East 72nd. From the opposite corner Jay watched Kelly alight and step into the Mark Hotel. He waited for ten minutes before paying the cab driver and crossing the street to enter the hotel. From a booth in the lobby he was put through to Kelly's room.

Disguising his voice with a midwestern drawl, tinged with a smooth hospitality note, he said, 'This is Steven, the concierge. I've got your tickets for tonight's performance of *Sunset*. You can collect them at the box office, the performance begins – '

Kelly cut him short. 'I didn't order any theatre tickets.'

'This is Mrs Newman, Room 589?' Jay said a silent prayer.

'No, it's not. I'm Mrs Prescott, Room 438, the same one as I always take. And I didn't order any tickets.'

'Sorry to disturb you, Mrs Prescott. I'm new around here – '

'Obviously,' Kelly said curtly and slammed down the phone. She didn't give the concierge another thought, until about fifteen minutes later when she stepped out of the shower with a suspicion forming in her mind. Wrapped in a towel, she walked to the phone in the corner of the bedroom and jabbed the concierge button.

'Steven, please.'

'Steven's off duty, Mrs Prescott – day off. He'll be back tomorrow morning. This is Joe, can I help you?'

She was about to ask how long Steven had worked at the Mark when the doorbell rang. 'No thanks, Joe, it was Steven I wanted to speak to.' She replaced the phone and securing the towel walked to the door. With her eye pressed to the security peephole, she could see the broad shoulders and back of a man who was holding a large floral arrangement that looked like an orchid. The man half turned and, hiding his face behind the arrangement, he rang the bell again.

'Delivery for Mrs Prescott.'

Not taking any chances, Kelly replied with, 'Leave it outside.' She waited; the man didn't move. She tried again. 'I can't open the door right now, please leave the delivery outside or take it to reception.'

Kelly knew something wasn't right; only uniformed concierge or housekeeping staff would deliver to the door. She watched the man kneel down. He was wearing a woollen hat pulled tight to his head and low over the top of his eyes; a black scarf covered the bottom half of his face. She continued to watch as he placed the plant on the floor, her eyes not leaving the peephole until he was out of sight. She waited for a few minutes, then very quietly she opened the door and a quick glance from right to left confirmed that the landing was empty apart from a laundry trolley.

When she knelt to pick up the package, Jay dived out from behind the housekeeping trolley. There was no time to protest as his bulk forced her back into the room, and the door slammed automatically behind them.

'Kelly, I've not come to hurt you I promise. But if you scream I might have to.' He saw her consider crying out for help, watched her lips trembling as she dismissed the idea, and suddenly he felt gripped by an unexpected erotic charge. In that instant Jay understood how psychopaths get off on power and dominance. It was an uncomfortable recognition that made him question his own motives; was it possible that he had some trace of psychosis inside his own head? Prison had changed him; had he succumbed?

He knew he hadn't when he felt ashamed for enjoying, however fleetingly, his power over Kelly. After that he kept repeating, 'I promise I won't hurt you.'

Kelly was cowering, her head bent in submission and he hated himself for making her feel that way. The desire to dominate her had left him as quickly as it had come. Nervously, Jay slowly lifted her chin until he could look her in the eye.

She was avoiding his pleading gaze, looking past him. Wrapped in a big bath towel tied above her breasts, limp tendrils of wet hair trailing across her neck, she looked very fragile.

'Please, Kelly, I only want to talk.'

Slowly her eyes moved. And then unflinchingly she looked directly at him, defiant now. 'We talked in the park. There's nothing more to say. I warned you, Jay, if you continue to follow me . . . I'll have to call the police.'

'Go on then, call them. Tell them I'm harassing you. You could do it easily, Kelly. And while you're at it, tell them how you know that I didn't kill Matthew Fierstein.'

'I don't know what the hell you mean.'

'Oh, I think you do. I think you know exactly what I mean.'

Kelly didn't trust her own voice, and she was beginning to feel strange again. That same sinking sensation of her limbs being pulled downward by an imaginary force – into something deep and dark and cloying. She began to tremble, and felt more afraid than ever before, except for the night of Matthew's murder.

'Jay, I – '

It was impossible to finish the sentence. The words would not come. Suddenly she felt a sharp pain shoot across her chest, and then her whole body turned cold. This was different from the previous times. Her panic attacks had never been accompanied by this extreme cold. She began to shiver uncontrollably and her head was jerking from side to side like a startled puppet.

Kelly felt her legs give way, and she slumped to the floor.

Jay fell to his knees to help her. Taking hold of her hands, he squeezed tight. 'Kel, what is it? What's wrong with you?' He thought for a terrible moment she was having a heart attack.

She tried to form the message, *I'll be OK. I've got some sedatives in the bathroom – please get them for me.* But she couldn't speak.

He stroked her hair. 'You're going to be all right, Kelly. Just take deep breaths. Fill your lungs and exhale slowly.'

She did as he bid, breathing deeply while he stroked her head and told her over and over again that she was going to be all right. His voice, calm and soothing washed over her and the quaking began to abate. In a croaky voice she managed to say, 'I've ... got ... tablets.' Another deep breath then, 'In the bathroom. In a blue ... wash-bag.'

Jay jumped up and almost immediately returned with a bottle of tablets and a tumbler half full of water. Shifting on to her elbows, Kelly took two tablets. Then with Jay's help she stood up. Using him as a crutch, she walked a little unsteadily towards the bed. He helped her on to it, covering her with a blanket, then sat on the edge holding her hand.

Now the shaking had stopped completely, leaving only a tremor in her left hand. He held it, stroking the back with his fingertips. 'You OK?'

'I'll be fine now. Sorry about that, stupid of me. I shouldn't have eaten a cheeseburger for lunch, must have had onions in it. I'm allergic to onions, they always have that effect.'

'Dogs with English mustard do the same for me.'

She smiled weakly. 'The trouble is I love cheese-burgers.' But then her eyelids drooped. 'This dope relaxes me so much I fall asleep.'

Jay watched her eyes close as the sedatives began to act. So as not to disturb her, he stayed where he was until she was dozing.

Kelly slept for an hour and ten minutes, during which time Jay went through her purse and suitcase. He found nothing that a woman of substance wouldn't carry. When she awoke he was sitting on a chair a few feet from the bed, a cigarette dangling from his mouth. His eyes, half closed, had lost their furtiveness and his face in repose looked younger, more like the Jay she had known and loved.

'When did you start smoking?'

Jay jumped, the cigarette almost dropping out of his mouth. 'How long have you been awake?'

'Just.' Then again, 'When did you start smoking?'

'After I'd been inside for a couple of months. Cigarettes are hot currency in prison, a sign of status and a comfort. After ten years I was a chain-smoker, that's when I could get my hands on them. I was introduced to these,' Jay showed her the pack of Ducados, '. . . by a young Cuban kid not much older than me. He was inside for killing his father.' Slowly Jay closed his eyes, the memory of his first meeting with Antonio as fresh as if it were yesterday. He'd already been inside for three years when he noticed the new inmate, a good-looking kid. They met in the exercise yard. Antonio had generously offered Jay a cigarette, and Jay had commented on the brand, saying he liked the strong acrid taste. An instant bond had developed between the two men and when Jay suggested they start up a small business importing Ducados, Antonio had eagerly agreed. The plan was for Antonio's brother, who visited regularly, to smuggle the cigarettes into the prison, so that Jay could then sell them from the library. It had worked like a dream, and within months Jay and Antonio had established a thriving business and became known as the Ducados Dudes. But demand had always exceeded supply.

He opened his eyes to find Kelly staring at him. 'Sorry! I was miles away, back there in the pen. I was kinda lucky. I worked in the library and got time to compose a lot of letters and poems for the inmates to send home. They called me the Poet. I would have preferred the Born Again Bard, but I doubt whether most of the guys knew who Shakespeare was.'

A silence slipped between them, both unsure of what to say next. Swinging her legs across the bed, Kelly stood up. The towel was loose and it slipped to the floor. She made no attempt to retrieve it.

Aware he was gawking with blatant admiration, Jay forced his eyes up her body, directing them on to her face. But not before he'd noticed her skin had a yellow tinge; her nipples were dark around the edge; and she had shaved her pubic hair to a narrow golden strip.

As Kelly walked towards him, she pushed all thoughts firmly out of her mind except the one uppermost. She held out her hand. 'I want you.'

He felt a tautness in his chest, like a tourniquet fastened

too tight. For the first time he noticed the different colours in her hair; he counted three as she got nearer: gold, yellow and platinum. Kelly was almost upon him when he stood up. He could feel her breath against his cheek, her warm nakedness against his arm. Very gently she touched his face with her fingertips, her arms encircled his waist, her breasts pressed against his chest. His hands found her ass and cupped her buttocks, gently at first, then harder, kneading, pulling her into him. Jay wanted to tell her how much he'd loved her, never stopped loving her, but no words came. Instead he found her mouth, it was half open, soft and warm and wet. The mouth of a woman, full of promise.

It started to snow while Jay and Kelly were making love; it continued while they slept. And by eight o'clock the following morning, the time Kelly awoke, Manhattan was drained of all colour except white. When she poked her head around the bedroom drapes, the city was hushed, cocooned under a four-inch spring blanket of the white stuff. And it was still falling, huge flakes spilling from a sky the colour of dirty dishwater. She made a shivering noise, and slipped back into bed next to Jay. He was sleeping, and she had the opportunity to observe him completely unawares. In her experience most men looked like little boys when they were in deep sleep. Jay did not. His face, creased and half hidden in drifts of white cotton, looked worn out. And his mouth curled up at the corners like the pages of a well-thumbed book. Her fingers itched to touch him in the hollow at the base of his neck, or where his hair was beginning to grow longer below his ears. But so as not to disturb him, she lay very still, listening to his breathing, shallow and even. He moaned softly and she was reminded of their love-making. Had she given herself to Jay out of a sense of guilt? Or had she been trying to control the situation? Seduction was an area she knew well, and in which she excelled.

No, the real reason was desire; a deep and profound need to fill a void. She sometimes felt that her whole life had been about running away. All the aspiring, achieving, the being on the treadmill, forever moving on and cramming as much superficial incident into her existence as she could.

She watched Jay stirring, consciousness slowly creeping over his lean body. He had lost twenty-six pounds in prison, and it was the first thing she'd noticed when she'd undressed him . . . Not an ounce of surplus flesh covered his frame, and every muscle was toned to perfect definition.

Kelly liked his body; she'd said so, commenting on his athletic shape. He'd devoured her compliment like a starving child offered a milky breast. Then his pleasure at her appreciation had saddened him, because it made him realize how much he'd missed being desired, how much they had missed together.

She saw one of his arms stretch across the space that separated them. He rolled over, his hand a hairy paw on her shoulder as he nuzzled into the space between her shoulder and neck. He was toasty, his breath tinged with Ducados and sleep. She could feel his mouth, at first dry, his lips cracked; then his tongue warm and wet, and licking.

He whispered into her ear. 'You are wonderfully, gloriously, amazingly fuckable. I want to love you, protect you for ever.'

She smiled, and it stuck.

Jay told her, 'Lying here with you, I feel better than I've felt for a very, very long time. I don't even want to dwell on how long.'

Her eyes slanted towards the covered window. 'There's a raging blizzard out there. New York is under inches of snow. We've got time to kill, so let's talk. Tell me about it, Jay. I want to know.'

He lit a cigarette, his mind rushing back to a place he'd sworn he'd never go to again. A useless vow. Where to begin? He supposed that to start at the beginning made sense.

'At first it was . . . I suppose *hell* is the only appropriate word. It's difficult to explain to someone who's never been inside just how bad it is. *Prison.* The place itself is so alien, it's like walking into another world on a different planet. All the rules of civilization don't apply any more. Everything I'd been brought up to believe suddenly became totally meaningless. I had to learn to live by a whole new set of values, and for a while I didn't think I'd make it.

'The first year was the most difficult. The new boy, the Harvard kid: young, good-looking. Fresh meat, fair game. The mothers wouldn't leave me alone. After a few weeks of being raped someone gave me some muscle relaxant.

I wanted to throw it back in his face. But he just said, "Wise up, kid, it ain't gonna stop. It's gonna go on, and hurt more, do you damage they won't be able to fix in the prison hospital."'

Jay ignored her shocked gasp. She'd asked for it, and he wanted her to know. It felt good to tell someone.

'Gradually, bit by bit I started to fight back. I used the only weapon I had at my disposal; intelligence will always conquer brute force. At first it challenged them, and made them want to beat the shit out of me. But soon the guys learnt I could be useful to them and I became a valuable commodity, just like cigarettes and drugs.

'I studied the psychopathic mind, it's fascinating. And I learnt how to use it to my advantage. Most of the inmates are egotistical maniacs. They get off on power –'

The ringing of the telephone intruded. Kelly wanted to ignore it, but Jay insisted she take the call. It was Todd.

'I saw on the news you've got some real bad weather up there, you think you'll get out of town today?'

'What do you think? It's New York, you know how they love any excuse to close JFK. It's still snowing like crazy and nothing's moving outside, but I'll keep you posted. How's the weather in DC?'

'Freezing, snow on the way, expected late tonight. So it looks like we're both going to be snowed in for God knows how long. I've got a lot of paperwork to catch up on, it'll keep me occupied. Wish you were here, honey. We could cuddle up together, like in January ninety-six when we were stuck in Toronto. Remem–'

Kelly interrupted, 'The other line's ringing, Todd. I'll have to go, speak to you later . . .'

She replaced the phone, glancing at Jay who was lying on his back still smoking. She had never in her life allowed a man to smoke in bed with her. It was a disgusting habit. Yet she felt only warmth and affection towards Jay as he lay pulling on another cigarette.

He exhaled. 'I assume that was your husband.'

'It was.'

'Are you happy with him, Kelly?'

'No.'

'So why stick around?'

'I'm the First Lady In Waiting, as Weston so eloquently puts it. Waiting my turn to become the most envied and powerful woman in the world.'

'Does that mean Todd's after the White House?'

'Exactly.'

'Will he do it?'

'Nothing's a dead cert but he's the most likely candidate.'

'Are you in love with him?'

'No.'

'Have you ever been?'

'No, not for one moment. But I care for him deeply, he's a good man and a good friend.'

'Have you ever been in love with anyone, Kelly? I mean really in love?'

She thought carefully about her answer, and replied honestly. 'I thought I was in love with you.'

Jay stubbed out his cigarette, and lit another. 'You didn't know for sure?'

'At the time I was sure. Yet on reflection our love seems like naïve teenage stuff. Perhaps if we'd been given the opportunity, it would've matured and grown.'

'It doesn't need time to mature, Kelly, it's either there or not. You feel it or you don't. But if you do, you nurture it. I never had any doubts. I wanted to make everything in our shared world good and fulfilling. Does that make any sense to you?'

'Yes.'

'Good. Now I want you to tell me about this Pact you, Weston and Beth made.'

Kelly sat bolt upright, catching her hair under his arm and feeling it tug. One minute she'd been feeling loved and cared for and the next minute . . . vulnerable. Not thinking straight, she blurted out the confirmation she should have withheld. 'How do you know about that? It's got nothing to do with you, Jay.'

He ignored the first question. 'That's the problem. I think it has.'

Now, on her guard, Kelly slid out of bed wondering what he knew about the Pact. She needed time to think, space to concentrate away from Jay's probing.

Following her with his eyes, he asked, 'Where are you going?'

'To the bathroom.'

Five minutes later when she emerged he was waiting outside the door. 'I want an answer to my question, Kelly.' He touched the collar of the towelling bathrobe

175

she had donned. 'Ha, armour! What are you hiding underneath?'

She shrugged. 'It's cold in here.'

'It's like an oven and you know it. Come on, just tell me the truth.'

'Goddamn you, Jay! Like I said, our Pact has got nothing to do with you. We made a silly, girlie agreement when we were in our sophomore year. A fun thing, you know, a crazy aspirational thing. Wes started it.'

'Weston Kane was, and I believe still is, a very powerful and insidious influence on you. Is she still pulling your strings?'

Kelly was angry. Two red patches flared on her cheeks as she snapped, 'Weston Kane is my dearest friend. We've been friends for nearly thirty years. I don't know what I'd do without her. She's been like a sister to me; better than a sister. She's a rock, always there. I can't imagine my life without Weston. In fact I hate to even think about it. And I resent you implying she's a bad influence on me. I'm a big girl, I make decisions for myself and I don't . . .'

Jay held up his hands as if to stave off a blow. 'OK, you made your point. You and Weston are bosom buddies, so tell me about the Pact. If it's just an innocent girlie thing, why are you so defensive?'

'Like I said, it started out as a fun thing. At college Weston was always talking about the feminist movement, and how she could beat men at their own game. One night she vowed to be in a position of supreme power by the year two thousand. Beth said that if Weston could do it, so could she. And then the two of them inspired me. We all got stoned, joined hands and agreed to keep in touch. We planned to meet every six weeks, wherever, whatever we were doing. We called ourselves sisters of supremacy, and named the bond the Millennium Pact. In the early years it was frivolous, meeting up, doing a little dope . . . swapping gossip.'

Jay raised his eyebrows. 'Is that all you did?'

'Yes, what else?'

'If I know anything about Weston Kane, I can't imagine her wasting any precious time on innocent girl talk. She never struck me as the frivolous type. And I'm sure her interest in you hasn't been entirely sisterly.'

'You can cut the innuendo and I don't really care if you believe me or not. We met last night at Weston's apartment, we drank some wine, dished the dirt on Beth's no-good husband who's playing around. Weston is between love affairs; and I'm – '

'Yes, Kelly. You were about to say?'

'Oh nothing, my life's boring. You don't want to hear about my problems.'

'That's where you're wrong. I do. And I doubt that being head of a successful media empire, about to launch a political tabloid and married to a future presidential candidate can possibly be described as *boring*.' Jay heard the bitterness in his own voice, his resentment surfacing. He was jealous of Todd Prescott. Not of the man himself, but of the years he'd had with Kelly.

Avoiding his gaze, she crossed the room. Jay had opened the drapes and she found herself looking out on a white landscape again. It was like a freshly iced cake. 'Still snowing . . .'

'Come back here!' It was a command.

She spun around. 'Wha . . .t?' Then she did as he bid, half automatically and half in anticipation. When she was standing in front of him, he grabbed the belt of her bathrobe, held the knot tight then used it to pull her towards him. With one sharp tug Jay had loosened the belt, and he fell to his knees in front of her. She could feel his fingers like talons digging into her buttocks.

Instantly Kelly felt safe. She was back on territory where she was totally at ease. Slowly she parted her legs and using both hands she opened herself up, inviting him to take her. As she felt, first his hot breath, then the tip of his tongue, she let out a long sigh. She held the back of his neck and pushed his head down hard, making him groan, feeling his shoulders quiver. Then all other thoughts fled as she gave herself up to his greed.

Kelly had just emerged from the shower when Weston called. It was six-fifteen.

'Hi, Kelly, fancy putting on some snow boots, and trudging over to my place? I've got pasta, and your favourite white Montrachet.'

Kelly, nervous that Weston might hear the movements of Jay still showering in the background, raised her voice and made an excuse. 'I, er, don't have any suitable outdoor stuff. This snow wasn't forecast until last night. I thought I'd be back in Washington.'

Undeterred, Weston went on, 'In that case why don't I come to you?'

'I don't think that's such a good idea, Wes. You might not get back.'

'So what, I can sleep with you. It won't be the first time.'

Panicking now at Weston's persistence, she feigned illness. 'Tell the truth, Wes, I've got a migraine. I'm going to order room service and have an early night. Hopefully by morning they'll have shifted some of the snow, enough to get me out or I can take Amtrak. Todd wants me back in DC for a supper party on Friday night.'

Weston knew Kelly was lying about the headache, and suspected she'd met some young guy in the bar and invited him up to her room. Weston knew that an uncomplicated one-night stand was Kelly's way of switching off when stress swamped her.

'OK, I get the message. Like Garbo, you vant to be alone.'

'Sorry, I just don't feel like company at the moment.'

'You all right, Kelly?'

'Of course I'm all right. For chrissake, Weston, will you stop treating me like a child.'

Hurt, Weston retorted hotly, 'I will when you stop acting like one.'

Kelly slammed down the telephone and stared at it for a minute, her face smarting as if she'd been slapped. Several angry replies leapt into her head, things she should have said, the 'wise after the event' remarks. She was thinking about ringing Weston back when Jay walked out of the bathroom, a welcome diversion.

His hair was wet. There was something deeply appealing about wet hair, she supposed it had something to do with little boys fresh out of the tub. Seeing him wrapped in a white towel brought back vivid memories of bathtime in her sister's frantic household. Of helping to bathe her two young nephews. The recollection brought a smile to her lips, she could still hear their laughter and squeals of delight when she'd made shapes from the suds: peaked hats and false noses.

Jay could see she was distracted. 'What are you thinking?'

'Oh, I was miles away. Believe it or not, I was thinking about my sister's two kids. They're both grown up now. Luke's out in California at UCLA, and Zach's working in a law firm.'

'I didn't ask, Kelly. Have you got any kids?'

He was pleased when she said no. At least she hadn't had the baby *he'd* longed to have with her – with someone else.

'Didn't you want children; it's not too late, is it?'

'Questions, questions, endless questions! Please, Jay, I don't want any more. Let's order something to eat, I'm starving. Making love always gives me an appetite.'

'Just tell me why you didn't have kids and I'll shut up. I promise.'

Raking her fingers through her hair, she flopped on to the edge of the bed, and not looking at anything in particular said, 'I had an abortion. It went wrong, horribly wrong, not the best experience. The doctor . . . well, you couldn't call him a doctor. This *butcher* –' she spat out the word '– was struck off for malpractice. He was doing illegal terminations, to make a few extra bucks.

'Anyway he made a mess of me inside. After that I tried with my first husband, but I miscarried a couple of times. And then . . .' she raised her hands in a hopeless gesture. 'I gave up and got on with my life. Beth is the only one of us who's had a baby.'

Looking impatient, Kelly picked up the telephone and holding it to her ear, said, 'Now, you promised no more questions.'

He watched her fingers jab the digits, his eyes not leaving her as she spoke to room service. *Turmoil* was the only word he could think of to describe the way he felt, and had felt since last night. His mind ran helter-skelter through the chain of events from meeting Kelly again to now. One thing was clear: Kelly had lied to him. He recalled the tape-recorded conversation between Kelly and Weston the day after he'd met Kelly in Fort Marcy Park. He'd played and replayed it incessantly until he knew it off by heart. She and Weston had been discussing him and he'd detected something in Weston's voice, something he recognized as fear. Why was she afraid if she had nothing to hide? Word for word, part of the conversation ran through his head. *He's just spent the majority of his adult life in prison for something he didn't do.* But if Kelly knew he hadn't killed Matthew, then Weston and Beth must have known too, and that meant the Pact had deliberately kept quiet.

So who *had* killed Matthew? Kelly knew. They, the Pact, they knew.

'Gary, make arrangements to go to Singapore as soon as this snow clears. We'll brainstorm the strategy over breakfast tomorrow morning. I think that concludes the meeting for today. Any questions?' Weston looked round the table at the Summit executive board, eight in all. There was silence. She nodded, collected the pile of files in front of her, stuffed them in her briefcase, then left the room.

Gary Powell caught up with her at the elevator. She was smiling. 'Thanks for the tip about the Nagiao, and Bob Hoffman. I've been waiting for months for a good excuse to get rid of him.'

He returned her smile. 'It worked like a dream.'

The doors slid open and Weston stepped into the elevator, leaving Gary outside. As they began to close again she said, 'Can't have dead wood littering the place. You're going to enjoy being vice president, sales and marketing. Get your office door painted asap.'

He grinned. 'See you tomorrow morning at eight sharp.'

Weston returned to her office. She was buzzing, flying, adrenaline popping. She loved a fight and now she wanted to make love, she always did after winning. For a split second she considered ringing Liz Sheen, who was usually grateful for a decent meal and a good bottle of wine. A vision of Liz the last time they'd been together – drunk, panties round her ankles, falling over and throwing up on Weston's rug – arrested the urge. Instead she called the Mark Hotel. There was no reply from Kelly's room and she left a message with reception: *Sorry about earlier, me and my big mouth, call me when you get in.*

Striding across her office she stopped at the window; from this spot on the forty-second floor she could see miles of concrete and glass, and pick out the detailed chrome work on top of the Chrysler building. This evening it looked like an enormous ice-cream cone. Weston glanced at her watch, it was almost six-thirty and the thought of going back to an empty apartment did not appeal. The snowploughs had been out in force all day, and the sidewalks were clear. She estimated it would take her, on foot, about thirty-five minutes to get across town to the Mark. As she struggled into rubber-soled boots, she planned to stop and buy Kelly a bottle of her favourite champagne. A peace offering and a nice surprise.

Jay dawdled down dark pathways, snaking through the drifts of snow that lay dirtied and surreal under the glutinous yellow light of a lumbering snowplough. The city had taken on a whole new identity. Vast flurries of white, like confetti, whirled around its snow-clad skyscrapers splendid in their eerie grandeur. Bulldozers cleared roads and sidewalks, ramming tons of snow into high piles ready for the scores of huge ten-wheel trucks which had been requisitioned to dump the compacted icebergs in the East River. He marvelled at New York's ability to galvanize itself. All it needed was the mayor's office to call a state of emergency and federal funding kicked in –

suddenly money was no object in getting everything back in action. It was as if the whole of Manhattan was being spring-cleaned by an army of metal-clad Goliaths.

He welcomed the relative silence. He'd been born in vast space, big sky country, in an epic landscape where you could travel for days without encountering a soul. As he was growing up the vastness of the Montana plains had made him feel small and insignificant, yet in touch with his inner self. In prison it was the one thing he'd longed for more than anything else, except Kelly.

His thoughts shifted to her. He'd been loath to leave her, but he had to meet Luther at his apartment at seven-thirty p.m. He'd promised to call her later. It would have been easy to tell himself it was fate that they had met hours before a snowstorm that had forced her to stay in New York. But all that schmaltz about destiny, paths crossing, meant nothing to Jay. They had spent most of the day talking. He had told her things he'd intended taking to his grave; she in turn had confessed to a life of networking, moving in the right social circles – mostly instigated by Weston Kane who was known for her lavish weekend parties at her parents' house in South Hampton. It had all amounted to a steady trawl through the ranks of eligible men and never a thought, he assumed from her cynical remarks, for love as the real reason for two people to share their lives.

Kelly didn't want the same things as him. She said she'd been conditioned to accept the life she had. She talked as if that life had been a fast-running river and she'd been in a boat cast off without a paddle or rudder. He doubted her honesty. There was a thread of steel running through Kelly; however much she might pretend to be a victim of circumstance. He was convinced she had not gone in any direction she herself was not content to follow. Her steel was the tempered kind, making her the type that is determined, and capable of being motivated to great things. It required a certain kind of skill – premeditation, manipulation and constant scheming – to stay afloat in the waters she'd chosen. In Kelly's case she'd used her exquisite face, lovely body and shrewd brain to get precisely what she'd wanted.

Jay wondered about the future. Meeting Kelly again, their love-making, the hours of talking, had somehow killed some of his passion for justice and for pursuing the truth.

He decided that if the movie on *Killing Time* went ahead and according to Ed it was a cert, then he would go to LA and realize his dream – write the screenplay on a terrace overlooking the sea. Who knows, Kelly might decide to join him . . . He stopped to light a cigarette as if to mark his resolve.

In the next instant Weston Kane rounded the corner and saw Jay's face. As he coughed to clear his throat, she ducked into a nearby doorway. First she watched him inhale, flick the match into a mound of freezing snow, and then she watched him pass, getting a closer look at his face. It was Jay Kaminsky, she would have recognized him anywhere. In fact he hadn't changed that much in twenty-five years.

Tugging at her scarf she covered most of her face,

then followed, making sure she kept a discreet distance. When he turned the corner into 68th Street, she stayed on First. Then she rounded the corner into 68th just in time to see him enter an apartment building. After five minutes she approached the entrance and checked the nameplate. 'Will Hope,' his pseudonym, lived in Flat 42a.

Making her way back through the semi-deserted streets to the Mark, she remained deep in thought. Jay Kaminsky was stalking Kelly, of that she was certain.

She called up from the lobby, 'Hi, Kelly, Wes here. Listen I'm sorry about what I said earlier.'

Weston heard a doorbell ring, then heard Kelly, 'Hang on, Wes, I think that's room service.' A couple of seconds later Kelly was back on the phone. 'Just ordered penne arrabiata with lashings of Parmesan, and a side order of French fries!'

Weston smiled. 'Well, I've got something to wash it down with – a bottle of your favourite fizz.' Her deep throaty laughter sounded then, 'Am I forgiven?'

'Nothing to forgive. Come on up.'

As soon as she entered the room, Weston knew Kelly had been making love. She could smell it. The mixture of stale sweat and scent mingled with the musky odour of body fluids and something else, acrid and earthy, something she couldn't place – like incense.

'Don't think it really needs the fridge,' she said, handing over the champagne. Her eyes had been taking in the dishevelled bed, and were now back on Kelly's animated face. 'Was he good?'

A quick peck on Weston's cheek and a whispered, 'What d'you mean?'

Weston looked at the bed again. 'Since when did one person leave a bed looking like that?'

Impulsively Kelly lied, 'Oh, I've been working in bed, had files and papers all over the place.'

'More like working out. Come on, Kel, this is Weston you're talking to.'

'OK so I met a guy a few months ago, we're having a very discreet fling.'

'Be careful, darling, affairs have a habit of becoming very indiscreet, very quickly.'

'I hear you, Weston, and I've decided to end it anyway.'

As she pulled off her gloves Weston asked, 'Anyone I would know?'

Kelly took her coat, saying, 'Doubt it, unless of course you're familiar with the University of Wisconsin science faculty.'

'Ha, that young?'

'No, a lecturer. Good brain, better body. Nice guy, married with two kids. All the best ones are.'

Wrinkling her nose, Weston picked a damp towel and a pile of clothes off a chair. She held the messy bundle away from her as if it were a baby that had just filled its diaper.

With a French fry, Kelly pointed towards the bathroom door. 'Stick them in there.'

'You do it, I hate the stench of sex.'

'Oh for God's sake, Wes, you're so fastidious. Drop them on the floor, housekeeping can sort it out.'

With deliberate distaste Weston placed the bundle on the edge of the bed, checking the chair wasn't wet before sitting down. 'You'll never guess who I've just seen.'

Kelly had opened the champagne and filled two glasses. Now she jabbed her fork into the penne, skewering several tubes. 'Surprise me.'

'Jay Kaminsky! Don't you think it's weird how we keep running into him? I've got friends who were born in the city, and have lived here all their lives, and I'm damned if I ever bump into them. Kaminsky's only been out of prison for a few weeks and all of a sudden he's everywhere. The next thing you know, I'll go into a board meeting and he'll be at the head of the table.'

Kelly pointed with her fork, dribbling tomato sauce on to white linen. 'You're getting paranoid. Are you sure it was Jay? You haven't seen him for twenty-five years.'

'Of course it's him, he's following us. Probably followed me from my office.' Weston made the suggestion knowing that he'd done no such thing. When she'd spotted Jay, he'd been walking in the direction you would take from the Mark Hotel to his apartment block.

Kelly swallowed a tiny piece of chilli, it burnt her tongue. She took a sip of champagne then in a voice deliberately casual, said, 'Did he see you?'

'No, at least I don't think so. There aren't many people out tonight, so I think if he had, it would have been pretty obvious. I followed him to an apartment building on sixty-eighth. I checked, he lives there. Now at least we know his exact whereabouts. I'm worried though. I think you should get some protection. Todd can get you a bodyguard, feed him some line about a screw-ball who's been making suggestive telephone calls. He'll swallow that.'

'Give me a break, Wes. I don't need some beefcake hoodlum watching me pick my nose.'

'Look, this is serious stuff. Just now, when I saw Jay on the street, I had the most terrible premonition.' She tapped her champagne glass. 'At the risk of sounding melodramatic, I really believe you're in danger.'

Pushing her plate to one side, Kelly threw her napkin on top, and leaned back. She looked unperturbed by Weston's fears. 'Quit worrying, Jay wouldn't hurt me.'

Weston was surprised by this complacency. 'Oh yeah?'

'But to please you, Weston, I'll be very careful. Apparently we can expect a thaw tomorrow afternoon, so I'll be outta here and back in the security of M Street. Todd's got that place geared up like Fort Knox.'

As Kelly stood up, her legs felt heavy and her heart fluttered like the wings of a trapped bird. *You're doing OK, doing just fine, stay cool.* She silently encouraged herself over and over again. Picking up Weston's bottle of Laurent Perrier once more, she urged, 'Forget Jay for the moment. Let's just enjoy the bubbles.'

# Chapter Twelve

The *New York Times* was neatly folded and delivered to Beth's door every day at six a.m. sharp. Douglas would read the headlines before he left for work, leaving it on the hall table for Beth to take to the office. It was a ritualistic thing, the same as her first double espresso and cigarette of the day. Apart from the front page and the share index, the newspaper was rarely read, but that wasn't the point – a day in the office without the *New York Times* was unthinkable. Today was different, she couldn't wait to read an article Weston had interrupted her breakfast to tell her about. Cigarette dangling from her bottom lip, Beth turned to a diary item on page 42, and began to read avidly.

In 1973 Jay Kaminsky, a twenty-one-year-old Harvard English student was accused of the murder of his room-mate Matthew Fierstein. After a controversial and lengthy trial, Kaminsky was convicted of second degree murder and sentenced to twenty-five years in Cedar State Penitentiary. He was released three weeks ago. But Kaminsky has wasted no time in making the most out of the lessons he learned from his years of imprisonment. In a whirlwind of activity, and to the delight of the parole board and penal reformers, he is about to prove that ex-cons can become productive members of society. How?

He shared a cell for three years with Alfonso Colacello, who worked for Mafia godfather Mario Petroni for twelve years. Al was a loyal and trusted lieutenant: bagman and hitman collector. He was convicted for the murder of three men, one a drugs enforcement officer in Queens. Kaminsky began a writing career in prison. His first novel, the bestseller *Killing Time*, was published in 1989 by Schnieder and Smith under the pen name of Will Hope. It is believed to be based on the life of Colacello, who is known to have kept secret diaries that have never been discovered and which have long been sought by FBI and Mafia bosses alike. Maxmark Productions are talking to several 'A' list stars about the lead rôle of José, a Mafia hitman not unlike Colacello and nicknamed the 'Teacher'. Media sources confirm that the author is due to fly to LA soon. So Kaminsky – novelist, screenwriter and, who knows, Oscar winner – is now set to become a fêted pillar of the Hollywood establishment.

And just to prove that he's not a one-book wonder, Kaminsky has another ace up his sleeve. During his trial and subsequent unsuccessful appeals, Jay Kaminsky repeatedly protested his innocence. He still does, and now claims to have uncovered new evidence in the Fierstein case and is currently working on a book that will demonstrate his innocence. *Remission*, due for publication in the fall, will no doubt cause considerable controversy among his fellow Harvard alumni. Literary agent Ed Hooper said, 'When I read the first draft of *Killing Time*, I knew I had discovered a great talent in Jay Kaminsky. He is a brilliant contemporary American writer, with a rare gift for combining fact and fiction in a fast-moving narrative. Anyone meeting Jay Kaminsky will be convinced of his honesty and his innocence. *Remission* is another wall banger.'

There was a small amount of pasta vongole in the bottom of the bowl. Mario mopped it up with a chunk of bread and licked his lips. He then reached into the inside pocket of his cashmere jacket, pulling out a thin silver case. It bore his initials in the left-hand corner, and as he flicked it open he thought about his daughter who had bought it for his birthday two years before. Taking out the eighteen-carat gold toothpick, he began to clean his teeth. It was a ritual he enjoyed. A narrow beam from an overhead halogen spotlight shone on his teeth, and a woman on the next table could not help staring. Mario winked at her and she averted her eyes. After five minutes he carefully wiped the toothpick and replaced it in the case. He then straightened his gaudy tie, patted his stomach and waited for his espresso to arrive. The waiters in Sandrinis knew they had to wait until Mr Petroni had smoked his cigar for precisely two minutes before serving his coffee. Once, a new waiter had been too prompt; the kid had got the coffee back – over his head.

His secretary, Rosa, was calling on his mobile phone. 'Sorry to disturb you, Mr Petroni, but I've just had a Weston Kane on the line. She said it was very urgent.'

The name rang a loud bell. It was the broad who'd just masterminded a six-billion dollar merger with Avesta – Sinclair Kane's daughter, a chip off the old block. Everyone had heard of Sinclair Kane – paparazzi fodder.

Mario was curious. 'Did she say what she wanted?'

'All she said was that you should read page forty-two of today's *New York Times*. And if you're interested in knowing where Will Hope is at the moment, call her on 798 2567.'

Mario put the phone down, and called to the head waiter, 'Sam, you got a *Times*?'

'Sorry, Mr Petroni, I'll send out for one.'

'Make it quick, Sam.'

Only minutes later Mario was holding the paper in front of his face. With each paragraph he was reminded of the first time he'd read *Killing Time*, and had realized that the godfather character was based on himself. As soon as he'd finished reading, he picked up the mobile and dialled Weston's number.

Al and Jay had been cell mates, he knew that for certain, and no doubt Al had sung sweet lullabies to Jay while getting his dick sucked, spilling out all he knew about yours truly. Did Kaminsky have Al's diaries, he wondered? The ones Al had used as a threat, the ones with information that could put him and several others inside for life? Mario had lost count of how many lives had been sacrificed over the years in the quest for the mythical Colacello diaries.

He waited impatiently to be put through to Weston, and when she eventually came on the line he spared no time for pleasantries. 'This is Mario Petroni. I believe you have some information for me.'

Weston was equally brusque. 'If you want to talk to Jay Kaminsky, he's staying at apartment 42a, 1597 Sixty-eighth and First.'

'Thank you, Miss Kane. I want you to know that I'm a very appreciative man, and I never forget favours.' With that he put the phone down. He then made another call; his instructions were brief and concise. 'A guy called Jay Kaminsky is staying at 1597 Sixty-eighth and First, apartment 42a. Bring him to me.'

Ed returned Jay's call from the side of the swimming pool of the Sandpiper Hotel in the Bahamas.

'Janet said it was urgent. What can be so urgent that you drag me away from my pina colada, and Jenni's ass?'

Jay was angry. 'The article in the *New York Times*. What the fuck are you playing at, Ed?'

'Look, the reporter called. I told him about the movie deal. I thought you'd be pleased; it's great publicity for the book.' Ed sounded nonplussed.

'Did you have to tell him Will Hope was Jay Kaminsky?'

Ed moved the phone to his other ear.

'I didn't. It just ain't a secret any more, man. Hell, you know what journalists are like – dogs with bones. They can extract information as easily as Carole can extract money from me.'

'It's not funny,' Jay said.

'So who's laughing?'

'Not me. The mob can read y'know. The *Times* has just told them my real name. As well as drawing their attention to the fact that *Killing Time* is their story, based on the diaries of my cell mate.'

Ed still wasn't sure where Jay was coming from. 'So it's non-fiction, tell me more.'

'The godfather character is based on Mario Petroni, who's probably gunning for me, like right now. If Petroni gets his hands on me, I'm fucked. Well more than that, I'm history.'

Ed dropped his feet either side of his lounger and sat up straight. 'You serious, Jay?'

'I don't have to tell you how tenacious the mob can be, or how dangerous. I would suggest you extend your vacation. They might come after you to get to me.'

Ed swallowed. He could feel sweat gathering in the centre of his palms and a nerve in his temple began to jerk uncontrollably. 'I kinda like it down here, and the weather's still shitty in New York. I think I'll hang out in the Islands for a while.'

'Very sensible. I might be joining you. You have my mobile number. Keep in touch, and be careful. Let's see how fast they read the papers. Meantime I'll make a few calls to some old friends from the pen, they'll know if the word's gone out on the street. If nothing happens in the next few days, it ain't gonna happen and we can get back to normal.' Jay rang off.

Quietly he sat calculating his next move. He had to think like Mario Petroni, try to put himself in the godfather's shoes. He knew Mario wouldn't come after him in person; he'd leave it to his henchmen – lookalike, talkalike, thinkalike Al Colacellos. Killing machines. Jay began to pace the floor. He knew he had to get out of town, snow or no snow.

An hour later when the intercom rang in his apartment, he was busy packing. At first he ignored it, then after four minutes of continuous ringing he looked out of the window on to the street. He saw Kelly stabbing at the bell, and he spoke to the intercom: 'Yes?'

'Jay, I need to talk to you.'

He pressed the buzzer to open the door. 'Come on up, fourth floor.'

When she entered the apartment the first thing she noticed was the open suitcase. 'You planning on going somewhere? It's just been on the news that there's no flights taking off before Friday at the earliest. I thought you were going to ring. I thought you might come back last night for a nightcap.'

'Like I said, I had to meet a friend. We had a bit of business to sort out. It went on.'

Again she glanced at the suitcase. 'So where are you going, Jay?'

'I'm going home.' He was lying and they both knew.

'In this?' She pointed to the window. Her speech was slurred and he suspected she'd been drinking.

'Yeah, with wheel chains. I'll head due south-west, and be out of this shit in a couple of days. I'm going to spend some time with my mother, like I told you she's not well. Then I'm going to LA, get me some rays, hit the beach, all the things I never got to do when I was young. Middle-aged adolescence, fun huh?' He felt edgy, strung out, and started jabbering to cover his nervousness. 'Get to do all those crazy things I missed, like hanging out in bars, skate boarding, making love on the beach, dancing all night in discos . . . doing drugs.'

Kelly was drunk, very drunk, and now she couldn't stop shaking. Her heart banged so loud in her own ears she thought she might be going mad.

'I killed Matthew Fierstein.'

She'd said it, at long last it was out. She'd admitted the crime she'd buried so deep. So deep she'd even begun to think it had never happened.

'What did you just say?'

Kelly couldn't meet Jay's eyes. 'I said I killed Matt. I came to find you and he was there. He raped me, we struggled, I – '

She let out a high-pitched squeal, a kind of animal noise between a yelp and a groan. Then her eyes closed, and she was back there. Back in Matthew's room, bound to the bed, rope burning the inside of her wrists and ankles as she struggled to free herself. She opened her eyes but it was not Jay's face she saw. It was Matthew's – contorted with a mixture of lust and barely contained rage. He was speaking very quietly and precisely, which scared her more than if he'd been yelling. 'I'm not going

197

*to hurt you, Kelly, I promise. First I'm going to open you up, and fuck you with my hand. You want me to, don't you? Tell me you want me.'* She saw him pull the knife from behind his back. *'This is to make you do as you're told.'* With the knife sticking in the side of her throat, Matthew hissed in her ear. *'Now keep quiet, you're going to enjoy this.'*

Kelly blinked several times and the scene inside her head went blank. She opened her eyes to Jay, his features frozen in shock. 'He raped me, he raped me I tell you! What was I supposed to do? Let him get away with it? He bound my hands and feet, he put his goddamn fist inside me.'

She was shouting now, out of control. 'I didn't mean to kill him. It was an accident. He had a knife, and I managed to free one of my wrists. I grabbed the knife or he would have killed me. I never wanted you to take the blame. It was Weston and Beth. They said no one would believe he'd raped me; they'd say I led him on. They told me terrible things about prison. I didn't expect you to be accused and indicted. And when you were, Weston said that if you were convicted you wouldn't get long. You had an exemplary character ... the prosecution had a weak case ... we all thought you'd be acquitted. I went along with it because I was terrified. You *have* to believe me, Jay. I had an abortion, I got rid of his baby.'

With both hands she gripped her stomach, long nails digging deep into the soft flesh.

'I ripped his baby out of me. Killed it like I killed him.' Suddenly her voice changed to that of a child's, a little girl pleading. 'I'm sorry, please don't hurt me. Say you love me still, I don't want to go away from home.'

She came towards him staggering, arms flailing, her head on one side, mouth slack. Saliva dribbling on to her chin, eyes rolling, she spouted, 'Kelly loves Jay, you forgive Kelly, don't you? Tell Kelly you forgive her. *Please.*'

The dramatic hush that followed her outburst was broken by the sound of loud banging on the apartment door. Jay somehow mustered his senses and crept to the window where he spotted a man in the street below. He couldn't see his face, only his brown overcoated figure hunched over the door of a Lincoln Continental parked outside the entrance to the building. It was then that Kelly tripped and, reaching out to balance herself, she caught her hand on the suitcase. It fell with a crash, the contents spilling to the floor.

A moment later the door of the apartment burst open, and two men were inside. The taller of them stood in front of Jay. He had a mobile genial kind of face, with ruddy cheeks and soft-focus brown eyes. It was the sort of face advertising execs love to use in commercials for life insurance, or real estate. A face to trust. 'You Jay Kaminsky?'

Jay thought about denying it, then decided that was stupid. He knew exactly who had sent these intruders.

'Yes.'

'Mr Petroni wants a quiet chat.' The voice matched the face, softly persuasive. 'You can either come with no fuss. Or the other way, which always makes a mess.'

Jay knew it was pointless to argue. 'Can I get my coat?'

The same man spoke. 'Sure.' With his eyes he instructed his accomplice to follow Jay into the next room, whilst he maintained a relaxed guard over a cowering Kelly. As Jay grabbed his coat, his mind was racing as to means of escape. There was one small window in the bedroom, with a fire exit leading to the street below. He assessed the man marking him: he was short, stocky, built like a small bull, and in direct contrast to his accomplice he actually looked like a hitman – with 'mean business' stamped over every inch of his killer-dog face. There was an acid taste in Jay's mouth, and he could feel the adrenaline pumping, driving fear out of his gut as he examined his limited options.

It was then that he heard the shots. And on re-entering the main room at a dash, the first thing he saw was a great splash of red daubed on the wall like scarlet graffiti. The tall man lay sprawled across the floor, his head was twisted at an odd angle and he looked like a half-decapitated rag doll. There was a gun next to his body, and another in Kelly's hand.

Clad in beige wool, she lifted her arm, displaying the front of her dress besmirched with blood. With a steady grip she directed the gun at Jay. 'I brought this along in case you wouldn't forgive me.'

Her voice sounded as casual as if she'd just suggested they go out for a pizza. Jay felt his heart leap into his throat as she fired two more shots. The first one hit the hoodlum behind him on the side of the temple; the second, a better shot, got the same guy straight between the eyes.

Shocked into total silence, Jay did not even notice that Kelly was bleeding. A moment later the gun slid from her hand, and she slumped to the floor. It was only when he automatically fell to his knees beside her, that he felt the wetness from the open wound in her chest seeping on to his hand, warm and sticky. Her eyes were closing, but her lips were moving and she was trying to say something. When he leaned closer he heard her murmur, 'Am I forgiven?'

Her eyes had shut, and he wasn't sure if she had heard his whispered, 'Yes'.

# Chapter Thirteen

'I know the Miranda rights. I refuse to answer any more questions until I've consulted an attorney.' Jay spoke with quiet conviction, a tone that completely belied the turmoil inside his head.

He was in the 19th precinct, midtown Manhattan, on 153 East 67th Street. He'd been there since his arrest four hours previously. The few moments after he'd discovered Kelly was dead were very clear. He'd felt overwhelmed by pain, then he'd felt completely numb as if he'd had an anaesthetic. And it was at this point that his survival instinct had kicked in, and the urge to run had taken hold.

He'd heard the thumping on his door, loud and insistent, then the voices of neighbours asking if everything was OK. He'd ignored them and run to the bedroom where he'd hoisted himself up to the window above the bed. It had been a struggle to wriggle through the narrow space but he'd made it, falling head first on to the fire escape. Scrambling to his feet, he'd seen a figure in the street below and a big black face staring up at him. It was shouting something Jay couldn't hear. Then he'd started to run, pounding feet on steel. He heard the shot ricochet off the wall a few feet from his face, then the same voice again. This time Jay had heard loud and clear.

'This is the police. Stop, throw down your arms, and put your hands in the air.'

He remembered obeying and standing motionless while he was approached, frisked, handcuffed and read his rights. The same detective who had made the arrest was standing closest to Jay now. The man was tall, broad-shouldered and black. With a sigh he turned to his partner, then he conceded, 'OK, Kaminsky, you got one call.'

Ed was out of town and the only other person Jay knew with any clout was Bob Horvitz, his publisher at Schnieder and Smith. He got the number from directories and prayed that Bob wasn't on vacation or away on business. His luck was in; the vice president was in town, but in a meeting. His PA promised Mr Horvitz would return the call asap. While Jay waited he felt his emotions undergo yet another reaction and he was consumed by an immense sense of loss. He was surprised he felt no anger at Kelly's admission. She had, after all, stood by and allowed him to take the rap for a crime she had committed. Yet he didn't despise her for it and he wished, oh God how he wished, he'd had time to tell her that he truly forgave her and that all his anger was reserved for the real criminal. Jay felt Matthew Fierstein was totally to blame for his own wasted life in prison and for Kelly's anguished existence.

So they had both suffered he thought, and he pictured the young Kelly trying to lead a normal life, tortured by her terrible secret. How far away it all was, he acknowledged, from the two young lovers they had once been.

The ringing of the telephone intruded and he was grateful for the digression as the detective handed him the telephone and he heard a female voice say, 'Mr Kaminsky? Please hold for Mr Horvitz.'

The day had not started well, had got progressively worse, and by two-thirty when Lauren Stone returned to her office she was feeling highly stressed. Justice Abe Simpson had been difficult to the point of impossible and her crucial witness for the defence had been injured in a road accident and was on life support.

Asking her secretary for a large pot of black coffee, she lit a cigarette, crushed the empty packet in her hand and vowed to give up smoking. She thought about her brother Tony who had recently undergone hypnosis and was doing well. He hadn't had a cigarette in five weeks, but his wife was considering filing for divorce if he didn't start again soon.

Since she wasn't married, or even dating, she didn't have to worry about taking her withdrawal symptoms out on anyone else. *Why aren't you dating?* she asked herself. Then: *When was the last time you got laid?* Exhaling, she tried to remember. Six months, maybe more?

It had not been the most memorable experience, done more out of necessity than lust, and certainly not love. The last time she'd done it for *that* reason had been three years ago, and she'd since made a solemn vow that she would never become involved with a married man again.

The coffee arrived exactly as she liked it, very black and very strong. As she took her first sip she smiled, hearing her father's voice, 'That stuff's going to take the lining off your stomach.' Thinking about her father reminded her she hadn't spoken to him in a couple of weeks, and she scribbled a note in her diary under Sunday's date: *Call Dad.*

Then she put a line through lunch at Melissa's, and wrote in capital letters WORK. Melissa Goodman would be disappointed, but Lauren knew she'd understand. How often had she heard her closest friend say, 'Lauren's work is more important than anything else,' and then with a proud smile add, 'That's why she's so successful.'

Lauren had also heard Melissa's husband on more than one occasion comment, 'That's why Lauren is never with a man.' In the best well-meaning, matchmaking fashion, Dale and Melissa had organized several dates – dragging along Dale's business colleagues and friends. Eighteen months ago it had started with Robert, an attractive thirty-eight-year-old business consultant. Recently separated from a stunning wife and five-year-old daughter, he was still an emotional wreck. Then, a few weeks later, it was Tom. He'd been interested in the occult, and had asked her to go to some weird séance. Finally there'd been Adam – at sixty-two a year older than her father and not so good-looking. He'd just had therapy for three years to try and control his obsessive desire for tidiness and hygiene.

The final straw had been a disastrous dinner when Adam had wiped crumbs, real and imaginary, off the table countless times, straightened the cutlery, neatly refolded all their napkins, and asked the waiter to change the table-cloth when Lauren spilt a couple of drops of coffee.

Lauren had spent the remainder of that evening convincing Melissa and Dale that she enjoyed her work, felt fulfilled, found celibacy a positive and therapeutic experience, and was perfectly happy . . . finally making them promise to stop fixing her up with blind dates. Absolute bullshit of course, but anything to stop herself being bombarded by needy, self-obsessed men who bored her rigid.

Work was preferable, and it was true she did love it. Lauren Stone had always wanted to be a lawyer. Well, ever since a momentous November morning in 1979 when she'd watched her father, in front of an all-white jury and a packed courthouse, present his closing argument in the defence of a twenty-four-year-old black man accused of the rape and murder of a middle-aged white woman. Lauren had never forgotten the look in the man's eyes when he'd been acquitted. Or the resounding media hysteria which followed.

Her father had wanted her to study law at Harvard, but she'd chosen Vassar where she was brilliant at debate in her mock trials, number three in her class and expected to graduate summa cum laude.

In her third year Lauren had been approached by Kaufman and Wolf, the second biggest law firm in New York. Josh Stone, certain that his daughter was being used as the gratuitous black female in a pool of white Anglo Saxon males, had tried unsuccessfully to dissuade her from joining the prestigious firm.

But Lauren wanted to fly high, and at twenty-seven she became the first female defence lawyer in Kaufman and Wolf to get an acquittal on a case of first-degree murder.

The media loved it. Lauren Stone, young and beautiful with *café au lait* skin . . . One columnist had described her as a 'supermodel lawyer'. It was at this point that she had turned her back on the uptown practice, on the spacious glass and monochrome office suite, on the million-dollar billings. All for a sole practice in a downtown, run-down 1930s building near the courthouse. That was nine years ago and she had never once regretted her decision. Lauren had proved she could be a high flyer. But once up there, the glittering prizes soon tarnished, and she had found herself losing touch with the real issues, real people, and had felt a strong desire to get back to her grass roots. Possessions were of little interest to her, she didn't own a car or an expensive wardrobe. Her apartment in Tribe-ca, though comfortable, was sparsely furnished with the basic requirements of living and no added frills. An old boyfriend had described her as the original minimalist before it became a lifestyle.

Lauren had ground her cigarette out and was pouring a second cup of coffee when the phone rang. It was Bob Horvitz. He introduced himself and then elaborated, 'You may or may not remember me. We met briefly at a Greenwich book fair in 1987. I edited a book your father wrote.'

Her father had written several non-fiction books. 'Which one?'

'*A History of Louisiana Law*. I'm vice president of Schnieder and Smith. I was an editor back then.'

Lauren frowned in concentration as a picture began to emerge of a short squat man, immaculately dressed and fast talking. Yes, she vaguely remembered him holding court at the Schnieder and Smith stand.

'I do remember a fair in the Village,' she said and added, 'So what can I do for you, Mr Horvitz?'

'You ever heard of someone called Jay Kaminsky?'

'Doesn't ring any bells, should I have?'

'No, not especially. Just thought you might have read something about him. In 1973 Kaminsky was convicted of killing his Harvard room-mate. He went down for twenty-five years, and while he was in prison he started to write. His agent sent me his first manuscript, *Killing Time*. It was great stuff, the best novel I'd read in years. I published it and we had an international best-seller for about eighteen weeks.'

Lauren put her coffee cup down. 'Yeah, I remember that book, I read it on vacation somewhere. But wasn't it written by someone called Hope?'

'Yeah, Will Hope – Kaminsky's pen name. He was released a couple of weeks back, and a couple of days ago there was a piece in the *New York Times* about him writing another book called *Remission*. He claims he didn't do the killing, and that he's uncovered new evidence to prove his innocence.'

'So what's this got to do with me?'

Bob had swung his feet off his desk and was leaning forward. 'In 1973 when Jay was convicted of the killing of Matthew Fierstein, he was a brilliant English scholar, and he was dating a girl called Kelly Tyler, same year at Wellesley. Apparently Matthew wanted Kelly and they fought over her. Anyway that was then. This is now and all I know they've got Jay downtown in the nineteenth precinct on suspicion of first degree murder.'

At her end, Lauren also sat up. 'Who this time?'

'That's the interesting bit. He was arrested while trying to escape from his apartment. I suppose when your apartment's littered with three dead bodies, it gets a little crowded. Two mobsters, Mario Petroni's hitmen so Jay says, and Kelly Prescott.'

'Senator Todd Prescott's wife?'

'None other, and guess what her maiden name was?'

Lauren didn't need to guess, she already knew. '*Tyler.*'

Standing poker straight, his back facing the prison bars, Jay didn't move when the door swung open.

'Jay Kaminsky?'

At first he still didn't move and when he did she was aware of the deep cut of his back muscles suddenly rippling under blue cotton denim. When he was in full view she could see that he had hard defined pectorals, and a washboard-flat stomach.

'You are Jay Kaminsky?'

'I am. And you are?' He faced her, rooted to the spot.

She moved towards him, hand outstretched. 'I'm Lauren Stone, criminal attorney.'

His eyes narrowed. 'Who sent you?'

As she stood in front of him he saw that her skin

was marble smooth, and she had the kind of mouth that usually only appeared in his erotic dreams – the luscious full-lipped dark red kind. It opened to speak, showing white teeth, the front ones slightly overcrowded.

'Bob Horvitz. He said you needed a good defence lawyer.'

Jay nodded. 'Yeah, Bob mentioned a female lawyer he knew, said you're choosy who you defend.'

She smiled, she had a nice smile, warm without being overpowering. 'I have to believe in who I'm defending. I know that might sound a bit corny coming from a New York lawyer . . . considering our reputations. I bill between five hundred and a thousand dollars an hour depending on the case, plus expenses. I'm focused, totally committed to every individual case, and I get results. I don't like losing, it doesn't happen very often because I'm good at what I do. You want to talk?'

Jay took one long step in her direction, now their faces were a few inches apart. 'Yes, I'd like to talk.' He was drawn to her obvious femininity and felt a slight *frisson* of attraction pass between them.

Lauren steeled herself to hold his steady gaze for a few moments. It was something she did with all her potential clients. Instinct, the gut feeling, the one that had only failed her once.

'Would you like to take a seat?' he asked politely, indicating a chair.

She nodded and sat down on one side of a dirty table, crossing her legs as Jay sat opposite on the only other chair. She was wearing a pinstripe suit with a pencil skirt and long boxy jacket that hung loosely on her narrow frame. Underneath she wore a white shirt with a tie at the neck. She was very thin and when she moved the jacket fell open, and he noticed that she had tiny breasts, small mounds like a pubescent girl.

Lauren took a pen and notepad out of her briefcase, then she opened a file and Jay spotted a photograph of himself taken during his trial. He ran a hand across his brow. It was wet and he wiped his palm down the side of his jeans. 'I can't believe this is happening to me again. It's like a repeat nightmare, only this time I'm accused of *three* murders.'

She noticed the hand he'd used to wipe his brow was shaking. 'Tell me exactly what happened.'

'You got a cigarette?'

She nodded and produced a pack of Marlboro which she threw in his direction.

He lit up, inhaled, exhaled, then began. 'Kelly came to my apartment to see me. Petroni's men came calling and –' Suddenly he stopped speaking, his mind went blank. All he could see was blood, Kelly's blood, spurting, soaking everything. 'It was like a running tap.'

Lauren asked, 'What was?'

'Kelly's blood, she was hit in the chest.'

'Yes I know. I've got the coroner's report. Who shot her?'

'One of Petroni's men I assume, I'm not sure, she could have shot herself.' He said the only thing he could, 'I wasn't there when it happened.'

'What were they all doing in your apartment?'

Jay looked down at his hands, then carefully placed one on each thigh, his fingernails digging into the firm flesh. He'd already thought about his reply, had practised it word for word. It was designed to test Lauren Stone's mettle.

'I shared a cell with Al Colacello for three years. He was Mario Petroni's trusted lieutenant for twelve years. Mario doesn't like to get his hands dirty, but Al was the opposite. Called himself "Teach and Reach"; there was no one he couldn't get to, no hit he couldn't reach. The man was a killing machine and the pair were a match made in true Cosa Nostra heaven. Al overdosed in the pen, but before he died he said that he wanted his ashes taken back to Naples, and that Mario would sort it out. He made me promise that if he died before me, I had to contact Mario when I got out, and that Mario would make all the arrangements. I did what he asked, and Mario sent his men round to collect.'

When Lauren looked up, her expression had changed from interest to irritation. 'Come on, Jay, you can do better than that. Two serious mob boys collecting ashes? Sounds like something out of your next novel. I want the truth.'

Jay was relieved at her response. Now he knew she was for real. Aware of his vision clouding, he blinked rapidly to clear his eyes. When he spoke his voice was very distinct like an actor repeating lines verbatim. 'I didn't kill anyone. Not then, not now.'

Lauren uncrossed her legs. 'I didn't say you did. I

simply asked for an explanation as to why two known Mafia men and a prominent senator's wife were in your apartment.' With a long sigh she suggested, 'Perhaps you'd like to start at the beginning, Jay.'

'By the beginning do you mean when I first met Kelly?'

Lauren replied, 'Yes. I want you to go back to when you guys first met, right through to yesterday. I'll try not to interrupt, and I want the truth, and nothing but the truth.'

'So help me God,' Jay finished the sentence and looking towards the ceiling said, 'Except that I'm going to need more than some fucking imaginary force to get me out of this mess.'

*Anger and bitterness.* Lauren had seen the combination many times before. But there was something else in Jay's expression, a profound sense of sadness, and for some inexplicable reason she found herself wanting to comfort him. With a dismissive shrug she leaned back, chewed her bottom lip and prepared to listen.

Squeezing his eyes shut, Jay rubbed the eyelids then opened them and in a methodical voice, he began to speak.

'OK, from the top. I met Matthew Fierstein when I went up to Harvard. As the whole world knows, we were room-mates. But we were more than that, we were best buddies . . .'

She listened intently to his voice. The timbre, deep and mellow, was very warm, very satisfying, and seemed incongruous in the shabby austerity of the prison cell.

His diction fascinated her, it was perfect, and his accent like nothing she'd ever heard before.

As Jay's voice filled the room, Lauren took notes. When he got to the part about seeing Kelly in New York after his release, he faltered and Lauren glanced up – detecting a change in both his tone and his body language.

Jay's neck muscles were protruding and his lips were stretched taut, like an elastic band. She found herself dwelling on his mouth, then reprimanded herself as he continued.

'She was meeting Weston Kane and Beth Morgan for lunch. I followed her to the restaurant, and sent a silly message to the table. I've always suspected they had something to do with Matthew's murder. No hard evidence, just a gut instinct. When I got out of the pen, I was hellbent on seeking justice, and I followed Kelly to DC, took an apartment opposite and bugged her house. I listened in to her telephone conversations – the most interesting were with Weston Kane. Several times they both referred to the fact that they knew I was innocent. I now know why, because Kelly admitted killing Matthew.'

Lauren looked stunned. 'When did she admit this?'

Jay lied, 'In a conversation with Weston.'

'Where are the tapes?'

'With a trusted friend, here in New York.'

Lauren sighed, 'I'd sure like to listen to them. But if we prove that Kelly killed Fierstein and then conspired against you, it only suggests more motive for you to have murdered her. Revenge, retribution. And who could blame you? Framed for a crime committed by the girl you loved, and had intended to marry. Anyone in your position would have wanted to do the same. Is that what you did, Jay?'

The sound of his bunched fists banging on the table startled her, and she flinched.

'No. That wasn't the way it was. Like I've told the police, when I came back to my apartment they were all dead.'

'But you did see Kelly again before that, didn't you?'

'Yes, I saw Kelly again.' Jay felt his chest tighten, and he was afraid he might begin to cry. He fought it by taking a deep breath. 'I found out she was going to a benefit in DC; I managed to wangle an invitation. She was shocked to see me there and accused me of following her. I begged her to meet me; she agreed and the following day we met again in the park . . . and talked.' At this point he stood up, almost as if he had to acknowledge the strength of his inner feeling by some physical gesture. Then he managed to carry on. 'For all those years in prison I carried a torch for her. And when I saw her again, she looked even more beautiful than I remembered and I realized that I'd never stopped loving her. Later I think Kelly realized that it was the same way for her, and that her whole life had been one long fucked-up lie. I now believe that in her own way she suffered as much as me for what she did.'

Lauren had stopped writing. A hush fell on the room, the only sound Jay's heavy breathing.

He sat down again, and when he resumed it was in a matter-of-fact delivery. 'I assume Mario Petroni sent his men for me because he wanted to call me in to talk about his old pal Alfonso. To see if Al sang sweet lullabies while penned up with me for three years. Kelly just got caught up in it, the wrong place at the wrong time. Ironic don't you think? Like history repeating itself. And that's it, Miss Stone, right down the line, no bullshit.' Jay made the sign of the cross on the breast pocket of his shirt. 'Cross my heart, and hope to die.'

Lauren shot him a quizzical look.

'Something else I picked up from a guy in prison.'

In reflective mood Lauren closed the file and placed it in her briefcase. Then she went straight into official mode. 'After I leave they're taking you down to central booking, where you'll be detained. And within twenty-four hours you have to appear before a judge to hear the charges against you. I could ask for bail, but I'm certain it'll be refused, so I'll reserve my right to request bail later. We've then got six days before the Grand Jury sit to vote for your release or indictment. Have you any evidence to suggest you didn't commit the murders? Anyone who could testify on your behalf?'

'My prints aren't on any of the guns.'

'You could have wiped them clean. Now, you were picked up leaving your apartment. The guy next door called the police, I believe.'

Jay nodded. 'Yeah, that's right.'

'Why were you running away, Jay?'

'I was scared. I've just come out of the pen; I didn't, I *don't* want to go back in. My first instinct was to get the hell out of there.'

'Before you got back to your apartment where had you been?'

'With a friend.'

'Name?'

'The same guy who's got the tapes; Luther Ross.'

'Would he testify that you were with him at the time of the murders?'

With more conviction than he felt, Jay said, 'Sure.'

'Great, where can I contact him?'

He gave her Luther's telephone number and address, not even sure if his old pal was still in the same apartment. Jay followed this up by asserting softly, 'I didn't kill anyone. I am telling the truth, do you believe me?'

Frown lines appeared between the lawyer's eyebrows; then her forehead relaxed.

'I believe that you're not telling me the whole truth. I think you're telling me what you want me to know. For now.'

For the first time since they'd met, Jay smiled with genuine warmth. Silently he admired her perception, his mouth curled at the corners before he said, 'I'm in deep shit, Miss Stone; I don't need to be told. I'm a convicted felon with traceable Mafia connections through knowing Al, and *Killing Time*. And I have a history with Kelly Prescott. I already feel like a dead man. All I can say is that I have never in my whole life killed anyone. I ask you again, do you believe me?'

Lauren held his searching gaze for a few moments before replying emphatically, 'Yes I do.'

# Chapter Fourteen

'Kelly Prescott will be sorely missed. All of you gathered here today must take comfort in the knowledge that she is leaving this mortal life to begin another one, a better one, in the Kingdom of our Lord. Now let us pray.'

As Father Denihan began the prayer, Weston bowed her head. At the same time, she felt Beth's hand reach for hers. She clasped it tightly and together they prayed. Weston prayed for a long and painful death for Jay. Since his arrest she'd thought of little else but revenge. Not since the death of her father had she felt as distraught as when Todd Prescott had called her with the news of Kelly's murder. At first she'd been in a state of total denial, unable to come to terms with the reality that she would never see Kelly again.

Lifting her eyes, Weston glimpsed the back of Todd's head. His shoulders were moving up and down and she knew he was weeping. A recollection of the Prescotts' wedding day flashed into her head. It had been blustery weather with showers. Kelly's dress had blown up, billowing around the top of her legs. And she'd held it down, throwing her head back and giggling in true Marilyn Monroe style.

'We will now sing Hymn number forty-three in your hymn books.'

As the first bars of 'The Lord is My Shepherd' rang out in the crowded church, Weston felt a great surge of sadness. It had been her father's favourite. She was afraid to look at Beth who she realized was crying silently. But she knew the words off by heart and she joined the choir in singing loud and defiantly, as if to ward off her own tears.

She loathed public displays of grief, much preferring to wallow in private. She'd been doing that for the last four days, and had told herself in no uncertain terms that it had to end. She knew anger would soon replace the grief, and that with it would come the positive will to avenge Kelly's death.

She was followed out of the church by Beth and they walked arm in arm to the grave. 'It was a beautiful service,' Beth commented.

Weston disagreed. 'It was, like all funeral services, depressing. The priest looked bored and rushed most of his sermon. He seemed pleased when it was all over. He's probably got something much more exciting to do later, like getting a blow job from one of his choirboys.'

At first Beth chose not to reply. It was typical of Weston to react in a flippant way when she was deeply upset. Then, staring at one of the pallbearers and recognizing him as Kelly's brother, she said in a quiet expressionless voice, 'I'm still trying to come to terms with her death.'

'I never will,' Weston returned and Beth knew she meant it.

At the grave they stood side by side: Beth with Kelly's sister-in-law on her other side and Weston alongside Todd's ageing mother, who was in a wheelchair. Weston could not bear to watch the lowering of the coffin, instead she watched a lone blackbird swoop from the branches of a handsome cedar tree. Like a sentinel it perched on top of a nearby headstone, beady eyes directed at the funeral party.

As the first soil hit the lid of the coffin, the bird cawed twice and was off, flying high above the graveyard, a flash of black on a watery grey sky.

As they trooped towards the cars it began to snow, white spots briefly speckling Beth's black felt hat before melting to leave a watermark. Weston wanted to go home and it was with dread that she climbed into the black funeral car that would take her and Beth to M Street and Todd's house, where they were expected to take part in a buffet lunch. She was tempted to instruct the driver to go straight to the airport, but the thought of Todd's displeasure harnessed the impulse. She pulled her hat off, and tried not to be irritated by the sound of Beth sniffling beside her.

Between nose blowing, Beth managed to say, 'I can't believe I'm never going to see her again. I said to Doug last night if it was my sister or my mother I couldn't be more upset. In fact I can't imagine feeling this bad if I lost Doug.'

*No loss*, thought Weston and said, 'It's the thought of

not having protected her that I can't come to terms with. I feel so full of fucking rage I could kill Jay Kaminsky with my bare hands.' She paused and her voice lowered, 'I knew he'd get her; I had a premonition about it.'

Beth looked out of the window. She didn't feel like talking about Jay at the moment. She wanted to fill her head with thoughts and images of Kelly. Wonderful memories of times they'd shared: the good times; fun times; times when they were young and all they had to worry about was what dress to wear to whatever party, and who was dating whom.

The car had pulled into M Street and parked behind Todd's limo. As Weston alighted she spotted Todd talking to a tall man with a shock of jet black hair. When he saw Weston he excused himself and turned to face her with open arms. She felt a sharp pang in her chest as she fell into his embrace, and with a loud exhale of breath began to cry. It was the first time she'd cried since Kelly's death. Todd stroked her head and muttered quietly, 'It's OK, Weston. It's OK.'

When her sobs had subsided, she wiped her face with the back of her hand and took a long breath. Todd noticed she'd lost weight, the skin on her neck was hanging as if it didn't fit properly.

'Sorry isn't enough, is it, Todd?'

'What else is there?'

Beth stood behind Weston. 'There's justice for the person who did this to her.'

Todd acknowledged this with a curt nod. 'I can't understand why anyone would want to kill Kelly. The police say that the man they're holding, this Jay Kaminsky, is a convicted felon. And he claims to have known Kelly when they were both at college. The other two men were hitmen, also known to the police. What on earth was she mixed up in, Weston? She always confided in you.'

When Weston shook her head helplessly, Todd continued, 'She gave me no inkling that there was anything wrong. Apart from the fact that she'd been on edge for the last few weeks. She'd put it down to hormone problems or something. Now I realize there was something much more sinister going on and I intend to get to the bottom of it. If this Kaminsky creep did kill her, I'll fight for the severest sentence.'

Weston knew that Kelly had always taken pains to put her involvement in the Fierstein trial behind her as far as Todd was concerned. She dropped her voice to a conspiratorial whisper as she enlightened him a little. 'When we were kids in college, Jay Kaminsky was in love with Kelly. His room-mate also had the hots for her. They fought over her and Jay killed the other guy. He was convicted and went to prison for twenty-five years. I believe he always blamed Kelly and when he was released he wanted revenge.'

Weston waited for her words to sink in before continuing. 'Kaminsky's got Lauren Stone to defend him. She's one of the best criminal lawyers in New York, only lost one case in God knows how many years. If he's indicted, we've got to get the best prosecution that money can buy. In my opinion there's only one man for the job: Richard McCormick. If anyone can beat Stone, it's McCormick.'

'Where can he be reached?'

Weston took Todd's hand. 'Leave it to me, I'll contact him and make all the necessary arrangements.'

'Todd Prescott is gunning for Kaminsky. Apparently he's taken advice from Rick McCormick, and if our man is indicted he wants no less than another life sentence. Not only is he playing the grieving husband out for justice, but he's also cast himself as the prominent politician, the potential Republican president who wants to use his own case as a stand in the fight against crime. Not just for himself, but "for the people of America". What bullshit!'

Lauren moved the telephone from her left to her right ear, and with her free hand she lit a cigarette. She was listening to Brad Lee, her clerk, and thinking about Todd Prescott. She'd met him once, a few years ago at a dinner she'd attended with her father in New Orleans. She'd found him very agreeable if a trifle bland.

'Prescott can rant and rave as much as he likes, let him get on with it. And McCormick doesn't scare me; I've been up against him before and won. Anyway Kaminsky hasn't even been indicted yet. The Grand Jury sit the day after tomorrow.' Lauren conveyed more confidence than she felt. 'That gives us loads of time.'

Brad cut in with, 'Forty-nine hours? You call that *time*, when we're sitting on fuck all?'

'Jay claims he was with a guy called Luther Ross, they met in the pen, but at the moment it seems like Ross has left town.'

'An alibi from a convicted felon is never gonna be watertight anyway, Lauren.'

Lauren sighed, nodding her head in acknowledgement. 'Tell me about it . . . In the meantime, what's the story on Kane and Morgan, did you dig up any dirt?'

Lauren heard a rustle of paper, then, 'Only that Weston was involved in a corruption case a few years ago. Under-age girls in pornographic videos. A dyke friend of hers was importing them, showing them at private parties. Weston was in the audience when the apartment was raided. The other woman implicated her, but she was fully acquitted. Other than that: *zilch*. Good pedigree, graduated magna cum laude from Wellesley. Phenomenally successful career, blah blah – '

'Anything on Beth Morgan that I don't already know?'

'Nothing, clean as a whistle.'

'And what about Kelly Prescott?'

'All I can come up with is that last year she had an affair with a young kid, he worked for her for a while. Twenty-two, half her age. But . . . there's no law against it.'

Making no comment, Lauren changed the subject. 'I want you to trace the principal of Wellesley, and any teachers that were there from seventy-two through to seventy-five. Find out everything and anything about all three girls, and do the same at Harvard. We know Kelly came up to New York a couple of days before the murders; find out where she went and with whom. Track down any of Kelly's other friends in Washington, her hairdresser, her trainer, her shrink. Get the toyboy lover if you can, and any others. See if she said anything to any of them. You never know, she might have let something slip.'

She heard Brad chuckle. 'It's us guys that usually let things slip, you girls keep a tight grip. At least Sharon does.'

'Well, most of us do if we've got any sense, but this Kelly broad seems to have had more beauty than brains. So who knows? She may have been having an affair with a Mafia boss, with Petroni himself. If she knew too much about the Dapper Don for her own good, sooner or later he'd want to take her out. Like who knows the reason people get killed every hour in this crazy town?'

Brad muttered, 'A hit of crack cocaine is usually enough.'

'Yeah, depressing, isn't it? I sometimes wonder what the fuck I'm doing here.'

'Same reason as me, you get off on the buzz. I can't imagine you anywhere else but right here, in the thick of the shit.'

'Thanks, Brad. And here's me thinking I'm living on the edge, finger on the pulse, making my mark. Even I occasionally want to pull myself out, take a long hot shower, smell something other than the stench of corruption. Talking of which, I must have a chat with Mafia maestro, Mario Petroni.'

'Think he'll talk to you?'

'When he hears what I've got to say, he might. Kaminsky shared a cell with one of his lifelong friends. A guy called Al Colacello. They went back a long way, Colacello and Petroni. Need I say more . . . ?'

She heard Brad whistle. '*That's* why Petroni sent his men for Kaminsky.'

'Exactly. Jay knows more than he's telling right now, but he's probably scared. It's no tea party dealing with the mob.'

Brad agreed. 'Go easy with Petroni, the man's dynamite. He'll have his own lawyers down on us before you can say go fuck yourself.'

'Thanks for the advice, junior. Got to go, catch you later.'

Keeping the phone glued to her ear, Lauren stubbed out her cigarette and lit another before punching out the digits to Mario Petroni's office. She was put through to his secretary. 'This is Lauren Stone, criminal attorney. I've left four messages for Mr Petroni, he hasn't got back to me.'

'Mr Petroni is very busy, Miss Stone. I'm sure when – '

The crisp officious voice angered Lauren. How could someone who worked for a known godfather be so damn prim! 'That makes two of us. So in order to save time, tell Mr Petroni I want to talk to him about a bird.'

'A bird?'

'Yes, a dead bird. When it was alive it loved to sing. This bird was called the Colacello canary.' Lauren paused. 'Have you got that?'

'Yes, Miss Stone. But – '

'Good. Just give him the damn message, you know where I can be reached.'

With that Lauren hung up. She waited an hour and when Petroni hadn't rung back, she went out to lunch.

When she returned her secretary gave her a message to say Mr Petroni had rung, and could she call him at four-thirty. It was a different number.

Lauren had a conference with a client at four, but at four-thirty she excused herself and used her mobile to dial Petroni from the hallway.

After two rings he replied. 'Petroni here.'

'Lauren Stone.'

'Ah, you wanted to talk to me about a bird.'

'Yes, the Colacello Canary. I'm not sure whether you know much about the species.'

'Enough, go on . . .'

'Well, this particular canary couldn't stop singing. It made friends with another bird in the same cage and sang to it every night. Unfortunately the canary died, but the other bird regained its freedom and now it doesn't want to go back in the cage. Nor does it want to die like the Colacello Canary.'

There was no animation in Petroni's monotone. 'What do you want, Miss Stone?'

'I want to know why you sent your men to Jay Kaminsky's apartment?'

'I felt like a chat with him.'

'So why didn't you go there yourself?'

'I was busy.'

'Did you want to speak to him or did you just want him dead, so he can't talk about Al Colacello and his connection with you and the underworld?'

Lauren held her breath, but Mario had hung up.

\* \* \*

'Why didn't you tell me you'd spent the night in the Mark Hotel with Kelly? The night before the murder, I mean.'

Jay, his eyes harnessed to Lauren's, answered dismissively. 'I forgot.'

With a flash of anger Lauren growled, 'Give me a fucking break! Come on, Jay, the doorman recognized you. He saw you go into the hotel. And the concierge spotted you coming out the following day. So it's hardly a secret.'

'OK, so I didn't exactly forget. What difference does it make?'

'I just had the coroner's report that Kelly had traces of semen in her. Was it yours?'

Jay shrugged. 'I assume so, unless she had sex with someone else straight after me, which I doubt.'

They were sitting in exactly the same positions as the first time they'd met, on opposing sides of a table. Jay looked haggard, the dark circles ringing his eyes suggested little or no sleep. And the taut skin covering his high cheekbones was drained of all colour except white. His denim shirt, dark with sweat under both arms, had a couple of grubby stains on the collar and a button missing.

'Was your love-making aggressive?' When he didn't reply, her voice became quietly persuasive. 'I need to know, Jay.'

'What is this? Some kind of pervert's interrogation? What comes next? *Was it good for me; was it good for her? Did I go down on her; did she go down on me? How many times did she come?* Jesus, three people are dead! I'm accused of killing them all. What does it matter what Kelly and I did between the sheets?'

With a deep breath Lauren controlled her rising anger and, adopting her best lawyer-to-client tone, explained, 'The Grand Jury are sitting in less than ten hours to decide whether to indict you, or not. As your attorney, everything I ask you has relevance to your defen–'

Jay interrupted. 'Don't patronize me with your lawyer speak. I'm not a child. I simply resent this extremely invasive line of questioning.'

'Tell that to the prosecution. For Christ's sake, Jay, grow up. I'm trying to help.' She pushed. 'Tell me about the love-making.'

Running a hand across his face, Jay looked over her shoulder as he spoke. 'OK, OK. After I met Kelly in the park in Washington I couldn't get her out of my mind. I followed her to New York, watched her leave Weston Kane's apartment and followed her to the Mark Hotel. I posed as a flower delivery guy to get to her. It worked. My initial intention was to interrogate her about Matt, to try and force her to tell me what she knew, what Weston and Beth were referring to in their telephone conversations. And if they all knew I hadn't killed Matthew, then who had.'

He hesitated. 'We were stuck in the snowstorm, we made love, and it was better than all my fantasies. I wanted to get close to her again, and I did. Afterwards I wanted to talk, needed to talk. And that's exactly what happened. I told her stuff about life on the inside, things I'd vowed never to tell another living soul, and she in turn told me about her life. How it had been empty and loveless, filled with running away from herself. All the men in her life had been about power, she got off on them wanting her. She needed to be desired, constantly. I think she felt strengthened by the fact that she didn't love any of them. She'd never been in love, never allowed herself to be that vulnerable. Kelly was chronically insecure. In the past she'd had dependency problems, drugs and drink, which you should be able to prove.'

'Were you in love with her?'

There was no hesitation in his definite '*Yes*.' Then, coming back to earth, 'I need a cigarette.'

Lauren passed him her pack. She sat silently while he lit up.

'When I left the Mark Hotel I walked back to my apartment. I'd arranged to meet Luther. I was still convinced that Kelly knew more about Matt's murder than she admitted, but I was no further forward and I was beginning to care less. Being with her had made me feel wonderful, given me back my self-esteem. I felt loved, it was a joy. I also felt more positive about my future than I have for many years. My book is being developed for a movie, and the producers have approached me about writing the screenplay. I was seriously contemplating relocation to LA, and asking Kelly to join me. I was beginning to believe we might have a future together. And that's when Petroni's men showed up.'

Lauren had stood up, and now she began to pace in front of the table. Jay sat very still watching her. He liked the way she moved, the way she held her neat head very high, always, and took small careful baby steps as if she was walking with a pile of books on her head. He also liked what she was wearing. Usually she wore city suits, mannish and hanging loose on her tall sinewy body. But today she was casually dressed in striped baggy pants held up with red suspenders over a tight three-button white T-shirt.

She was very beautiful yet seemed totally unaware of her physical attributes. Jay found that very attractive. He guessed the tough exterior had been carefully constructed to hide what he suspected was the little girl inside. The first time he'd met her, Jay had recognized the signs: her habit of abruptly changing the subject if he touched on something personal; her tense body language if confronted with anything other than the business in hand. Somewhere, somehow, she'd been deeply hurt.

Abruptly Lauren stopped pacing, she scowled in concentration. 'You say the sex was great, so perhaps Kelly fell in love with you again and realized what she'd missed. What you guys could have had, how it could have been. Plagued with guilt about the past, she loses it, gets smashed and ends up confessing. According to the doorman, Weston Kane showed up at the Mark after you. I wonder if Kelly told her you'd been there?'

'It's possible. Kelly had an unusual relationship with Weston; she loved her but she was also intimidated by her. If she was in trouble it was Weston she'd turn to, and if she needed emotional support Weston was always there for her. That's probably why she was so screwed up!'

'Were the two women lovers?'

Jay shrugged. 'Not sure, it's possible they could have been.'

Lauren sat down digressing now from the subject of Weston and Kelly. 'I spoke to Mario Petroni yesterday. He told me exactly nothing.'

Jay shot her a quizzical look. 'What did you expect?'

'Don't know, but I had to give it a shot. I thought it might just shake him up a bit, get a reaction, you can never tell.'

Jay grunted. 'With thugs like Petroni you can always tell. I've spent the best part of my life banged up with the psychotic. They have a weird code – a twisted morality – and usually no conscience. Al Colacello was a perfect example of the species.'

Lauren leaned forward, resting on her elbows. 'So tell me about Colacello, did he spill anything about Petroni?'

Jay thought carefully. 'Let's just say I know too much about Mario Petroni for my own good. He wanted to find out what, then eliminate. He's probably still deciding, as we speak, whether to chain-saw me into nice disposable pieces, or use some other form of waste disposal.'

Lauren tried again. 'So our Dapper Don wants rid of you, why? What exactly do you know about him?'

Jay cleared his throat. 'It's all in *Killing Time*. I changed names, dates, places etc. But the fundamental plot is non-fiction. During his entire time with Petroni, Al kept diaries. Precise and accurate records of transactions, meetings, banking accounts, the works. All Al ever said was that they were somewhere very safe. But he talked me through them. Mario knows of their existence, and presumably tried to trace them after Al's untimely death. When the book was published it must have been obvious to Petroni that Al had either talked to the author, or that the author had enjoyed access to the diaries.'

She felt very hot. 'No wonder you hid behind a pseudonym.'

'Yeah, I didn't much want to compare notes with Petroni. The mob don't waste time talking for long, they have an action speaks louder than words routine. So when that stupid dickhead reporter ran the piece in the *New York Times*, I made plans to leave town.'

'Can you trace the diaries?'

Jay pondered. 'Not sure where to look after all this time.'

'But if we had enough to indict Petroni, would you be prepared to join the Witness Protection Scheme and testify against him? You would get a new identity, go on to another life.'

'Somewhere warm and obscure in no-man's-land?'

Lauren decided to be frank. 'If you're indicted it doesn't look good for you, Jay. The prosecution will have Weston Kane, Beth Morgan and Todd Prescott all baying for your blood, and right now we've got very little evidence to get you released. I can't trace your Mr Ross. According to the guy in the apartment next door, he hasn't seen Luther for a couple of weeks.'

Jay said *shit* in his head then told her, 'Look, I'm paying a lot to have you defend me. It's your job to prove I'm innocent. If you think you can't do it, then say so right now and I'll get someone else who believes they can.'

Lauren could hear his anger rising as he continued. 'Shit, I've just got out after two and a half decades! I was actually beginning to live again.'

'If you agree to testify against Petroni, I'm certain we could do a deal. Think about it, Jay. You're a writer, you can write anywhere. You've got no family to worry about, no wife and kids to relocate. You could walk away from court to a new life.'

Lauren glanced at her watch, she was due in court in less than half an hour. She rose, saying, 'It's a chance, a good chance. The judicial system let you down once before. This way you could come out on top.'

As Lauren picked up her briefcase, Jay stood and took a step towards her, 'After the Grand Jury hearing, I'll consider talking about the Petroni deal. I promise.'

Side by side, Lauren and Jay walked down the steps of the Central Booking jail. With her body, lawyer shielded client as they faced a barrage of press and television reporters all clamouring, pushing and edging closer. A flashbulb exploded making Jay cover his eyes.

As soon as he uncovered them he saw Weston Kane. As their eyes met and locked he detected a flash of fear, then a split second later it was replaced by contempt. The desire to throttle her was overwhelming. His hands began to shake and he felt his spine stiffen. Todd Prescott was standing on Weston's right, and Beth Morgan on her left. *The Gang of Three*, Jay thought. *All out to get me, to see me go down for yet another crime I didn't commit. Well this time, it's different; this time, it's not going to happen.*

He'd just had time to register that Todd Prescott looked genuinely distraught, and to feel a pang of sympathy for him, when Lauren swept him further through the throng. Then he became aware of someone behind him, so close he could feel hot breath on the back of his neck. He spun around to face Todd. Now, there was a steely calm about him that Jay found slightly unnerving but, determined not to be intimidated, he pulled himself up very straight and faced him square.

Todd was emphatic. 'You haven't been indicted, but the battle is far from over. I intend to see justice done.' He jabbed his forefinger in Jay's chest, oblivious to the cameras of the press pack, and raised his voice. 'Today we have not seen justice done – a murderer is allowed to go free. That's the problem with this country, we've become too lenient.' His voice gathered momentum. 'This man is a convicted felon who killed his college room-mate. He's only been out of prison for a short time and he's already been arrested and charged with triple murder. When are we going to clean up the streets of America? I've lost my wife at the hands of this killer.' With another vicious poke in the centre of Jay's chest, Todd repeated, 'This killer.'

The cameras flashed as Jay swiped at the jabbing finger and Lauren stepped between them. 'Senator Prescott, I would advise you to – '

Todd growled, 'I don't need advice from you, Ms Stone.

And I'm warning you, I'll stop at nothing to see that Kelly's murderer gets what he deserves.'

'A Grand Jury has decided not to indict my client. I advise you to keep your comments and opinions to yourself.' Lauren spun on her heels, intending to usher Jay out of the fray, but she was too late to stop him confronting the senator.

'I loved your wife, Prescott. I wouldn't have hurt her for the world. Kelly was my . . .'

Before anyone could stop him, Todd's hands were fastened on Jay's throat and he was squeezing as if his life depended on it. 'You bastard! You killed her because you were jealous!'

As the hands tightened, Jay felt his throat close, then a great rush of blood to his head. There was a loud pinging in his ears and he was only vaguely aware of various frantic pulling and chopping movements in front of his face.

Suddenly the pressure released and he fell to his knees spluttering. Lauren crouched down beside him, her hand on his back. 'You OK?'

Jay, his head bent, coughed into his hand. He mumbled, 'Yeah, I'll live.'

Todd, his neck infused scarlet, as if he'd been the one that was throttled, used the flat of his hand to smooth his hair, straightened his tie, and without another word turned slowly on his heel. He was quickly swallowed up by a gaggle of reporters. Weston Kane and Beth Morgan did not follow him.

As Jay was helped to his feet, Weston moved quickly in

his direction. He didn't see her at first and was surprised to find her right next to him when he regained his balance. She spoke in a hushed whisper, for his ears alone. 'You won't get away with it, Jay. I'll make certain of that.'

Rubbing his neck, he was aware of her eyes upon him in a brittle blue gleam. 'I could say the same to you, Weston.'

Mario Petroni flicked the remote control button and the television screen went blank. He sat motionless, lost in thought. The result of the hearing was good news; an indictment would have meant Kaminsky was inaccessible.

The telephone rang close to his right hand and he picked it up after the second ring. It was the call he'd been waiting for. 'Yeah, I just heard the news. Find out where he is, and this time no mistakes.' As soon as he replaced the telephone, it rang again. This time the caller brought a warm smile to his lips. 'Anna my baby, how are ya?'

'Great, Paps.' 'Paps' was one of the first words she'd uttered and even now after almost thirty years, it still made his heart ache to hear her say it.

'Just wanted you to know that I made the reservation today. We're flying Concorde to London, then Paris, Florence and Rome. Neat trip, huh? I'm *so* excited! My first trip to Europe, and my honeymoon. You're so generous, Paps. I know Danny doesn't know how to thank you.'

Mario managed to respond with enthusiasm, and hoped

it didn't sound as forced as it felt. 'Wonderful news, my princess. You'll love London.'

There was silence on the other end of the phone. 'Sorry, Paps. That was Danny coming in, gotta go. Speak soon, big kiss.'

Mario didn't get a chance to reply and, rising from his desk, he stretched his short torso. His lower back ached and he had the beginnings of a headache. Very few people had his private number and when the phone rang yet again, he cursed, 'What is it with this fucking line today . . .' Then he growled, 'Yes.'

'Mr Petroni?'

Another curt 'Yes. Who is this?'

'Weston Kane. I thought you might like to know where Jay Kaminsky is staying at the moment. For how long, I'm not sure.'

'I shall be making immediate contact.'

'Hope so.'

'And what else do you hope, Miss Kane?'

'To see his head on a plate.'

'Literally?'

'I don't care how it's done.'

'I do, Miss Kane. I do.'

The apartment Lauren had found for Jay was located in Tri-be-ca, two floors below her own. It belonged to a friend who'd gone on a screen-writing course in LA for three months. It had lofty ceilings, exposed joists painted dark green and wooden floors sparingly furnished.

Jay was in the glass brick circular shower when Lauren

rang the doorbell. Wrapped in a towel, he spoke into the intercom then opened the door. Discreetly averting her gaze from his clearly defined abdomen, she smiled and asked, 'Can I come in?'

'Make yourself at home, I'll throw some clothes on.'

As Jay ducked out of sight, Lauren meandered into the living room carrying her full briefcase. In her other hand she carried a bottle of red wine. Familiar with the apartment, she headed directly to the kitchen and located a bottle opener.

After a few minutes Jay reappeared, barefoot but dressed in faded 501s and an oversized beige sweater. His hastily dried hair stuck up and out from the top of his ears like porcupine spikes.

Lauren poured wine into two tall glasses, one of which she handed to Jay. 'Congratulations.'

He clinked the side of her glass. 'Thanks, you did a good job. I really thought I would be indicted.'

'I'll let you into a secret . . . so did I. And it's not me you should be thanking. I did shit. It was Bob Horvitz who dug out your buddy Luther just in time *and* who got several prominent citizens to vouch for your integrity. Boy, has Horvitz got a lot of clout in this town. And it doesn't hurt that his wife is deputy editor on *Time*.'

Jay grinned. 'It sure feels good to know people like Bob and Luther are there for me.' He sipped his wine, watching Lauren move across the room from under narrowed lids.

She was wearing tight black jeans and a white T-shirt

under a kind of floppy grandad-style cardigan. It was the first time he'd seen her in tight pants, and as he followed her towards the sofa he decided that she had a cute ass, high like a shelf and very protruded. As they sat side by side, they seemed to generate a cosy atmosphere. Outside, through the long floor-to-ceiling window, it was raining – fine misty droplets. And the view was clouded and dark.

Lauren was undeniably attractive, yet he felt no attraction. She wasn't his type, he'd never wanted a black girl. Sure, some guys in the pen had joked about black chicks being hot, and great lays. But then most of the guys inside were misogynists who used women like Kleenex.

Lauren placed her glass on a sculpted table in front of the sofa, and snuggled into the cushions. Turning her chocolate gaze directly on to Jay, she asked, 'You feel OK here at Tara's?'

'Yeah! The apartment's cool, apart from the doormen.'

'How many more times do I have to remind you that you're in danger. Real danger. You've got Godfather Petroni on your back for taking out two of his men *and* for writing a book loaded with enough information to put him away for the rest of his life.'

'I didn't kill his men. Remember?'

'He thinks you did. And then there's Todd Prescott, he's already almost throttled you. And just to make up the numbers, there's this Weston Kane after your blood as well. So don't get pissed about the security, you should be grateful I'm looking after you so well.'

Reaching into her briefcase she pulled out a stack of papers. They included her secretary's transcript of the tapes which Jay had got Luther to make of Kelly's telephone conversations. She'd been able to plunder the material for crucial background information, but told Jay that she'd been left disappointed in one area. 'The tapes tell me that the three women were worried about your release, and that they were great friends, particularly Kelly and Weston. But there's no confession from Kelly on any of the tapes.'

Jay did not bother to prevaricate. 'I lied. She told me the night she came to my apartment, the night of her death.'

Lauren could not disguise her concern. 'Is that all you lied about, Jay?'

His eyes narrowed when he replied, 'Yes.'

Lauren wasn't sure whether to believe him or not, but she chose not to pursue it for the moment. 'Do you know anyone I could contact from their student days, anyone else they may have kept in touch with? Brad, my clerk, has come up with very little, and if we're going to take a shot at a retrial we need more evidence.'

Jay racked his brain. 'They always hung out together – you got one, you got all three. I don't recall any other friends.'

'Boyfriends?'

'Beth was fat, and short on dates. And Weston's gay.'

'I know, but she may have had a regular girlfriend. Do you think she and Kelly were lovers?'

Jay shook his head. 'You asked me that before. I really

241

don't know, but I doubt it, Kelly was straight, but there may have been the odd occasion, perhaps when Kelly was at her most vulnerable.'

'Tell me more about Weston and Beth, all you know.'

'Both high flyers, Weston in particular. Old money. Sinclair Kane, her father, had his finger in several pies. Chemicals, mining, banking. They had a huge property on the beach at South Hampton, and a smart westside apartment. How the other half lives. Weston has always been very poised, very polished, with a lot of attitude. In her junior year at Wellesley she created a TV station, and produced several documentaries. She's a natural leader – domineering, single-minded and determined. She was always very ambitious and in my opinion manipulated both Kelly and Beth. As you know, she's been phenomenally successful and has recently master-minded a brilliant merger between her own company, Summit, and the media giant Avesta. Beth is British and president of Hamtrust, a multinational merchant bank. She has a school-age daughter now, I gather. I think she's still unattractive, small and barrel-shaped. On campus she was considered a bit of a curiosity with her English accent and dated dresses. She's now married to Douglas Morgan, the – '

Lauren was there before him. 'I've had dealings with him in the past, he's a creep! He came on to me, big time, a couple of years back. One of those arrogant guys who can't take no for an answer. It's like they're so self-opinionated they can't believe you don't want to go to bed with them. Patronizing prick.'

'I don't know him, but can't say I blame him. If I was married to Beth I'd probably be coming on to other women.'

'She that bad?'

Jay just pulled a long face in answer. Then he continued, 'Beth is very influenced by Weston, too. She'll do what Weston says, and they'll protect each other and their own hides until the bitter end. They're a couple of tough cookies. Weston especially, and she hates me. She's always hated me, ever since I first started to date Kelly.'

Lauren bent her head. He studied her neat crown covered in soft waves, black and very shiny like polished jet. She had a long neck and an oval-shaped skull, and he imagined her in indigenous African dress – something stunningly bright, with one of those thick tribal chokers of beaten metal around her neck.

At that moment Lauren looked up, instinctively aware that Jay was scrutinizing her. Feeling uncomfortable she kept her voice businesslike. 'Remember you promised to discuss the possibility of testifying against Mario Petroni.'

'I've thought about it a lot. But without Al's diaries, I don't see how there's much chance of proving that *Killing Time* is not what it was published as – fiction.' Jay bit his fingernail then, picking up a box of cigarettes, he handed her the pack.

She took one, looking at it with approval. 'Good cigarettes.' She waited while he lit hers, and his own, with a disposable lighter. Then, through a plume of smoke, Lauren said, 'Well obviously it's no good going into court with charges we can't prove. But if you're willing to testify, we might be able to prove Petroni's men killed Kelly, and Kelly killed Matt. That way you could prove your innocence, get a new identity and a new life. It's your best bet.'

'Do you really think you can pull all of that off?'

'If we can prove that it was the material you collated from Al Colacello against Petroni that caused him to send his men after you, yes it's possible.'

'And Kelly?'

'Kelly got in the way.'

'What about the stuff I told you I sent to the women – cards, weird gifts?'

'So what, they don't prove you murdered Kelly.'

Jay grimaced as he took a sip of wine. 'Afraid I didn't acquire a taste for wine in the pen,' he admitted. Then placing the glass on the table, he said, 'My mother's dying. I'm not sure how much longer she's got – months, weeks maybe. Who knows with cancer? She believed I killed Matthew. She never said, but I know. And that hurts, it hurts like hell.'

Suddenly Lauren felt very sorry for Jay, not the superficial kind of sorry, it ran much deeper. Surprised by the emotion, she tried to keep her sympathy out of her voice when asking, 'Is your father still alive?'

'Could be, I haven't seen him since I was a kid. He left one day and never returned. It's an age-old story, and one I got over years ago. But my mother's different. She was good to us, my sister and me. Brought us up well, considering she was on her own, and had very little money. We never went without. Home was frugal, but it was clean. During the first few years in prison I used to imagine that she was out there gunning for me, you know . . . the kind of woman who fights tooth and nail for her kids. It wasn't true of course, but it felt good to pretend. I now know she buried her head in the sand, became a virtual recluse, and I'm sure went a little nuts. I wanted to prove my innocence before she dies. But there seems little chance of that now.'

Lauren sighed, and drained the last of her wine.

Then out of the blue, Jay asked, 'You ever been married?'

'Almost, once when I was younger.'

'How old are you now?'

'Thirty-six, almost thirty-seven, May twenty-sixth.'

'That makes you a Gemini?'

'Yeah. And you, Jay?'

'I turn forty-six in May.'

She watched the smoke spiral out of his mouth as he said, 'The first day we met, in the holding cell after my arrest, you said that you believed me. Were you telling the truth?'

'Yes, I was. Call it instinct, call it gut feeling. But I did, and I still do believe – '

Before the words were out of her mouth, he'd leaned forward to kiss her. Not a passionate kiss, not a fleeting one either, just a warm kiss full of affection. It took her completely by surprise and she was left breathless and blushing.

As abruptly as he'd started, he stopped. 'I want you

to know you're the first person to believe in me since Matthew was killed. The first person, that is, with nothing to gain. It deserves a lot more than a kiss, but it's all I've got to give right now. And my thanks.'

Lauren just wanted him to kiss her again, wanted him to want her, to take her, there and then on the sofa. *He's a client, stop this before it's too late; you can't do this, Lauren.* She listened to the reasoning in her own mind, but chose to ignore it for a minute as she allowed Jay to take her hand in his. He looked at it closely then raised it to his lips; he pecked first the back, and then the palm. It was a gesture of affection, as from a brother to a sister, or between close friends. And with a start she realized she'd misjudged his intent. The knowledge made her blush even more.

'By the way did anyone ever tell you that you're very beautiful?'

She grinned. 'Only my daddy.'

'Well, he was right.'

# Chapter Fifteen

Weston looked at the digital clock by her bedside. It read three ten a.m. Wide awake, she sat up, rearranged her pillows and stared into the darkness. The sedatives her doctor had prescribed after Kelly's death weren't working, he should have given her something stronger. After all she still had a business to run, life had to go on. Like her father had always said, one door closes, another one opens. *Think positive.*

Her stomach made a rumbling noise, reminding her that she hadn't eaten much for days. The sight of food was nauseating and it got in the way of alcohol. She knew she was drinking too much. It had been the same when she lost her father, six months of boozing, smoking and getting laid with any old slag she could lay her hands on. Then all of a sudden she'd woken up one morning recovered, the grieving over. It was like a dose of flu: you don't realize how bad it was until you feel better.

But this was different, because Kelly's death was different. Kelly had been shot, brutally murdered. Beth had dared to use the word 'retribution', and it had taken all of Weston's will not to slap her face. Kelly had been abused and raped, she'd done what most girls would have tried to in the same circumstances. Matthew had deserved to die. And now it was Jay's turn. An image of Jay outside the courtroom filled her with fury. So fucking smug. And that black lawyer bitch with the triumphant tilt of her head and the insolent body language. Weston heard her maternal grandmother's deep Alabama drawl again, *'Give blacks a bit of power, and they get to thinking they're as good as us.'*

It had cost a lot in bribes to find out where Jay was staying, but as far as she was concerned it was money well spent. If Mario Petroni got to Jay direct, and she was certain he would, Jay Kaminsky would be history. Then they could all get on with their lives and live happily ever after.

Whilst Weston was thinking about Jay, he was packing a small bag. Where he was going he wouldn't need much – a pair of jeans, three Ts and two warm sweaters. He zipped the bag and crept to the bedroom door. He'd deliberately left it ajar so as not to make any noise. As he entered the living room he heard a muffled snort followed by two loud snores. A peek at the security guard, chin on chest, saliva hanging from the side of his mouth like a silvery shoelace, confirmed that the drug in his coffee had worked.

When he left the apartment building on Hudson Street, Jay glanced at the clock in the lobby. It was five a.m. Nodding briefly to the doorman, he said, 'Can't sleep . . .'

'I've got the same problem, buddy. Ever since my wife died. That's why I work nights.'

Jay slunk into a darkened doorway as a car slid past,

then he crossed the road and walked two blocks. He was looking for the first easy ride he could find and soon struck lucky with a 1986 Oldsmobile. Like most ex-cons on the streets, he carried the right hardware and knew what to do with it. As he slipped behind the wheel, he felt a loose spring poke into his left buttock. The car seemed reluctant to start, but after several cursed attempts the engine groaned into life. There was very little traffic on the Westside Highway. And when he crossed the George Washington Bridge, the sun even made a brief appearance, dappling the windscreen while Jay cruised at a steady fifty m.p.h. towards Route 80.

Jay enjoyed driving. He supposed it was because his life hadn't given him a chance to do much of it. When he hit the freeway he opened the engine up. The best it could do was a shaky eighty miles an hour, however hard he put his foot down. Dawn broke as he crossed the state line into Ohio, where he stopped for gas and a pee. Before getting back in the car he watched the light streak the sky in three stages – from white to yellow to the washed-out blue of faded denim. At three p.m. he reached Mansfield in Indiana. The sun was high now, glinting on the bonnet as he drove into an underground car park.

Jay wiped the car clean, inside and out, then headed for the drugstore he'd spotted on the opposite corner of the street. An old timer, who looked only half alive, directed him to Arnie's second-hand car dealership located a little out of town.

Arnie wasn't in but his assistant, who introduced himself as Clive, showed off several vehicles that he said were all 'great bargains'. Jay paid for a nine-year-old jeep in cash. It had one hundred and sixty thousand miles on the clock, yet rode like new. Anything would have felt good after the wreck he'd just abandoned. And he didn't want stolen goods on his hands as he headed west.

He drove out of the lot past a beaming Clive and on to Route 90, towards Illinois. The sun was warm, and the air at last had a distinct whiff of spring. He felt optimistic. He supposed that had something to do with the fact that for the first time since his release there was one thing he felt absolutely certain about. *He was not going back inside.*

'He's gone, disappeared . . .' Lauren was back in her office, from where she'd called Jay several times earlier that morning. When she'd eventually gone downstairs to the apartment, the private detective had opened the door with a groggy explanation and the doorman confirmed the time Jay had left the apartment at five a.m.

Brad was leaning on the side of her desk, drinking coffee from a paper cup and wearing what he always wore – a black suit and tan boots. His fresh face held a scowl which made him look older than his twenty-eight years. 'What do you mean he's *gone*? How did that happen?'

'He drugged the security guy, gave it to him in his coffee. Not the guy's fault; why would he be suspicious?'

'So Kaminsky's on the run. It says a lot for his motive. Perhaps he did take the mob boys out, and that Kelly broad. Perhaps he's got a hidden agenda.'

'This case is more than just straightforward murder. Kaminsky was talking about joining Witness Protection and testifying against Petroni. He's got some pretty heavy-duty tales to tell against the don. If we could make them stick as evidence, we could go for an indictment against Petroni.'

Lauren heard Brad wheeze in response. He was asthmatic and she knew in a few minutes he would be rummaging for his steroid inhaler.

'Why didn't you mention this before?'

'Because I wasn't sure myself. We only talked about it briefly.'

'So have you seen the evidence?'

'I've read his novel, *Killing Time*, which he wrote as "Will Hope". That's the point, it isn't any old novel. It's nearly all true, and it's based on diaries kept by Kaminsky's one-time cell mate. None other than Petroni's lieutenant Al Colacello.'

Brad had read *Killing Time* and he let out a long low whistle.

Lauren elaborated. 'I mentioned testifying against Petroni. At first he was reticent, then when we started talking about plea bargaining he seemed keener. Of course he's determined to prove he didn't kill Matthew Fierstein, that seems to be his priority, and when I suggested a retrial in exchange for the goods on Petroni he was interested. Jay's obsessed with clearing his name before his mother dies. Apparently she's got cancer and hasn't got much longer.'

'That's probably where he's gone,' Brad commented

before pushing the inhaler spout in the side of his mouth and depressing the lever.

'He could be anywhere. He's got money, underworld connections no doubt, and sufficient reason to get out of the country. He's been convicted once before for something he didn't do, he sure as hell doesn't have a lot of faith in the judicial system. OK, he didn't get indicted, but he seems to think it's only a matter of time before Prescott or Petroni get to him one way or another. Can't say I blame him for getting the hell out.'

'You still believe he's innocent then?'

'Yes I do.'

'But there was ample motive for killing Petroni's men if they were out to get him for the Colacello stuff.'

'You're right, but you only have to spend a short length of time with Kaminsky to know he's no killer. How the hell he's maintained his sensitivity after all those years in the pen is nothing short of a miracle. I've spent most of my life involved with murderers, one way or another. My father always told me to look them straight in the eyes and listen to my gut. When I did that something just told me Jay was innocent. But I agree it doesn't look good for him now.'

Brad coughed. 'He's probably right to run. With a combination of Petroni and Prescott gunning for him, the poor bastard doesn't stand a lot of chance.'

'His only chance was the Witness Protection Scheme.' An image of Jay when she'd first met him entered her head. So tense and so determined. Lauren lowered her voice, 'Believe me, we haven't heard the last of Jay Kaminsky yet.'

On the morning of Jay's disappearance, Todd Prescott was on the golf course. It was the first time he'd played since last fall. But when he'd risen to the brilliant sunshine and spring-like temperatures, he'd decided to take up Bill Forsyth's daily offer of twenty dollars per hole over eighteen.

It was only a couple of weeks since Kelly's death, yet the pain he felt made it seem like it had all happened yesterday. Most mornings he awoke from the same dream, the one in which he was fishing off the Maine coast, where his father had taken him as a child. It was always the same time, mid-summer and a cloudless horizon. The only sound, water licking the side of the boat and the occasional cry of a lone gull.

Then suddenly the peace is shattered by a loud splashing in the bay. At first he thinks it's a big fish, but as it gets closer he can see a person swimming fast towards the boat. He's on his feet when the swimmer comes alongside the boat.

A hand reaches up out of the water; he grabs it and a moment later is pulled in himself. Gasping for breath, he emerges from below the water to see Kelly. Her face is very glossy as if covered in oil. She laughs and tells him that she didn't die, she's been on vacation to an idyllic island and she wants him to join her.

The dream always ended the same way, with Kelly pulling him under water. Resisting, thrashing about as water begins to fill his lungs, Todd would wake up with flailing arms, gasping for air. His doctor assured him the dreams were normal and would stop with time. He wished for it to be soon.

Now as Todd swung the club and drove the ball down the fairway to within a few yards of the ninth hole, Bill Forsyth's eye followed the shot. 'Good one, that's going to take some beating.'

They both fell silent as Bill lined up to take his own shot; it landed a few feet behind Todd's ball. 'Not bad, close enough.'

The two men climbed into the buggy, and started to descend the fairway to the ninth.

'I hear that Kaminsky guy escaped charges.'

Todd looked straight ahead, but Bill could sense his tension as he answered. 'He won't be free for long if I've got anything to do with it.'

With a sideways glance, Bill observed his companion. 'How long have we been friends, Todd?'

'Thirty-two years at the last count, why?'

'You want a little advice?'

'No, but that hasn't stopped you in the past.'

'Leave it to the police, think of your career. Kelly's dead, going after this guy isn't going to bring her back.'

They had reached the hole. Todd stopped the buggy then announced, 'Career or no career, I won't rest until Jay Kaminsky goes to trial. I want my pound of flesh.'

Beth was secretly pleased Jay had not been indicted. She hoped that he would leave New York; even better, leave the country never to be seen again. Then they could all get on with their lives.

Kelly's death had affected her more than she could ever have imagined. It wasn't only that they'd been lifelong friends, or that she'd loved her like a sister, but also the fact that she could not rid herself of the sense of retribution being served. An eye for an eye, biblical justice stuff. Until now she had never believed in such 'stuff and nonsense' – as her mother had always referred to any form of superstition. Nor had she ever even given it much thought.

But Kelly had killed, and been killed, and Beth couldn't help feeling that it wasn't just coincidence . . . that she'd got what she deserved. And from there it was only a short step to wondering when would it be *her* turn. The thought, ever present in her mind, filled her with impending dread.

Several years before she'd read a book about a family having committed a terrible crime, their dark secret had been held to be the cause of their eventual destruction as each one died in a more terrible manner than the last. Beth's paranoia even extended to fearing for her daughter; was poor Clara destined to suffer some terrible fate because of what she and Weston had helped Kelly to cover up? The logic in her head told her that she was overreacting and that she had nothing to worry about. But if what Weston said about Jay having a price on his head was true, he did not have long to live, trial or no trial.

Even that bothered Beth. Hadn't Jay Kaminsky suffered enough? If Kelly had confessed to killing Matthew, who could blame Jay for retaliating by killing Kelly? Beth, consumed with an urge to confess, had tried to talk to Weston about how she felt. As expected, Weston's response had been to exhort her to keep quiet and wait. According to her, Jay Kaminsky was a menace and had to be eliminated.

Beth was afraid, and scared that she was cracking up. Yesterday her shrink had said that she was going through a mid-life crisis brought on by Doug's constant womanizing. But then Doc Phillips didn't know about Jay. Twice in the last few weeks she'd been tempted to tell her, it had been on the tip of her tongue, ready to spill out. But each time the voice of Weston Kane had intruded, and she was more afraid of Weston's wrath than her own troubled mind.

Her thoughts digressed to her father whom she was due to visit in London in two weeks. He was eighty-seven, riddled with rheumatoid arthritis and critically ill. Sometimes she wondered if he would last until the end of the year. But then the cantankerous old goat had said that last year, and the year before. A month ago his doctor had told her that the old man had vowed to hang on until the millennium. Beth believed he would, stubbornly refusing to die until he had seen in the new century.

Thinking of her father encouraged thoughts of London to surface. The last time she'd stayed with him it had been springtime, the apple blossom outside his sitting-room window only slightly obscuring an otherwise uninterrupted view of Albert Bridge and the Thames. She recalled shopping in Sloane Street and Brompton Road, and an awareness that London was the place to be, the It city. It had offered the same buzz that had intoxicated her when she'd first lived in New York. She missed London, and for the first time in years considered moving back. What if she bought a house there? The idea came out of the blue, but it was her home after all.

As for Clara her daughter had always wanted to go to school in England. And the UK branch of Hamtrust could use a shot in the arm. She could get rid of its chairman, Charles Ryan, he was near retirement anyway, and take over the London office. The more she thought about the idea, the more she liked it, and for once in her adult life Beth decided not to mention her decision to Weston.

She would just go quietly. Douglas was a waste of space, and would soon find another woman to play his sadomasochistic games with him. Christ, she'd been doing it for years and for what? Good sex, the desire to be desired by a great-looking guy – a man whom other women wanted – in order to bolster her own low self-esteem. It was wearing thin, Doug had ceased to give her what she needed. Much more appealing was the thought of a new direction, a new life. The plan soon took hold and grew. In London she could start again. No Weston, no threat. And no Jay Kaminsky.

The wedding reception was held in the banqueting suite at the Four Seasons Hotel. It wouldn't have been his choice, but then he'd had very little say in the arrangements. It was a woman thing, and Isabella and Anna had planned all the minute details. All he'd had to do was pay. And he'd doled out dutifully; painless extraction. It was for his princess, she was worth every penny and more. *Ah my baby, my beautiful baby*.

Mario could hardly take his eyes off his daughter. Swathed in ivory tulle and lace, she was swirling around the floor in the arms of her new husband. His princess was happy; Mario was happy. It had been a good day and he had to give Isabella credit – she'd done a fine job. The food was superb, better pasta than his own mamma could have produced, and that was saying something. Fleetingly, his eyes covered the room. Yes, all was well. Not a drunk in sight yet.

Mario's fingers crawled across the white tablecloth towards a bowl of sugared almonds and grabbed a handful. At the same time he spotted his brother Gianni striding across the room, heading in his direction. There was something about the purpose in his step that alerted Mario. Something was wrong.

Gianni sat down next to his brother. 'Great wedding, Mario; Anna looks beautiful.'

'She is. So what is it, Gianni? You look like you've got something on your mind.' Mario slicked his tongue across his bottom lip, pink with almond stain.

'Didn't know whether I should bother you at this moment, but we've located the car he used. An eighties Oldsmobile. It was in an underground car park in Mansfield, Indiana. An old guy in the local drugstore directed him to a used car lot where he paid cash for a jeep. The salesman said he thought he was heading west.'

His face impassive, Mario said, 'Isabella's done a great job here, don't you think?'

'The best, Mario, the best! And you look great.' He whistled. 'Like the suit.'

Mario ignored the compliment and looking at his daughter again, said, 'You did right to tell me.' He licked his fingertips and wiped them on the edge of the table-cloth. 'My beautiful princess is going on honeymoon to London tomorrow. I think you should also take a trip, Gianni. I can't trust anyone else.'

A look of mutual understanding passed between the two men before Gianni stood up. 'I'd rather be going to London.'

Mario grinned. 'But just think of the fun you'd miss.'

# Chapter Sixteen

The house in Sand Springs, Montana looked exactly the same, apart from the paintwork. It had been a dirt-brown colour when he'd left, now it was green. Not the green of grass, more like jade. A relentless sun had burnt huge patches in the patina, revealing some of the original brown visible underneath. Weeds poked through the slatted wooden steps which creaked underfoot. The once familiar sound made his mind flood with a vivid image of himself racing up the same steps, bursting with the news that he had come top of the class in his end-of-semester exams.

As he rang the front doorbell, Jay could still hear his mother's voice reprimanding him for coming home late, and drunk, from his first teenage party. Then his father's controlled anger, which was far worse, and always preceded a beating. When he got no reply, Jay walked round to the back of the house. He stopped at the kitchen window, pressing his face close to the glass. There was no sign of life. All was scrubbed scrupulously clean. No crockery or cutlery, no newspapers. There were two small plants on the windowsill, one was dying, the other dead. Jay circled the house twice. The sash windows facing the back yard were locked, curtains drawn. He peeled back a strip of paint and watched a platoon of ants march down the architrave for a few seconds, before he noticed a chink at the bottom of the drapes. He fell to his knees and peered through apprehensively. He could see a set of table legs and the base of a sofa whose faded peach upholstery was worn thin, loose threads hanging as if a cat had been using it to scratch. As he stood up, Jay considered his next move.

It was obvious his mother wasn't home, and hadn't been for some time. He decided to call Aunt Emily, his mother's sister. They were close; if anyone knew of Rebecca's whereabouts, Emily would. It was only as he drove in the direction of town, searching for a telephone booth, that he realized he didn't know Emily's number. He hadn't had any contact from her since she'd moved house, several years before. He muttered a silent prayer that she was still in Montana, and then hoped she was still alive.

A few minutes later he spotted a gas station. He pulled in, parked the jeep out of sight behind a car wash, and entered the telephone booth. He got lucky: Emily was living at a new address nearby. But she wasn't at home, so he left a message on her answering service, then he returned to his jeep and drove off the road into a wooded area. He parked under a bush and slept for a couple of hours. It was fitful sleep, interspersed with ragged semi-conscious dreams.

At seven-thirty p.m. he tried again. This time Emily answered; she was shocked. 'That you, Jay? Jesus boy, where are you?'

'Emily, I want you to know – whatever anyone tells you, or you read in the newspapers – I haven't killed anyone. And I didn't kill Matthew Fierstein either. I'm involved in something out of my control. It's dangerous and that's why I'm on the run. I need your help.'

'I never thought you'd killed that young buddy of yours, Jay. Always told your ma that boy wouldn't hurt a fly.'

If his aunt had been close he would have hugged her. Instead, choked with emotion, he struggled to speak, 'Thanks, Emily, I really appreciate what you've just said. More than I can express right now.'

'So, boy, what can I do for you?'

'Do you know where my mother is?'

There was silence and Jay feared the worst, that his mother had died.

'Your ma's real sick, son. I just came home from the hospital. I've made arrangements to have her here with me when she's discharged next week. They operated a few days ago, but it didn't go so well. The tumour has spread, it's in her kidneys. I don't know how much longer she's got, a few weeks, a couple of months at most.'

'Where is she?'

'Mount Vernon Hospital in Great Falls, Room Four, Ward Twenty-nine. Under Doctor Cornwell.'

'Thanks, Emily, and God bless.' As he put the phone down, he realized it was the first time he'd used the term 'God bless' since he'd been sentenced and had stopped believing in God.

Ready to walk back towards the jeep, he caught sight

of a car a mile or so up the road. It was travelling at high speed, a wide arc of dust flying from the back tyres. As it came closer he could see it was a black Lincoln Continental. Not a typical Montana vehicle. He squinted to read the licence plate, and dived back into the booth when he realized it had New York plates.

The car cruised to a stop in front of the pumps and Jay held his breath as he saw a man get out and refuel. He watched him pay and then get back into the car. That was when he overheard him speak to his male companion who was behind the wheel.

'Cashier thinks the Kaminsky place is a couple of miles from here, says to ask directions in Sand Springs.'

Sprinting to the jeep only when the Lincoln had driven off, Jay reckoned if he put his foot down it would take him less than an hour to get to Great Falls.

He did it in fifty-two minutes. Mount Vernon Hospital was well signposted and he found it easily. From the age of four when his mother had taken him to visit his grandfather after a hernia operation, Jay had harboured a fascination for hospitals. Until he was fourteen he'd wanted to study medicine. What a pity he hadn't stayed with his first ambition and gone to Cornell instead of Harvard . . . Ward 29 was on the fourth floor, and with a confident stride he marched past the reception desk and located Room Four.

The room was spartan, the white walls unadorned, as was the narrow steel-framed window that overlooked the car park. There was one sit-up-and-beg wooden chair placed opposite two beds. They were separated by a bedside table on wheels. It held a plastic water jug, two glasses, three Get Well cards and a bunch of half-eaten grapes, the skins shrivelled and brown. One bed was empty and unslept in, the other contained Rebecca Kaminsky. She was fast asleep, but just one look told him of the rapid deterioration there'd been since their last meeting.

Without moving Jay stood at the bedside, and for the first time in as long as he could remember he wanted to hug his mother. He kneeled and very gently picked up her hand. It felt very small and frail. With his lips he brushed her cheek and felt her stir. There was a rapid fluttering of her eyelids and a slight movement of her mouth, then she awoke. A look of amazement filled her face when Jay came into focus.

'Sorry to wake you, Mom,' he said, still holding her hand.

Struggling, she tried to sit up. 'How long you been here?'

'A few minutes.' He helped her, propping her up with two pillows.

'How did you know I was here?'

'I went home, and when I found the house empty I called Emily.'

'I told Emily not to tell anyone. Folk only come to see you cause they feel pity, or worse out of guilt. I want to die in peace.'

'What about Fran. Has she been to see you?'

'Your sister's dead, died in a car accident eight years ago. She was pregnant, first baby, hit and run, they never caught the driver.' Rebecca spoke in a detached voice, as if she was talking about a complete stranger.

Jay felt like he'd been hit by a truck himself. 'Why didn't you tell me, Mom?'

'Figured you had enough trouble on your plate. What good would it have done? You couldn't pay your last respects. She didn't suffer, that's a blessing. Funny, I dreamt about her the other night. A wonderful vivid dream, I didn't want it to end. She was leading me through a garden, it was so beautiful, like paradise. It was full of flowers, all kinds of exotic blooms, the scent like nothing I've ever smelt, like it was dripping from the petals. The birds were singing, and so was Fran, in her lovely melodic way. Like a nightingale. In fact that's what your grandma used to call her, remember? The Kaminsky Nightingale.'

With scrawny fingers Rebecca began to pluck at the blanket, clawing at the fabric like a cat. She was looking straight ahead towards a blank wall; there was a vacancy in her staring that Jay had not noticed when he'd last seen her in New York.

'Mom, remember when I sent you a box with some of my research and my stories?'

She nodded. 'That made me very proud, son, you writing all those pages. I always said you were clever, even as a little boy you used to write stories and poetry. You wrote me a poem once on Mothering Sunday. Remember? And painted pretty flowers all around the edge.'

'Think back, Mom, to when I sent the package. I asked you to put it into a safe-deposit box in the bank.'

Still staring at the wall, she said, 'Oh, the bank, I took everything out of the bank. Never liked that manager Philby, never trusted him for a goddamn minute.'

'When you took everything out, what did you do with the box?' Jay had taken up a new position at the foot of the bed so that he could look directly into her face.

Rebecca's eyes widened and to his horror he saw what he'd dreaded. *Madness.* He'd seen it before – in Al Colacello, and in other longterm inmates who should have been registered insane and hospitalized.

'You do look like your grandmother, just like my old mom. I always said so, but your father wouldn't have it, said that you were the spit of him. Said you got your good looks from his side of the family.' She spat and the spittle landed on the front of her nightdress. 'Ha! The Kaminskys were a motley crew. His mother was gross, big fat titties.' Rebecca giggled. 'Looked like a lady wrestler.'

At that point a nurse appeared. Briefly she glanced in Jay's direction, then directing her gaze at Rebecca said, 'Mrs Kaminsky, blood pressure time.'

Dutifully Rebecca held out her arm. It was stick-thin and grey, one long tangle of vein visible through the papery skin. With a jabbing finger, she pointed to Jay, 'He killed my son.'

The nurse tut tutted. 'Now, now, Mrs Kaminsky. Stop being foolish.' Then to Jay, 'Sorry, she gets like this some days. Usually after chemotherapy. It passes, tomorrow she'll be fine.'

Jay nodded his understanding and said, 'By the way I *am* her son.'

'Good to meet you; she's talked about you a lot, said that you're a writer.'

'That's right, I'm a novelist.'

'What books have you written? Would I have read any of them?'

'You might.' Jay invented a couple of titles. '*Circle of Dreams*, and *Killer Mountain*.'

She shook her head. 'Sorry, never heard of either. But I'll look out for them. *Killer Mountain* sounds like something my husband could get into. Anything to get him away from the ball game!'

Undoing the tourniquet, she patted Rebecca's hand. 'Blood pressure normal.' Then, taking the patient's temperature, she declared that normal as well and scribbled some notes on the clipboard at the end of the bed.

Before leaving the nurse glanced in Jay's direction. 'You know you look kinda familiar, must have seen your face on the cover of one of your books some place.'

'Yeah, probably,' Jay said, turning to face his mother once more.

'I'm mighty tired, Jay,' she said, running a tongue across her lips and pointing with her eyes to the water jug.

Jay filled a glass for her and encouraged by her saner demeanour, he tried one last shot. 'Mom, they're going to make a movie of *Killing Time*, the book I wrote and sent to you, and listen to this, Mel Gibson is going to play the lead.'

'My favourite.'

'He's agreed to star in the movie of the book, but I can't start writing the script until I have the manuscript – the one you kept safe for me. The one I sent you when I was in prison.'

'Is Mel Gibson really going to be in the movie?'

'Yes, Mom, he's signed the contract.'

With feeble pressure she squeezed his hand. 'Emily's got it. When I took everything away from the bank, Emily said that she would keep things safe. You'll have to ask her. She likes Mel Gibson as well, but I don't think he's her favourite, the last I heard it was Kevin Costner. Who do you like the best, Jay, Kevin or Mel?'

'It's gotta be Mel.'

'Would I get to meet him?'

'Course, Mom, we can arrange that.'

She was smiling, and for an instant she looked like she'd done in the days when she'd meet him from Sunday school and they'd walk home hand in hand.

Jay fell to his knees; he rested his cheek on hers then he kissed her on the same cheek. It was very warm, and very dry. 'I didn't kill Matthew, Mom.'

Her eyelids fluttered shut. 'I was never sure, son.'

'Are you now?'

Without opening her eyes she said, 'Yes.' Then suddenly her eyes did open – two bright buttons, clear and alert when she repeated, 'Yes, absolutely sure.'

Jay felt his chest fill up with warmth. It was like nothing he'd ever experienced before, this sense of relief, and for a few wonderful moments he was consumed with joy. He longed to cry, and for her to comfort him. To take him in her arms, like she had done when he was a very small boy. But she looked too frail to move, so he made do with holding her hand, happy to sit at the bedside in silence. He knew that the two heavies from the Lincoln could burst in on him at any second, but nothing and no one was going to stop him savouring this time. He'd waited too long for it to let it go. Anyway for all he knew, the guys on his tail were already sitting outside waiting for him. Eventually he placed his mother's hand next to the one folded across her chest, and planted a kiss in the space between her eyebrows. The skin felt puckered, dry and hot.

'I love you, Mom,' he whispered. Not sure if she had heard him he repeated, 'I love you.'

This time he knew she'd heard. A flicker of a smile crossed her lips, and she reached up to touch his face. With feeble fingers she stroked the unshaven skin below his jaw and opened her mouth to speak. He lowered his head in time to hear her say, 'I love you too, son.'

Home to Emily and Ted Crawford was a house called Ducksberry Point. It sat on a grassy promontory, bordered on three sides by water, at the end of a long tree-lined drive.

Ted and Emily had bought the house eight years ago. It had long been their dream to retire to Fort Peck Lake where Ted had been taking fishing vacations ever since their son Saul was five. The wooden house had been built in the late 1920s.

It was painted a warm cheery yellow, and Jay almost

269

expected to see an Anne of Green Gables lookalike appear in a red gingham dress at any moment. But Emily was not wearing gingham, nor did she look remotely like the fictitious character created by L.M. Montgomery when she opened the door.

She looked exactly like a younger version of his mother, only with fuller cheeks, broader hips, bigger breasts and a warmer smile. Rebecca had long since lost her youthful sparkle, yet Emily had retained all of hers and had the body language of a woman half her age.

Jay couldn't remember exactly how old she was, but his cousin was a few years younger than himself and somewhere in the deep recesses of memory he recalled his mother saying that Emily had had to get married at eighteen because she was pregnant with Saul. It made her about sixty-two.

'Jay, good to see you!' Emily embraced him, her full bosom pressing hard against his chest.

Jay stiffened, out of embarrassment more than distaste. Yet his rigid pose did not seem to worry her. She held him at arm's length, regarding him with affection.

'Come on in! Ted's out fishing as usual, he spends hours on the water, never gets bored.' She winked. 'So he says. As for me I git bored trying to think of new ways of cooking the damn catch. There are only so many ways to skin a chicken.'

She winked again, this time it was accompanied by a smile and Jay felt himself warming anew to this aunt he'd always been very fond of as a child.

'You look tired, you want something to eat, drink?'

'I don't have a lot of time, but I could use something to eat, and a hot shower would be great.'

Leading him into a pretty floral bedroom, she pointed to a door on the right. 'In there you'll find all you need, hot water, towels, shampoo and the like. This is our guestroom, but most of the time it's used by our granddaughter, Cindy. That's her there.'

She picked up a photograph frame, and Jay felt a sharp pang of envy as he gazed at the family snapshot. Cindy had a mop of tight blonde curls, and a gap between her two front teeth. He wouldn't have recognized Saul, who had lost not only his puppy fat but also most of his hair. Jay had never met the petite female Saul had married. In the photograph she looked elfin in oversized dungarees, her hair tied in a topknot like Kelly's.

'Cindy was only eight when that was taken, she's a big girl now – thirteen next month.' Emily dusted the frame with the flat of her hand before replacing it on the chest of drawers. 'While you shower, I'll make you some eggs and bacon. How do you like your eggs?'

'Sunny-side up, and by the way, Emily, *thanks*.'

'Don't you mention it, you've had a rough time, boy. I want to help.'

The smell of bacon greeted him fifteen minutes later as he walked into the cosy kitchen. It was decorated in English farmhouse style, with oak units, a scrubbed pine table and six chairs in the centre. Four slices of bread popped out of the toaster as Emily ladled two eggs on to a plate.

'Good timing, sit yourself down,' she said, placing

the plate next to a tall white ceramic cruet set. All done, she placed the stack of toast in a wicker basket close to Jay's right hand, and sat next to him. 'You said on the telephone last night that you wanted your manuscript back?'

'Yeah, but it's more than just wanting it. I need it, it might save my life.'

'You in a lot of trouble, Jay?'

Pouring himself a cup of coffee from the large pot she had made, he decided to confide in Emily. 'The person who really killed Matthew Fierstein framed me with the help of a couple of friends. It was my old girlfriend, Kelly, who was raped by the bastard. She confessed – in my apartment in New York – and asked me to forgive her. For most of her life I think she's been tormented by the crime, and seeing me again made it worse. I always suspected she knew something, but I didn't think for one moment she'd done it.'

'But to let you go to prison to take the rap! That I can't understand.'

'You would if you met Weston Kane.'

'Who's that?'

'Weston was Kelly's best friend. She persuaded Kelly to do a cover-up, convinced her that she would never survive prison and that I would get off with a light sentence at most. Weston never liked me. She was jealous, she was in love with Kelly herself.'

Quietly sipping coffee, Emily managed to hold her silence.

'You know the story of *Killing Time*, so I don't need to

272

go into detail. The characters were based on real people, and the godfather is someone called Mario Petroni. He found out that Will Hope was my pen name, and sent a couple of his men to get me. By coincidence or bad luck – the story of my life so far – Kelly turns up at my apartment minutes beforehand. She winds up shooting both of them, and then herself. Either that or one of them got a shot at her after he'd been hit. I'm not sure. I was in another room at the crucial time, and didn't see it.' Jay rubbed his eyes. 'I can't believe this is happening to me all over again. Far-fetched, huh? A repeat nightmare! I couldn't dream up better fiction.'

Emily looked very serious. 'Can you prove Kelly killed Matthew?'

'I've got a tape recording of her admitting that she knew I was innocent. And two other people know that: including Weston. The problem is that proving Kelly killed Matt just gives me a motive for killing her. Revenge stuff. If I'd been indicted, the prosecution would have had a field day, aided and abetted by Weston for one. And on top of everything else I've got the mob after me. You'd better take a long hard look at me, cause I may not be around much longer.'

Emily stood up, as if taking him at his word. 'I'll get what you came for.' With that she left the kitchen and returned a few minutes later carrying a brown laundry box labelled, 'Sam's Cleaning Services'. Moving Jay's empty plate, she dropped the box on the table in front of him. 'It's all there, exactly as your mother gave it to me. Still tied with the blue ribbon she used.'

When he opened the box Jay felt his hand quake. With his forefinger he touched the top page, then looked underneath. 'Is this all she gave you?'

Emily shrugged. 'I never opened the box. She said it was your work, that you'd asked her to keep it safe until you came out of prison. Is there something missing?'

With a deep sigh and a nod Jay replaced the lid. 'Yes, but it's too late to do much about it now, at least I've got the original factual version of the manuscript. It would have been a lot easier on disk, but when I wrote *Killing Time* they didn't have laptops. At least not in the pen.'

Suddenly brusque, Emily said, 'Look, Ted doesn't know you're here. Under the circumstances I wasn't sure how he'd react, best not to involve him. He'll be back in half an hour, Jay.'

Jay understood. His Uncle Ted had never liked him, or believed in his innocence. Jay was on his feet with the box tucked under his arm before she'd finished speaking. He extended his free hand in her direction and she used it to pull him into an embrace. For a few moments he allowed himself to be hugged, then he drew back.

Emily had speckled eyes, like a brown egg, it was something he'd never noticed before, and they were glittering now with unshed tears. 'Don't cry,' Jay said. Then with more confidence than he felt, 'I'm going to be OK.'

'Good luck, boy. Don't let them get you this time. If you need me you know where I am. And don't worry 'bout your ma, I'll look after her.'

'Thank you, Em. I'm sure as hell going to need some of that good luck.'

# Chapter Seventeen

The boat was the type used for day sailing and line fishing. It had a 95 horsepower inboard, a steel hull and deck. It was painted blue and white, and was called *Sea Spray*.

Jay watched it bob up and down in the water, then read the crudely painted sign pinned to the hull. 'Day and week charters, fishing, cruising in the calm waters of Fort Peck Lake. Call Charlie Stansfield on 6875432.' Jay memorized the number and was about to find a phone when a man came up behind him. 'You interested in a charter?'

Jay turned to face a big barrel-chested man, with a thin white moustache, who introduced himself: 'Stansfield's the name; she's my boat.' The man's face was partially obscured by a peak-brimmed hat and, lifting his chin, he peered at Jay from under the peak.

Directing his attention on the boat, Jay enquired, 'How much for a week?'

Stansfield calculated in his head. 'Two thousand five hundred dollars.'

'*How* much?' Jay was incredulous.

'I can hire her out for a hundred dollars an hour, and by my reckoning, average of five hours a day for seven days, you gitting a bargain.'

'You reckon you can charter for five hours a day at this time of year . . . the season's barely started.'

'Fish biting, lots of folk down last weekend, got a lot of catch. Only this morning I had four enquiries for the weekend,' he raised four fingers. 'All of 'em wanted *Sea Spray* – she's solid and reliable, nice cabins, good galley.'

'I'll give you two thousand, that's all I've got, and it's more than I can afford.'

'Done.' Touching the brim of his cap, Stansfield jumped on deck and, squinting into the sun, called to Jay, 'Come on board, take a look.'

Jay hated boats, they made him seasick, and it was with a weak smile that he followed Charlie Stansfield on to the boat.

'She's full of diesel, been winterized, all her ass is fine and ready to go. You familiar with boats? You got sailing hours in?'

Jay lied. 'Yeah, my daddy took me fishing and sailing when I was a kid, and I've had a couple of boats myself in the Keys. I chartered a sixty-foot Boston whaler one time down in the Bahamas.'

'Good, so you know how to navigate.'

Jay didn't have a clue but he nodded enthusiastically. 'No problem.'

Charlie demonstrated the equipment in great detail, explaining everything as he went along. Finally, with a sense of pride he showed off the galley. 'Just refitted her, nice job don't you think?'

Jay looked around the neat galley; it was fitted in

highly polished cedar, with gleaming stainless steel fittings. 'Very nice,' he commented, following Charlie past a teak table surrounded by fitted and upholstered seating. Aft, there were two small cabins, both containing two bunk beds, a shower and toilet.

Dumping his bag on the bottom bunk bed, Jay took an envelope out of his back pocket. He withdrew two thousand dollars in hundred notes and handed Charlie the money. 'This will do me just fine.'

'Good, I just need you to sign the charter agreement, then you can be on your way. Decided which way you're heading?'

'Don't know yet. Thought I might just cruise around some, catch a few fish, get a little peace.'

'Wish I was coming with you, can't think of anything better. I caught a big kingfish last week. A thirty-five pounder, a real beaut! He put up a good fight but I hauled him right on in, then got mighty drunk to celebrate.' Stuffing the money into his own back pocket, he said, 'Come on then, let's git them papers signed.'

The two men walked side by side down the dock. When Charlie opened the door of his office, the rank smell of rotting fish and detergent greeted them. Jay wrinkled his nose and grimaced. Charlie noticed and, oblivious to the smell himself asked, 'Something wrong?'

'Just got a headache.'

'Fresh air will clear that. Once you get out there, you'll forget all your problems.' Rummaging in a drawer, Charlie pulled out a slip of paper, then rummaging some more he found a pen. 'Name?' he asked.

Jay supplied his cousin's: 'Saul Crawford.' And he used Emily's old address.

'Chartering for a week, right?'

'That's right.' Trying to contain his impatience, Jay watched Charlie finish writing and then he signed 'S. Crawford' in a sweeping scrawl.

'ID? Driver's licence?'

Jay was ready. 'Had a little problem a few days back, speeding offence. They still got my licence, waiting for a fine. The cops were real bastards, I was only ten miles over the limit.'

'Don't talk to me about cops. Last year I had a boat stolen, the cops didn't do a darn thing to help. I caught the guy myself in the end.' He handed Jay the keys. 'Go on git going, get some water under you before nightfall.'

'Thanks and don't worry about *Sea Spray*, I'll look after her.'

'I ain't worried, she's well insured. Made sure of that after losing my other boat. You have fun now, watch out for the currents. And sometimes at this time of year it can get a bit squally. You got bait and tackle on board. Extra blankets if you need 'em, stored in the left cabin aft.'

Swinging the keys, Jay walked outside. Charlie followed. Thick cotton wool clouds littered the sky, covering the sun, and the darkening light suddenly seemed almost foreboding. They walked side by side to the bobbing white craft where Jay jumped on board and Charlie stayed on shore.

'Anything else you wanna know?'

'Yeah, where can I hire scuba equipment? Did a bit of diving when I was a kid, thought I might try again.'

'You got your certificate?'

Jay didn't need to lie. 'Yeah, I got it in Florida in seventy.'

'There's a shop a few doors down from me, they've got all the stuff there.' Charlie licked his lips, he was thirsty and his thoughts had digressed to wanting a beer. 'You want me to cast off when you done that?'

Fervently Jay willed Charlie to go away. He wanted to acquaint himself with the boat before he set sail. 'I'm going to settle in first, probably set off a little later.'

'OK, I'll leave you to it. Call if you've got any problems. You've got the ship to shore, and the radio. Have a good trip.'

'Thanks! See you next week.'

The persistent knocking woke Ted Crawford from his afternoon nap. As he struggled to his feet, a quick glance at the wall clock told him he'd been dozing for more than two hours. That meant Emily would be out at her Yoga class by now.

Walking down the hall he passed a window facing the front door. First he saw a black car, a Lincoln, then a male profile. Someone short, with close-cropped hair and a flat nose. For some inexplicable reason Ted felt a quick *frisson* of unease, and he opened the door only a fraction.

The man spoke in a gravelly voice and his pleasant smile made Ted's fears disintegrate.

'Sorry to disturb you, but we're looking for Roy Bannerman's place. Something Creek, I think?'

Opening the door wider, Ted said, 'Never heard of him, have you got the full address?'

The caller began to forage in his pocket, and a moment later pulled out a gun. 'Step inside, no noise, no fuss, just do as I say.'

His face a frozen tableau of fear, Ted Crawford stepped slowly back into the hall. Immediately another man appeared, much taller and handsome in a swarthy Latin way – olive skin, black hair and piercing peppermint-green eyes. Ted found him more menacing than his friend.

The green-eyed man took control. 'We're looking for a friend of ours, it's imperative we reach him; life and death. His name's Kaminsky, Jay Kaminsky.'

The look of amazement on Ted's face was genuine. 'Jay is my wife's nephew, we haven't seen him in years. He's been in prison, my wife visited a few times but I haven't seen him since he was convicted – '

The blow to his face was sudden and unexpected. Ted felt a ringing in his temples, then a sharp pain across his chest. He vaguely heard the short man say, 'You're lying, we know he's here.'

Through a fog Ted heard himself reply, 'You can search the house, there's no one here except me.'

'If he's not here now, tell us where he's gone.'

The second blow sent Ted crashing into the wall. He heard the sound of his skull crack on contact with the plaster, then felt something wet trickle down the back of his neck. Wincing, he touched the wound and when he lowered his arm his hand was covered in blood. The pain in his chest increased and, panic-stricken, he clawed at the neck of his shirt. He was having difficulty breathing and struggled to speak. 'I swear I haven't seen Jay Kaminsky since – '

Ted never finished the sentence. His eyes closed and he saw a rush of unconnected images; then a white light, brilliant in its brightness, and warming . . . welcoming . . . like being enveloped in a wide ray of sunshine. He didn't feel the barrel of the gun thrust into his gut. All was calm, no more pain, death felt good.

'Somebody got there before me.'

'What do you mean?'

'There was a stiff in the house, and it was crawling with cops.'

'The mob.'

'Yeah, I figured that. But I did some sniffing around the area, and found out that a man fitting the right description chartered a private boat for a week. The owner was very helpful, and for a price agreed to contact the boat, and get its exact whereabouts.'

'Where are you now?'

'In a bar close to the marina.'

Todd said 'Keep in touch' before hanging up. Leaning back in the deep-buttoned leather chair, he plaited his fingers and put his hands behind his head, feeling his shoulder muscles stretch. He felt confident that if anyone could outrun the mob and get to Jay Kaminsky, ex-FBI special agent Dexter King could. The urge to fly over to Montana and join Dexter was almost overpowering. He'd thought of little else all last night, and all morning.

Still full of the anger that had consumed him since Kelly's death, he wondered whether even killing Jay Kaminsky would make it go away. The question had been haunting him for days, and the answer was always the same. He wasn't sure. But the prospect of sitting back and doing nothing was worse, and filled him with a sense of hopelessness. Yet creeping to the surface was the other doubt, the one he'd refused to confront until now.

What if Jay Kaminsky was innocent? What if he was telling the truth: the mob had been after him and Kelly had got in the way. His brain was worn out with trying to understand what Kelly had been mixed up in. Weston and Beth had closed ranks and were saying only that Kaminsky must have killed Kelly. Weston was adamant; Beth less so. The last time he'd spoken to her, the day after Kaminsky's disappearance, he'd detected a slight hesitation, and something else that he'd recognized as fear.

With this recollection in mind he picked up the telephone and dialled Beth's private line. It was engaged, so he tried the switchboard, getting through to Beth's secretary who informed him Beth was engaged on an overseas conference call and couldn't be interrupted.

Beth called back twenty minutes later. 'Todd. How are you?'

'As well as can be expected. And you? Doug and Clara?'

'We're all good. Clara is adolescent, that says it all. And Douglas, the last time I saw him, seemed fine.'

'You OK, Beth? You sound tired.'

'I am. I'm working on a big deal right now, and I'm not sleeping so good.'

'You and me both. In fact I haven't had a natural night's sleep since Kelly died.'

The last thing Beth wanted to talk about was her dead friend, and she was about to invent an important meeting she had to rush to, when Todd said something surprising.

'Do you believe Kaminsky killed his old room-mate?'

On her guard, Beth chose her next words carefully. 'A jury convicted him of manslaughter. A guy in the next room at Harvard gave conclusive evidence that on the night of the murder Jay and Matthew had fought over Kelly. We all knew they were both in love with her, and that Matthew was jealous of Jay. Who else could have done it? Who else would have had the motive?'

'You haven't answered my question. I said do you think Jay did it?'

'Yes, Todd, I do.'

'Something's been bothering me for a while, something I remembered a few days after Kelly's death. I'd been unable to sleep and you know how it is in the middle of the night when everything gets out of proportion.'

Beth knew exactly.

'I was trying to figure out what Kelly was doing in Jay's apartment, and it suddenly dawned on me that she may have been in love with him. When she was having difficulty conceiving, I overheard Kelly talking to the obstetrician, something about having had an abortion when she was a student. I questioned her and she freely admitted that she'd had a fling at college and had secretly aborted a baby. The operation went wrong, and her cervix was damaged in the process. Do you know about the abortion? Do you think it may have been Jay's baby?'

Beth decided there was no harm in telling the truth. 'Yes, I knew she'd had an abortion. Weston arranged it.'

'Who was the father?'

'I don't know.'

Todd felt she was lying. 'I think you do.'

Beth held her breath, she could feel the panic rise. 'What makes you say that?'

When he replied his tone held a distinct threat. 'Stop playing games with me, please. I don't like it. I want the truth. I know you know, so cut the crap.'

'It was Matthew Fierstein's baby.'

'Thank you, Beth.'


Luther Ross played and replayed the tape, methodically transcribing it word for word on to a small notepad in case he missed anything. When his mobile telephone rang, he had in front of him all the conversations he'd recorded over the last two days. 'Jay, man! You OK?'

'Fine, like your new job as a telephonist?'

'Pays better than waiting table.'

Jay grinned. 'OK, brother, fire away.'

'The mob know you took the boat, and have bribed someone called Charlie to get your exact location. Morgan has just admitted to Prescott that Kelly aborted Fierstein's baby. And yesterday afternoon he took a call from Weston Kane – they're due to meet in New York the day after tomorrow, that's Wednesday. And the ex-FBI guy – that Dexter King – is hot on your tail, man you're gonna have to move it.'

At this point Luther hesitated, unsure whether he should tell Jay the next bit. But decided it was important he knew what he was up against. 'And, sorry, man, I guess one of your relatives is dead.'

Jay had a sinking feeling in his gut. 'What do you mean?'

'All I know is that the Dexter guy said the house in Montana was crawling with cops when he got there. Said the mob beat him to it, and killed whoever was inside. There's one stiff.'

'Did he say a man or woman?'

Luther couldn't remember. He scoured his notes and not finding any reference either way, he made a guess. 'I think it was a man.'

'My Uncle Ted.' Jay had no fond childhood memories of Emily's husband whom he had found distant and bad-tempered. Later, when he was convicted, Ted Crawford had spoken to the press – saying he'd never liked or trusted his wife's nephew. Yet Jay was filled with an indescribable sense of guilt and sadness. A picture of Emily's concerned expression entered his head, her kind words ringing in his ears as she'd wished him goodbye and good luck.

'Shit, Luther, when is this garbage going to end!'

Luther was tempted to say, *When you stop running*. But he held back. What good would it achieve? And anyway he understood what Jay was doing, he would do the same.

Jay felt his anger begin to surface, gobbling up the guilt and sadness. Reminding himself that there was no time to feel sorry because right now he needed all his energy to survive, he embraced his anger. It would keep him alive. 'Did Prescott mention where and when he's meeting Weston Kane?'

'Yes, they're due to meet at her apartment at six.'

'Does that give you time to get in and out of her apartment?'

'It depends, man, I'd need to case the place, but I've got somebody good I could use.'

'Do you trust him?'

'He's cool. I saw him last week and he was desperate for work.'

'OK, Luther, I'll leave it with you. And by the way I'd love to listen in to Petroni's calls. Can you do it?'

With a deep sigh Luther said, 'I don't want to die just yet.'

'Nor do I. I'll call you the same time tomorrow.'

'You going to dump the boat?'

'It will be a pleasure. I've been seasick for forty-eight hours.'

As he pressed the off switch on the mobile telephone, Jay heard the faint noise of an outboard engine. Pricking up his ears, he grabbed a pair of binoculars from the wheelhouse and crossed to the stern. Pointing them south in the direction of the sound, he caught sight of a speedboat heading towards *Sea Spray* at breakneck pace. He was anchored at least ten miles offshore, so escape by swimming was out of the question. Struggling out of his clothes he threw them overboard and quickly stepped into the wet suit he'd bought from the shop recommended by Charlie Stansfield. He strapped the aqualung, which he'd bought from the same shop, to his back, and jumped into the water. The last time he'd used aqualung apparatus he'd been a teenager and on vacation from high school but he prayed that, like riding a bike, he would be able to remember what to do.

When he hit the water he heard Sean's voice flooding back, doling out instructions just as it had done back in that Florida summer of his youth. Diving to approximately twenty feet, he waited. It didn't take long; about six minutes later the speedboat pulled up alongside *Sea Spray*.

From his position underwater Jay could just make out the underneath of both boats. After another ten minutes or so, he very slowly drifted to the surface – emerging on the far side of the speedboat.

Cautiously he peeked over the edge. The only signs of human occupation were a pack of Marlboro Red and two empty beer bottles. Then, scanning the dash, he spotted a key chain dangling from the ignition. It was all he needed. Hoisting himself on board, he crouched in front of the wheel and started the engine. Its powerful 200 horsepower roared into life as Jay pushed the throttle down hard and on to full speed.

The boat leapt forward, two wide arcs of water spraying from either side. He didn't even hear the first shot as it skimmed past his right temple, and hit the windscreen. He heard the second all right, but didn't see where it went. He had retreated to underneath the seat and was steering with his fingertips. Until he was confident he was out of firing range, he did not dare glance back.

When he did so, *Sea Spray* was a mere dot on the horizon. So he made himself more comfortable, pulled the throttle back to lower the speed and ten minutes later was cruising into a small lakeside harbour.

With great relief he unstrapped the aqualung, and left it in the boat. Clad in his wet suit, he attracted a few curious glances in the harbour store but was able to buy the clothes he needed: a sweater, waterproof chaps, plimsoles and a windcheater. Leaving the shop with them on, he sprinted to the nearest bus stop and caught the first bus that pulled up a few minutes later. It was going to Three Forks.

The journey took fifteen minutes and as the bus pulled to a halt Jay spotted a sign saying, 'Maritime Hotel, Vacancies, B&B.'

'Guess what? They found me.' Jay was calling Luther from his warm and cosy room at the Maritime.

'You still in one piece?'

'Just, but it was close. I'm gonna have to move fast. Send him the tapes.'

Luther understood. 'Consider it done, man.'

Cutting the connection, Jay began to dial another

number. The telephone was a fifties reproduction model, cream coloured and bulky, with a circular brass dial like the telephones he'd used before prison. Jay found it awkward to use, and this time his heart was beating very fast as he waited for the connection.

'Yes?'

'Mario Petroni?'

'Who is this?'

'Jay Kaminsky . . .'

'What do you want?'

'I want my own life, and enough money to enjoy it. I've got a proposition for you, Mr Petroni.'

'I'm listening.'

'I don't go for being hunted down like an animal, and I'm sure as hell not going back inside.'

'You're a convicted killer, Kaminsky. Prescott's out to get you, if I don't get there first. What do you think your chances are?'

'They're great if I agree to testify against you. With the evidence I've got, I can join Witness Protection and while I'm enjoying my new life you'll be inside for the rest of yours.' Jay paused. 'Ever been in the pen, Mario? It's not a lot of fun, unless of course you enjoy being systematically buggered and – '

'Spare me the shit, Kaminsky, I know what happens inside and I've no intention of going there. So what's the deal?'

'It's simple. I give you the original manuscript of *Killing Time*, the factual version with all the actual dates, names and places Al told me about. Those diaries he kept . . . they made very interesting reading. Some very useful research there.'

'You got the diaries?'

Jay felt a quick thrill of triumph as he detected a hint of fear in Mario's voice. Not replying directly, he continued, 'We became big buddies, Al and me. He trusted me, told me everything.'

'That fucking scumbag Colacello . . . should have finished him off when I got the chance back in seventy-one.'

'Oh, but then we wouldn't be having this interesting conversation. Let me make it a bit more interesting for you . . . The Trident Packing Company, Long Island, MD Richie Evans. I'm sure the Food and Drugs Administration would love to have examined the crates that arrived every second Wednesday in the month, supposedly full of bananas from St Lucia – funny how they got trans-shipped via Columbia. And that other neat little operation in Texas. Sweet Success, your sugar importation company; great name, it shows wit and panache. Again, funny how refined sugar looks exactly like cocaine and smack. I bet the FBI would enjoy a chat with Fernando Mendoza, whiz-accountant in charge of offshore portfolios based in Panama. And with our very own home-grown New Yorker, Roberto Cappellini, the money-laundering genius. I can name at least six legitimate companies he's set up for you: one in nineteen eighty – '

'*Enough*. What do you want?'

'I want five million dollars deposited in the Cayman

Islands. I want Weston Kane and Beth Morgan indicted on whatever charge you fancy. And I want you to call off your mastiffs. When you've done all of that, I deliver.'

'How do I know you won't double-cross me?'

'You'll have to trust me, Mario. Just like Al did.'

# Chapter Eighteen

Weston was standing in front of the floor-to-ceiling glass wall of her apartment. She'd lost count of the times she'd stood in exactly the same spot admiring the view, and congratulating herself on having made it her own. But today she wasn't in a self-congratulatory mood. Today was another dark day, one of the many blackout days since Kelly's death.

Soon Todd would arrive, and they'd make small talk, swop a little business, a little gossip, until the conversation got round to Kelly and Kaminsky.

Lunch earlier with Beth had been the same. Lots of enforced banality to mask the emotions they were both experiencing. Beth was obviously in denial. Pretending everything was all right and hunky dory. Just lock the demons away, don't feed them and eventually they'll die. But the problem was they didn't. Instead they lay dormant and festered, taking on a life of their own and breeding.

Weston had found Beth's trivial twittering pathetic, and had responded angrily to her on several occasions. The meeting had ended on a sour note, with Beth storming out of the restaurant in tears. Weston had stayed, got drunk, and had come straight home instead of going back to the office. She'd fallen asleep on the sofa and had woken in a slumped position, her chin on her chest, her neck twisted. Minutes later she'd been sick, heaving over the toilet basin. And it was in that moment she'd decided to stop drinking. *Kelly was dead. Jay was alive.* These were the two incontrovertible facts that haunted her. Whether she was drunk or sober, the truth was the same.

The doorbell intruded. It was Todd, ushered in by her new maid Elsa. He crossed the room to greet her with a light peck.

'Good to see you, Weston.' If he said she was looking well, he would be lying. And he supposed the same would apply if she said it about him.

'How are you, Todd?'

'Keeping busy, there's always plenty to do. I even got out on the golf course the other day. Lost, as usual, to my old pal Bill. And you?'

'Same, I'm always busy. On the treadmill, can't get off, not even sure I want to. What would I do? Sorry, Todd, I didn't offer you a drink. I've given up. Five minutes ago.'

Waving his hand, he refused. 'No thanks, I've been drinking too much lately.'

'Join the club.' She had a glass in her hand, she lifted it saying, 'Water from now on.' Then, 'You want to sit?'

They sat side by side on the deep sofa. Weston was wearing blue jeans and a white cashmere sweater over a white button-down cotton shirt. Her hair was loose and unkempt, thick curls framing her washed-out face.

Todd couldn't remember ever seeing Weston look so distraught. Not even after her father had died.

'Todd, is this a social call or something else?'

'It's something else. I want to ask you a few questions and I need you to be candid with me.'

Weston scrutinized his face as he continued. It wore the solemn look of the recently bereaved but there was something missing, something she'd seen the last time they'd met. At first she wasn't sure what it was, then she realized the anger was gone.

'As I'm sure you're aware, I loved Kelly very much. I know she didn't feel the same way about me.'

Weston peered at him over the rim of her glass. 'Why do you say that?'

'Oh, lots of little things. The usual cliché – I think she loved me, but wasn't in love with me. But it didn't matter, I loved her passionately, to distraction. Under the brittle exterior she was so fragile. I think things would have been better had she had a baby. A child would have occupied her mind, helped her forget whatever demons she suppressed under the controlled surface. I now know that in the seventies she aborted Matthew Fierstein's baby. But why did the fact that she was pregnant never come out in the Kaminsky trial? And why did Kelly in a conversation with you say that Kaminsky was innocent?'

Shock registered on Weston's face, yet her even voice denied it. 'I don't know what you mean.'

Todd fished in his pocket and brought out two tapes. 'I think you do, Weston. These arrived by special courier this morning. My phone has been tapped for some time.

I'm not sure since when exactly, but these recordings date from some weeks ago. There are several conversations between you and Kelly. In one Kelly speaks of Kaminsky being innocent of the Fierstein murder, and in most of them you're both worried about his release and subsequent presence in town. Why are you afraid of the guy?'

Todd let his words sink in, then took Weston's glass from her hand to claim her full attention. 'Tell me who killed Fierstein. And don't give me any shit, Weston, I want the truth.'

After a long silent moment of considering, Weston gave up her initial intent to prolong the deception. 'Kelly killed him in self-defence.'

Todd was clearly winded by these six words, but he managed to say, 'Now, I want the whole story. I think I deserve to know.'

Deprived of her glass, Weston walked to a nearby console table and lit a cigarette. Then she walked slowly back and sat down in the seat she'd vacated. Inhaling deeply, she let smoke curl out of her mouth, and pushing all other thoughts out of her mind she travelled back to 1972.

'It began in the fall of seventy-two, when Kelly and I first met Jay. It was, as they say in the movies, love at first sight. They were like a couple of lovesick puppies. So much so, it made Beth and I want to throw up. *Jay this, Jay that, Jay the other*. Kelly talked of nothing and no one else. They dated all year, and by next fall we could hear the definite chime of wedding bells. She was too young, much too young, and Jay wasn't right for her. He was a country kid, bright but a hick, he would have ended up as a stuffy professor in some obscure faculty, Kelly deserved greater things. With her beauty she could have anyone. She'd worked hard to get into Wellesley, and she was determined to get to the top. I helped her get through all her exams, I didn't mind. You see, Todd, I was in love with her myself.'

He was not taken by surprise. 'I suspected as much.'

'Matthew Fierstein was a jerk, and a mean bastard. I knew that from the first night when we all went out to dinner. He had set his sights on Kelly, and he was determined to have her. He had a dark side, problems with his mother, probably sexually abused when he was a kid – I'm not sure. But what I am certain of is that he was seriously fucked up. Kelly tried to let him down lightly, but he wouldn't take no for an answer. He just pursued her. She didn't tell Jay because he was Jay's best friend and she didn't want to come between them. On the night of the killing Matt and Jay had quarrelled and Matthew called Kelly from some bar threatening to kill Jay and then Kelly herself. She went to find Jay in his room but when she got there she found Matthew, very drunk; he raped her, abused her . . .'

Faltering now, Weston ground out her cigarette. 'Matthew Fierstein got what he deserved – Kelly was lucky that she was the one that got out of there alive. When I got her call I was with Beth, and together we went to Matt's room.' Shutting her eyes, Weston visualized the scene, reliving the fifteen minutes it had taken to calm the hysterical Kelly and wipe all the surfaces clean, including the handle of the kitchen knife.

'Kelly was distraught, and wanted to call the police. I admit I was the one that stopped her. At that point we were all more concerned with covering up than actually framing anyone else, and when Jay was arrested we were shocked. Kelly in particular. Again she wanted to confess, and once again I talked her out of it, certain that the prosecution had insufficient evidence to convict Jay.

'I was wrong, I know. I don't make any excuses for what I did, what we all did. We were just kids, hedonists, and selfish in a way that's exclusive to the young.'

Weston cleared her throat. 'I don't think Kelly ever recovered from Jay's conviction – she lost something inside and then she buried her guilt. We all did, it was a shared bond, the unspoken secret. And it's a large part, I believe, of what's kept us together for the last quarter of a century.'

Todd searched Weston's face. 'How could you live with yourselves knowing an innocent man was serving time, twenty-five years of time. Have you ever been inside a prison?'

Weston shook her head.

He sighed. '*Not* pretty, it's no picnic in there. The poor bastard! A brilliant young kid, a Harvard scholar. A lifetime wasted . . . and for something he didn't do.'

'*Exactly*. That's why he's killed Kelly, and would kill Beth and me if he gets the chance. Somehow Jay must have found out, or just suspected. Or maybe Kelly confessed to him, I don't know.'

'And who could blame him?' Todd's expression had changed, the anger had returned, only this time it was directed at Weston.

'What are you saying, Todd? He's killed your wife – your beautiful, beloved Kelly. He shot her, blew half her body away.'

'Give it a rest, Weston. There's no definite proof of that. And how can you talk as if you've no sympathy, no regrets?'

With an impassive expression and an icy cool, Weston said, 'I've only one regret: that Kelly's killer is free. And I won't rest until Jay Kaminsky is brought to justice.'

'For God's sake, woman, don't you think you've interfered with the course of justice enough! Hasn't it ever occurred to you that Jay could be innocent of this crime as well, that he might be telling the *truth*?'

'Not for a moment. I know he killed Kelly.'

'Well, I've got no stomach to hunt him down any more.'

'Chickening out? Feeling sorry for poor old Jay who was in the wrong place at the wrong time, once again. The story of Jay Kaminsky's life. Don't waste your sympathy, Todd; it's happened to thousands before him, and no doubt will happen to thousands more. How many convicted felons do you think are innocent victims of circumstance? Life sucks, we all know that. What happened way back in the seventies has got nothing to do with now, you're confusing the two issues.'

'I'm not confused, I've just lost the anger that's been gnawing away at my gut for the last few days.' He snapped his fingers. 'It's gone, and I feel much better. Kaminsky's a fugitive, on the run from the mob. It's only a matter of time before they catch up with him, poor sonofabitch. Maintaining one's anger can be extremely debilitating. If you could get rid of yours it might help.'

Jumping to her feet, Weston screamed, 'Help me to do *what*! To forget Kelly? To come to terms with never seeing her again? Only time will help that. Anger can also be positive, mine is, and I need it right now – it's all that's keeping me going.'

Todd rose to stand next to her. 'Leave it, Weston, let it go, get on with your life. If you don't you'll destroy yourself.'

'You're a coward Senator Prescott, a fucking lily-livered coward! God help Uncle Sam if you ever get into power.'

The colour drained from Todd's face, and as soon as he began to speak she knew she'd gone too far. 'I won't forget what you've just said, Weston. Not ever. And I warn you, you've just made an enemy.' He strode to the door. 'I'll let myself out.'

Weston stood in the centre of the room where she remained motionless and for the first time in her life felt very afraid.

He was in Great Falls Park, Montana. It was a warm day. Jay felt like a jerk in the shin pads and roller blades. It would have been OK if he could skate. It had seemed like a good idea at the time – the time being earlier that day when he'd been desperate to mingle inconspicuously with the crowd in the park.

From under the peak of his baseball hat, he'd seen the same black Lincoln that had been following him pull into the car park. Sitting on a public bench he took off the blades, replacing them with his trainers. Tying the laces, he slung the boots over his shoulder as he watched four men get out of the car. They were all wearing dark suits. Initially they huddled in a conspicuous bunch, smoking and talking in hushed voices. If he hadn't felt so nervous he would have found the entire scene hilarious. It was like something out of a gangster movie, only real.

When Jay got closer, a man whom he recognized as the second-hand car dealer he'd seen in the garage back in Indiana looked up and fixed him with his gaze. A few feet from the group Jay stopped. They all turned and he felt panic-stricken; *it's like being up against a firing squad*, he thought.

One figure stepped forward, while the others stayed in a line behind. Jay didn't recognize the man as Mario Petroni. There was little resemblance to a photograph he had seen of Mario and Al Colacello, taken before Al's arrest. Either Mario had undergone cosmetic surgery, or Al had shown him a picture of someone else. Then Mario opened his mouth and his front teeth were revealed. Gold capped, glinting in the sun like a pair of gilded tombstones, they immediately jogged Jay's memory.

But the rest of Mario was a surprise. The photo had been of an archetypal Latin: swarthy and heavily built. Petroni was none of this. Instead he had inherited his mother's refined Venetian features, visible in his greying blond hair and sapphire blue eyes. Almost as tall as Jay, he wore his charcoal suit with sartorial elegance – it was beautifully cut and hung perfectly on his well-proportioned slim frame. He was also wearing a silk tie, and a matching handkerchief poked out of his breast pocket. With the palm of his left hand, Mario smoothed the front of his suit, a four-carat diamond glinting on his little finger.

'You Jay Kaminsky?'

'You Mario Petroni?'

Mario had evidently taken this as a statement, not a question. 'I believe you've got something for me.'

'Before I hand it over, I want proof that the money has been transferred.'

Taking a slip of paper from his pocket, Mario handed it to Jay. It was a fax from a bank in Grand Cayman detailing a transaction for five million dollars deposited in the name of Jay Kaminsky.

'The money arrived yesterday afternoon, four-thirty Cayman time. If you want any further confirmation, go call. The number of the bank, and the guy to speak to is all on the fax.'

Jay stuffed the fax in his back pocket; he sucked in his breath, he needed a cigarette. 'What about Weston Kane and Beth Morgan?'

'No problem, I've got that covered.'

Jay took a second deep breath, willing his heart-rate to slow down. 'Another copy of my unedited manuscript is in safekeeping. If you're lying, or I'm double-crossed, or

301

in the event of my death, that copy will be sent to Lauren Stone. She's a criminal attor– '

Mario interrupted, 'I know who she is.'

'Like I said, if anything happens to me, like anything at all untoward, she'll produce her copy of the goods.' Jay was nervous, and it showed. He was aware of babbling, talking too fast.

Mario looked perplexed. 'That wasn't part of the deal. I don't like sudden changes in plans, it makes me nervous.'

'I need insurance,' Jay said.

Mario took a step closer to Jay and surveyed his manicured nails. Using a toothpick he began cleaning them and without looking up said, 'Don't fuck with me. What is it with you, you don't trust me? You got your money, I want my goods. And I want to sleep nights.'

'I need insurance,' Jay repeated. 'If all goes to plan the other manuscript will be destroyed.'

'You got the diaries?'

'No, I don't know where the diaries are, they disappeared after Al died.'

'So what about Mario's insurance?'

'You've got my word.'

Still Mario didn't look up. But when he finally did, Jay was surprised to see him smiling. The smile stuck clown-like, as if painted on, and it didn't move as the toothpick was flicked into Jay's face. 'If you want to stay alive long enough to enjoy your cash, I suggest you keep that word. Because if you don't, I promise wherever you are in the world . . . I'll find you. Understood?'

Jay experienced a sinking sensation deep in his gut, then the urge to shit. He nodded.

Mario held out his hand, palm up. 'The goods.'

Fumbling in the inside pocket of his windcheater Jay pulled out a disk. 'It's all there.'

Mario looked at the disk then, with his eyes narrowing, back to Jay. '*Everything?*'

'Everything, I promise. The diary material intact.'

'Talking of promises, I want to repeat mine just so you don't forget. You fuck with me,' he pointed to Jay's crotch, 'and you won't have anything to fuck *with*. Understood?' He was grinning, gold teeth gleaming. 'Happened to a guy I knew once, a scumbag who caused trouble, tried to be clever. When the cops found him they thought he still had a dick.' Warming to the subject, Mario began to laugh, 'Cause by then he had real flies.' Making a ball with both hands he elaborated, 'Hundreds of 'em feasting in the hole where his schlong had been.'

There was a long moment of silence before Mario turned on his heel and walked towards the car. His three stooges followed. The car doors shut with muted clunks, then the driver did a three-point turn, deliberately reversing a little too close to where Jay stood. As he watched the Lincoln drive out of the car park and out of sight, there was no doubt in Jay's mind that Mario Petroni had meant every word he said.

# Chapter Nineteen

Ed was having lunch poolside, he was eating what he had every day – a BLT sandwich, with French fries and mayonnaise. He flicked an insistent fly off his bare forearm, and took a sip of rum Collins. Idly he watched an old woman rub sun cream into her wrinkled thighs and wished, not for the first time, that he was freezing his balls off in New York instead of taking too much sun, getting smashed and losing money in the hotel casino every night. At least he was getting laid, regularly, some consolation, but not enough to interrupt the monotony of life in the Sandpiper Hotel, Grand Bahamas.

From behind his shades, he saw Ricky the head bellman heading directly towards him with a package. 'Special delivery for you, Mr Hooper.'

Ed was wary. He looked at the handwriting and the postmark: Montana. He smiled; it was from Jay. Handing over a five-dollar note to the bellman, and pushing his plate to one side, Ed tore open the parcel's wrapping. Underneath was a brown box and inside a manuscript with a handwritten letter placed on top.

*Dear Ed,*
  *Here is the original unedited manuscript we talked*

*about on the phone. Sorry to have to implicate you
in all of this, but like I said I haven't got a whole
bunch of people I can trust. I won't bore you again
with the 'wrong place at the wrong time' bullshit,
suffice to say I'm innocent. You believed in me before,
I'm asking you to do so again. Take the manuscript
to Hayward Trust bank, located on 289 South Shore
Drive, Grand Cayman – account number 7827508.
Stick it in the safe deposit and if anything happens
to me or alternatively if you don't hear from me
in the next two weeks, make sure Lauren Stone
gets a copy. That's it, Ed, simple. I'll say thanks in
anticipation. I think you're one of the good guys,
and there aren't many of us left. Hope you're getting
laid regular, and hope to see you again in the not too
distant future.*

   *Yours,*

   *Jay*

Ed reread the letter then looked at the manuscript.
Intrigued, he began to read and at the end of the
second chapter knew this was, as Jay had claimed, the
factual version of *Killing Time*. It was a devastating
piece of evidence against several prominent underworld characters – Mario Petroni in particular. Dropping the A4 sheets of paper like they were red hot, Ed
closed the box, paid his bill and left the table to pack
his bags.

  When he checked out of the hotel an hour later it was
raining. The taxi was late and Ed jumped into the back

with an urgent, 'Put your foot down; the airport as fast as you can.'

The car, a 1970s Ford bumped forward, throwing its passenger into the air as it hit a rut in the road. 'Bad storm brewing, man, you goin' have a rough ride.'

Ed grinned. He'd heard it all before. West Indians loved to talk, about anything and everything. 'No shit, it ain't hurricane season.'

'Believe me, when ma cow Molly gits skittery and won't eat, always it storms, man, real bad.'

Ed ignored this, and concentrated instead on watching the scene outside. It never failed to amuse him how West Indians reacted to rain. They were afraid of getting their heads wet, believing it gave them a cold. He watched a woman, her arms outstretched, holding a black bin liner like a tarpaulin over her head.

The taxi had joined a queue of traffic stopped at a set of lights. Ed glanced at his wristwatch and told the driver he had to catch the twelve-fifteen to Grand Cayman, rain or no rain. Then he dropped his head back against the seat and thought about Jay. The boy was in deep shit, there was no doubt about that. But Jay had made big bucks for him and he was more than happy to help him if he could. He heard Jay's calm voice speaking to him in his head. It was something he'd said the first time they'd met in the pen. He'd thanked Ed politely for coming to see him, and Ed recalled being surprised by his perfect diction. He had asked him if he was American, and where was home. It was then that Jay had uttered something Ed had never forgotten. He'd said, 'Home is where the heart is, and I hope to get there some day.' With Jay's voice whispering in his ear – *you're one of the good guys* – Ed once again urged the driver to step on it. He received a grunt in return, yet felt the engine rev up as the car turned left on to a dual carriageway.

It was the lorry driver's fault, he was busy looking up the billowing short skirt of a long-legged young girl who was waiting at the crossroads. He didn't see the taxi before it was too late.

The lorry's front bumper hit the car head-on, killing the taxi driver instantly. Ed was catapulted into the front of the Ford where the open glove compartment on the dash punctured his spleen a split second before he went through the windscreen. As he hit the bonnet with a dull thud, Ed could taste something wet, warm and sticky in his mouth. He didn't hear his own screams, or the combined shouts of pedestrians and drivers alike. He died before the ambulance reached the hospital.

'Kelly killed Matthew Fierstein.'

Trying not to look surprised, Lauren said, 'How do you know?'

She was surprised not by the statement, but by the person uttering it. His call yesterday had come out of the blue, and she'd been intrigued to find out why Todd Prescott needed to see her so urgently.

They were sitting in her office, side by side on the beat-up old leather sofa that had been her daddy's. A legacy she cherished.

With a long sigh, Todd repeated, 'Kelly killed him after

he'd raped her. She covered up the murder with the help of two friends and allowed Kaminsky to go to jail. I can't stop thinking about how it must feel to go down for twenty-five years for something you didn't do. The whole thing stinks.'

'You have evidence, I assume.'

'I've got tape recordings, and I can testify that Weston Kane and Beth Morgan were involved.

'Weston admitted the truth to me at her apartment yesterday. She thought that telling me would convince me that Kaminsky killed Kelly. I'm not so sure any more. Weston's obsessed with finding him, and bringing him to justice, so much so I think she's losing her marbles.'

'The tapes could be admissible evidence, and you say you'd be willing to testify?'

'Absolutely. And I'm sure Beth Morgan would crack under cross-examination. I think you'd have enough for a retrial.'

'But it still doesn't solve the problem of Kelly's murder.'

'Do you think Kaminsky killed her?' Todd asked.

'No.' It was emphatic. 'I've got no evidence, but I believe what he told me. The mob were after him, and Kelly got in the way. Caught up in something that had nothing to do with her. Ironic isn't it? *What goes around comes around.* I don't know who said that, my dad I think.'

'*Fact is stranger than fiction*; that was *my* pop's favourite,' Todd added. Then with a quick glance at his watch he stood up. 'I've got to go, got lunch with the state governor at twelve-thirty, and the traffic's hell.'

Getting up also, Lauren walked with him to the door of her office. 'Thanks for coming to see me, Senator Prescott. I appreciate it.'

'This thing's been hanging over me ever since Kelly's death. At first I was so mad I wanted to kill someone myself. But when I listened to Kelly's voice on the tapes, I just felt profoundly sad. Kelly must have lived her entire adult life in the shadow of her guilty secret. It coloured every aspect of her existence. I now know I was married to a stranger, someone I never really knew at all.'

There was nothing more to say and as Lauren held out her hand to shake the senator's, she felt a wave of sympathy. 'I'll keep in touch.'

After Todd left Lauren could not concentrate on her brief. She sent out for a Coke, a large cappuccino, a tuna sub and a pizza – her favourite pepperoni with extra chillies. She pigged out, eating the lot without stopping for breath. When she'd finished, instead of the satisfaction she'd anticipated, she felt bloated and lowered by having done the very thing she'd promised herself she would never do again. 'Emotional eating', her shrink called it. Thank God the urge was rare, and the desire to throw it all back up never came in her case.

Pushing the debris to one side of her desk, she took out the letter Jay had sent her before he'd left New York. She'd read it several times and now she reread it once again.

*Dear Lauren,*
    *Sorry I had to split, but I had pressing business*

309

*elsewhere. My lack of faith in the judicial system
was one reason, and the other I hope to sort out
in the next few days. If I don't, and there's a
strong possibility that I might not, please contact
my agent Ed Hooper. If I don't make it, he will
have a gift for you.*

*I want you to know that you've got a very cute
ass. I bet your daddy never told you that? And
like I said before, a great smile. So keep right on
smiling.*

*Take care, love,*
*Jay*

'Jay Kaminsky is dead.'

Beth thought she was hearing things. 'Come again?'

Weston's voice was resigned. 'I said Jay is dead.'

'*How; when; where?*' The questions tumbled out of
Beth. She was in her office and had been sorting through
her correspondence, a prospectus from St Paul's School in
London on the top of the pile.

'His body was found in Montana last night, near Fort
Peck Lake. I just caught it on NBC and I suppose it'll hit
our newspapers tomorrow morning. I don't know all the
details yet.'

Beth felt a great surge of relief, accompanied by a sensation of light-headedness. As if she'd been carrying a huge
weight on her shoulders, and it had suddenly been lifted.
She said, 'How do you feel, Wes?'

Weston thought about lying to Beth, saying that she
felt elated, but in truth she felt the opposite and said as

much. 'It's strange, but I feel sad. Don't ask me why. The only explanation I can offer is one that scares me.'

In a small voice Beth said, 'Tell me.'

'Well, when I first heard, my initial reaction was *Thank God*. But since then I feel like I've come in a complete circle. I truly believed that punishing Jay would make me feel better about missing Kelly, but his death has made it worse, much worse, and I'm not sure why. For the first time in my whole life I'm not sure about anything. I've walked round the apartment a dozen times, touching all my beautiful possessions – and they mean nothing.'

Beth had never heard Weston sound so despairing, and she wasn't sure how to react. 'Losing Kelly has been very traumatic for me too, I've not been well since. Perhaps now that Jay is dead, we can at least put the past behind us, and get on with our lives . . .'

'That's the problem, Beth, I don't feel positive about my future. I've got everything most people aspire to, all the trappings of wealth and success. But suddenly I feel totally detached, empty. It's like I'm living in someone else's apartment, like I don't belong any more. I think that I'd better go away for a while. I'm not sure where at the moment, I may go to Europe, do the Grand Tour, all that upwardly mobile American's thing. Might even find myself a beautiful senorita in Italy, someone to give me back some purpose in life.'

'That sounds wise. How long is it since you had a vacation?'

'Four years ago, when I went skiing.'

Beth thought it was a good time to mention her own forthcoming travels. 'I'm on the move, too. I'm going to London. I've decided to leave Douglas and go back home to live in England. My father's not getting any better, and he can't have much longer.'

Weston made no attempt to hide her surprise. 'When did you decide all of this?'

'After Kelly's death. It was like an omen, a turning point. I felt I had to go in a different direction. I didn't tell you before, Wes, because you had enough on your plate, and I knew how cut-up you were over Kelly.'

'I see,' was all Weston could find it in her heart to say. She knew if she said what she really felt, expressed her hurt and loss, she would regret it later.

'Look, Wes, I'm sorry I didn't tell you, because, well, like I said . . .'

'Don't worry about it, Beth. So you didn't tell me, so what? It's all over now anyway – the Pact, the bond, the friendship. It died with Kelly, and now it'll be totally buried with Jay.'

# Chapter Twenty

It was late morning when Lauren located her Corvette convertible hire car in the Hertz compound. It was blood red and brand spanking new, with just three hundred miles on the clock.

Yesterday when she'd heard about Jay's death, she'd been shocked and saddened. Then later her shock had turned to anger and suspicion. She'd called his agent only to be told by a tearful secretary that Ed Hooper had been tragically killed in a car crash while on vacation in the Bahamas. The whole thing stank, and it was the nagging doubts in the back of her mind which had driven her to make flight arrangements to Montana. Though she was still asking herself what good she could do as she drove out of the airport terminal heading towards Fort Peck Lake.

She was convinced the mob had got to Jay, and if she could pick up one lead, one shred of evidence, she was determined to prove it. It was one of those 'good to be alive' days, high sky and cloudless, warm but not too hot. A day of promise. On days such as this, Lauren often thought of her childhood, of growing up in the warmth of a devoted family, of the idyllic weekends spent at her parents' summer house in Pawleys Island on the South Carolina coast.

Last night she'd spoken to her father, asked his advice. It had been as usual, sound and constructive: *drop the Kaminsky case*. Let it rest, he said. What could she hope to gain from chasing ghosts? If it was true that Jay had been executed by the mob, then there was no doubt they'd have left no trace.

During a sleepless night Lauren had pondered her father's wisdom. She'd risen at dawn, jogged for a mile around her neighbourhood, picked up fresh croissants for a rushed breakfast . . . before taking a cab out to La Guardia.

Her thoughts digressed to Jay's wasted life and her anger returned. She was still feeling angry when she entered the small town of Great Falls forty minutes later.

Lauren found the local police precinct easily and was lucky to find a parking space right opposite the building. Inside, her flat rubber soles made little noise as with two purposeful strides she approached a young man who was standing behind a long wooden counter. He had a telephone pressed to his left ear, and with his eyes he indicated a bench seat to his right.

Lauren sat down, glancing briefly at the headline in the local newspaper: 'Ten-year-old Local Boy Battered to Death by Gang of Youths'. There was a photograph of his distraught parents holding each other, their vacant-eyed bewilderment staring out of the page. She felt a wave of disgust for the sort of world that made killers of children. How did it happen she wondered; were these young murderers born that way, was the urge to kill inherent? She doubted that, and had spent enough time with people who had killed to know that society was the real villain, the ultimate perpetrator.

She listened to the police officer's voice. The sound, like subdued murmuring, was more suited to seduction than small-town police affairs, and seemed incongruous to Lauren. At last he concluded and turned his attention on her with a slack smile.

She rose and approached the counter. 'My name is Lauren Stone, I'm a lawyer. I've got an appointment with the DA, Mr McCabe.'

Abruptly the young man's body language changed. He straightened his back and tilted his chin in a kind of standing-to-attention pose. 'Yes, Miss Stone. Mr McCabe is expecting you. Follow me.'

She followed him down a long windowless corridor to a door where he stopped and knocked twice.

'Come.'

'Miss Stone for you, Mr McCabe.'

Jim McCabe rose from behind a mountain of papers. Sunlight streamed from the window above his head, lighting his mop of hair. It was white and wiry, and reminded Lauren of the candyfloss she'd had at funfairs when she was a child.

'Pleased to meet you,' he bellowed.

'Likewise,' Lauren said. 'Thanks for agreeing to see me on such short notice.'

'My pleasure, sit down. Drink?' When she declined, he added, 'You don't mind if I do . . .' And he proceeded to pour neat whisky into a teacup. 'You like Scotch, Miss Stone?'

'Not my poison, and call me Lauren.'

He grinned. 'Well, in that case you can call me Mr McCabe, or sir.' He winked, his open eye blue and twinkling. 'Only teasing, call me Jimmy. It's a long time since a pretty little filly called me that.'

Lauren said reluctantly, 'OK, Jimmy it is.' She resented being referred to as 'a pretty little filly' – it was not how she perceived the image of a tough uncompromising lawyer. But at this juncture she chose to ignore his patronizing comments. She'd met the Jim McCabes of this world before. Invariably they talked a lot, rarely listened and were often complete misogynists.

Jim looked down at the notes in front of him, then up at Lauren. 'You said on the phone that you were acting for this Kaminsky fellow?'

'That's right, he was accused of killing three people, including Senator Todd Prescott's wife.'

With a dismissive wave of his hand, he said, 'Yeah, I've got all the background. Convicted felon gets out, revenge trip, the usual.'

'That's where you're wrong, Mr McCabe . . . Jimmy, if you don't mind me saying. Jay Kaminsky was not "the usual". First and foremost, I believe he was innocent of the crime he served twenty-five years for, and I also believe he didn't kill Kelly Prescott. In fact I don't think Jay ever killed anybody. He had vital evidence that could indict a well-known Mafia don, and I think he was murdered because of that.'

'Well, it don't make no difference now. He's dead.' The District Attorney had downed the remaining whisky with a loud slurp.

316

'Finding out who killed him might make a very big difference.'

With his finger curled around the handle of the empty cup, McCabe asked her, 'To who?'

'His family, Todd Prescott, the Feds, the FDA . . . Need I continue?'

Placing the cup down, he plaited his fingers across his chest. 'There were no suspicious circumstances, it was a straightforward crash. Car spun off the road down a ridge and blew up. We figure he was on his way to his aunt's house. Probably driving too fast, wet night, who knows, it happens all the time.'

'When the mob make a professional hit, they leave no trace. It's invariably a thoroughly clean job. Another unsolved crime, just one more for the record books.' She paused. 'I gather his body was charred beyond reasonable recognition?'

'Yeah, burnt to a crisp.'

'Don't you think it strange that his ID was conveniently close at hand? Has it not occurred to you that it was probably planted?'

'No, young lady, it has not. To be perfectly honest I've got a lot of real unsolved crimes to be getting on with. This Kaminsky was a convicted felon, on the run from the police. I don't hold with this cockamamie story about the mob after him. There's a young local kid just been battered to death by a gang of boys he called his friends – barely out of diapers, average age twelve. And old Molly Searle was robbed and raped last week by some black kid from South Dakota for ten dollars. That's all she had in the house. Molly's seventy-two, going on seventy-three, she's lucky to be alive. How does a twenty-four-year-old kid rape a grandmother? It's sick, all belly-aching, shit-stirring sick!

'So if this Jay Kaminsky gets out of the pen and then gets himself finished off by driving off the road, good riddance I say. One less killer roaming the streets.'

Lauren could feel her pent-up anger start to release, like a valve on top of a pan of boiling water emitting spurts of steam. 'I work with criminals all the time, Mr McCabe, and I don't need to be reminded of how sick the world is. This is a serious investigation and I expected professional co-operation, not rednecked speechifying.'

Jim McCabe, accustomed to generating respect, fear and obedience, had a bully's resentment of confrontation – always exacerbated if his adversary was female. It was, after all, the fault of women that the world was in such a mess as he'd conceded only last night over supper with two male friends. Kids were forced to grow up without feminine nurturing. Where were all the mothers? Out working their pretty socks off to jump into the shoes of some unsuspecting male colleague.

His voice turned ugly. 'This is my patch, Miss Stone. Small-town hicksville to you, from your fancy uptown law firm, but still my beat. As far as I'm concerned the Kaminsky case is closed.'

As if to emphasize his point he pushed the papers on his desk to one side and stood up. It was a definite dismissal and inwardly Lauren reproached herself for having rattled the autocrat's cage. *Should have known better, should have sucked up, crept a little, flattery gets you everywhere. One last shot?*

She stood up too. 'Hey, Jimmy, sorry I was a bit sharp. My daddy always says my tongue runs away with me, maybe that's why I'm a good lawyer. I screwed up on the Kaminsky case, like big time, and I'm trying like hell to put it right. You know how it is.'

She gave him her practised smile, the one her father always said made her look like a little girl in need of help. It didn't work. Jim McCabe still looked noncommittal and unco-operative.

'I don't really give a shit if you screwed up or not. Like I said, Jay Kaminsky was found dead in a car smash six miles south of the lakeside. The accident happened in normal circumstances. There is no tangible evidence to suggest foul play of any sort.' His voice rose. 'The case is closed.'

But not for Lauren. 'Jay Kaminsky was eliminated by the mob, of that I'm positive. I know why, and if I can prove it I might be able to bring down a Mafia godfather who's responsible for drug importation, killing and corruption on a scale that goes off the Richter. I would like to see the body, and talk to the coroner.'

'Miss Stone, I don't think you are hearing me correctly. I said the – '

'I heard you the first time, Mr McCabe. If you are intent on being unco-operative, I'll have to go over your head.'

Gritting his teeth, he snarled, 'And what exactly do you mean by that?'

Lauren bluffed. 'The FBI.'

The mere thought of the sleepy banks of Fort Peck Lake crawling with Feds was enough to make McCabe so incensed he wanted to throttle Lauren's long slim neck. Slowly he sat back down behind his desk, extracted the whisky bottle out of the drawer, poured a four-finger measure into the cup and took a sip. Then with a heavy sigh he wagged a finger at her. 'So you tell me what you know, and I'll consider giving you what you want.'

There was a thicket of dark trees beyond her window. Lauren stretched, watching the sun steal through a gap in the evergreen blanket. A dog barked, the plumbing groaned on the floor above, and she thought about Jay. What a waste. Just a few weeks of freedom – big deal – then game over. *Life sucks*. Well, she knew that – but shit, the phrase could have been invented for Jay. The thought made her angry, and she backtracked to yesterday and McCabe. After establishing an uneasy truce with the DA, she'd had to give him credit for his co-operation. The threat of bringing in the Feds had been the deciding factor in his about-face.

McCabe had driven her to the scene of the crash. The police had cleared and cordoned off the site, and the burnt-out vehicle had been removed for forensic evidence. There was very little to see, save a scorched patch of grass. An open-and-shut case according to McCabe – with everything pointing to a genuine car crash, not a carefully contrived Mafia hit. Yet Lauren wasn't really convinced of either scenario, a nagging doubt tugged at her, something didn't quite fit.

As she rose and dressed in brown wool slacks and a big cable-knit sweater the colour of egg yolk, she thought about McCabe's behaviour when he'd dropped her off at the hotel last night.

She had been forced to agree, that the case did *seem* to be that of a straightforward accident, yet still the hint of doubt kept pressing. 'Before I go I'd like to talk to the pathologist,' she had said.

It was then that McCabe had turned nasty again, insisting she was poking her nose into something that had nothing to do with her. He told her she should get on a plane back to New York and leave well alone. If he hadn't been so belligerent, that is exactly what she might have done. But she hadn't been nicknamed 'Stubborn Stone' for nothing and his attitude had merely fuelled her dogged determination.

Tom Currigan, the local pathologist, had agreed to meet her this morning at ten. It was now eight-thirty, she had an hour and a half to kill. Before going to bed last night she had wandered through the hotel, a converted early nineteenth-century merchant's house. Beyond the cosy sitting room, there was a wide conservatory filled with potted plants and trailing ivy. It was here they served breakfast, and the thought of warm toast and eggs in the sunny dining room appealed.

There was one other occupant present when Lauren entered ten minutes later. A blue rinsed lady, with a slash of scarlet lips and periwinkle blue eye shadow applied very thickly. She was picking crumbs from her plate with delicate bird-like movements and nodded to

Lauren as she sat down, a thin smile breaking her face.

'Good morning, young lady, lovely morning, don't you think?'

Lauren returned her waning smile. 'Yes exceptional, one of those feel good days.'

'We get lots of them here in Great Falls. You not from round these parts?'

Lauren was tempted to avoid her prying by simply saying no and burying her head in one of the newspapers. But something stopped her. A reporter had once told her that one of the best sources of local information was lonely old ladies who adore gossip and chatter.

'No, I'm from New York; down here on a case.'

Lauren actually saw the old woman's ears prick up, and was amused by the discernible interest suddenly sparking in her bright eyes.

'Not that terrible Molly Searle case?'

'No, I heard about that. But I'm here investigating the death of Jay Kaminsky. He was killed in a car crash a few days ago. I knew him, he was a friend. It's tragic.'

The old lady fixed her with a long hard stare, then in a dramatically changed tone said, 'I don't think that's so tragic. Kaminsky was a felon, a killer. Got what he deserved. I told Emily Crawford what I thought, that it was probably him that killed her poor Ted. A regular psychopath if you ask me.' With that, the other woman got up and without so much as a glance in Lauren's direction left the breakfast room.

Before Lauren had time to ponder on this outburst, a young man appeared at her table.

'Morning, miss. I'm Elton, what can I get you? We've got fresh blueberry and apple muffins. Or there's the usual wholemeal toast, eggs any way you want them, and . . .'

Lauren interrupted his flow. 'I'll take the muffins, scrambled eggs, some coffee. And I'll try your fresh kiwi juice.'

'Coming right up.'

Six minutes later her breakfast arrived, and as Elton served her, Lauren asked, 'Do you know anyone here-abouts called Emily Crawford?'

'Nope, never heard of her, except the surname rings a bell.' The young man appeared lost in thought for a few moments before he added, 'A man called Crawford died recently, some place near here, it was in our local paper. Perhaps she's a relative?'

Lauren said her thanks and made a mental note to call the DA straight after breakfast. If there was some connection between this Emily Crawford and Jay, she wanted to know about it, and if necessary she would wring the information out of that bastard McCabe.

'The body was charred beyond recognition, but what about dental plates?'

'This corpse had no teeth, and from what I've ascer-tained they had only recently been extracted. He may have had dentures that were destroyed, I can't be sure.'

The pathologist was as pleasant looking and as genial as

his job was grisly and unappetizing. Tom Currigan looked like the archetypal small-town storekeeper or bank clerk who had a couple of fresh-faced kids and a homespun wife who baked a lot of pecan pie. He was in fact single, in between gay lovers, and snow-boarded like an Olympic champion.

They were in his small office, next to the lab. It was painted in muted greens, the furniture functional rather than decorative.

'Do you know the time of death?' Lauren enquired.

'The body was badly burned, there was very little left to work with. Death could have occurred any time between noon Thursday and midnight Friday.'

Shifting in her seat, Lauren said, 'The smash-up was discovered early on Saturday morning, about seven?'

The pathologist nodded. 'By a couple out walking their dog. I got there round about eight.'

'Were all of the corpse's fingers burnt?'

Currigan nodded again. 'All except for the left thumb.'

'Is it possible to take a thumb print?'

'It is, but not in this case. The pad had been cut.'

Lauren leaned forward. 'What do you mean?'

'I mean someone had sliced off the entire thumb pad making it impossible to get an imprint.'

It was spotting with rain when Lauren stopped her car in front of Ducksberry Point. A single black cloud was strung like a tarpaulin across the wide expanse of water in front of the house. It had been easier than she'd anticipated to get the address of Emily Crawford.

McCabe had been surprisingly co-operative after his first growled, 'Thought you'd be on your way back to the big city by now. Don't say you've got to liking the country life better.'

Lauren had her response ready. 'With good-looking, charming men like you around, Mr McCabe, I just might.'

McCabe had chuckled, easing some of the tension between them, only to reinstate it a moment later by saying, 'Must say you're a feisty little filly. Give as good as you get.'

Lauren had bitten her tongue and asked him about Emily Crawford.

'They had a break-in, she was out at the time. Her husband took a beating, died of a heart attack. Emily found him dead when she returned. There was no robbery, no prints, no one saw anything untoward. The local cops have got all the details. For Chrissake, why do you want to talk to Mrs Crawford?'

'I think she knew Kaminsky.'

'You're wasting your time. The poor dame's just lost her husband, and I think if she'd known Kaminsky we would know about it.'

Lauren had ignored this, asked very politely for Emily Crawford's address, then thanked him when he'd complied. She had slammed the phone down after he'd insisted she promise to be off his back within twenty-four hours. Or else.

As soon as she stepped out of the car, Lauren spotted a woman sitting in a cane chair near the water's edge.

Assuming it was Mrs Crawford, she began to walk towards the figure. When she got closer she realized that the woman was quite old and that what she had assumed was a hat was in fact a bald scalp. It was as smooth as an egg, with just two sparse tufts of white hair below each ear.

The woman sat motionless like a statue, her hands were laid neatly side by side resting on her lap, and she was wearing a long plaid dress and a woollen cardigan. Lauren walked around to face her. 'Mrs Crawford?'

There was no response; Lauren tried again. 'Are you Emily Crawford?'

With watery eyes trained on something in the far distance, the old woman ran her tongue over cracked lips and whispered, 'I like the seaside, don't you?'

'Yes I do very much, I love being beside the water.'

'I forgot my bucket and spade, and Mommy smacked me. But Daddy promised to buy me a new one. Do you think he will?'

'I'm sure he will,' Lauren said carefully. It was beginning to rain hard and she was about to suggest they go inside when she saw a female figure running across the lawn towards them. She was out of breath and panting when she reached the old lady, and with a slight reprimand said, 'Rebecca, there you are! I've been looking everywhere.'

Then turning to Lauren with a quizzical look, she asked, 'Can I help you?'

'Are you Emily Crawford?'

'I am.'

'I'm Lauren Stone, we spoke on the telephone earlier. You did say four o'clock?'

'Oh, yes! I hadn't realized the time. My sister's just come out of hospital, and needs looking after all the time. It means I lose track . . .' Putting her arms around the seated woman, she said, 'Come on inside now, Rebecca. I've got some fresh carrot cake and your favourite cookies.'

Rebecca shrugged off her sister's arms with a petulant pout. 'I want a bucket and spade, then I'll play.'

With controlled patience Emily replied, 'The bucket and spade are indoors, if you come inside I'll give them to you.'

This seemed to do the trick and Rebecca began to giggle – girly high-pitched laughter that made Lauren shudder as she followed the sisters into the house. When they were in the cosy cluttered kitchen, Emily sat Rebecca down in an easy chair, making sure she was comfortable before turning her attention to Lauren who was standing awkwardly at the kitchen door.

Lifting a kettle off the stove, Emily asked, 'Tea, coffee?'

'Coffee would be great, thanks.'

'Please sit down.'

Lauren did so, saying, 'Are you sure this is a convenient time for you? I can come back, if you'd prefer.'

'It's fine, don't worry, once I've given Rebecca her tea we'll talk.'

As Mrs Crawford busied herself with boiling the kettle, and taking cups, saucers, tea, coffee and cookies out of a nearby cupboard, Lauren observed the older sister. The vacant look she'd noticed earlier was slowly being replaced by an awareness, eyes darting from side to side.

Emily had already laid a tray and placed it on Rebecca's lap, and now she placed a steaming cup of coffee in front of Lauren, pushing milk jug and sugar-bowl towards her before sitting down opposite.

Cradling her own cup in both hands Emily began, 'You said on the telephone you wanted to talk about Jay?'

'Yes, I know it must be painful, but it's important.' Lauren ploughed on, 'As you know, I'm a lawyer. When Jay was accused of killing Kelly Prescott, I was assigned to his defence. I believed in his innocence, I still do. I want to prove he didn't kill her, and that's just for starters. I believe he was himself killed by the Mafia because he knew too much about a man called Mario Petroni.'

Rather dumbfounded, Emily shook her head. 'Well, whoever killed my husband was after Jay, of that I'm sure.'

Lauren looked surprised. 'I don't understand.'

'Jay was here last week. He came to collect his original version of *Killing Time*. Years ago, before it was published, Jay sent the first draft to his mother, urging her to keep it safe. She did as he asked and put it in a safe deposit in her local bank. Some time later she had an argument with the manager, I really can't remember what it was all about now. Anyway in a fit of pique she withdrew her savings and transferred her valuables to my bank. It was during a period of her life when she was considering selling up in her part of Montana, and coming to live where we were in Lewistown. Anyway she changed her mind, but I always kept the manuscript safe for Jay. Until last week when he spent a short time here, and then left with it. About half an hour later I went out to my over-sixties yoga and was gone a couple of hours. When I returned my husband was dead. He'd been beaten about the head, but the cause of death according to the coroner was heart failure.'

'Did you tell the police about Jay coming here?'

'No. They believe that my husband must have startled an intruder, who attacked him and escaped.'

'Did Jay ever talk about a man called Al Colacello?'

'No, before Jay came here we hadn't spoken for several years. When he was first imprisoned we exchanged letters once a week. After a few years that petered out. For a while I visited him a couple of times a year, then my husband got sick and I had to care for him. Then my son got married and he and his wife lived with us for a while, and communication with Jay got less and less. Nobody's fault, life goes on, you know how it is. But I never believed Jay had killed that Fierstein boy. No one who knew him like I did would have believed it either. He couldn't hurt a fly. He was a sensitive soul, the literary type, loved to read and write.'

'You talking about Jay? Is he here? Tell that boy to come downstairs, his father wants to talk to him.'

Both Emily and Lauren looked at Rebecca, who was on her feet, her hand clawing the back of the chair.

'Jay, git your ass down here! Your pa's got something to tell you. Jay boy, you hear me?'

Emily was on her feet and in one long stride she was next to her sister. 'Jay's not here, Rebecca.'

'Is he coming back? Cause I've got something for him. And where's Fran?'

Emily covered her sister's hand. 'He might be, but I'm not sure when. And Fran's not coming back, ever.'

'Well if you speak to him, tell him they're safe, the books that is, the ones he sent me, the ones bound in leather. He begged me to look after them and I did. Clever boy, top of the class, all his teachers said Jay would go far.'

'You gave me the book, Rebecca, don't you remember, after you had the argument with the bank manager. You took the book out of the bank, along with your valuables, and gave everything to me for safekeeping.'

Rebecca looked annoyed, and with her free hand she gave her sister a sharp smack on the wrist. 'I know exactly what I'm talking about, Emily, why do you insist on treating me like a child?'

It was a perfectly reasonable question, delivered in a sensible articulate way, and for a moment Emily looked nonplussed.

'If I treat you like a child, Rebecca, I'm sorry.'

'OK, now like I was saying, if Jay contacts you, or asks about the books, tell him they're all at home.'

Emily slowly repeated what she'd said earlier. 'Rebecca, you gave your things to me, after you took them out of the bank.'

Rebecca began to laugh, only this time it wasn't the girlish giggle, but a deep heart-warming sound. She started to shake, then stopped abruptly, and once again her voice was calm and articulate. It was as if she were two different people. 'I know that, I'm talking about the bound books – the ones I gave to Francesca. I kept them for Fran, of course Fran didn't come back for them, you know what happened to her, silly girl. Anyway like I said, if Jay comes back tell him I did good. And will you also tell him his ma loves him.'

# Chapter Twenty-One

She wasn't sure what she'd expected, she'd had no pre-conceived image of the house. Yet when her car bumped down the dirt path towards the wooden shack where Jay was born, she was suddenly filled with remorse. Crowning a slope beyond a scrubby patch of grass, the two-storey house stood alone in a kind of forlorn decay – paint peeling, grimy windows and missing roof tiles. It was as if no one had ever lived there.

As she stepped out of her car, she tried to imagine Jay as a little boy running up to the front door after school, or playing some childhood game in the front yard. But she was unable to conjure up any happy images. Lauren solemnly mounted the first step leading to the front door, the key gripped firmly in her hand. When the next step creaked, she jumped – turning to look over her shoulder, overcome by the distinct feeling of being watched.

There was nothing but a gentle rustling in the cluster of pine trees to the left of the house, then all was still. The door opened easily, and she stepped into a small glass-partitioned lobby leading to the kitchen. It was sparsely furnished with the bare essentials for eating and drinking, a means-to-an-end place. Now she had an image: it was of Rebecca doling out food on the pine table, her pinched face and harsh voice demanding Jay eat every scrap, or else.

Slowly she moved towards the staircase. The stairs were uncovered and uneven and as she began to climb she steadied herself by holding on to the wall on either side. At the top there was a half step to a square hall and three doors leading off – Emily had said Fran's bedroom would be directly in front of her at the top of the stairs.

The door was ajar, sunlight somehow filtering through a thick film of dirt on the south-facing window. There was a bed with a crudely carved pine headboard, and a matching wardrobe; an old cane chair holding a cushion with a faded bird print; and a sixties-style chest of drawers in melamine with brass handles and a glass top.

When questioned as to whereabouts in Fran's old room she had put Jay's books, Rebecca had retreated into her infantile state, arguing about who should play with the dollies first – herself, Lauren or Emily. Kneeling down, Lauren looked under the bed first. There was nothing there apart from a thick layer of dust, and some dead insects.

The floor was pine-planked, each plank about ten inches wide. She thought about the possibility of the manuscript being hidden beneath, but after testing each plank realized they were all solid. Next, she searched the chest of drawers thoroughly; it was empty save for two threadbare sweaters, and a few handkerchiefs.

The wardrobe held an assortment of clothes, some obviously Rebecca's, and a heap of old bed linen. There

333

was a small bedside table, painted in moss green with a single sunflower in the centre of the door panel. Kneeling, Lauren opened the door, a short gasp escaping her lips as she peeped inside to see, sitting on the solitary shelf, a set of leather-bound diaries. Carefully she lifted them out, there were five volumes. Sitting gingerly on the bed, she opened the first one. It was dated '1974–1978'. Lauren felt her heart hammering very fast as she began to read the exceptionally neat hand, realizing after a couple of pages that here were the diaries of Al Colacello.

After reading a particularly explicit piece concerning a huge narcotics importation, her head was filled with a wonderful vision of Mario Petroni in court, squirming under her meticulous cross-examination. The urge to whoop was overwhelming, and with a loud smack she kissed one of the worn leather covers. Then holding the diaries high above her head, she shouted, 'Thank you, Rebecca! Thank you, Jay!'

She left the room with her trophies, and was about to walk downstairs when she was drawn to the room next door. Instinctively she knew, before she entered, that it was Jay's old room. The single bed was unmade and the blue and white ticking mattress had two big brown stains. There was a similar chest of drawers to the one in Fran's room, and a larger version of the same pine wardrobe. Lauren opened the wardrobe door: two items of clothing hung lopsided on cheap wire hangers. One was an old overall covered in paint stains, and the other a brown jacket. Both were dusty and smelt damp. She was drawn to take the jacket out – it was small and made of a cheap synthetic fabric. It had a name tag on the collar, 'Jay Kaminsky', hand sewn in red thread. Feeling moved, and about to put it back, she saw a notepad poking out of the inside pocket. It was a school exercise pad with Jay's name and class written on the front.

Flicking through the pages like a ghost, she realized it was a book of verse. Lauren was arrested by the title 'Elevator to Heaven', dated 16th September 1965, and she began to read.

> *Walking south against his will*
> *Stirred by turmoil of the mind*
> *Whirled by words of good, and still*
> *Trampling to dust for all mankind*

Jay would have been eleven or twelve when he'd written the poem. *Shit, what a waste*, she thought as she held the notebook tight to her chest. Even then he'd shown great talent, he could have become one of America's great writers if only fate had been a little kinder.

On the flight from New York to Montana, Lauren had been consumed with thoughts of Jay, of his background, his mother, his lost life. Now it was very clear what she had to do. Not only must she prosecute Petroni, but she also had to prove Jay's innocence. However long it took, whatever the cost to her own career, she would clear his name.

Still holding the diaries, she made her way back downstairs and outside. But before getting into her car, Lauren looked back towards the house. With her eyes trained on Jay's bedroom window, she whispered to herself, 'Wherever you are, my friend, I hope you're safe. And happy.'

Jay turned to look at the moon, a swelling ball of powdery white partially obscured by feathery wisps of stray cloud. His eyes had got used to the darkness and from where he stood, at the entrance to a disused hangar, he could see the narrow airstrip as a string of white cutting through the blackness.

He was early, and he didn't expect Red for at least fifteen minutes. *Red Conway*, he said the name in his head, then smiled a secret smile, thinking about how he and Red had met again. Pure chance, the best things in life always are.

Jay was to pinpoint it, much later, as the turning point in his life. It had happened the day after he'd met Mario Petroni in Great Falls Park. From there Jay had checked into a cheap motel, where he'd been unable to get to sleep, plagued by his thoughts.

*How much longer could he hold out? Would Petroni keep his word, or would he come after him? At least the godfather hadn't lied about the money. It was where he'd said it was, and had been transferred that morning to another account in the name of Luther Ross. Had Ed got the manuscript, was it safe?*

Finally at three thirty-five a.m. Jay had given up, and left the shabby room, grateful for some fresh air. It was damp but not cold. Zipping his jacket halfway, he'd lit up and walked aimlessly down the street at the back of the motel. It was deserted and dark, and he'd enjoyed the silence.

Jay didn't notice the body at first, not until he was almost upon it. And even then, in the darkness, it was almost impossible to distinguish the shape of a man. It was lying in the foetal position, legs pulled up into the chest. At first Jay thought it was a tramp sleeping rough, until he got closer and saw the blood teeming from two gaping holes in the stomach. As he kneeled down beside the prone figure, Jay had noticed that the man was of a similar height and build to himself, and about the same age.

The man stank of alcohol, it smelt like whisky. Jay listened for a heartbeat; hearing none, he'd frantically searched for a pulse. After holding the lifeless wrist for several minutes, he realized the owner was dead. Loath to leave a dead body in the street, but with no real option, Jay had started to walk away. It was then that the idea had struck, and he broke into a fast sprint back to the motel car park.

Grabbing his stuff from his room, Jay had jumped into the jeep, driving back to where the body lay. Carefully he'd loaded the corpse into the back of the car, covering it with his windcheater. Then he had driven out of Great Falls, heading for Fort Lake Peck itself. A few miles before the turning to Ducksberry Point and his Aunt Emily's house, Jay had turned off into a deserted lane. Carefully he'd dressed the man in his own clothes – they were an almost perfect fit. Then, one by one,

337

with a Swiss army knife he'd sliced off each finger pad and somehow steeled himself to extract the man's teeth. The second-hand jeep must have belonged originally to a car-maintenance fanatic, because its repair kit included a pair of pliers.

The first extraction was the worst and Jay had gagged. When a particularly strong upper back molar snapped in half almost like a carrot, he'd felt a wave of nausea travel up his body, then the acrid taste of bile. Swallowing hard, he'd had to stop for a few minutes to steady his shaking hand.

After completing the grisly task, there only remained to prop the body behind the wheel of the jeep and to jump in the passenger side himself.

Still with a less than steady hand, Jay had started the engine and slowly let the car move to the very edge of the road. Then he'd jumped out and had stood motionless, a silent prayer on his lips as the car careered over the edge to plummet down a sixty-foot drop. It had rolled a couple of times then burst into flames. Jay had watched the burning wreck for a few moments before starting down the hill on foot to reach the smouldering vehicle. He'd stood back and waited for the flames to subside completely before peering inside the shell of the car. The body was, as he'd hoped, totally incinerated, the face unrecognizable.

Having removed his money, Jay had then set light to his wallet, burning half of his Social Security card and part of his driver's licence – but not enough to obliterate his ID number. What was left of the wallet was thrown in to the car, where it had landed on the floor in the back. Shivering in jeans and a sweater, he had thankfully scrambled back up the hill and walked for miles cross-country until he felt he had put enough space between himself and the site of the crash.

In the small town of Wolf Point he'd boarded a train for Seattle, where he'd changed to one bound for Tacoma, and onward to Portland. He wasn't sure where he was headed, he'd simply had the urge to head out west.

At Portland he decided to take the bus, and climbed aboard a Greyhound headed for Sacramento. The bus was deserted, except for two teenage girls and a young kid with cropped hair and a sullen expression. Jay sat alone in the front seat, turning every few minutes to watch the sun beating down on pale green fields, the repetitive rumble of tyre on tarmac lulling him to sleep.

He'd slept a little and dreamt of his sister Fran, only in the dream she was very old. Dressed in a long shabby skirt that was bloodstained, she was crying.

When he awoke the bus was stationary at a depot, and still in Oregon. Rubbing his eyes and aware of a pain in his neck, Jay watched a heavily pregnant woman walk towards the door of the bus. He felt a rush of tenderness, there was something about pregnancy that could still fill him with hope.

It was then that he'd seen him. Just his back at first, next to the ticket booth. Who could miss a red-headed, six-foot-eight-inch mountain of a man ... When the mountain turned Jay saw that his shock of carrot hair had become grey at the temples, he was slightly heavier around the girth, and a good shoemaker could have made a pair of decent leather boots out of his skin. But the bright blue eyes seemed brighter than ever, a mischievous twinkle still evident, and he had the same hangdog expression Jay had never forgotten.

As the bus began to move, Jay had jumped up, waving. Running to the door, he had ignored the driver's protests and forced it open with the side of his foot. With a deep breath he'd jumped, landing on the flat of his feet. Then he was up and running, running fast towards Red Conway who was watching with a puzzled look. It wasn't until Jay was very close that the puzzlement turned first to surprise, then genuine pleasure.

'Well, I'll be damned! Jay Kaminsky, you old son-of-a-gun!'

Jay stepped forward out of the hangar, ears pricked as he heard the faint drone of engines. A moment later he saw the wing of the plane. As he watched it land he was filled with a great surge of sweet sadness, quickly gobbled up by an even greater sense of optimism.

When the plane had taxied along the runway to a smooth halt, Jay began to run towards it. He could see Red's face smiling and yelling something he couldn't hear. Then as he climbed aboard, Red greeted him with, 'Sure hope you feel happy flying with me? Haven't done much since 'Nam.'

'I'd be unhappy flying with anyone but you, Red.' Slapping the pilot's shoulder affectionately, Jay settled into the cockpit next to him.

As they began to taxi down the runway, it was Red who said, 'Feel like Humphrey Bogart in *Casablanca*?'

This made Jay laugh. 'No, I feel more like Columbus about to set sail.'

# Epilogue

In January 2000, Mario Petroni stood trial by Grand Jury on eight counts of corruption, tax evasion and the illegal importation of narcotics. He was convicted on six, and sentenced to serve fifteen years in the state penitentiary. His appeal against the sentence was revoked, but two years later he won a second appeal and his sentence was reduced to five years. Three years later he walked. Lauren Stone had tried, and failed, to indict him for the murder of Kelly Prescott. The case was lost on insufficient evidence. With Todd Prescott's help the Matthew Fierstein case was reviewed. Weston Kane and Beth Morgan were both charged with corrupting the course of justice and perjury, sentenced to serve six years in prison. Jay Kaminsky was posthumously cleared of killing Matthew Fierstein. Unfortunately Rebecca Kaminsky died before the hearing. After her release, Beth Morgan divorced her husband and left New York for London. Two years later she remarried. Weston Kane led a revolt against the conditions in prison. During the fracas, she injured a prison officer who later died. Weston is serving a life sentence for manslaughter.

The postcard arrived two days before Christmas 2000. Lauren looked at the image. It was a typical paradise beach scene, with the obligatory swaying palm trees, aquamarine sea and curved white sand. A solitary figure of a bronzed man was strolling in the shallows. Flicking over she read the back.

*I could use a little turkey right now, and snow would be nice. That was a great job on Petroni, and thanks for what you did for me. I suppose you're still working too hard, and looking for Mr Right?*

*Like my old grand daddy used to say. The past always has a future.*

*Merry Christmas.*

# The Nursing Home Murder

## Ngaio Marsh

### A Roderick Alleyn Mystery

Sir John Philips, the Harley Street surgeon, and his beautiful nurse Jane Harden are almost too nervous to operate. The emergency case on the table before them is the Home Secretary – and they both have very good, personal reasons to wish him dead.

Within hours he does die, although the operation itself was a complete success, and Chief Detective Inspector Alleyn must find out why . . .

'Nobody begins to touch Ngaio Marsh's skill at creating corpses and suspects . . . her dialogue is a continuous delight.' *New York Herald Tribune*

ISBN 0 00 612396 1